AWAKEN

A Soulkeepers Novel

Book Two

Lori Adams

Spyhop Publishing

Praise For
FORBIDDEN Book One

"An action-packed, satisfying love story gets this supernatural series off to a rousing start." — *KIRKUS REVIEWS*

"In a clash between heaven and hell, no one raises the heat like Sophia and her Guardian Angel, Michael." — CECY ROBSON, **award-winning author of the WEIRD GIRLS series**

"One of the best angel books I've read. Lori Adams' writing is *entertaining* and *SMART*...man, oh man, the emotional rollercoaster for this book was loopy and thrilling and had me back to read it the moment I finished. (And *I will marry Michael in my book fantasy world.*)" — *CASSIE MAE, author of FLIRTY THIRTY*

"I read Forbidden in one day because I just could not put it down." — *GOOD CHOICE READING*

"Simply put...this book was amazing! Not only was it captivating, but it was intriguing as well." — *JUST US BOOK LOVERS*

"I *strongly recommend* this book if you are looking for a well-developed paranormal romance...can't wait for the next one!" — *TJ LOVES TO READ*

AWAKEN Book Two

USA TODAY lists *AWAKEN: THE SOULKEEPERS (#2)* as a summer read for *hot-new-romance-book-releases* in July!! (2015)

"Dual plotlines of good and evil provide a well-rounded universe; *Hell never seemed so charming.*" — *LIBRARY JOURNAL*

"The emotions I experienced, though, while reading this book were completely all over the place. I went from sighing from the beautiful love between Michael and Sophia, to anger, to fear, to pride, then, the ending, when *my jaw hit the floor.*" — *CAROL, GOODREADS ADDICT*

"What I love about the writing in this series is the completely simple way things are drawn out, yet it's so captivating...*these characters are so alive to me.* And when an author can get that from a reader, that's pretty darn special." — *CASSIE MAE, author of FLIRTY THIRTY*

"Adams' *writing style is fantastic.* It's engaging, gripping, thrilling and the book is full of twists and turns. I could hardly put this book down, I was hooked trying to guess what would happen next." — *ROSIE, GOODREADS*

"I literally *stalked Netgalley for this one*, guys. Once again, Lori has drawn in her readers with such expressive and personal writing." — *M. BENSON, GOODREADS*

Spyhop Publishing

All rights reserved.
SPYHOP PUBLISHING 2022

ISBN 978-1-7371312-8-1
ISBN 979-8-9868812-1-8
ISBN 979-8-9868812-2-5

Originally published by **Random House 2014.**

First published in the United States by FLIRT, an imprint of Random House, a division of Random House LLC, a Penguin Random House Company, New York.

This book contains an excerpt from the third book in
The Soulkeepers Series, *Unforgiven*, by Lori Adams.

Also By Lori Adams

~Young Adult Books~

The Soulkeepers Series

Forbidden

Awaken

Unforgiven

Kate March Mysteries

Speak Easy, A Kate March Mystery

~Middle Grade~

Avalina Jones Series

Avalina Jones and the Eye of the Storm

LoriAdamsBooks.com

To Danielle and Sierra

~For Chelsea King, Forever Seventeen~

Chapter 1
A Lady in Waiting

I clutch the gun to my chest and carefully slide my finger over the trigger. The constant throbbing of my second heartbeat is distracting and making me tremble. With my back against a tree, I should feel the gnarled bark cutting at my shoulder blades, but I don't. It's early December in Haven Hurst, Connecticut, and an unforeseen snowsquall caught everyone off guard. So I don't feel anything but the bitter cold. And fear.

I exhale a cloud and scan the woods. I can sense someone out there. Watching. Waiting.

An army of winter trees surrounds me like frozen enemy soldiers stuck in the very places they died. The storm ended two days ago but left snow packed on branches, a burden they can't shake loose. The battleground is mounds of smooth white drifts, tempting the child in me to dive in and frolic. Lay flat and make wings. But I can't because I'm not alone. I'm being hunted.

He's going to kill me.

It's an understanding that sprouts desperation and a need for sanctuary. A high snowbank thirty yards to my right will do nicely if I can reach it in time. So I rescan the woods, only to sense it again—the frost has eyes. I'm being watched by something or someone hiding in plain sight. It's a familiar sensation, yet I can't identify it. I strain to hear anything unusual. What eventually seeps through is the murmur of voices behind me, not beyond me.

"You're not really gonna kill her. Are you?" Raph demands.

"Yes," Michael answers dispassionately.

I squeeze my eyes shut in frustration, in denial. I don't want to know that it's finally come down to the inevitable outcome I've dreaded. I don't want to hear Michael say it's unavoidable or for my own good. I don't want to hear any of it. So I shove my earbuds into my ears and then tap the phone in my pocket. Music is set to play "Christmas in Hollis" by Run-DMC.

If I'm gonna die, I might as well go out to a funky holiday jam.

I map out my course over the uneven terrain. It'll be disorderly at best, trampling over things I can't see and sinking into things that can't adapt to me. Nature has conspired against me like I'm forever intruding on life.

When the tune accelerates, I bolt forward and take off running. The virgin snow is not smooth and penetrating but packed and crunchy beneath my boots—the earth's hard crust that I was not engineered to overcome. The sound must be horrifying for someone trying to sneak. I'm doomed.

A black streak flashes in my peripheral, so I know they're coming. Fear rises in me because they move with unnatural speed.

Just keep running!

I navigate haphazardly around misshapen lumps and

scrappy saplings determined to slow my progress. The wall of snow is less than ten yards away. I'm almost there.

When I'm within range, I bound off a log and launch myself over the wall. I sail parallel to the ground and fling out my right arm, firing recklessly. I rotate a quarter turn just as two shots slam into my chest. One stops the music, and the other knocks the wind out of me. I rotate again, face up and splayed like a sacrifice. I glimpse the bright blue sky as I land—not on the ground, but on a pile of writhing bodies.

"What the hell, Sophia?" Duffy hollers from somewhere beneath me. Angry, muffled voices shout and curse because I have inadvertently flung myself onto my friends' mosh pit of a hiding spot.

"Sorry!" I say, riding the wave of people jostling me to the edge, where I am unceremoniously dumped to the ground.

Bailey, Rachel, Duffy, JD, Holden, and Casey James are a pile of fat ski jackets, chunky boots, paintball guns, and masks. As usual, they have appropriated a hiding spot without telling me.

Somewhere in the tangled heap, Casey yelps. "Hey, somebody's got a hand on my butt!"

"Not me!" Bailey says, and the hand is swiftly removed.

"Who said I didn't like it?" Casey grumbles, and everybody laughs.

The bodies crawl apart and sit back, staring at one another. Well, mostly staring at me. I've blown their cover by invading their frozen foxhole. Everyone is sporting splattered paint. But again, mostly me.

I pull off my mask and toss it aside. "Thought we were

speedballing, not hiding in bunkers," I say, checking my pack. "I'm out of pods anyway."

"How is that even possible?" Holden asks. "I don't think you hit a single person."

A burst of laughter brings all eyes up, and there are Michael and Raph, standing over us, paintball guns resting casually against their shoulders. Their pale blue eyes practically glow with amusement. The sun halos their blond heads, reminding me of their secret identities. Angels. *Real* guardian angels living right here in Haven Hurst.

I discovered their secret a couple of months ago, and now I can't see them as anything but truly mystical beings. I'm amazed the others can't tell.

Of course, it doesn't help that Michael and Raph are a bit cocky and laughing at us losers splattered with colorful splotches. As usual, neither of them has a drop of paint.

"Hey, look!" I sit up, smiling. "Michael only hit me twice!" I show off the two red spots on my jacket like war ribbons. It's amazing, considering how many rounds I heard flying past me.

"*Everybody* hit you twice," JD teases, and they all laugh again. I slump and inspect myself. This is true. I have more paint than Sherwin Williams. More color than a Jackson Pollock masterpiece.

"Somebody even got you in the foot." Rachel points, and we all look.

"No. That one's mine," I mumble. Michael laughs again, and I shoot him a warning look. Michael Patronus may be a six-foot-four guardian angel, Born of Light and trained to protect human souls, but he is also my boyfriend. My *secret* boyfriend.

Michael's laughter melts into a seductive grin just for me. A grin that sends electric flutters through my entire body because he has a powerful effect on me—a physical effect, as though I can feel his eyes caressing my skin or stroking my hair. I would think he was standing right behind me, touching me, if I wasn't looking at him twenty feet away. I will never get used to this, and it brings a flush of heat to my cheeks. I have to look away before Raph sees or senses my emotions and traces the origin back to his brother.

Michael won't come over and sit next to me because we have to keep our feelings secret. In doing this, we've established ourselves as friends, no different than everyone else Michael interacts with. Except I require copious amounts of tutoring in astronomy class to explain our need for private time. There can't be a hint of inappropriateness between us, especially in front of his family. Luckily, the ruse is working.

I think I've gotten the hang of things, despite those sexy smiles Michael gives me. At first, I thought he was testing my ability to deaden my emotions around others. But Michael says that he just can't help himself. That he is forever fighting the urge to touch me or kiss me. I love when he says that. And I know exactly what he means. Since we worked out the mechanics of kissing without killing me, it's been torture keeping our hands to ourselves. But sometimes, it's nice to know his struggle is as difficult as mine.

On the other hand, Raph's friendship has evolved into something in the overprotective brother category. So he comes over to help me up even when I don't need it. It's kind of sweet.

"You okay?" Raph asks, throwing his brother a reprimanding look for laughing at me. Michael's heated gaze cools but never leaves me.

"Yeah. Thanks, Raph." I smile smugly at Michael while Raph brushes snow from my shoulders. Michael tilts his head and cocks an eyebrow, saying I'd better not enjoy Raph's attention too much. I look away to hide my smile.

The game is over, so we fall in line and trudge through the woods, heading back into town. It's times like this that I hate hiding my feelings for Michael. I know it's forbidden for an angel to love a human. I understand Michael would be called before The Council of Guardians and sent back to Heaven. But sometimes a girl just wants to hold hands with the guy she loves.

Everyone is chatting about lost opportunities to beat Michael or Raph and strategizing for next time. I'm not listening because my mind has drifted back to that time alone in the woods. I know I felt someone watching me. If my friends were hiding in the foxhole and Michael and Raph were behind me, who had I sensed out there?

My second heartbeat grows stronger, indicating Michael is walking close behind. No longer a pain in my chest, our unique connection is comforting, and I soon forget my suspicions. Then I feel three gentle tugs at my heart. Michael is using his supernatural link to say: *I. Love. You.*

I smile. Loving a guy like Michael is like swallowing the moon. I'm glowing on the inside.

"Hey, Sophia?" Michael says in his casual *We're just friends* voice.

"Yes, Michael?" I answer in my best *I don't love you* tone.

"You kinda suck at paintball, huh?"

"Yes, Michael."

"Hey, Sophia?" It's Duffy mimicking Michael.

"Yes, Duffy?"

"You're buying, *again*." He swings an arm around Bailey's shoulders and rubs invisible money between his fingers and thumb. Bailey gives me a sympathetic look.

"Lara Croft wouldn't have shot herself in the foot, Soph."

Ouch. Bailey hits my hero where it hurts.

Losing at paintball is getting expensive. I wonder if the Soda Shoppe will take Dad's debit card.

We cross the street and troop into the park—the heart of the town square. Haven Hurst is a quintessential small town heavily into tourism. Flanking the park is an array of old-timey shops: the Naughty Nectar Café, the Aunt Tik furniture store, the Hickory Stick, the Words 'N Water bookstore, and the Soda Shoppe at the far corner. Opposite are Viktor Vogue's Haberdashery, the Sugar Shack, and the Cut 'N Dye hair salon. Among others.

At the south end of the square is Hadley's Market where Dad and I buy our groceries. At the other end is the courthouse. I have a keen dislike for the old Federal-style building with its red brick and white columns. Last Halloween night, three demons posing as high school students—Dante Dannoso, Vaughn Raider, and Wolfgang—held my dad on the third floor of the courthouse and tried to Take his soul.

It was mine Dante really wanted.

It started back in Los Angeles when I dated a loser named Steve. Pretty quickly into our relationship he got abusive, and I did something kinda freaky—I slipped out of myself and became someone else. Someone with warrior-like skills that almost killed Steve. It really shook me, and I wasn't the same afterward.

Before I had time to fully process things, we up and moved to Connecticut. Which wasn't unheard of since Dad is a pastor, and we move around a lot. What I didn't know was that Dad intentionally hit Steve with the car and killed him. But the whole thing was really my fault. I should've listened when Dad told me not to date Steve. He knew there was something off about him, but I was too stubborn. I put Dad in an impossible position.

So, when the demons found us in Haven Hurst, I wasn't going to let them take Dad's soul for a mistake *I* made. I bargained with Dante, the demon who claimed to love me. The demon who insisted we shared a past life.

Dante believed my soul was the reincarnated soul of his lost lover, and he was only too happy to accept my deal. So he administered the kiss of death and killed me. But while I waited for him at the spiritual Borderlands, my mom appeared.

Mom died two years ago, so I was shocked and overjoyed to see her again. And then she told me I was Taken before my time. She said I was to become a spiritual warrior—a spirit walker—and I was experiencing the first signs of my

Awakening, which explained my hallucinations and ability to see into the spirit world. Mom insisted I return to my body and begin training to help lost souls cross over.

But I missed her so much; I didn't want to leave. And then her friend, some frosty spiritual guy named Armaros, joined us at the Borderlands and helped me betray Dante.

After Michael and his brothers destroyed the demons, Dante arrived at the Borderlands to Take me to Hell. He became enraged at Armaros's interference and my willingness to break my promise. Dante was dragged below, shouting threats that things were not over.

Michael and his brothers drew my soul back into my body, and here I am.

I haven't seen Dante since that night. Nor have I heard anything about this Awakening business or any form of training. Even if Michael could help me find answers, he probably wouldn't. He has been very open about his feelings on the subject. He doesn't want me to fulfill my Awakening. He says it's far too dangerous.

Michael's mother is a Seer for The Council of Guardians, and his father is a Messenger, but even they can't explain why I haven't been assigned an Ascended Master. Why I haven't begun my training.

I am left to cling to Mom's words—I come from a long line of spiritual warriors, and I am supposed to be one myself.

Since I can't call on my fate, I wait for it to call on me. In the meantime, seasons change, and I move through life, waiting for something fantastical to arrive.

It's a gorgeous afternoon with holiday music crackling over the speakers as Dean Martin sings it's "A Marshmallow World." I almost believe him. The town square is a winter wonderland, bustling with commotion: kids building snow-people, shopkeepers clearing sidewalks, tires sloshing along the streets. The old-fashioned streetlamps are crowned with pine wreaths and bright red bows. Storefronts are framed in bushy garlands and holly. Every door jingles with shiny brass bells while mistletoe graces every doorframe. Window displays contain various renditions of Santa Claus with accompanying elves.

A towering Christmas tree stands naked in the center of the park. The town council is huddled beneath it, debating which decoration colors to use this year: red and green, silver and blue, purple and gold...

Abigail Monroe, the reigning dictator, is shaking a finger in Mayor Jones's face. Whatever colors she is insisting upon, it's safe to assume she'll get. Fair or not, Abigail Monroe usually has her way.

Dean Martin is interrupted by the courthouse bells, reminding us that it's noon. We're starving, so we cut across the park, heading for the Soda Shoppe. Vern Warner, our mail-carrier-cum-bandleader-cum-snow-shepherd, is herding snow from the sidewalk. He's wearing a combination Davy-Crockett-meets-Russian-czar fur hat and floppy galoshes. Then, out of nowhere, a snowball smacks him in the head, and Vern flails dramatically like he's been shot. My friends explode with laughter. Vern is always the punchline to someone's joke—usually Duffy's.

Vern throws Duffy an accusatory look as he whips off his hat. He shakes out the snow like wrestling a rabid Russian raccoon and then smacks it back onto his head. Duffy raises his hands, pleading innocence.

"Hey, man, all my balls are accounted for!"

Duffy has been on his best behavior lately, hoping to avoid Mayor Jones. Around Thanksgiving, Duffy decided it was a *fowl* thing to sacrifice turkeys for the locals' carnivorous cravings. He released thirty toms into the town square. As penance—otherwise called community service—Mayor Jones ordered Duffy to wear a giant turkey suit and stand on the corner to greet tourists. Humiliated to the point of molting, it's quite possible that Duffy has learned his lesson.

Vern scopes out the park for possible pranksters. There is a pack of kids digging out tunnels and stockpiling snowballs for serious winter warfare. Nearby, the McCarthy twins, Norah and Gracie, walk their ducks, Romeo and Juliet. The twins, like Abigail Monroe, are members of the Red Hat Society, meaning they always wear some style of red hat and purple clothing.

Today, they are sporting red pom-pom beanies and puffy purple snowsuits that would do nicely if they decided to hop a space shuttle. Even the ducks are subjected to the fashion fascism. They're wearing red and purple capes like two fowl superheroes.

No one claims the hit against poor Vern. But I do notice an impish grin on Gracie's chubby little face.

We all file into the Soda Shoppe, a fifties diner packed with my schoolmates. A hip, soulful song is playing on the jukebox, "Back Door Santa" by Clarence Carter. It seems to be a local favorite. My friends start singing and grooving and dancing through the restaurant. For no apparent reason. I laugh and look around for the cast of High School Musical.

As the song fades, Bailey and Rachel jive over to our usual booth by the window. Holden and Rachel are a couple now, so he follows like a dutiful puppy. The freshmen occupying our favorite booth haven't eaten yet and Bailey hones in on their leader.

"Hey you, slowest common denominator. Take your emojis and squiggle. Senior priv. *Comprenez vous?*" The kids scoot out, knowing it's a lost cause. I give her a look to say, *Quit being such a bully.*

"What?" she says. "I'm not here just for my blinding good looks." She slides in and pats the seat next to her.

Fifteen minutes later, the holiday cheer escalates because we can't leave well enough alone. Jordan the Leerer, whose favorite smile is of the cynical persuasion, loads his spoon with whipped cream from Lizzanne's shake. He flings it across the room. Frothy shrapnel doesn't discriminate, and everybody gets hit.

There is an instant uproar that triggers round two. Pacer fires open ketchup packets, hitting JD and Sarah. And then Harper Rose shoots root beer through the gap in her teeth. She hits Duffy in the face, but he likes it and opens his mouth for more. Casey's grandma, Nana James—ever the tolerant Mrs. Claus—serves a tray of food. Everybody piles over to snag the fries. Most are devoured, but some are launched across the room in retaliation.

Bailey and I start noshing on burgers while Rachel enjoys her vegetarian avocado wrap with a dreamy smile.

"Mmm, this is absolutely delicious," she says. "You guys should try it. Even Holden likes it."

Bailey snorts. "There goes your man card."

Holden just smiles and eats what he is told. He and Rachel were announced homecoming King and Queen last month. They've gone Siamese twins on us, so it's no surprise.

I ask Bailey if she wants to ride with me to this Friday's basketball game. I'm taking photos because I'm the *Gazette's* only photographer. It's a small local newspaper just around the corner from the Shoppe. I'm also the official school photographer, meaning I'm obligated to attend *every* game.

This week we're playing Glastonbury. I've never been there and would love company on the drive. Plus, I know Bailey has been bummed since Vaughn Raider left town. She never knew he was a demon and had it pretty bad for him. I'm not sure how serious things got between them. But lately it seems that Duffy hasn't been enough to satisfy her.

"Might as well," Bailey grumbles. "Duffy's been a full-blown nincompoop these days."

"Did you just say, 'nincompoop'?"

"Yeah, I'm bringing it back. Anyway, I wouldn't ride with him if he was driving the Anheuser-Busch beer wagon. Which reminds me. I'll see if I can score a geriatric bypass. Snag some brewskies after the game. I know some frat guys throwing a party after. Yeah?"

Rachel scoffs and snaps a photo of her avocado wrap with

her cell phone. "Oh yeah, that's just what you need. Get caught using a fake ID right before finals."

"Don't be a fusspot. You know I'm dying from boredom in this town. A little customized stupidity never hurt anyone. And since when did you start taking pics of your food? It's just an avocado wrap, you know. Not a newborn."

"It's for my foodie followers. We're documenting our diets. You know, it wouldn't hurt you to pay attention to what you—"

"Are you calling me fat?" Bailey wails in mock horror. She viciously bites into her burger and moans like it's Brad Pitt's neck.

Rachel rolls her eyes and shakes her head.

I'm full, so I push my empty basket away and gaze out the window. Those kids stockpiling snowballs are in the throes of battle, pelting enemies far and wide. Beyond them, I see that Dad has joined the town council conference to offer his advice on trimming the tree. This is good.

Dad has recovered nicely from his brush with death in the courthouse. Michael and his family compelled him to forget the details. Namely the part about The Council of Guardians and that Michael's entire family are angels. Dad's overall mood has done a U-turn. He is out and about more often, putting on some weight, and looking like his former handsome self. More like his wedding photo of seventeen years ago. And his sermons have positively exploded with enthusiasm. Dad tells me he views every day as a gift.

I start to wave at him, but a strange thing catches my

eye. There is a guy strolling around the park with a look of sheer wonder.

Who in the name of Jason Momoa am I looking at?

He's a big, broad-shouldered guy with a goatee, long dark windblown hair, and a huge smile on his handsome face. If Jason Momoa had a twin, the similarities would end there. This guy seems to be a man of his own.

If I look closely, I can just make out colorful braids hidden throughout his shaggy mane. The rest of him plays out like that educational game for kids: One of these things is not like the other. In the aftermath of a snowstorm, where everyone is sporting winter paraphernalia, this guy has the audacity to wear a short-sleeved Hawaiian shirt. And not the current touristy Hawaiian shirts you can pick up at the grocery store. This looks like an original Aloha shirt—the real deal. The kind the beach boys of Waikiki used to wear when surfers were golden gods and longboards owned the waves.

Not only that, he's wearing vintage boardshorts that look like they've battled one too many riptides and crappy huarache sandals—all legit.

He's wandering around while nodding back and forth like a pigeon. To say he is completely enthralled by his surroundings would be an understatement.

He is by far the oddest tourist I've seen yet—and the competition has been tough—but I don't have time to alert the others. Michael walks by our booth, making his way down the hall toward the restrooms. I know because I can feel an intense tugging in my chest. Michael is asking me to follow him. Follow, or he'll drag me out of the booth by my heart.

"Back in a sec," I say as I start sliding effortlessly to the left. I hurry so I don't stumble over my feet. This has happened before when I didn't respond quickly enough to his supernatural tugging.

As a guardian angel, Michael Patronus is extraordinarily patient and immensely peaceful. Usually. Lately, he's been acting…I don't know. Different? Serious? Impatient? I'm probably the only one who has noticed.

By the time I turn the corner, Michael is leaning against the far wall at the end of the hallway. His arms are crossed, and he's sporting his *What took you so long?* look.

"What? Ten seconds not fast enough?" I tease.

Michael lowers his chin and shakes his head, making my pulse flutter and my cheeks flush. The tugging in my chest snaps like a whip, and I'm airborne, flying down the long hallway until he catches me. His arms wrap tightly around my waist as he holds me up.

I am always momentarily stunned when Michael makes me fly. It's hard to describe the feeling, like my body rushes to catch up with my mind. Or vice versa. But we are not supposed to be doing this very thing, so I raise an eyebrow at his brazen antics.

"Sorry, I couldn't help myself," he says. He blinks lazily, allowing me to watch his eyes churn from pale blue to deep indigo—Michael's supernatural sign that tells me he's enjoying our closeness. A lot.

I grin and carefully place a chaste kiss on his lips. We have to be cautious with this. The wrong kind of kiss from Michael can suck the life from me. The first time we kissed, I fainted. Thankfully, I recovered without complications, but it scared the life out of Michael. Since then, we have learned to regulate our affection. And I learned to read the warning signs. Angels were never meant to kiss humans, so Michael and I have been educating ourselves. With copious amounts of practice, of course.

"I wish we could be alone," he murmurs in my ear. "Please, babe?" He trails soft kisses down my neck and then takes a bite.

I gasp because my body responds so sharply to his touch. As strange as it sounds, his teeth sinking into my skin devastates my equilibrium, sending shockwaves down my spine. I feel shivers in places I didn't know could shiver. Private places that make me squirm.

I'm surprised Michael would do this now. Aside from the pale blue streak his kisses and bite will leave on my skin, he said we could never be affectionate in public. He's lectured me countless times on the importance of keeping our emotions in check. Especially while his family is nearby. It's harder for them to read me, as opposed to normal humans, so they have to look directly into my eyes. But Raph is in the restaurant and could easily detect Michael's forbidden emotions. I doubt hiding around the corner is enough.

I pull back and look at him in question. Usually, *I'm* the one pushing the limits. After all, Michael Patronus is the hottest guy around. In fact, he's famous for his hotness—the most elusive, most eligible hot guy in the tri-state area. At least, that's what I overheard the visiting cheerleaders say at the last basketball game. I had no idea Michael's hotness exceeded the boundaries of our quaint little town.

When *I* look at Michael, I see so much more than his classic beauty. I see deep into the layers of his life, his love for humanity, and his quiet strength. I see his struggle against the holy vows he continually breaks because he refuses to give me up. He won't deny his desire for me, and for that, I am forever grateful. It humbles me to know what he is risking to be with me.

Michael and I have spent the last few months growing into best friends. Now I can't see him without seeing myself. I can't remember who I was before. There is only the *me after Michael* that I know. It has been exhilarating but lonely at times. Michael is forced to leave me without a moment's notice. When he receives a spiritual call for help, he is gone in a flash of blue light.

Sometimes, when we're around others having a private visual conversation, Michael steps away and vanishes with a shimmer in the air, and I am deserted in the crowd. It's not easy. And I understand he is choosing to go and help those in need. As it should be. I would never ask Michael to stay when others need him.

The rules of Michael's life are predicated on his willingness and choice to obey. Michael has free will, the same as I do. But he has fallen in love and found a secret way to disguise his emotions around his family. He is far better at it than I am. It's a discipline I can appreciate. Lately, though, Michael has changed. He's had less patience, and right now, his desire for me seems magnified beyond reasonable proportions.

So why is he taking risks when he said we shouldn't? What's changing?

"Please, babe," he begs sweetly, resting his forehead against mine. "I just miss my candy kisses." He grins and then brushes his lips lightly across mine, igniting soft sparks. "And stop being so suspicious. We're fine. Now, may I see you tonight?"

I smile cautiously and consider. I love when Michael asks to spend time with me. But sometimes, I have to be the practical one. So I tell him I'm drowning in homework. My academic adviser has recently tossed out a life raft, and if I hang on, I might still have a decent college application.

This is all true. But, if I'm being totally honest, this waiting around to start my spiritual training is driving me mad. I have no idea when or *if* it will actually happen. To keep my sanity in check, I decided to move on with life and stay on track as though I'm not anticipating a life-altering event just around the corner. As a result, I've become annoyingly tenacious about my future college plans. It's a fine distraction when it works.

"I'm sorry. I have so much homework and…"

Michael nods. "Human obligations. I get it. I shouldn't have asked."

Dang it!

I hate this. Michael is so patient and understanding. His time is so precious, like a gift I should never take for granted.

"Actually," I say, rearranging my thoughts. "If I leave now and work on my essays, we can hang out later. Around nine?"

He looks up, hopeful. "How about eight?"

I laugh and pretend to consider how difficult that would

be. "Well, maybe I could manage eight forty-five, but—"

"Eight-thirty?" He grins and pulls me closer.

"Okay. Eight-thirty. But I'll drive to you. And promise you won't try to make me stay too long."

"No promises," he says and then crushes his mouth onto mine in a quick, demanding kiss that buckles my knees.

.

Chapter 2
Michael

The faded red barn at the edge of the Patronus property was glowing. Or, more precisely, blue light was shooting through cracks and around the doorframe—something of a lightning show inside. Luckily for Michael, only otherworldly entities could see the light. It was a spiritually enhanced barn where all manner of mystical training took place. Humans saw the barn as an aged relic and nothing more.

There was no official training today, just Michael letting off steam. A few weeks ago, his forbidden desire for Sophia began growing deeper and stronger than he'd imagined. It had become a daily struggle to hide his excessive energy from his family. Even now, he could feel Raph, Gabe, and their young cousin, Uriel, assessing him from across acres of peaceful meadow inside the barn. It didn't help that Michael had destroyed three spiritually enhanced punching bags in four days.

For three hours he went at it, killing time until he could be with Sophia again. When he finished a series of bare-knuckle haymakers that rocked the bag sideways, Michael finally stopped to catch his breath. Chest glistening with sweat, he grabbed a towel from a nearby tree and wiped down.

"Is there a problem?" he tossed out to anyone who cared to challenge him.

"I'd just like to know what that bag ever did to you." Raph laughed, drifting up a tree in the center of the meadow. A bubbling brook encircling the tree stirred up the sweet heady aroma of honeysuckle. Raph reclined on a branch, tucked his hands behind his head, and situated himself for a nap.

"Why don't you come down here and take its place?" Michael said, spreading his arms to allow Raph a free shot.

His brother scoffed. "I wouldn't face you if we were shadow boxing. What's got you so fired up these days?"

When Michael didn't answer, Gabe decided he knew.

"It's the Halos, isn't it? You haven't heard anything yet." Gabe tied the gold belt around his fighting garb as he and Uriel prepared for a sparring lesson with cane poles. Uriel, who was fourteen and obsessed with animals, brushed the Forest Owlet from his shoulders before it got in the way of his exercises. The owlet flitted to a nearby tree.

Michael moved away, refusing to answer Gabe. He had failed to release enough energy to power down, so he paced. And raged inside. Gabe's question had turned Michael's frustration into anger. He was so sure he'd be recruited for the Winter Trials this year. A dream he'd had since the day he began saving human souls. Passing the Trials meant joining the Halos of the Son, an elite team of angelic warriors.

But it was early December and the candidates must have already been notified. Winter Trials were surely in progress, and yet Michael had heard nothing.

He threw the towel aside and stalked to the sound system. Scrolling down the playlist, he tapped a song that suited his mood. "Fire It Up" by Thousand Foot Krutch. The music swelled like his energy, and he marched back to the bag. As the song exploded, so did Michael, slamming his fists into the stationary enemy. Over and over, he jabbed and punched.

After a series of violent uppercuts, hooks, and stiff jabs, Michael switched to Pankration, an ancient Greek-fighting technique. He bounced on his toes and then viciously kicked the bag, simulating a crippling liver punch. Then he swung around, destroying the legs of any potential opponent. The pounding continued until shards of light shimmered through the bag. The destruction only added fuel to Michael's fire. He pulverized the bag until too much light escaped, and it became a blinding nuisance. He tore it down and hurled it into the bushes.

"Uriel, fetch me another one," he called to his cousin, who was the closest to the supply chamber. But before Uriel could obey, a deep voice bellowed from above.

"I have a better idea."

Michael swung around. Up on a stone balcony, hidden among climbing vines, stood a warrior in a black cape and a black and gold breastplate. A broadsword was strapped high on his back, and the shield on his shoulder bore the sigil of the Halos of the Son. The man was a Halo warrior.

Excitement swelled inside Michael. He stood tall and proud, and then remembering himself, waved a hand and killed the music. Raph had bolted upright at the bellowing voice and dropped to the ground next to Gabe and Uriel. All three stared in awe. Gabe recovered first by lowering himself to one knee. He pulled Raph and Uriel down beside him.

"Michael Patronus," the man called as he descended an invisible staircase in midair.

When he drew closer, Michael took a knee and bowed his head.

"Sir."

The man stopped before Michael and motioned for everyone to rise. "I am Scout Master Haniel. I am in charge of finding possible recruits for the Halos of the Son. As such, I am here to inform you that you have been scouted, vetted, and nominated as a candidate for the Winter Trials with the sole purpose of becoming a spirit warrior for the Halos of the Son. Do you accept the challenge?" He held out a golden scroll.

Michael stared at it, speechless. He had dreamed of this moment for years and could hardly believe it had finally arrived. But he hesitated as an unexpected thought crept in; he would give anything to have Sophia here to witness this, to share in the start of his future.

"Hell yeah, he accepts!" Raph blurted out when Michael failed to answer. Gabe elbowed him to stay quiet. "Well, he does."

Michael's mouth twitched with a smile, and then he steeled himself, gripped the scroll, and looked Scout Master Haniel in the eye.

"Yes, sir. I accept."

At the moment of his consent, several other candidates about Michael's age appeared along the balcony where Haniel had stood. They were accompanied by two more Halo warriors who led them down the same invisible staircase.

"This is Chief Master Sachiel and Squad Master Camael," Haniel announced. "Chief Master oversees training for the trials. Squad Master will assist and assess." Haniel turned toward Michael, who had taken a knee again. "This is candidate Michael Patronus. He has accepted the challenge." Michael stood and nodded his affirmation to the Halo Masters.

Chief Master Sachiel was a hardened man with a closely cropped red beard and sympathetic eyes. He looked Michael up and down in close inspection. Squad Master Camael sported black cornrows with colorful tribal beads that brushed his shoulders. He scratched his soul patch and strolled around, scrutinizing Michael.

"You are the one who killed Demon Knight Dante," Camael stated with a gruff, commanding voice. Michael nodded, ready to explain the details of killing a Demon Knight from the Royal Court, but Camael continued, "Maybe next time, you will do more than just decapitate him, yes?"

Michael frowned and glanced at his brothers who had also killed Demon Knights. *What was better than decapitating a demon?*

Raph and Gabe were just as clueless.

"Well, Camael," Scout Master Haniel called out cheerfully as he ascended the stairway like an escalator. "These are all the suitable candidates so try not to destroy *too* many before the final trial. *This* time. I'm going on hiatus and don't plan on returning just to track down replacement recruits."

Camael threw back his head and laughed. Chief Master Sachiel cleared his throat and turned his attention to Michael's family. He nodded his approval to Gabe and Uriel in their training garb.

"I am pleased to see young guardians working your skills, but if you don't mind, we will be conducting the Winter Trials here in the *Sanctus Horreum* this year. Please give us at least three hours of privacy today."

Raph and Gabe broke into wide smiles. They hadn't heard the holy barn's spiritual name in years. It was an honor for the Halos to select it for training, so they quickly gathered their things and ushered Uriel out.

When the barn was cleared, the five candidates fell in line and stood at attention, hands tucked behind their backs. Squad Master Camael stood aside as Chief Master explained the three-trial process.

The first trial was the Test of Spiritual Commitment. The candidates were instructed to disregard all earthly distractions. To leave behind memories of saved souls. To abandon all pride from defeating evil entities. In short, they would need total concentration and devotion. Or they would fail to prove their commitment.

"To begin, you must harness your spiritual energy and retain it here." Chief Master thumped a fist against his heart. "*All* of your energy." He spoke directly to Michael, prompting the others to look down the line at him. Michael was the only one radiating a cerulean light. His energy was still high, and he shifted uncomfortably, forcing himself to deaden his feelings for Sophia, where his mind had wondered. He'd been imagining their date tonight, when he would tell her about his candidacy. He wanted to impress her. To make her proud. But none of that would happen if he couldn't control himself during the first trial.

With concerted effort, Michael cleared his mind, deadened his emotional slate, thus dimming his light.

"It's important to learn to narrow your energy," Chief Master continued. "This is different from when you feel it gathering for the purpose of soul saving. Yes, you must let the energy expand inside you, but then you must control it. Turn it back on itself. Allow it to flow freely without obstruction throughout your system. But always under your command."

He strolled among the candidates with his palm out, feeling the power of each individual's life force. He nodded encouragingly as each young candidate—two females and two males—struggled with the internal exercise. And then he reached the end, where Michael stood.

Oddly enough, this was a technique familiar to Michael. He'd already been training himself to do exactly as Chief Master had instructed—not for the Halos but for Sophia. It was the only way he could control his emotions around her. His overwhelming love for her translated to a dominant pulsating energy force. This was also the kinetic instrument he used to pull Sophia to him when he wanted her close.

Chief Master looked highly impressed, but Michael knew it was a false read. It wasn't spiritual commitment Chief Master sensed, but Michael's love for Sophia. Okay, maybe the first trial wouldn't be as challenging as he'd feared.

"This one has a powerful commitment already," Sachiel

murmured to Camael, who appeared skeptical.

Squad Master Camael grunted and strolled around the candidates, taking his own read. "Let's send them up." He raised a hand and levitated each candidate in turn.

Michael caught his breath. It was an odd sensation, being elevated by another spiritual entity. He and his brothers had horsed around with levitation over the years. Tried to hurl each other across the room as easily as they could a human. But they usually had control over themselves. The energy it took for one angel to levitate another was substantial. Squad Master Camael must house an enormous amount of power, but you wouldn't know it by his calm demeanor. Michael was excited by the prospect of gaining similar strength and control.

Four candidates were placed in a square configuration in the sky with Michael, as the fifth, positioned in the center. They hovered above the grassy meadow.

"You will stay aloft until I give the command to descend," Squad Master Camael called up. "And no back wings! Only fetching!"

The candidates engaged the fetching on their forearms and idled in the air with nothing but blue sky above them. Squad Master slowly waved his arms as though pulling energy from the air. He began a chant that opened the sky and unleashed black roiling clouds that engulfed the candidates. Lightning flashed, and thunder boomed, rattling the old barn.

Up in the storm, Michael jolted to attention. Earlier thoughts of breezing through the first trial vanished as he struggled to stay aloft. All around him, his fellow candidates dipped and turned like boats tossed on the sea. The unexpected power surge had thrown them for a loop.

Michael closed his eyes and narrowed his thoughts. He spread his arms, allowing the fetching to stabilize his body. It worked, and he regained balance.

Then a lightning bolt struck his leg, and his eyes flew open. He flailed and dropped, only stopping himself at the last moment. Fighting through the pain, he forced himself to recover and float back into position.

That's when the air began to swirl. Hard, gale-force winds to shame any hurricane hit them sideways. They twisted and tossed in a blur. Michael heard a swift rustle as a candidate tried to unfurl his wings in a desperate attempt to stabilize himself.

"I said *no back wings!*" shouted Squad Master.

The dry wind swirled, creating super-charged static. It stirred up random bolts of lightning and deafening cracks of thunder. Lightning struck Michael's back, and his head flew up, his body arching in pain. A growl rose in his throat, but he gritted his teeth and contained the rage. Again, he closed his eyes and searched for a mental focal point. Something to divert his attention from the searing pain radiating inside him.

Sophia.

He saw her smiling face so clearly. Saw her sitting in the snow, covered with paint splatters. She was laughing at her precarious predicament...

Lightning zapped Michael's shoulder, spinning him around as white-hot pain shot through him. Another hit. Followed by another and another. One to his thigh, his arm, his chest, and then his calf. Each one excruciating and crippling. He spasmed back and forth, fighting for control. It took every ounce of energy and focus to stay aloft.

Next came the sacred red rain used only for training and warfare. Torrents of it hit Michael, sizzling against his skin. Smoke rose from his open wounds, a sure sign that regeneration would be slow and painful.

Once the candidates were sufficiently soaked, the roar of wind and rain dissipated. The barn became deathly quiet. And then snow fell like tears, sticking to their skin and packing on layers of frost. As the temperature dropped and the fetching on Michael's forearms became crisp, he felt a slow building of awareness. He was receiving a call for help. His eyes churned to a kaleidoscope of colors as panic rose inside him.

He had to stop the trial! He was needed to save a soul!

Michael glanced at his fellow candidates. They were exhausted and tortured, but each was sensing a call for help. Their eyes were churning. Their focus faltering.

Should they stop? Should they alert Chief Master? Was this part of the trial?

The candidate in the northeast corner began to lower himself. He would stop his trial and answer the call.

Michael trembled violently from the cold but raised a shaky finger at the candidate and shook his head, hoping the guy would understand.

Follow orders. Do. Not. Descend.

The candidate stopped. He stared at Michael and then reconsidered. Shivering uncontrollably, he returned to his position.

For the remaining two hours, all five candidates stayed aloft to endure whatever torture the Halo Masters devised. Through it all, Michael used his vision of Sophia to calm his center. To find his balance and control his energy. Everything he'd wanted was coming together—enduring the trials to join the Halos *and* being with Sophia. Always Sophia. It seemed her Awakening had been denied. Or perhaps, it was never supposed to unfold in the first place. Why else the delay?

If they could keep their forbidden love a secret, they could have it all. With Dante and his dregs out of the way, Michael saw no reason to fear for Sophia's safety. They would finally be together.

Chapter 3

Dante

Bone-crunching screams echoed down the stone corridors of Hell's Death Bunker. Blazing whips of fire snapped through the air, striking flesh already shredded to ribbons. Black blood pooled on the gritty stone floors, seeping into groves. Now and then, a chain rattled against bony wrists and brittle ankles. Night after night, the condemned suffered.

The Death Bunker was a maze of chambers with iron cages, where nefarious henchmen lurked in shadows, eager to deal out pain. Only the wailing cries of their victims drowned out their sadistic laughter. No one but the henchmen enjoyed the Death Bunker. Dante would not argue this point.

The moment he, Vaughn Raider, Wolfgang, and Santiago failed to Take the souls of Pastor St. James or Sophia, they were dragged back to Hell and locked in the Death Bunker. The daily torture had begun without a word from Lord Brutus, the leader of The Order of Reapers.

Truthfully, Dante had expected some kind of personal reprisal from Lord Brutus. Perhaps a verbal lashing at the very least. Before the real torture began. It was a curious thing that weeks had passed with no visit from any member of The Order.

Dante feared they had finally had enough of his lies and deceptions. They had finally judged him and his men unfit to reap. There was nothing left but unmerciful suffering until they were stuffed down the chute and dumped into the Nether Region.

If they were to land in the Nether Region, the torture would continue because they were Demon Knights, cursed with personal demons living inside them. Trapped in the Nether Region, their demons would devour them from the inside out until nothing remained but crispy ashes.

It was not pretty.

But Dante wasn't going down without a fight. Even now, with his wrists and ankles chained to the wall behind him, he stood proud and peered through the bars of his cell, scrutinizing the dank chamber for a way out. Day after day, he searched as he suffered.

A particularly loud cry from the chamber on the opposite side of the stone wall pierced the air, making Dante twitch. He had no sympathy for the damned soul because he was next. He could feel it. And his skin crawled with dreaded anticipation.

Black blood streaked his naked torso like ribbons of ink. Little remained of the clothes he'd worn at the haunted house party in Haven Hurst; his black peasant shirt hung in rags from his waist, and his black riding pants were sliced open, allowing a steady stream of blood to fill his tall riding boots.

One of the torches along the wall sputtered unexpectedly, adding light to the dim chamber. Dante's eyes shot across the aisle. It was finally bright enough to see his old friend, Vaughn Raider, in the opposite cell bound to the wall like a man crucified, but for a few exceptions. Vaughn's shackles were softly padded and offered no pain whatsoever. Vaughn was never whipped. Never cut. And he was dying because of it.

"You awake?" Dante called softly.

Vaughn's head had been sagging in defeat for weeks. With the Demon of Affliction living inside him, Vaughn needed to inflict pain on others. Or himself. Denied since his return below, his demon was consuming him from the inside.

"Talk to me, Vaughn," Dante ordered. He released his demon, Persuasion, to tap into Vaughn's subconscious. "Tell me what to do."

As if he could do anything.

The sight of his friend slowly dying was gut-wrenching, and Dante took full blame. Well, perhaps he would share the blame with Wolfgang this time. Wolf had tried to Take the pastor's soul too soon. He had succumbed to the nature of his demon, Impatience, and ruined everything. Dante knew he could've stopped him. Could've controlled the situation if he hadn't been so devastated by Sophia. Her failure to remember their past life had shocked him. The way he saw it, two possibilities were at work: She had help keeping the memories at bay, or she *had* remembered and still refused him. An idea he couldn't take seriously.

No, someone in the spirit world had helped her, and in his book, that just wasn't playing fair.

Vaughn's head stirred as he tried to lift it. The task seemed a great effort, and he gave up, letting it fall forward again. "I'm done," he whispered hoarsely. "They're letting me fade. It's over."

"No!" Dante jerked against his chains. "Lord Brutus will not let that happen. He has always liked you. It's me he hates now. Trust me. You will be released soon."

Vaughn snorted, and Dante grimaced. Okay, perhaps "trust me" was a poor choice of words. It was Vaughn's trust in Dante that had gotten them into their current situation. But he wouldn't let Vaughn give up. Not yet.

Dante glanced around for a distraction. Something to change the subject or make small talk. Anything to divert Vaughn from the unbearable weakness he must be feeling. Demonic fading was particularly agonizing for most Demon Knights, but Vaughn had described his experience as slowly growing numb, inch by inch. His muscles could not ache. His stomach could not growl with hunger. Nothing was allowed to make him uncomfortable. Vaughn would cease to feel anything and eventually collapse.

Dante failed to find a diversion because they were alone in this part of the Death Bunker. Not even Wolfgang or Santiago to argue with.

Footsteps scraped along the stone hallway. A key was thrust into the lock, turned, and the outer door opened. Skaw, the Demon of Torture, walked in.

Skaw was a retired soul seeker who found the work of chasing lost souls too exhausting. He'd been relegated to the Death Bunker, where he preferred to punish stationary targets. Skaw loved his work and always wore a sadistic smile.

Dante stiffened as the six-foot-seven albino in black robes approached. His eyes dropped to the coiled whip at Skaw's side.

Glowing with fire, it hummed with dark energy.

Two attendants scurried in behind Skaw, twins who had been skin-stripped centuries ago. Hideous creatures, they barely reached four feet tall and were covered with patches of red, raw muscles. Their organs and veins were visible, and here and there a bone poked through. Each had a crop of black hair protruding from the top of their gray skulls. They sloshed when they walked and were always losing organs. Plus, they reeked.

The twins crept forward, nervously fumbling with the key to Dante's cell. Behind them, Vaughn struggled to lift his head.

"Why don't you send Thing One and Thing Two over here tonight? I've been a bad boy. Could use a good spanking." He laughed, but it turned into a coughing fit. Skaw's greedy eyes sliced through the bars.

"Believe me, Demon Knight, there is nothing I'd like more than to beat you senseless. But since you would enjoy it too much, I'll give your share to your friend."

The twins chittered with approval and then slid open Dante's cell door. Dante bared his teeth and snarled at them. Fear had them twitching and bumping into each other. One dropped an organ and then they scurried away, jabbering and arguing.

Dante leaned into his chains and kicked the dark, bloated liver. "You're not leaving that in here."

One of the twins scooped it up and screeched incoherently as he shoved it awkwardly under his ribs. His brother tried to help, but they ended up slapping and hissing at each other.

"Not hungry, then?" Skaw asked with a greasy smile. He stepped into the cell as his whip began unfurling on its own.

Dante's chin went up with a stubbornness borne out of sheer pride. "Why don't you put aside the whip and let us go at this like real men?" he taunted. "Ah, but I have forgotten. You were never a *real man*." He smiled cruelly, knowing his insult stung worse than any whip.

There was a general hierarchy in Hell; entities who were once human but turned evil thought themselves above those created by the Master. Since everything in nature had an opposite—Heaven to Hell, angel to demon—soul seekers, like Skaw, were created as a dark opposite to compete with spirit walkers who were Awakened to the light.

Unfortunately, most dark opposites become jealous of their light counterparts. As a soul seeker, Skaw had spent decades fighting spirit walkers for lost souls and grew envious of their ability to walk the earth as humans. Skaw, like most who were created in Hell, hated anyone who had been born human.

Skaw's expression hardened, and his whip pulsated with the need to strike. Dante knew better than to provoke a henchman like Skaw, but what the hell. He might as well get a bit of pleasure before the inevitable pain.

Skaw snapped his fingers, and the jittering twins rushed back to Dante's cell. They approached cautiously and grabbed the chains. Tugging and shuffling, they worked the pulleys and forced Dante to turn around. Skaw moved forward, eager to enjoy the bloody sight of his handiwork across Dante's back.

Instead, the Demon of Torture growled his displeasure. The long gaping wounds from the last beating were already regenerating. It appeared that Dante had richer demon blood than most Knights. Perhaps two beatings a day would speed along his demise.

Skaw wrapped a pale hand around the whip's handle. The merciless weapon sensed its target and uncoiled on its own. Wave upon wave like a ribbon of fire, it moved through the air, fervently searching for Dante's flesh. Skaw licked his lips, savoring the impending pain he would unleash.

With a sudden jerk, he snapped the blazing whip across Dante's back. A streak of flames sliced him open from shoulder to hip. Dante's head went up, and his body shuddered in pain. He bit off the scream in his throat and squeezed his eyes shut. Skaw's hollowing laughter echoed in his ears, while the twins gurgled and clapped with delight.

Again and again, the fire whip cut into Dante's flesh. Black blood poured from the wounds as his skin was slowly flayed like a steak. Dante trembled but remained quiet.

Determined to provoke some sound from the arrogant Demon Knight, Skaw hauled back, gathering all his strength behind the next blow. But before he could strike, the chamber door was thrown open with a resounding boom. Skaw whirled around to Lord Brutus standing in the doorway.

Shrouded in a gray cloak, the leader of The Order peered from beneath his hood and scrutinized the two Demon Knights. Vaughn was slumped forward and unresponsive in his chains, while Dante's back sizzled like burning orange lava. Lord Brutus's ashen face and black eyes showed no sign of emotion. He moved over the stone floor with arms crossed and hands tucked inside the opposite sleeves. Behind him came six members of

The Order like a trail of foul monks.

Skaw withdrew from Dante's cell and bowed submissively to the Demon Lords. The twins hid behind him, nervously peeking around his cloak.

"Leave us," Lord Brutus ordered, to which Skaw hurried from the chamber with the twins at his heels.

Dante heard the commotion behind him and struggled to lift his head. His back pulsated with white-hot pain that sparked whenever he moved. Hair fell across his forehead, dripping sweat into his eyes. By sheer will, he forced his shaky arms and legs to turn the chains.

Lord Brutus and six members of The Order stood outside his cell. Even shrouded inside their hoods, Dante recognized them as Viperon, Kruell, Malachi, Hailu, Stivell, and Sultar. They were the six who had convened and voted on his petition to resurface. Lord Brutus had given the final vote, tipping the odds in Dante's favor. He eyed each one in turn. It didn't take a genius to guess their mood. Even so, Dante would make no assumptions.

"So, you have finally come to release Vaughn Raider, yes?" Dante struck his point like a hammer and then forced a smile while his back sizzled and smoked.

Lord Brutus lowered his hood, revealing a face so pale it appeared gray. His bloodshot eyes swept over Dante. Dry, flaked lips parted to reveal yellowed teeth.

"How very touching that your first concern is for your *friend*," Lord Brutus said, his gruff voice thick with sarcasm. "Better for you to worry about your own fate, I should think." He stepped into the cell while the others leered through the bars.

"Very well, I will worry about myself after Vaughn is released. Are we in agreement?" Dante pushed his shackled hand forward as if to shake hands and seal a bargain. Lord Brutus did not find him amusing.

"My servants tell me you have not mentioned the name of your *other* friend since your return. No concern for him?"

Dante became still and stared with dead eyes. Wolfgang had betrayed him by going after the pastor too soon. He had nothing but contempt for the Demon of Impatience, who could not control his demonic urges. Skaw occasionally repeated news from the gossipmongers, who said Wolfgang was locked in solitude several chambers below them. With any luck, his demon had already destroyed him. As for Santiago, Dante wasn't surprised that he'd gotten off light. Santi was an underling sent to the surface to watch and learn. There ends the lesson.

Dante lifted his chin defiantly. "I would think you would have more concern for him than I. After all, it was Wolfgang who lost the pastor's soul for you. No doubt he is receiving your special brand of punishment?"

The old man's crusty lips curled against his teeth as he snarled. "If not for Wolfgang's attempt at the pastor's soul, we would never have known *your* true intentions!"

Dante's jaw muscle flexed violently. If the old man thought to provoke a reaction, he would have to try harder.

"So, am I to understand that your real purpose for resurfacing was not to Take the pastor's soul, but to Take that...that girl's soul?" Lord Brutus snapped his fingers to gain someone's attention. "What was her name, that girl in Haven Hurst?"

The members of The Order exchanged glances, trying to produce an answer. Dante scrambled for an idea.

"Release Vaughn and I will tell you everything you want to know," he lied.

Lord Brutus looked aghast. "*You* dare to bargain with *us*? After what you—"

"Sophia!" Lord Malachi jumped in as the name came to him. "Sophia St. James." He locked eyes with Dante and grinned cruelly.

Dante considered Lord Malachi for a moment. He was not an ally per say, but close enough in the game of politics that reigned over everyone in Hell, including the Royal Court. In fact, Dante had used Persuasion on Lord Malachi to convince the others to vote in his favor. It was Lord Malachi who was responsible for Dante's trip to Haven Hurst, whether he knew it or not. Apparently, the Demon Lord had not liked being made to look a fool.

"Yes, *Sophia*," Lord Brutus repeated slowly. "Now tell us, what was so special about this girl?"

"As I said, release Vaughn, and we will talk."

Lord Brutus narrowed his eyes. "Did you know what she was when you resurfaced?"

Dante faltered. "What...do you mean '*what* she was?'"

"Let's not play games, Dante. I never trusted you and your men to resurface alone. I had a spy in place before you even got there. Imagine my surprise when a report came back indicating that an Awakening was in progress in the very town named in your petition—Haven Hurst. Of course, you understand there is no such thing as coincidence."

Dante's head was spinning as one thought split into another. *A demon spy in Haven Hurst?* Impossible. He and the others would have sensed it, would have known if another demon was present. And Michael Patronus and his brothers would have mentioned it if they had known. Unless...

Dante stumbled onto a horrific thought, and his eyes snapped to Lord Brutus. The old man was grinning.

"Ah, the look of a man well played." He chuckled dryly and then shrugged in surrender because the game was up. "Yes, I admit it was an old trick, sending a demon to inhabit a human vessel. But sometimes, the old ways are best."

The realization hit Dante hard: *Someone in Haven Hurst had a demon living inside them. A demon spy who could kill Sophia without a second thought of where it would send her soul.* The vessel would have to be someone close to Sophia. One of her friends perhaps.

He ran down the list of names, everyone he'd met in Haven Hurst. *Who could possibly be a vessel for a demon?* Unfortunately, a few people came to mind.

Even so, Lord Brutus was not making sense. What did Sophia have to do with an Awakening in Haven Hurst? He couldn't possibly think...

"A pathetic trick, old man. Sophia is no more Awakening to the spirit world than you will enter the gates of Heaven." Dante tried to effect confidence because he knew spirit walkers had a price on their heads. He didn't want Sophia associated with them. And yet, something didn't feel right. A look of awareness passed over the Demon Lords. *They knew something about Sophia that he didn't.*

"You would have us believe that you petitioned this court, put your friend's life in jeopardy"—Lord Brutus gestured toward Vaughn's slumped body—"just to Take the soul of an inconsequential human girl? That you were ignorant of her true identity?"

The insinuation was an insult to Dante's intelligence, but that hardly mattered at the moment. He was too busy grappling with this newest revelation.

Sophia was experiencing an Awakening? She would become a spirit walker? How was it possible? And why didn't he know?

The truth rocked him to the core. He *did* know. Somewhere deep inside, he knew Sophia was different. It would explain her odd behavior. And those hallucinations he had suspected she'd had but never admitted to him.

A black knot formed in his stomach. He now had more questions than answers. *What happened to Sophia when she waited for him at the Borderlands? How did Armaros know she was there? And why had he helped her return to her body?*

If Sophia was Awakening to the spirit world, it would explain why her soul was retrieved. That part made sense now. But what part had Armaros played? Grigori had no allegiance to spirit walkers. Why would he have helped her?

"Tell me which way her Awakening is likely to go," Lord Brutus demanded as though Dante had known all along.

Dante looked up. His mouth opened but nothing came out. He understood all too well what it meant for Sophia to experience an Awakening. Training to become a spirit walker was a precarious time. Any demon or reaper could lure her away from the light and into darkness. If one succeeded, Sophia would bond to it. She would be loyal only to the one who turned her dark. Sophia would never again have the ability to love Dante. And the memories of their past life would burn to ashes inside her.

But if Sophia could not be turned, she would become a spirit walker. She would be hunted for her unique light. Hunted and destroyed.

"Tell me!" Lord Brutus demanded again, jerking Dante out of his disturbing thoughts.

"I have nothing to tell you," he said coldly.

"Then you will remain here to suffer until I run out of patience or the girl has been turned. Make no mistake, Dante, you and Vaughn will be cinders in the Nether Region while Sophia St. James sits at my feet!" Lord Brutus swung around and yelled toward the door. "Bring in the witch!"

The chamber door opened and in walked one of The Order's mute servants. Shrouded in the customary black cloak and hood, the Marrow Man was comprised entirely of brittle bones from the Death Bunker's boneyards. Slowly, he escorted the witch into the bunker and then left, his duty completed.

As a Mistress of the Dark Arts, Isatou was occasionally called upon to administer specialized effects. Members of The Order of Reapers might hold powerful positions in the Royal Court, but even they could not conjure or cast spells. A witch was needed. And Isatou was the best.

She moved through the chamber in a gossamer dress shredded just below the knees. Once resplendent in delicate pastels, it now appeared to have been dragged through a swamp, chewed by something subhuman, and hung out to dry. Somehow, it still looked lovely on her shapely frame, hugging her full chest, and clinging to soft round hips. Long hair colored by brushes dipped in pale, polluted colors fell down to her waist. Chalk residue covered her bare feet because she often followed in the Marrow Men's wake.

"I want something to contain them," Lord Brutus explained, indicating each Demon Knight. "I want them physically bound to Hell. You understand?"

Isatou's pink lips spread into a smile while her hands curled into fists. When she spoke, her voice was slow, soft, and rich.

"*Si, signore. Catene che legano.* Chains that bind. It shall be done."

Isatou turned to Dante, and for the briefest moment, he thought he saw pity in her eyes. And then she closed them and began stroking the air around her.

Isatou chanted methodically, reciting the list of mystical items required. Then the air began to open in starts and stops until a three-foot-long crevice appeared. It rippled and split, folded in on itself, and then split again. She opened her eyes and reached inside the quivering fissure to retrieve a long iron chain, a pinch of green fire, and an obsidian handle. The items secured, she waved a hand across the fissure, causing it to slam shut like elevator doors that ruffled her clothes and hair.

Dante's eyes fell on the sleek obsidian object that resembled the hilt of a dagger. As beautiful as it was, he didn't like the look of it.

Isatou positioned a link of chain close to the tip of the black handle. It snapped together as if by magnetic attraction, creating a chain whip. Taking the pinch of green fire, she lit the last link in the chain, watching it glow strong and bright. Green flames traveled along each link, burning and hissing like a holiday sparkler. Dante looked at Lord Brutus. The old man was grinning with gathering excitement.

"Enjoy." Was all he had to say.

Isatou raked the air, fingers twisting as she used her dark energy to tighten the manacles at Dante's wrists and ankles. Spread eagle, he became Hell's Vitruvian Man.

Dante grunted as his appendages stretched beyond their limits. An inch more and he felt sure his arms would snap from their sockets. His chest pumped feverishly as he held still, unable to fight the constraints. Instead, he looked across the aisle.

Wouldn't Vaughn love a taste of this?

Isatou worked the whip back and forth, leaving streaks of green fire in the air. Then she honed in on her target and cracked the chain around the soft flesh of Dante's left bicep. Snake-like, it coiled into a circle and burned while Dante contorted in pain. Green smoke hissed and the unmistakable scent of burning flesh tainted the air. Dante spasmed and then went rigid. His eyes slammed shut while silent tears seeped down his cheeks. The remaining links scorched a path down the outside of his arm and across his elbow where it came to rest on top of his wrist. Once the links had adhered to his flesh, the unused portion fell away and retracted into the handle.

Panting and trembling in excruciating pain, Dante

forced his eyes open to find Isatou stepping toward him. She grasped his chin and squeezed tightly as if suddenly enraged by his very existence.

"Tethered. Just like the Master," she said loud enough for all to hear. Then she released him and winked.

Dante frowned. The whites of Isatou's eyes were decorated with sadistic runes meant to distract. Sometimes, they pulsated. Sometimes, they rotated like tumblers in a lock. It unnerved most, but Dante wasn't like most. He always saw the real Isatou behind them. But he had to admit that he didn't know how to interpret the wink, or this manufactured anger she was displaying.

Isatou had been human once, same as Dante. They had known each other for centuries, and he had always considered her a friend. They had jokingly called themselves Hellmates. But that was ages ago. She had just chained him to Hell, so why the wink? Why so happy to see him burning in agony?

Dante glared at her, remembering that allies were few and far between in Hell. Because Isatou was post-human, she was more susceptible to his compulsions. Without wasting another minute, he released his demon and infiltrated her subconscious. Isatou was compelled to quickly gathered her things and hurry to Vaughn's cell. Dante watched with relief as the witch seared a matching tattoo into Vaughn's arm. The chain of fire burned with such intensity that Dante half-expected the limb to fall off. Not that Vaughn would've minded.

Persuasion urged her to extend the process, adding to Vaughn's pain and pleasure. Hopefully, he would regain his strength. But through it all, Vaughn failed to move.

"Enough!" Lord Brutus shouted when he realized what was happening. He was furious to have momentarily forgotten the nature of Vaughn's personal demon. The last thing he wanted to do was give comfort to prisoners. Even if torture *was* the comfort.

Isatou blinked out of the trance and looked sharply at Dante. She had no idea she'd been under his influence.

"Now, as Isatou has said, you are bound to Hell. Just like the Master," Lord Brutus proclaimed with an air of triumphant. "Should you change your mind about revealing information regarding Sophia St. James, the servants know where to find me. In the meantime, remember, this is not the worst you will suffer before the chute opens and you are sucked into the Nether Region." He turned and led the others out.

When the chamber door closed behind them, Dante's eyes cut to Vaughn. His friend had shown no signs of life during the branding. Dante feared it was too late.

"Vaughn! Lift your head. Your hand. Anything. Show me a sign that you've survived." He stared hard at Vaughn and released his demon. Maybe Persuasion would have better luck rousing his friend from the edges of madness. The chamber fell quiet as Dante closed his eyes, narrowing his concentration in Vaughn's direction.

"Get out of my head," came a low grumble. Vaughn slowly lifted his eyes and grinned sideways. "You know it makes me all giddy with bromance when you do that."

Dante's eye opened, and he slumped forward with relief.

"It worked. The chain tattoo was enough to bring you back."

"It was a nice hit." Vaughn looked at the green chain links burned around his arm. "Thanks, by the way."

"Don't thank me. It was Lord Brutus. Or didn't you hear?"

"Yeah, I heard everything. But I figured you compelled Isatou to give me an extra helping."

"Are you okay?"

"Not great."

"We'll have to risk it. This is as strong as you've been in weeks, and we need to get out of here."

Vaughn struggled against the chains. "Look, it hasn't been *A Night at the Roxbury* over here. I'm weak as hell." When Dante frowned at the reference, Vaughn rolled his eyes. "Didn't you watch *any* cable TV when we resurfaced?"

"We have to get out of here. Now," Dante repeated. He worked his hands against the shackles, hoping the fresh blood would make them slick enough to pass through. No such luck.

"What's the sudden hurry, besides the obvious?"

"You heard what Lord Brutus said about Sophia. She is experiencing an Awakening. If the demon spy can't turn her, it will kill her. And by the looks of Lord Brutus, he's lost his last charming quality. Patience. We have to go after her."

"Listen, Dante, we're seriously screwed here. No one's ever escaped the Death Bunker. But just for grins, let's say we do get out. We can't cross the gates now. We've been branded. The mother of all tats."

"I have to try. Besides, what more can they do to us if we're caught?"

The realization set in. They had nothing to lose.

"Yeah, well, we still have no way to get—"

Grinding footsteps along the briny corridor interrupted Vaughn's argument. The door hadn't opened, so they scanned the bunker's blackest corners and crevices, verifying they were alone. Still, the sound continued. And then slowly, something stirred in the darkness just beyond their cells, a silhouette borne out of shadows. Dante squinted and leaned in for a closer look. The silhouette shoved his hands into his pockets and sauntered into the dim light.

"'Sup, guys?" Santiago asked with a wry smile.

Chapter 4

All Things
Are Made to Fall

The temperature has dropped with the sun. I'm blasting the jeep's heater and bouncing in my seat, singing back-up to "Christmas Wrapping" by The Waitresses at the top of my lungs. It's a great way to stay warm and burn off nervous energy. Even if I look like an idiot. Which I know I do because I can see Michael standing on his porch laughing as I pull up to his house.

I stop and cut the engine. My cheeks grow hot with embarrassment as I climb down. Michael meets me in the yard, smiling.

"Well, that was entertaining," he says. He takes my hand, leading me around the side of the house.

It's cold, and I start shivering. "Aren't we going inside? We can tell your family you're still tutoring me in astronomy. Which nobody ever seems to doubt, by the way." I give him a perturbed look. Michael isn't paying attention.

He stops beneath a tree and pulls me into his arms. He crushes me against him until I can't breathe.

"Michael!" I grunt, and he relaxes a bit. Then I snuggle myself more comfortably against him while he buries his face in my hair, inhaling.

"Mmm, you smell so good," he murmurs.

"Who can smell in this cold?"

"So good, in fact, I'll forgive you for being three minutes late. It was excruciating."

"Poor baby," I say, giggling.

Michael leans back and looks at me. His eyes are cobalt and full of secrets. He gives me that slow, sexy grin, and I feel myself growing warm from the inside out. He is trying to stay calm but is excited about something. His chews the inside of his cheek, contemplating.

"Come," he says, taking my hand again.

We continue toward the back of the property, where the land slopes naturally and runs a hundred yards until it meets the forest. Everything is bluish white under the moon. Spectacular. A Currier and Ives Christmas card.

Michael stops, and we stand, hand in hand, gazing appreciatively at the winter wonderland. It's quiet because winter has stripped away its sins, and Heaven has thrown a mantle over everything. Hope hibernates deep underground.

"I imagine this is what Heaven is like," I say. "Calm. Pristine. Covered in a bluish-white blanket of frozen precipitation." I peek up at Michael to gauge his reaction. He is staring ahead, grinning. Michael has yet to confirm or deny any heavenly descriptions I've tossed out. He is forever withholding details of his spiritual life. Michael tries to forget he is an angel when I'm around. The irony is blinding. I'm determined to start my supernatural life while he is determined to be as human as possible. At least when he's with me. The grass is always greener, I suppose.

Michael looks down at me. "I thought my California girl might like to sample the local flavor."

"It's magnificent," I say. *Being here with you, Michael. Not just the view.*

"Yeah, well, this ain't it." He laughs and tugs me along, and we're off again.

We take a path through the pasture, where I walk in giant footprints that have gone before me. They're at least a foot and a half deep. I have to step up and over, or I'll miss.

We pass through the edge of the forest and come out the other side to a red barn. I stop. In front of the barn is a beautiful palomino hitched to an old-fashioned sleigh.

"Michael!" I breathe out.

"Happy anniversary."

Oh crap! Really?

I feel my eyes swell. I have forgotten our…wait—how long have we been dating? I must look panicked because Michael says, "Eight weeks, Sophia," in his no-nonsense voice.

"Oh." I scramble to check his math. "When did you start counting?"

"That night in the courthouse. When you went *flying squirrel* on me and jumped out the window."

I cross my arms and give him a look. "Flying squirrel? Really? That's what we're calling it? I thought maybe it was the night I went *all in* and called your bluff."

Michael cups my face and gazes into my eyes. He is serious and calm. "Babe, I don't care what we call it. I'll always remember it as the night you changed my life forever. I became yours."

My tummy shivers because that is the most romantic thing I have ever heard him say. I throw my arms around his neck, and he wraps his around me. I can feel him smiling against my cheek. Then he lifts me up and walks to the sleigh, letting me dangle against his body. He sets me onboard, where a plaid blanket and a thermos of hot chocolate await. The horse has a string of bells attached to his white tail.

"You know, people write songs about this kind of stuff." I laugh and pat the horse's rump.

"His name is David."

"Hello, David."

Michael watches me, evaluating my reaction. He's always curious to know if he has done the right thing—the right *human boyfriend* thing. For all his confidence in the supernatural arena, Michael has serious doubts about human relationships. Which only makes him adorable in my book.

"Okay?" he asks.

"Perfect," I say.

"Good. Now please stop looking at me like I'm some adorable puppy. Trust me, being *adorable* is the last thing I have in mind." He gives me a wicked grin and then snaps the reins. We take off with a quick jerk, and I have to look away to hide my blushing smile.

Michael relaxes and sits back, wrapping an arm around

me. I snuggle beneath the blanket as we glide smoothly over the gleaming snow. I'm trying to find a safe place in my head for his seductive comment, but it's a labyrinth up there.

David trots and bells jingle. The air is frigid as it dances across my face, insisting that I taste its coldness on my tongue. If snowfall had a sound, it would sound like bells—God's salt-shaker tapping down grains of Heaven. I grew up along beach cities, so I've been pleasantly surprised to learn snow has a fragrance. But it's not altogether unfamiliar. I remember Armaros, the frosty apparition I first saw in the library basement, and then again at the Borderlands with Mom. He smelled just like our recent snowsquall.

Armaros has been a curious thing for me—his unusual warrior clothes and mismatched eyes. One blue. One brown. Michael doesn't like to talk about him, so I keep my thoughts to myself.

We slide into the forest, making our own path. Moonlight flickers on and off as we sail in and out of clearings. We turn right at a huge boulder covered with a pad of snow like an old man's toupee. A long river gleams before us, a sapphire ribbon under the moon. Like everything else, it is frozen and still.

I notice the first lantern perched on a rock next to the river. It's exquisite and unique. Some handblown European glass set adrift in an ocean of frothy whiteness. I sit forward and "Oooo" at its glowing purple light under a blue moon.

The next lantern comes as we climb higher. We're following a trail of glowing purple lanterns like illuminated crumbs in the forest. And then we round a corner, and they appear all at once in a glorious display up the side of a cliff.

The sheer wall is looming but high in the center is a giant waterfall—milky white and frozen. Snow has found places to land on each side of the solid cascade. It drapes over lumpy boulders, towering pines, and stubborn brush borne in crevices. Tiny purple campfires nestle on every available ledge because Michael didn't know when to quit. I imagine him meticulously placing each lantern for maximum effect. He has succeeded. It's beauty repeated over and over.

The sleigh slows to a stop, and I jump to my feet, gaping in wonder. Time is frozen here as though someone hit the Pause button. Thin ribbons of water have halted progress and become jagged stalactites suspended above a wide pool. Life is standing still as if a winter witch cast a spell against Mother Nature's decree that all waterfalls must drop. It's breathtaking. And I'm speechless.

Michael hugs me from behind and murmurs, "I knew you'd like it." Words are not necessary, and I shake my head in wonder. *I've never seen anything so amazing, and he knows it.*

Michael laughs and hops to the ground. He lifts me out of the sleigh to stand beside him. "I learned something today that I'd like to try." He holds out his hand. "Trust me?"

I give him a look that says, *Do you really need to ask?*

"Good," he says and leads me to the edge of the deep pool at the base of the waterfall. I can almost see our reflections in the icy surface. Michael puts a lantern in my hand and steps away. He rubs his hands together like they're cold, his eyes never leaving mine. Michael's hands aren't cold—this is T-shirt weather to him—so I know he's gearing up for something. I'm nervous. The last time I saw this look, fetching appeared along his forearms, and he took me flying over Haven Hurst.

"Take a closer look." He nods at the frozen waterfall. I frown suspiciously at him and then turn and look up.

"It's the most beautiful thing I've ever—whoa!" I'm slowly lifting off the ground. My head whips around to Michael with his right arm pointed in my direction. He's staring with serious concentration as he levitates me.

Okay, so he doesn't *always* want to do the *human boy-friend* thing.

"Babe!" My voice wobbles like my body, so I lift my arms for balance.

I rise higher and higher, gliding over the pool that turns dark from this angle. Up I go, drifting toward the waterfall like a moth to a flame. Because I know all things are made to fall, I'm afraid. A terrified sound I've never heard before escapes my mouth. I wish Michael was with me, but he remains where I left him.

The pressure of his meditation finds the deepest part of me. It denies gravity its job, lifting and pushing and maneuvering me higher in the air. I pause, hovering before the cliff, where the river tips over and becomes the massive waterfall. Layers of frozen water glow purple under my lantern.

"Do you see them?" Michael calls up. I try to twist around and look at him but can't.

"What?" I wail.

"Look! In the water!"

I raise the lantern and squint into the murky light. Vague shapes appear in the frozen water. Sticks, leaves, various debris, and fish. Lots of fish. Their eyes bulging and mouths open.

"Holy crap!" I holler down. "It's like they're petrified!"

Michael uses both arms now, turning me around to face the wide expanse of countryside. Lights live in the distance beneath a dark sky that seems to go on forever, as though it was told not to stop, no matter what.

I fill my lungs with cold dry air and then gaze down. Michael's face breaks into a wide smile. He looks so proud. I have to laugh.

"This is pretty cool but why didn't you just fly us both up here? Two is better than one, you know?"

"Because I really wanted to do this." He whips his arm to the left, flinging me toward a patch of snow-covered trees.

"Ahhh!" I scream and crash into the softness. I don't fall because he is spinning me around as snow rains down. I burst out laughing and accidentally drop the lantern. It sails into a snowbank and disappears. "Again!" I yell.

Michael flings me back across the clearing and into bushes on the opposite side. I'm a marionette with Michael pulling the strings.

He tosses me in the air, doing flips and spins and dangling me upside-down. I fear we're pushing our luck. I fear gravity will eventually demand to be obeyed. But Michael is relentless. He sends me to the top of the hill, skirting me across the snow until my boots skim the surface. I'm snowboarding without the board! Down into nature's half-pipe and then back up, high into the air in a double backflip. I cry out, arms flailing, but I never lose balance because the puppeteer is in control.

I drop fast, zooming at an arc to slide across the crystallized pool on my bottom. I fly along the frozen river, bouncing down a few mild waterfalls. I'm laughing so hard my tears are running horizontal from my eyes. *Six Flags never had a ride like this! Just sayin'!*

I hit the next waterfall but take flight instead of dropping. Michael returns me to the top of the cliff, where I hover over the wide pool with arms flung out. Slowly, I rotate a three-sixty while a cold breeze lifts my hair. Michael gently sets me down, and I clutch the ice so as not to slide over the edge. Feet dangling, I'm panting great swells of fog. My heart is a jackhammer. Michael finally lowers his arms. The maestro, smiling in satisfaction at the end of a well-played concert.

I hold out my hand, begging him to join me. Fetching instantly rises on his forearms, and he drifts up the face of the cliff to sit next to me. Once he's settled, the fetching retracts so it won't cut me. Then he slips an arm around me.

"Thank you so much," I say. My nose and ears are frozen, but I don't care. Next to flying with Michael, that was the most overwhelming experience of my life.

"A bit of the local flavor," he says, and then tugs my heart three times.

"I love you, too," I say, dropping my head onto his shoulder.

We fall into a comfortable silence, letting our eyes drink in the natural beauty. So high up, the views go on forever. As far as the eye can see there is only white. Blankets, mounds, clumps, crevices, and valleys of white. If Heaven doesn't look like this, they're getting gypped.

"How is it that you just *now* learned to do that? I thought it would come naturally, making people fly."

"Not exactly. During a fight, guardians can throw an enemy around. Knock them into things. Destroy them. It doesn't require as much control. With you, I was concentrating my efforts into a pinpoint target. Making you rise and fall at a slower speed. And then turn and twist without making you hurl your guts out. Pretty cool, huh?"

I laugh and say, "Show off."

He laughs and says, "Yup."

"Hmm." I ponder things.

"Are you complaining?"

"Nope."

"Actually, I had a point to all this. I brought you here to tell you something." Michael turns, so I lift my head. He is serious but practically bubbling over with news. "I made the Winter Trials."

My heart stutters, and I take a moment to let this sink in. Then throw my arms around his neck. "Ohmygod! I'm so happy for you! You've waited so long for this!"

I hug him tightly for a minute and then, because I'm absolutely so thrilled for him, I clutch his jacket and growl and shake him. "You did it! You did it!"

He laughs, happy that I am so happy for him. I get control of myself and sit back to give him room to talk. "Okay, now, tell me everything. I wanna hear all about it."

I stay quiet with a silly smile and crinkly eyes as Michael explains in detail. About the Halo Master elevating all the candidates, which gave him the idea to try it on me. About the storms and the lightning and the subzero temperatures. He endured terrible pain but is trying to play it cool. He managed far better than the others, and I can tell he is pleased with himself. Michael impressed the Halo Masters and is ready for the next trial.

I sigh wistfully. I'm so happy and excited for him. So proud he excelled on his first day. Michael's dream is finally coming true, whereas I've been plagued with doubts that I have lost my chance to become a spirit walker. The idea nearly chases away every joyous thought in my head. I fall back onto the snow before Michael can detect anything.

Of course, he picks up my shifting emotions before I even hit the ground. I stare up at the night sky and blink back tears that threaten to spoil everything.

"I'm sorry, babe," he says earnestly. "I should've realized—" He scoops me onto his lap, and I snuggle my head into his neck.

"No, it's fine."

"No, it's not. I should have...I can't believe it never occurred to me. I feel like a jerk."

"Don't say that, Michael. You're the best boyfriend, human or otherwise, a girl could ever hope for."

"Human or otherwise," he muses softly. "Still, I should have been more thoughtful."

"But you know what it's like. All this waiting around to

start a new life. Waiting for your chance to start training. It's so hard not knowing when or *if* it'll happen. I haven't had a single word or sign."

He strokes my head, and we sit quietly for a while, rocking back and forth in the comfort of each other. After a while, Michael sighs. "You know, maybe it's for the best. If it doesn't happen. I've told you before, this kind of stuff isn't for everyone. Sometimes an Awakening just doesn't come to fruition. It's nothing personal." I lift my head and give him a look. "Okay, so it is personal. But there are a million reasons why it doesn't advance beyond visions. Besides, you know I don't want you involved in the spirit world. It's too dangerous."

"But it's what I want. And besides, it's not your decision."

Michael growls in frustration because I am the broken record he can't bear to hear again. We've been over this a hundred times before.

Michael looks out across the valley, lost in thought. I know he can't help the way he feels. I understand he knows things about the spirit world that I don't. Scary things. Unpredictable things. But it's not enough to dissuade me. I can't help the way I feel any more than he can.

This is not how either of us expected the evening to go. I feel bad. Michael has great news, and we should celebrate.

"So, these Halo Masters don't suspect anything about us? They don't know you're in love with a human?"

This brings him around, and he looks at me—his eyes so beautiful and pale. The blue almost appears white beneath his thick black lashes. But then he lowers his chin and gives me a look. Michael speaks with his eyes, telling me so much as the pale blue beings to churn.

The change is quicker this time, almost bypassing cobalt and flashing straight to indigo. Michael's desire is palpable, and my whole body is responding. My second heartbeat drums feverishly. My tummy clenches because I am aching with some strange, ethereal need. Michael pulls me closer.

"They don't know anything," he murmurs. "I've learned to harness my feelings for you and use them for another benefit." While he says this, he is pulling aside my collar, where he bites down on my neck. I catch my breath as a warm blue flower blossom across my skin beneath his teeth. I can see it so clearly behind my closed eyelids; pale blue petals unfolding and spreading like wings. It's a delicious sensation, filling me with longing.

A shiver runs through me, so Michael pauses, assessing my emotions. It's not the cold that makes me tremble, but I almost wish it was. I'm nervous. I'm starting to want things, intimate things, I'm not sure we can have. Sometimes, I wish Michael and I were just two ordinary people who fell in love. Ordinary people facing the same ordinary concerns and expressing our love like everyone else. Without fearing for my life. Without putting me in danger.

If we have to be so cautious with kissing, I can't imagine how dangerous it would be to take things farther. I don't know if he's even considered it.

Michael has finished his assessment and withdraws to gaze back at the view. I can't see his eyes, but I suspect they are returning to normal. The deep purple lanterns flutter below us, matching his eyes when his emotions for me escalate. Are the lanterns a coincidence or a subtle hint?

"You're scared," he says. "Don't deny it. You know I know." There is concern and disappoint weighing down his voice.

"I'm sorry," I murmur.

"Don't be sorry. I'm scared, too. I want things I'm not supposed to have. Things I'm not *designed* to have. But I still want you, Sophia. God help me, but I do." He looks at me so deeply tormented that I know he must have been wrestling with this issue long before tonight. This is not a new concern for him. And his unrestrained honesty is undoing me. I drop my head into my hands. I feel awful. For Michael. For me.

What have we done? We have put ourselves in an impossible situation.

He holds me curled against his chest, his chin resting on my head. "Please don't torture yourself, babe. We'll think of something. Go slowly. Step by step, if we have to."

I frown. Go slowly? What does that mean? Is he willing to risk my life to test the limits?

"And please stop dissecting everything I say," he says. "You're getting as bad as I am." He lifts my chin and lowers his mouth onto mine in a soft, sweet kiss. "Mmm," he murmurs across my lips, grinning. "Just like candy."

I lean into the next kiss, welcoming the familiar sparks. We turn our heads, breaking the connection before deepening the kiss in the opposite direction. Over and over, we pull back, rotate, and adjust so the electric charge doesn't tap into my circulation. So it doesn't change the course of my blood.

Michael pulls me closer, sliding his mouth down my neck. He tugs at my sweater so he can reach Michael's Hollow, that tender place along my collarbone he claimed as his.

He turns my head, exposing my throat, where he nips and bites. Tingles flood my body, making me arch and press against him. Michael bites hard and pulls until I feel my pulse gather in his mouth. I groan, and he releases his bite. A river of blood rushes into my head.

"Whoa," I whisper languidly, guiding his head up. "That felt—" I start to say *different,* but Michael's eyes are strange again. For a moment, I think one has turned...brown. I blink and squint, but it's changed again. Both eyes are the same. It must have been a trick of the light. Or lack of light.

"You good?" he asks curiously because I've been staring.

I nod. This time, I shiver from the cold, and he rubs my arms to warm me.

"Maybe this *is* too cold for you, after all," he says.

"But I've always longed to be a Popsicle." I snuggle my frozen nose against his cheek.

"Well, if we're going slow at this, I suppose there is something I should ask you."

"What?"

"Will you go to the Winter Carnival dance with me?"

I lean back and look at him. I've heard everyone talking about this at school. It's the biggest, most spectacular event of the year. Bigger than prom because it involves the entire town. It's a black-tie, fancy-schmancy affair. I heard the governor and a senator showed up last year. It's the only event that Michael's parents attend.

"But how…wait, I'm confused. Raph told me your parents will be there, so how can we go together?"

"Why were you and Raph talking about the dance?"

"What? Oh, I don't know. Everybody was talking about it. He said you guys never go."

"We don't, but our parents do. There's a lot of local and state politics that goes on there."

"Like on golf courses?"

"Something like that. And I thought you and I could go. We just couldn't show up *together* together. But we could dance." He smiles playfully, so I consider it.

"But to avoid suspicion, you would have to dance with other girls, too, wouldn't you?"

Michael nods gravely. "Yes. I suppose I would be forced to."

"What a sacrifice." I roll my eyes, and he grins. "Well, I suppose I'll have to dance with other guys, too." I sigh like it's a chore.

Michael growls his objection and buries his face in my hair. His lips move down my throat, teeth scraping my skin before sinking into the long thin muscle. I gasp but keep the shudder in my mouth, keep the pain to myself. It immediately turns to pleasure anyway. My eyes close because they aren't needed. Michael is all I need to know…

He eventually finds my mouth again, kissing deep with a longing that can't be satisfied. At least not with a kiss. We break apart because nature demands it. And then we find each other again. His arms tighten possessively around me as if to say *Here is where I am meant to be.*

Longing that is denied leads to frustration, and I feel it in Michael's lips. In his hands. His kisses have an urgency that fuels the sparks. They're so strong this time that I flinch and clutch his shirt. Then comes the familiar sensation singing through me. All my blood is rushing back to my heart. My arms and legs tingle from the sudden loss of circulation. We are rushing toward the point I recognize as dangerous. But why isn't he slowing down?

He'll stop any moment. Like he always does. He knows when to stop now.

Michael moans and deepens the kiss. The pulling grows stronger as my heart rages inside me. My lungs feel as though they're collapsing inch by inch. Michael's energy, his desire, gradually draws the air from me.

Stop! Stop! Michael, why aren't you stopping?

I struggle against him, but Michael cups my head and eases me onto the ground. He pins my hands over my head. I know he can sense my fear, but he seems lost in his own world. Lost to the dangers. My eyes fly open to a hazy vision. Everything is white around the edges. A tremendous buzzing in my head says we're too late. I'm going to faint. Again.

Michael suddenly startles as though I've cried out in panic. He lifts his head, and his eyes spring open. For the briefest moment I see that one is churning darker than the other. It doesn't take hold in my muddled brain because my head is swimming. My vision blurring.

Michael is trembling. He clutches my shoulders, sitting me up. "Stay with me, babe! Stay with me!"

My head flops back and darkness shrouds my world.

Tiny drops of water sprinkle my face, making me twitch. I blink and eventually come around. A hand taps my cheek. A voice murmurs my name until I open my eyes. Then I grimace because I have the mother of all headaches. Not only that, my chest hurts like it's bruised. Like the night I died and Michael and his brothers had to draw my soul back into my body.

I take a moment to remember what happened and where I am. And then I'm not sure which emotion to act on first. Fear—because Michael almost killed me and had to save my life all over again? Or anger—because *Michael almost freakin' killed me and had to save my life all over again!*

I bolt forward and find that I'm back in the sleigh at the waterfall with the plaid blanket wrapped around me. Fresh anger is on the tip of my tongue, but the moment I see Michael, I freeze. His eyes are shimmering prisms. He has received a spiritual call but hasn't left yet. He was waiting for me to wake up.

"Ohmygod," I whisper.

Michael jumps down from the sleigh, and I catch a flash of controlled rage in his face.

"David will take you home," he says, his voice choking. "I'm so—" He glances toward the trees, unable to finish. Without another word, Michael turns and disappears in a flash of blue light.

Chapter 5
Michael

The yellow and black school bus lay in a ditch, hissing and steaming like a dying beast. Young bodies were sprawled across the icy road illuminated by flashing red and blue lights. Six patrol cars, two fire engines, and four ambulances were on the scene. Paramedics and EMTs rushed in every direction, overwhelmed with the magnitude of wounded. Raph and Gabe stood aside in spirit form, methodically assessing the damage.

Raph moved among the children who just hours ago sang Christmas carols at the Danbury Fair Mall. He sensed their needs, zeroing in on one. Head injury. Concussion—the brain already swelling. He placed a hand on the boy's forehead, meditated, and drew out the damage as a thin silvery ribbon.

Gabe knelt beside a little girl groaning in pain. An EMT spoke to her, asked her name, while gliding his hands along her body, checking for injuries.

The rib cage. Gabe pushed his suggestion into the man's head. *Get her on the backboard. Gently. Her rib is broken and will puncture the liver if you're not careful.*

The EMT quoted his concerns to his partner. Together, they followed Gabe's silent dictation.

Raph sprang to his feet and spun around. Two paramedics were bent over the bus driver. The first medic said, "Work him up," and the second quickly cut away the driver's sweater and attached twelve electrode pads to his chest, connecting him to a heart monitor. It registered faint, erratic heartbeats—signs of a heart attack. The first medic started an IV in the man's limp arm while his partner prepared to insert a tube down his throat. The monitor's alarm went off. "We're losing him!" the second medic barked. He began CPR.

While the medic pumped the driver's chest, Raph flashed over. *Sixty-nine-year-old male. Heart attack. Lost control of the bus. Slid on the ice. Hit the culvert, rolled, and plunged into the ditch.*

A burst of blue light flashed down the road, and Michael emerged from the epicenter, marching in hard, powerful strides. He was furious with himself, evident by the energy radiating around him like heat sizzling above a long stretch of desert road. His translucent eyes raced over the scene. In an instant he knew: twenty-four children—fifteen female, nine male. All under twelve. Two adult females. No life-threatening injuries remained.

"Where have you been?" Raph demanded, walking over. His prism eyes blazed with rage. Michael stalked past him without answering.

"You have her?" he demanded of Gabe crouched by the girl. Raph was on his heels, yelling and pointing to the dead driver.

"We lost one! It wasn't his time yet!"

Michael stepped back as though he'd been sucker

punched. Had he miscounted? He whipped around and headed for the bus driver. *Male. Sixty-nine years old.* The heart had stopped so Michael hadn't picked up his presence in the initial scanning.

Michael glared at the paramedic who had decided the bus driver was beyond help. He yelled, *"Try again!"*

"What are you doing?" Raph grabbed his arm. "It's too late! You've lost him!"

Michael jerked free. *"Keep trying!"* he shouted into the medic's head.

"He's gone, Michael! It's too late! *You* were too late!"

Michael grabbed Raph by the collar. "Do not tell me it's too late!"

"It *is* too late!" Gabe said. "He's already here."

Michael shoved Raph away and swung around. The faint imprint of the bus driver, Jimmy Doogan, was standing in the road. He appeared bewildered by the scene, all those children in his care, bleeding and crying. He grimaced and wiped away a tear that wasn't there.

"What are you doing here?" Michael demanded, startling Jimmy. He stalked over and took him by the arm. "Get back in there!" He shoved Jimmy toward his dead body.

It was a desperate move, and Michael felt himself spiraling out of control. He'd never lost a soul before. And he wasn't about to let one slip through now.

"Use the defibrillator!" he yelled into the medic's head. *"Try again! Try again! Try—"*

"Stop!" Gabe shouted. "You'll scar the medic for life!

He'll think he didn't try hard enough! He'll think—"

"He didn't!" Michael yelled, pushing past his brother. Using his newly discovered manipulation, Michael narrowed his concentration and forced his energy into the medic. The guy looked at his partner and then at the bus driver. He frowned and glanced curiously at the defibrillator.

"Push the button!"

As if in a trance, the paramedic mumbled, "Clear," and then reached out to push the button.

His partner grabbed his arm. "What are you doing? I've got the epinephrine ready."

"I think…I don't know. I think I've got to shock him." He pushed the button and the bus driver's chest spasmed. They watched the monitor. Nothing changed.

"Again! Try again! Don't stop!"

"I think I'd like to stay," Jimmy Doogan's imprint said. "Please. I want to go with you. It's so warm and peaceful and…" He looked up at the night sky already beginning to swirl into a supernatural, cosmic blackhole—an open door just for him. "I want…I'm ready to know—"

"It's not your time yet, Jimmy."

Gabe sucked in a breath. "You can't tell him that! You know it's forbidden!"

"We're wasting time here," Raph growled, glancing around. "The longer that imprint hangs around, the more likely we'll have reapers or soul seekers raining down on us. I like destroying them as much as the next guy, but we've got a lot of kids in pain here. Michael, you have to take Jimmy Doogan

Home. He was *your* responsibility. You blew it. Escort him Home. Now."

Michael's temper flared. This couldn't be happening. Not when he'd worked so hard to save every soul. The full expanse of the bus driver's existence spun through Michael's subconscious. He understood the meaning of the man's life in an instant. *Jimmy Doogan was a good man. He had lived a good life. But it just wasn't his time yet.*

Michael stepped toward the paramedic, intent on yelling another instruction. Then he sensed an intrusion. He turned to a figure in spirit form walking up the road. A good-looking guy, about twenty-five with shoulder-length brown hair. He wore a brown leather jacket and jeans.

"Hey, guys, remember me?"

Raph walked closer, eyeing him curiously. He seemed pretty cool, like an old friend. But something was off.

"You sound familiar."

"Yeah, it's me. I picked up some new threads. No more grungy jeans and T-shirt. Not too shabby, huh?" He smiled, brushing his hand over the soft leather sleeve.

"Degan," Raph said flatly. "You just can't take a hint, can you?" The last time Raph and his brothers had seen the soul seeker lurking around a car accident, Raph had snapped his neck and sent him back to Hell.

Degan laughed softly. "Aw, c'mon, guys. You knew I'd snag another body as soon as I could. Besides, we're all working stiffs here. No pun intended." He grinned. "You know, I really hated using that kid's grungy body. So, I wanted to stop by and say thanks for killing me. I was due for a change. And might I possibly pick up a little roadkill while out and about? It's nearly Christmas."

He sounded too casual, like he was just doing some late holiday shopping before the stores closed. Then he found Jimmy Doogan's imprint, and raw greed climbed into his eyes.

"You really think you're getting past all three of us?" Michael asked dispassionately.

At that moment, Jimmy's imprint began to make an odd oohing noise. Degan curled his hands in anticipation. If he could only touch the imprint, it was his to Take.

Jimmy's eyes widened in surprise at the same moment the medic hit the defibrillator again. The monitor registered a sharp spike in sync with Jimmy's imprint being sucked back into his body—vacuum style. The monitor fluttered and fell into a steady rhythm.

Michael smiled at Degan while Jimmy's heartbeat grew stronger. "Sorry for the wasted trip." He crossed his arms, posturing confidence. What Michael really wanted to do was exhale with relief and collapse from sheer emotional exhaustion. That was the closest near-loss he'd ever had.

"Hmm." Degan frowned pensively. "Mind telling me how that happened?" Michael glared at him, so he raised his hands. "Okay. Never mind. Not my problem. You don't have to explain your freakiness to me. Now, *him* on the other hand..." He nodded toward the trees where Dimitri Patronus stood, watching his sons work.

Chapter 6

The Inside of
All Things Out

I'm sitting in bio class, typing two pages of notes and have no idea what they say. My fingers are on autopilot, and my mind is on Michael. I haven't seen or heard from him since he abandoned me in the middle of the countryside last night. David took me back to my jeep, as Michael said he would. But I waited up most of the night, hoping he would pop in and let me know he was okay. He was so upset when he left that I wanted him to understand I was fine. But I *am* wondering why he didn't stop the kiss sooner.

I peek sideways at Raph because I've caught him covertly watching me throughout class. No smile. Just intense curiosity. I worry he's growing suspicious of Michael and me. I try not to make eye contact for too long. I'm on guard, especially today when I'm preoccupied with thoughts of Michael.

I fiddle with my stylus and try to cook up an innocent reason to interrogate Raph about Michael's whereabouts. And then Mr. Wagner says five words I've never heard before.

"When we dissect the body—"

I startle, and my stylus flies out of my hand, but Raph snags it lightning-quick, and our eyes lock. The room falls silent.

"Is there a problem?" Mr. Wagner turns from the grease board, where he has been divulging a plethora of information I've been tuning out.

Raph hands over the stylus, so I take it and whisper, "Did he say, 'When we dissect the body'?"

"Yes. I did," Mr. Wagner answers impatiently.

I slide down in my seat and feel my armpits tingle with sweat.

What body? A frog? Are we dissecting a frog? Why doesn't he just say frog, then? Maybe it's a pig. Maybe—

"Miss St. James? Is there a problem?"

Everybody is staring. I look at Bailey who understands I've been caught unaware. She is biting her lips together to stop from laughing. Her eyes bulge, begging me not to speak. But I have to because, well, I'm me.

"I guess I don't understand what we're really dissecting."

Mr. Wagner scoffs. "You don't *understand?* We've only been talking about the evaluation of the human body *all* semester. We've discussed our future journey through tissue, veins, organs, and the general body cavity as a way to realistically observe human life. Have you paid attention *at all?*"

"I thought you were speaking metaphorically just now," I say. About half the class groans. Okay, I understand this is biology, and we have been delving deeper into the human anatomy than a typical senior class. But I don't recall anyone ever mentioning dissecting a *real* human body.

Wait—I do remember my first day of bio. Bailey had jokingly said we were prepping for an autopsy.

Crap.

Mr. Wagner reiterates that we've been on standby for an impromptu field trip to the morgue. Apparently, Christmas has come early, and we're off to the New Haven Hospital morgue this very afternoon.

Oh, what fresh Yuletide hell is this?

After lunch, the entire bio class clomps across the snowy parking lot. "All aboard the poor man's limo," Bailey grumbles, leading the way up the bus steps.

I've given up on seeing Michael today or discreetly discovering his whereabouts from Raph. I'd hate for him to become more suspicious than he already seems to be.

Bailey sits beside me and starts griping about Duffy. How irritating he's been lately. "It's like that time he pulled an Adderall-nighter. All hopped up to cram for that astronomy test when we had to chart the constellations."

I'm scanning the parking lot for Michael's truck and only half-listening. The bus lurches forward, and I slump in my seat, disappointed. Then we stop short, and the door opens, and my second heartbeat springs to life. I hold my breath as Michael climbs aboard.

He is greeted with an array of teasing and grumbling for playing hooky most of the day. He jokes with the guys, laughing like he's in a pretty good mood. I try to catch his eye, but he doesn't even look in my direction. He slides down the aisle, scowls at Raph, and then collapses into a seat somewhere behind me.

I sit still, searching for signs that Michael misses me. The second heartbeat is slow and steady. But there is no tugging at my heart, and I feel a terrible letdown. I gaze dismally out the window and bury my hands in my coat pockets. I've been worried about so many things lately. How does Michael feel about having to stay and watch over me when he received a call for help? Does he think our relationship is getting in the way of his duty? Have I become a distraction? A burden, because I can't handle a simple kiss? Is he regretting us?

The sky is slate gray with a promise of more snow. The bus heater is doing its best, but I shiver anyway. My phone vibrates in my pocket, so I pull it out. The word *Indigo* appears, indicating Michael is texting me. It's the only word suitable to identify him since I can't possibly use his real name. I thought it was very clever of me, but Michael is embarrassed and wants me to change it.

I read.

Michael: *Can I assume by your pouting attitude that you are upset with me?*

Hmm. I narrow my eyes.

Me: *Can I assume by your audacious display of ignoring me that you haven't missed me?*

I wait and realize Bailey is still complaining about Duffy and expecting me to confirm that he *is* being an asshole. She is seriously annoyed this time, so I agree wholeheartedly with whatever she's said.

"Wow. Yeah. That's ridiculous," I mumble.

My phone vibrates and I read.

Michael: *Ah, so you are confirming the pouting attitude comment. Fine. Pout away. It's freaking adorable anyway. As to my 'audacious display of ignoring' you, it should be clear by now that it's an unfortunate necessity in our situation. It would hardly be appropriate for me to pounce on you at every given opportunity. As much as I would love to.*

I smile and clutch the phone to my chest. *As much as I would love to* runs around my head, making me warm inside. I look back out the window before Bailey gets suspicious and grabs my phone. Okay, I'm feeling somewhat pacified. Michael doesn't seem upset about leaving in a rush last night. And besides, I love when he says things like that.

But honestly, we still have the issue of the kiss. Why did he refuse to stop in time? He ignored the warning signs. He ignored me pushing him away. I've never seen Michael like that, so insistent, so demanding. So full of need that he put my life at risk.

I know he must feel bad about it. But why didn't he come over last night to check on me or even apologize?

I tap the screen and type.

Me: *I have seen 'As much as I would love to' firsthand. It put me in a dead faint, and I think I'd like an explanation.*

The bus hits a pothole, and we're jostled up and down. Bailey almost drops her phone and snaps, *"Son de la bitch!"* She eventually juggles it to safety in her lap. Duffy throws her a scowl.

"See that?" she whispers hotly. I nod. Duffy is giving both of us the stink eye. It seems to be catching because Jordan the Leerer, Pacer, Casey, and JD are now staring. I can't shake the feeling that they know something we don't.

My phone vibrates again.

Michael: *This hardly seems the time or place to discuss our lack of restraint, now does it? I'm sure we can find appropriate accommodations later. Somewhere dark and quiet perhaps, to go over the issue in greater detail?*

Our lack of restraint? Our lack?

Why, that little Casanova. He's flirting about something he insisted was dangerous. How can he be so *blasé*? So…unconcerned? I can't wait to hear his excuse.

Everybody starts talking about this week's basketball game. And then Casey cranks up his iPhone. Duffy starts singing "Who Spiked the Eggnog" by Straight No Chaser. It sounds like a forties throwback, but Duffy whips it into a rap. The guys stand up, singing and clapping. They're actually not bad, but everybody laughs at them anyway.

By the time we pull into the New Haven hospital parking lot, Duffy has changed his tune. He's irritated by the Christmas cheer he's created, so he starts singing homegrown lyrics in the key of Suck the Magic Dragon. Everybody groans. We all file out and head into the building.

We are introduced to the director, a severe-looking lady in a white lab coat who leads us into the dark underbelly of the hospital—otherwise known as the bowels of the morgue. It's a cold, sterile place. I can feel Michael walking some distance behind me as we trail through a labyrinth of long sanitary corridors. I'm glad he's here, if only for some vague comfort. I don't like this place. It reeks of disinfected death.

Below us are gleaming white tiles and above are bright

florescent lights that make our eyes squint involuntarily. I am a mouse inside the maze box. It's claustrophobic, and I whisper to Bailey, "Exactly, *why* did we agree to this?"

"Because we need to pad our college résumés like a preteen's bra. Plus, I need to meet some seriously hot doctors."

We stop outside the autopsy room, where the director tells us we are looking at a state-of-the-art facility. "With negative pressure ventilation," she says. We all nod knowingly as though we're impressed. Because we aren't medical students, we can't enter the actual autopsy room. We file into the observation room and peer through a wide window that takes up most of the wall. The director stands in the adjoining autopsy room and communicates through a speaker.

She introduces Dr. Marks. He is youngish and seems good-looking, although it's hard to tell because he's wearing the full monty of protective garments: blue surgical gown, cap, face shield, gloves, and matching shoe covers. I can hear Bailey purring, so I elbow her, and she stops. She grins with a look that says, *He's yummy*, so I laugh. Then I feel a sharp tug in my chest that yanks me backward. I flail but JD catches me before I fall.

"Sorry. Slippery floor," I mumble, embarrassed.

"No problem," he says, smiling. JD is one of those guys who is so quiet you wouldn't know he's in the room. I look past him to Michael, lounging in the back because he doesn't really need to pay attention. He's just going through the motions of being a typical high school student. And maybe he's a little bored. I mean, he can't seriously be concerned if I find the doctor attractive, right?

I give him a look that begs the question: *Do you honestly think I'm the one fawning over a grown man wearing a thin blue dress?*

Michael just grins.

Dr. Marks says he's ready to begin, so I refocus my attention. The class huddles against the glass wall, and I put on my studious face, determined to focus and get the best out of this.

The autopsy room is lined with shelves and countertops laden with jars, metal bowls, and scales. There are carts serving an array of torturous steel devices, not unlike those at my dentist's office. The room is dominated by a long stainless-steel table on which lays a body draped with a cloth. I'm suddenly thankful for the wall of glass separating us.

"At least we can't smell all the putrid stuff, right?" I mumble to Bailey.

"Don't tell me you have a weak stomach," she says.

I shrug. "Guess we'll find out."

We all pull out notebooks and pens in eager anticipation like the sadistic little voyeurs we are. This feels wrong and highly intrusive, and I realize how much I don't want to do this. I don't want to be here, and I wonder why no one else seems bothered.

Raph slides in next to me, so I look up at him. A moment is all he needs to sense my emotions. He offers a sincere smile.

"Stop worrying, okay? Try to think of it in medical terms. An evaluation of disease. The extent of that disease into tissue and organs and so forth. Now, take a deep breath. Good. You'll be fine."

Stop worrying. Yes, that's what it is. Not queasiness for

what I'm about to see but actual concern that we are interfering with this person's personal space, the intimate details of someone else's life. I understand it's necessary for the medical community and society as a whole. I get that. But it still feels too invasive, too...

Raph elbows me and nods with understanding. I forgot he is gifted in the human anatomy area. He told me as much the day we met. Of course, I didn't know then that he knew humans on a molecular level. Not to mention being on friendly terms with their souls.

I take another deep breath and think, *Well, if a guardian angel says it's okay to slice open a dead human and peek inside, I guess it is.*

The white sheet is removed by one of two assistants and there it is, the body. We are not told his name, but Dr. Marks says he is a white male in his mid-sixties. I wouldn't have guessed his age because any laugh lines have lost their humor. But he does, or *did*, have a full head of dark hair, a thin mustache, and a goatee. Also, he is as naked as the day he was born. This guy is so dead he doesn't look real. Most of us recoil involuntarily but Bailey is craning her neck to see everything. Nothing seems to faze her.

Dr. Marks begins his observation, while I clutch my pen and stare at the cadaver. I pretend this is an episode of "CSI" and it's simply routine.

The body is a bit paunchy around the middle with a dull grayish pall. His head is resting on a block, while his profile shows an aristocratic nose and strong chin. His skin seems waxy and dry at the same time. His lips are a thin gray line. Lips that once laughed and smiled are stilled forever. This is a man no longer, but an empty shell left on the beach. I can't help wondering...*Did he take with him the words he spoke, the love he gave, the cruelness he inflicted? Where is the heart of the shell?*

Looking at him makes me feel small and humble, similar to when I'm standing before the ocean. I realize that no matter what our age, we're all just children with nothing but potential. No matter what we think we've accomplished or come to know, we are naïve and altogether basic. Not inconsequential but wholly unprivileged to the scheme of things. We are a grain of sand with the entire universe inside each one of us. We are the excess of our emotions. But aren't we more than the nerves in our skin? More than the fluid in our spine, and the blood in our hearts? The value *must* lie in our souls, not our muscles.

I remember the vision of Mom at the Borderlands, that in-between pathway of Heaven and Hell. It was there she showed me the lost souls wandering aimlessly. They were sad and scared—afraid they would be swept up by dark forces and dragged to Hell. But still, they roamed, searching for their answers, refusing to be escorted into the folds of Light. Of safety. They cried for answers, and I felt their pain.

I'm so lost in thought that I've missed the first incision, a long Y shape from both collarbones to the breastbone down to the pelvic bone. Dr. Marks has laid open the chest and is examining things on the inside. We watch through the mirror above the table.

"Lung sections demonstrate excessive pulmonary vascular congestion with inflammatory cells..." The two assistants slide their gloved fingers into the area. Dr. Marks fiddles inside and removes the heart, lifting it up for all to see. There is little blood, but my throat constricts because I can see the heart feverishly pumping in his hand. Still alive.

But of course, it's not. And I have to blink hard to make it stop. My mouth waters as a lovely wave of nausea rocks my stomach. I lean my forehead against the cool glass pane and close my eyes. It's too confined and hot in here. I can't breathe.

I feel Michael's gentle tug on my heart. I almost turn and say I'll be fine but catch myself. I'm not thinking clearly.

"You okay?" a voice beside me says. A hand squeezes my shoulder, and I look over. It's JD, frowning with genuine concern. Bailey looks, too, and now she is worried.

"Yeah. I just need some air." I head for the door and glance back at Michael and Raph. They step forward but I shake my head, telling them not to follow. I'll be fine.

I move into the corridor and inhale deeply, but it smells like antiseptic and doesn't really help. I hate being the first to wimp out. I figure if I can get some water I'll be fine to return. Without hallucinations.

Around the corner is a vending machine, so I insert a couple of bucks and punch the button. When I'm finally chugging down water, I give myself an internal pep talk.

I can do this. There's hardly any blood. And besides, I'm pretty sure the grossness of it isn't my problem. I just don't know what is.

I feel a little better, and then I turn around and spew water all over the floor. I embark on a coughing fit and nearly drop the bottle. Not ten feet away is a man in a funky burgundy jacket and black silk lounging pants—one of those smoking-jacket outfits you see in late-night movies. He has a full head of dark hair, a thin mustache, and a goatee. He's a bit paunchy around the middle. I recognize him instantly, and my hands begin to shake.

"Fancy a chat?" he asks pleasantly enough. I stare without blinking. Then he gets irritated and snappy. "Well? Who are you? How does this work?"

"I'm uh...uh...but you're..." I point in the direction of the autopsy room.

"I should think so, love," he says.

Aside from the British accent, he sounds rather condescending. He steps closer, and I wheel backward, slipping on the water I've spilled. I land hard on my tailbone. He continues, so I do the backward crabwalk to get away. He stops. I stop. He starts forward again, and I start backward again.

"Oh, for the love of God! Get up!" he says.

I scramble away and race into the women's restroom and bolt the door. *What in the actual hell! Okay, this was stupid! I should've run to Michael! Now I've locked myself in.*

"Ahem." The man clears his throat, and I whirl around. There he is, standing by the sinks. I gasp and fumble with the lock. "Really?" he says. "I mean, really? Are we going to do this...really?"

I stop and reconsider. Then I force myself to calm down. After all, I've dealt with angry demons and a temperamental guardian angel boyfriend. Surely, I can handle an insolent apparition.

My phone vibrates in my pocket, but I ignore it. My mind searches for something to say, but the man speaks first.

"Well, who are you?" He is very impatient.

"I'm, uh, uh—"

"Yeah, I think we've already established that you are 'uh, uh'. Let's move on, then, shall we? Tell me how this works?" He shifts his weight and then peruses my clothes. I'm wearing a gray teddy jacket, black T-shirt, and ripped jeans. He scowls as though I didn't get the memo that it was time for a wardrobe change. "Thank God I perished before *this* became all the rage."

I pull my jacket around my shoulders and ignore his rudeness because this is weird enough. "How does what work?"

"Well, my goodness, love, don't tell me *I've* got to explain this to *you*." He puts his hands on his hips and gives me a haughty attitude.

This guy is really starting to piss me off.

I regain myself and move deeper into the bathroom. We circle each other, both curious and slightly concerned.

"You're dead, right?"

"Don't be cheeky. Of course I'm dead. You think I'd consort in the women's toilet if I weren't?" He snarls with distaste. "Now tell me how this works. You can help me cross over, yes?"

My heart jumps a beat. *He thinks I can help him!* I'm excited beyond words but also confused. This shouldn't be happening yet, right? I'm not ready.

"Well, I—wait—why do you think *I* can help you?" Maybe he knows something I don't. Maybe this is how it all begins.

"Because you can bloody well see me!" he yells.

"Oh." That wasn't the answer I was hoping for. "But when you died, didn't you see anyone, you know, hanging around that could—"

"You mean like an angel? Yes, well, I did. I just wasn't..." He puts on a pout and inspects his nearly translucent fingernails.

"Ready to go," I finish for him.

This is where spirit walkers come in. Michael explained that some souls are reluctant to let go. They think they have unfinished business and demand to stay behind, earthbound. Even after death, there is a form of free will. Michael's father jokingly calls them Free Radicals. They inhabit the spirit world but are in more danger now than when they were alive. One touch from a soul seeker and the apparition is dragged to Hell. No questions asked.

And, of course, there is always a reaper's snare to be wary of. If the lost souls can't find a spirit walker to help them cross over, they're left to wander. Or hide from evil entities. Honestly, I'm surprised this guy is still here.

"You have unfinished business?" I ask, and he nods. He's become quiet and, dare I say, humbled, by his predicament?

He takes his time, telling me his name is Colin Firth, to which I choke out a laugh.

"Of course, not Colin Firth the actor," he says sullenly. "Everybody *loves* him."

I detect a note of cynicism but tell him to continue. He briefly describes his life in London as a theater actor. He came to New York for a while, appeared in various productions, and was playing a part in the New Haven Theater when he suffered chest pains. He refused to go with his guardian escort because he wanted to return to England with his body. As a policy of the hospital, a routine autopsy is performed. He's been stuck around, waiting.

"I'm sorry, Mr. Firth," I say with all sincerity. "But I don't know what I'm supposed to do."

I explain about my training as a spirit walker, or lack thereof. I tell him I haven't a clue how to help him. I tell him to be very cautious until he finds the right spirit walker. I believe he'll know them by the light in their palm.

"It's called a Chelsea Light. It will distinguish spirit walkers from the evil entities trying to trick you." I look at my palm, remembering the light I saw there at the Borderlands. The one Mom kissed into existence but disappeared right after. It's never reappeared, and this has me worried.

Colin Firth nods sadly. I offer to introduce him to Michael and Raph, but he refuses. "That train has left the station, I'm afraid. There is nothing anyone can do. My fate lies in the next spirit walker I find, I suppose."

All I can say is, "I'm sorry." I feel horrible for failing him and angry that I haven't been trained yet.

My phone vibrates again, reminding me that I should head back before they send someone to find me. I unlock the door, and we walk out together. Michael and Raph are waiting in the corridor, their eyes sliding from me to Mr. Firth. They say nothing, but I know they see him. I wait for a reaction. When no one speaks, I make the introductions with a brief explanation of Mr. Firth's dilemma.

"You should go back now, Sophia," Michael says without acknowledging Mr. Firth or his problem. "Mr. Wagner is asking about you."

I frown and make a swift gesture toward the apparition that says, *Don't be rude, at least say hello to the man.*

Raph strolls over and says, "Hey, what's up?" to Colin Firth. Then he looks hard into my eyes, assessing me.

Mr. Firth smooths out his lapels with a forlorn expression. "My mistake, mate. I thought perhaps the young lady could help me cross over. Apparently, she can't."

I flush with humiliation. Raph understands my distress and wraps an arm around my shoulders.

"It's okay, Sophia. I know how much you want to help. When you've become a spirit walker, you'll get to help lots of lost souls. Just be patient."

I smile tightly and peek at Michael. He is stoic, and I repeat what he's told me.

"Michael said it probably isn't going to happen anyway. That sometimes the process just doesn't come to fruition and..." I feel a lump building in my throat that's making it hard to talk. I don't think I knew how much I wanted this until now. Until I felt this insatiable need to help someone and couldn't.

"*Why* would you tell her that?" Raph demands. Before Michael can answer, Mr. Firth clears his throat.

"I don't mean to interrupt but would someone kindly direct me to the best place to hail a spirit walker. I would like to begin my journey Home. I feel my time is running short."

"It doesn't work like that," Raph says, keeping his eyes

on Michael. "But stick around, if you can. Sophia may be able to help *when she is ready*."

"No, she won't," Michael says, pushing away from the wall he's been leaning against. "She's not experiencing the Awakening anymore. So if I were you, Firth, I'd get the hell out of here. A hospital morgue isn't the safest place to hang out. You're on your own."

"What's *with* you?" Raph says. "First last night and now this?"

"What about last night?" I ask.

They clam up and glare at each other. There is an argument simmering between them, and I only hope it doesn't have anything to do with Michael arriving late after receiving a call. I'm sure he didn't tell anyone he was with me at the waterfall so...

"Michael, what's he talking about?"

He shakes his head, refusing to answer. But Raph has no qualms about opening a can of worms in front of me or Mr. Firth.

"He almost lost a soul."

I clench my jaw and stare at Michael. That's why he didn't come over after his call. That's why he didn't let me know everything was alright. It wasn't. I can see the truth written all over his tight expression. *But why didn't he tell me?*

"He's gotten careless lately," Raph continues with a challenge in his voice. It's almost like he's purposely inciting Michael's temper. Their energies rise to the point I think they might fight and then it abruptly recedes. They relax and a second later Bailey comes sashaying around the corner.

"Man, you guys are missing the best part," she says and then stops to assesses the situation.

I look at Colin Firth. He shakes his head. Bailey can't see him. He walks straight through her, and I give a soft yelp of surprise that prompts her to cock her head at me.

"*What* is going on out here?" she asks as she shivers. "Geez, it's colder than a witch's tit out here. C'mon, Soph, you're fine, right?"

She doesn't wait for an answer but snakes her arm through mine and leads me away. I glance over my shoulder at Michael and Raph. I want to know what Michael won't tell me. And why I feel Raph knows exactly what secrets we are keeping.

Chapter 7

Dante

"You look like a big heap 'a douche," Santiago said. He was standing between the two cages that held Dante on his right and Vaughn Raider on his left. He was talking to Dante, whom he'd never really liked. Then he turned to Vaughn, the first guy to show him any kind of sympathy when he arrived in Hell. He gripped the bars and peered inside. "You don't look so hot either."

Vaughn gave him a loose smile. "Aren't you a little short for a storm trooper?" he asked and then chuckled at the kid's melancholy expression. "You wouldn't have a Wookiee or a lightsaber on you by chance?"

Santiago had been stoked to introduce the Demon Knight to America's most epic space opera. He missed their late-night binge parties.

"Sorry, I didn't think..." He grimaced. "I didn't know if the rumors were true. They said Lord Brutus went all zombie apocalypse on you guys. At least you're still standing. You wouldn't believe what I've stepped over just getting down here. Raw meat hanging off people. Or what used to be *people*. No offense, but spoiled demon blood stinks like putrid in a can, ya know?"

"We need to get Vaughn out of here," Dante said, leaning into his chains.

"You mean *you* want out!" Santiago accused savagely, flipping long jagged bangs from his eyes. The tips were bloodred and matched the spiked ends in the back. His black Metallica T-shirt looked like a zombie chew toy but seemed better for it. His skinny jeans and multicolored high-tops were splattered with some grime best left unidentified.

"Everybody knows what you did," he said. "How you got Wolfgang crucified. How you got Vaughn sent to the Nether Region."

"Uh, still here, kid," Vaughn said.

"Who said Wolfgang was crucified?" Dante asked, narrowing his eyes. Skaw had implied Wolfgang's punishment had been severe, but he hadn't provided details.

"I gotta a source in with the gossipmongers," Santiago said, arrogantly. "Word is that Wolfgang wasn't just crucified once, he hit the daily double. At midnight, he's nailed to a cross and impaled with iron hooks. All over. Every inch of him. And the hooks are heated to cauterize the flesh. He's left simmering in his own blood. And then when he's good and baked, the hooks are ripped out and the wounds left to fester. Some say he's dragged through the lava pits. Some say Lord Brutus allows his vultures to peck at the wounds and nibble on his eyeballs. Then at midnight, the party starts again: wash, rinse, and repeat. All because of you."

"You've gotten your facts wrong, kid. Wolfgang is getting his due," Dante said and then looked over at Vaughn, weak and shattered. Hardly recognizable. Dante felt sick with guilt—for Vaughn. Who had always stood by his side, no matter what. But Wolfgang? He could rot.

"I'm not here for you, by the way," Santiago said, glowering at Dante. "I'll do whatever Vaughn asks because he was nice to me. I'm still pissed about what you did on the surface. What you let happen to Vaughn. He didn't deserve this."

"I had more important issues to deal with than your feelings," Dante said tightly. He wanted to remind the underling he was speaking to a member of the Royal Court. But since Santiago might be their only hope of escaping, he held his temper in check. "My apologies if you were put out. But some of us received more than a tongue lashing and sent to our caverns without supper." He rustled his chains to mark his point and then nodded toward Vaughn. "He's in a bad way."

Santiago gave Vaughn a grim look and murmured, "I figured as much."

"So, kid, you gonna be the Igor to my Frankenstein?" Vaughn asked, hoarsely.

"Whatta ya think I'm doing down in this stinkthole?"

"You will have to steal a key from the guards," Dante said. But Santiago was already digging into his mouth. "What the—"

The Demon Knights watched in disgust as Santiago pinched a string tied to his tooth and then carefully pulled something up from his stomach. He gagged a couple of times but eventually hacked up a black key covered in thick yellow stomach acid. He held it up, grinning.

"Eeew!" Dante and Vaughn grimaced.

"Hey, it worked," Santiago grumbled, disappointed they weren't impressed by his ingenuity.

"How did you come by the key?" Dante asked.

"You know how the twins are always dropping things?"

"Eeew!" They grimaced again.

"You assholes want out or not?" he snapped.

Dante seethed at the insult but said nothing.

Santiago went to work. After cleaning the key, he opened their cells and unshackled them. In less than five minutes, the Demon Knights were walking free—Dante in a rush and Vaughn, not so much. He was too weak to move on his own, so they supported him while he dragged his feet.

"You have a plan?" Dante looked over at Santiago struggling under Vaughn's weight. He couldn't have sympathy for the kid when his own back was still sizzling. Not to mention the burning chain tattoo on his arm.

"Yeah, through here," Santiago grunted and jerked his chin toward the corner from where he'd come. "By the way, I know about Sophia. How you want to go after her."

Dante didn't acknowledge anything but wondered who else might know. Was Lord Brutus spreading the word like a plague? Just how many demons or reapers would he send to turn Sophia dark?

"I need a fix or somebody's gonna lose an arm," Vaughn said. "Seriously, man, I'm holding back the urge to throw one of you into the wall. Demon's got the munchies."

When neither one offered themselves, Vaughn shrugged

free and pushed Santiago out of reach. He turned to Dante and gestured toward the wall. "Do it."

"We don't have time for this. Can you hold off a little longer?"

Vaughn let his eyes answer for him. They were swirling. His demon was rising.

Dante yanked the tattered remains of his shirt from his waistband and threw it aside. Then he fixed his eyes on his friend and prepared himself. "I wish I could say this was going to hurt me more than it hurts you, but..."

In one quick movement, Dante grabbed Vaughn and spun him around like throwing a discus. Vaughn sailed across the chamber and smashed into the stone wall. A resounding boom shook the bunker. Dust sprinkled down. The stones crushed around Vaughn's large frame, while the Demon of Affliction let go a wail of pleasure. Vaughn flopped to the floor and rolled over with a dreamy smile. "Ahhh."

What should have broken every bone in his body only caused minor damage. The pain was pure joy. Vaughn slowly climbed to his feet, yelled a battle cry, and then rammed two fists into the wall. They sank elbow deep, and his head rocked back in satisfaction. He wanted to go again, but Dante restrained him.

"You broke your hands," he complained, inspecting the damage. They were two black, bloody mounds. "We needed these to get out. How long will it take you to regenerate?"

Vaughn blinked lazily and gave him a sappy grin. "I dunno but I *lack* it," he slurred, and then snorted a laugh.

"Oh, great!" Santiago said, throwing his hands in the air. "He's stoned! And we gotta long way to go!"

"How long?" Dante asked, suspiciously. He didn't fully trust or understand the kid's adoration toward Vaughn. He also had trust issues which didn't discriminate.

"Too long to stand around bitchin' about it. C'mon." He grabbed Vaughn and led him down the back corridor.

They snuck past three guards playing keep-the-spleen-away-from-the-twins, and then slipped into a dark hallway that rose two levels higher and split into ten different directions. Dante inspected the slimy tunnels critically, but Santiago never wavered. He followed the third from the left, pulling Vaughn along when he veered off in distraction.

"Just how long till he's back to normal?" Santiago muttered, heading down another tunnel.

"He should regain his composure when the effects settle in his system." Dante grasped Vaughn by the scruff of his neck to keep him moving forward. "Right now, he's swimming in it."

Santiago paused at the end of the tunnel and peeked around the corner. He pulled back and whispered. "Guards at the end. We gotta wait till they pass."

"Just where are we going, anyway?"

"You guys are planning to resurface, right? Yeah, I figured. Well, I want in. For real this time. Not jackin' around and watchin'. I liked it up there. I mean, being dead and in spirit form and all. It was pretty sweet, actually. And I wanna go back."

He had a confidence that Dante found both amusing and comforting. It meant he and Vaughn weren't being led into a trap.

"In exchange for what?"

"I'll give you what you need. And you'll let me go along."

"And just what do we need?"

"You'll see." He checked around the corner again. "Let's hit it."

They snuck across the hall and down a narrow shaft that brought them to another tunnel. They traveled on for thirty minutes in relative silence, constantly changing directions. A stream of murky water ran beneath them, and a new malodorous stench hung in the air. Not that there was much air to begin with. It was stifling and getting darker until they rounded the last corner. A circle of light shone from above. There was an opening at the top of a metal ladder attached to the wall.

"C'mon." Santiago started up the ladder, with Vaughn following and Dante up last. Vaughn fumbled awkwardly but eventually hung on.

"My hands hurt like a sum'bitch," Vaughn said as he gripped the rungs.

"Happy now?" Dante smirked.

Vaughn laughed and started singing, "Hurts So Good" by John Cougar Mellencamp. "C'mon baby, make is hurt so good."

Dante rolled his eyes.

Santiago stopped and yelled down at him. "Shut your rat trap! Wanna get us caught?" His agitation only served to amuse Vaughn. He smacked Santiago's legs, and the kid flailed and kicked him in the head.

Vaughn squeezed his eyes shut and shook his head clear. "Ah, that's better. Thanks, kid."

"Ok then, listen up. We're sneaking in the back way so move aside."

They were still perched on the ladder, halfway up the wall. Dante and Vaughn leaned aside while Santiago swung his leg out so his foot tapped a lever on the opposite wall. A secret door drifted open, and he stretched forward, grabbing it. Gaining his balance, he hauled himself across the threshold, stuck the landing, and spread his arms saying, "Tah-dah." It was pretty clever. A concealed entrance behind anyone climbing up the ladder.

The Demon Knights looked less than impressed, so Santiago continued. "Anyway, the front is always guarded so we'll hoof it around back." He stepped aside, allowing them to follow his lead.

Once they had crossed over, a short walk down a dim tunnel brought them to the back entrance. It was a wooden door covered with thousands of needles and no handle. Obviously, no touching was allowed or desired. Santiago pulled out a heavy stone pestle from behind a brick and began pressing imprints into the needles. Five round impressions across and two below it.

"What are you doing?" Vaughn asked.

"What's it look like? I'm knocking." He inspected the seven indents and then sang out, "Shave and a haircut, two-bits." He grinned. They didn't.

The door opened inward, grating against the stone floor. The Demon Knights followed Santiago inside.

By all appearances, it was a college dorm room—if *Battlestar Galactica* had exploded inside Hogwarts. Beneath the rough stone ceiling was a twin bed with rumpled *Star Wars* sheets pushed against a stone wall. Along the walls were various posters: Einstein sticking out his tongue, Geeks Gone Wild Comic-Con 2000, a *Big Bang Theory*'s Friendships Algorithm chart, and a high-gloss rendition of *Star Trek* Emojis, alphabetized.

Shelves were lined with *Game of Thrones* mugs next to a row of shot glasses etched with the four main houses: Stark, Lannister, Targaryen, and Baratheon. This was followed by a collection of intergalactic bobbleheads. A Tardis mini fridge sat in the corner piled with various gadgetry, and a smart can was maneuvering around the floor, hoping to catch any trash thrown in its direction.

Farther to the left, however, was a whirling, flashing conglomeration of flat-screens, computer towers, and remote cameras with tons of video and audio devices. At the epicenter sat Julian Wexler, a twenty-two-year-old boy genius and former grad student.

"What the frak? You're late!" Julian stuffed a cigar stub between his teeth and thumbed the remote, shutting the door behind the Demon Knights. He wore a black cowboy hat, white boxers, Ewok flip-flops, and a ratty red robe over a T-shirt that said MEGABYTE MY ASS!

"Hey, I told you it wouldn't be easy," Santiago said.

"Well, we're mega-short on time. Let me see your arms." He gestured impatiently at the Demon Knights, who exchanged bewildered looks. "Santi! Didn't you tell them why they're here?"

Santiago grimaced. "Guys, meet Julian Wexler, boy genius and destroyer of all good moods."

"What do you do down here?" Dante cast a suspicious eye around the room. He recognized the locations visible on each surveillance monitor as the five gates of Hell.

Julian rocked back in his chair and began massaging the magnetic stress ball in his hand. "Look, we can spock, paper, scissors this to see who gets to play twenty-one questions, but like I said, we're mega-short on time, so if you'll just—"

"You will answer my question!" Dante shouted, startling Julian. "I am a member of the Royal Court, and I expect you to follow my orders. Now, tell me what, *exactly*, you do here. And who you work for."

Julian blinked rapidly, visibly shaken. "My apologies. I work directly for Lord Brutus and The Order. Um, as you can see, I'm on surveillance and all things high-tech on this level of Hell. I've recently developed a new identification system that makes the old system obsolete. A facial recognition for DOIs that now extends to iris and retinal scans. Voice and demonic recognition. Code like that."

"DOIs?" Vaughn asked.

"Demons of Interest. And you two have been DOIs for about four hundred years. The difference now is that you'll no longer have permission from Lord Brutus or The Order to re-surface. Just like before, you've been grounded. Only this time you're on the short list. The permanent list."

"But we passed through the gate unharmed last time," Dante said, scrutinizing the monitors.

"That's because The Order gave you a death contract. And they gave *me* your permission to resurface. I let you pass through my gate. Now, your access will be denied. Meaning, you can't even sneak across the gates of Hell. You see, in about thirty minutes my new system will be implemented. The moment you reach the gates, an algorithm will scan these digital readouts here"—he indicated one of the monitors— "and identify you two as DOIs. In the past, all the gatekeepers had was word sent down from The Order to stop anyone grounded from passing through. Now, biometric features are applied, along with a key code; it's a two-factor authentication process. You need a key code to go along with your biometric ID."

Dante frowned because this was more or less gibberish to his traditional senses. Ignoring progress on the surface, as he had hoped to do, had not done him any favors. The world outside his own had not only advanced beyond recognition but had passed him by while he had been consumed with tracking his lover's soul. He could see now that he had a lot to learn. Quickly.

Vaughn chuckled at Dante's confusion and clapped him on the shoulder. "Well, if that don't smoke your hard drive. We're gonna need a password to get out of Hell."

Julian laughed but stifled it when Dante's scowl landed on him. "Yeah, anyway, you guys would flame out with those tattoo leashes. But I figured we have a narrow space of time to get you through the gates undetected."

"And there's more," Santiago jumped in. "Tell them about the weapons."

"There's weapons?" Vaughn perked up, practically beaming at the mention of the word.

"Not just any weapons," Julian said arrogantly. "Mystical

binary weapons. But it's completely beta. You gotta understand, nothing's been tested. Theory is, my new weapons will
kill demon hunters."

"And angels!" Santiago blurted out.

Dante and Vaughn froze and stared at Julian.

"I never said it would kill angels," he snapped at Santiago, and then glanced uncomfortably at the Demon Knights.
"I said if the bugs are out and it's code, it could take one down.
Meaning, if my recipe is correct and galbanum was the missing
element, it *might* have the *possibility* of debilitating an angel
long enough to drag it to Hell. Otherwise, the whole thing
could crater." He shrugged, unwilling to brag so easily in front
of members of the Royal Court as he had to Santiago.

Dante had never heard of such a thing. Vaughn was too
intrigued to be suspicious.

"So, where is this little she-devil?" Vaughn poked around
the room, tossing crap aside.

"Doesn't work like that," Julian said, snatching the
lightsaber chopsticks and Wookie coozie that Vaughn was
holding. "Look, I have to embed them, okay? And we're running outta time, seriously, man."

"What do you mean 'embed them'?" Dante asked.

Julian took Vaughn's arm. "I mean embed them, here,
inside the forearm. It's optimal placement."

"Hey, if it's gonna hurt, make mine a double." Vaughn
held out both arms.

"Yeah, I figured you'd say that. People don't call you Sir
Bleeds A Lot for nothing."

"People call me that?" Vaughn flashed a smile at Dante. "Well, hell, let's get it on or should you buy me a drink first?"

"We have to agree on a *deal* first," Julian said, returning to this chair. "Here it is in a nybble: I load you guys with some high-tech, black art weapons that amp your fighting skills on the surface." He glanced at his digital clock. "We've only got fifteen minutes left until I shut down the system while my new security algorithm is implemented. It'll take thirty seconds. During that time, you two will pass through the gates, taking Santiago with you. Once you're topside, you take care of your business while Santi takes care of mine. But remember, because you leave through gate five, you *must* return through gate five. Anything else is sub-optimal. I'll be wired in. But if you try sneaking back through another gate, that gatekeeper will fry you. The plan will crater. Roger that?"

Dante scrutinized the monitors while considering the plan. Once again, most of Julian's instructions were foreign to him, but one thing struck a chord. "Why the weapons?"

Julian became coy and shrugged. "I've been heads down on this for a while. Could make an impression at this year's Demonic Games and...well, my bandwidth doesn't allow for testing down here so..."

"And why should we trust you? Why do you not embed one of these homegrown weapons in yourself and resurface?"

"Totally boss questions, but it'd be a waste of prime time to embed the weapon in myself. First off, I couldn't take the subcutaneous pain. And second, I can't resurface. I'm a gate-keeper." Julian shrugged out of his robe and revealed a green chain tattoo emblazoned around his bicep. It was identical to the ones Dante and Vaughn had just received but without the extension down their arms.

"Isatou brands all gatekeepers. We're stuck in this black hole forever. Whereas you guys got a bit of tether, at least ten links down to your wrists. I heard the witch proclaim you bound to Hell, 'just like the Master.' Well, Isatou was trying to clue you in. She did you a favor. The Master has a very long tether. And if your brand is like his, you could probably resurface without much restraint. I mean, you can't go continent hopping like before, but I bet it'll get you where you wanna go."

So that's why Isatou had winked. She had deceived Lord Brutus *and* did Dante a favor.

"How do you know about a conversation that happened less than an hour ago?" Dante asked.

Julian tapped one of the touch-screen monitors. It sprang to life and revealed a live stream of the Death Bunker—the two empty cells that previously held Dante and Vaughn.

"I was on TV this whole time and didn't know it." Vaughn laughed and smoothed back his hair.

"Do you know why Isatou would help you?" Julian asked, but Dante turned his back on him. He knew exactly why the witch would have helped him, and it was nobody's business but his own.

"She got a thing for you?" Vaughn elbowed him and grinned.

"I would hardly call it a 'thing,'" he said, shrugging it off.

"Well, how 'bout it then?" Santiago asked. "Is it a deal?

'Cause if we're gonna do this, we gotta make like a tree and get outta here."

Dante contemplated and then looked at Vaughn. "I am going either way, but you...must decide for yourself."

Vaughn grinned. "Hey, we're dead either way, right?" He understood Dante's concern, his guilt over their current situation, and he appreciated the gesture.

Dante chuckled and laid a hand on Vaughn's shoulder. His old friend was himself again, even repeating that ridiculous saying he'd worn out ages ago. "Grazie."

Once Julian got the nod of approval, he began peeling back the Einstein poster. Carved into the wall was a secret shelf that held a black velvet bag. He emptied the contents onto his palm, an obsidian handle similar to the one Isatou had used to create their tattoos.

"This is gonna burn like before, only worse. I'm not using a fire chain but direct pressure."

As much as Vaughn wanted the pain, Dante insisted he be tested first in case something went wrong. Steeling his nerves, he offered his arm. Julian grasped his wrist and then shook the obsidian handle like a spray can. When the tip glowed bright red, he carefully placed it against the smooth skin of Dante's left forearm.

Dante flinched as his arm sizzled and smoked. His body began to tremble while Julian went to work, etching an exotic-looking dagger into his skin. Blazing heat raced through Dante as though his blood was boiling. Sweat broke across his forehead, and his eyes rolled back. Like all his torture sessions, he forced himself to escape the pain by focusing on Sophia.

By the time Julian started on his right forearm, Dante was lost in his self-induced visions. Thanks to Persuasion's hypnotic powers, he could remove himself from the pain his body endured. He was with Sophia in the courthouse, feeling his arms around her slender body in the lavender dress. He reveled in her warm, sweet kiss as she offered herself in complete submission. She was his. As it was always meant to be.

I'm coming, Sophia. And this time, I will not be asking your permission. You will come home with me.

"There! It's done." Julian sat back, panting. He wiped his forehead and studied the elaborate artwork on Dante's arms.

When Dante roused, the burning sensation came flooding back and snatched his breath. He doubled over and balled his hands into fists. His forearms sported twin dagger tattoos. They were deep purple at the hilt, fading into red blades with gold tips. Swirling black lines overlaid the daggers like coiled snakes.

"Now what?" Dante said through clenched teeth.

"Shake your arms down like you have something up your sleeves."

Dante shook his arms, forcing excruciating pain from his forearms, down to his wrists, across his palms, and into his fingertips. Again and again, he shook until the tattoos began to slide beneath his skin. It was almost unbearable, and he had to stop for a moment to compose himself.

"Maybe it's like a Band-Aid," Santiago offered. "Just give it a good, hard—"

Dante flicked a cold look that stopped further suggestions.

He eventually took the unsolicited advice and snapped his arms, first one and then the other. The dagger tattoos ploughed through veins and tissue in sporadic jerks until they shot out his wrists and landed in his palms.

"Well, I'll be a monkey's uncle," Vaughn said, his eyes alight with excitement. "It was excruciating, wasn't it? Please say it was."

Dante tested the weight and balance of the daggers. They fit perfectly in each palm. He tried to rotate them, but they were stiff on the spin.

"Oh, yeah," Julian said. "They won't rotate too easily, but with practice I think they'll loosen up. And you can't throw them. They're obviously attached to the body."

"Okay, my turn." Vaughn forced his way between them. "Hit me with your best shot."

Carving the tattoos for Vaughn went much faster. Julian didn't have to work slowly to regulate the pain. Once done, Vaughn easily shook them into his palms and worked on rotating them.

"Seriously man, I think I love you," he said, strolling around and whipping the daggers in and out of his flesh.

Julian began stuffing various items into a backpack. "Now, listen up," he told Santiago. "I have a list of everything I want in here, so don't lose it. This won't hold it all so get another bag, okay? I don't want the circuit boards damaged. And if you can't find the electric conductive ink pens, don't get the solar ones. Kinda useless down here. I'll take a bag of quantum bits instead. And don't forget the case of Top Raman and the

Death Star soccer ball." Santiago gave him a look, so he said, "What? It's an icebreaker for hittin' on underlings when I'm in flirt mode."

"Wouldn't want you to have an intergalactic episode when you're trying to hook up." Santi smirked and then fell on the bed as Julian punched him in the arm.

A scraping sound like a guillotine being dropped brought them around, and Julian rushed to his keyboard, tapping a button to kill the noise.

"That's the alarm. You have two minutes to reach the gate before it's shut down and the new system is installed. So get through the gate as quickly and quietly as you can. Once you're over the bridge and through the Badlands, well, you know the rest. Up and around until it spits you out at the Borderlands, and then you flash to Haven Hurst. Just remember, you must return together through gate five. Good luck."

Chapter 8

Get Thee to a Bakery

The moment I turn off the shower I hear it, the faint thumping of drums. I didn't leave my music on, so I dry in a rush, pull on sweats and a T-shirt, and twist my hair into a small towel turban. I open the bathroom door as the beat climbs an octave higher. It's quick and familiar, but I can't figure why I should be hearing it now. I hurry down the stairs and catch Sundance, my golden retriever, at the bottom. I ruffle his ears and then we follow the wailing cry as the lyrics begin.

Dunna dunt, dunna dunt, dunna dunna dunt, dunna dunt dunna do.

"What the heck?"

I stop in the kitchen doorway and there is Dad and Bailey dancing their hearts out to "Chelsea Dagger" by the Fratellis. They are wearing frilly pink aprons and wielding spatulas. The kitchen smells of sugar, fresh bread, and honey. The countertops are a wild concoction of various ingredients. Something is sizzling in the deep fryer, but nobody seems to care.

Bailey's spatula is a microphone, and she sings at the top of her lungs. "*Well, you must be a girl with shoes like that...She said, you know me weeeell...*"

I break up laughing. Dad is radiant in his absurdity because he never could dance. He used to be a punk rock devotee back in the day. I was raised on the Violent Femmes, The Clash, and The Kinks. It's no wonder he's euphoric over The Fratellis. I can hear the similarities.

I am spotted and dragged into the kitchen, my turban tossed aside. I can't help but join in, bouncing and singing and laughing. Dad leads us in pogo dancing and then goes old *old* school in some contorted combination of the mashed potato and the twist. Pointing index fingers seem to be an important requirement. It is such a joy to see Dad happy! But seriously, I wish he could dance.

When the song ends, Bailey and I fall into each other laughing. Dad takes a proper bow. Then I ask what's going on, and Bailey presents their culinary clutter with a grand flair and a fake Russian accent, "Ve are mak-ink *chak-chak!*"

"What? What?" I ask, peering into the deep fryer.

Dad says, "Here, try one," and offers a plate. There is a stack of short stick-like treats that have been fried and bathed in warm honey. They are rich and dreamy and make my eyes roll around.

"We're testing out treats for the Winter Carnival," Bailey explains, shoving a *chak-chak* into her mouth and licking her fingers. "You've heard everybody talking about it—the big winter *prazdnik,* where we haul out the ol' *valenki* and *ushanka* and take *troika* rides through the snow?"

I raise my eyebrows in question. "Share with the class, please."

"Boots, hats, sleigh rides."

Ah.

"So any-vay," she continues, playing the czarina tour guide, "the dance is the highlight, ah-v course, but the *prazd-nik*—the festival—itself, is pretty ama-zink. It ah-vayz starts in December, and it ah-vayz has a Slavic influence. Vee are steeped in the Slavic culture all through Christmastime." She helps Dad remove the last batch of goodies from the fryer. Things are hot, and they have to be careful.

"I offered to cook something," Dad says proudly. He settles the treats onto a fresh plate and beams at me. I have a vague memory coming back to life. Dad used to love to cook. Before Mom died. Dad used to love music. Before Mom died. I'm ashamed to have forgotten that Dad used to be a normal guy, before our lives were upended by her death and the nightmare with Psycho Steve. Seeing him so happy again, dancing and cooking and…well, it's enough to make me tear up.

"Hey, none of that," Dad says, pulling me into a hug. He strokes my wet head and shushes me. "It's all good now. It's time we were happy again, right?"

I sniffle and say, "At least you've moved on from The Kinks," and Dad's face lights up.

"Hey, there's an idea!"

"You never told me *ser* papa could cook," Bailey says, snagging another *chak-chak*. "Of course, I had to teach him how to make these. Just be thankful he wasn't asked to make the borscht." She fakes a convulsion, and we laugh.

Bailey gives Dad the final approval on his first round of specialized desserts. Then we traipse upstairs, so I can continue my morning ritual before school. The kitchen goes quiet for a moment, and then we hear "All Day and All of the Night" by The Kinks, grooving from the speaker. I smile, feeling so grateful all of a sudden.

Bailey lounges on the bed, while I sit at my desk and squint into the mirror, applying a bit of mascara. I'm almost finished when she rolls over and asks a question that snaps my eyes open.

"What?" I croak, trying to pretend I didn't hear.

"C'mon, Soph, I know something was going on at the morgue. Sister ain't no dummkopf. You were so pale, like you'd seen a ghost or something."

I drop my head and make like I'm searching for something in the drawer. Bailey gasps. "Ohmygod! You *did* see a ghost! That's it, isn't it?" She marches over and swivels my chair around, forcing me to look at her. She reminds me about our little tête-à-tête in the library basement back in October. When Abigail Monroe and the McCarthy twins tried to hypnotize me, so we could put a hex on Psycho Steve. Bailey is not beyond believing I could've seen a ghost.

I scramble for an excuse, but my thoughts are somersaulting all over the place. I end up scrunching my face.

Bailey whoops and hollers and flings herself around the room. "I knew it! I mean, I can't believe it, but…I knew it! People are always seeing weird shit in hospitals." She flops back onto the bed and demands that I spill the beans. Every last little legume.

So, for the next thirty minutes, I tell Bailey about Colin

Firth dying—which she finds hilarious—not him dying but being called Colin Firth. And I remind her of the way she shivered from the sudden chill in the hallway. It was Colin walking through her. Then I explain that he thought I could help him.

"I don't get," she says. "Why would he think you could help him cross over? Just 'cause you could see him?"

I consider my answer for a long moment. I want so much to tell someone what I've been going through. How I've been desperately waiting for someone to come and explain how things work. Michael and Raph have their opinions, but it's not the same as sharing with a girlfriend. I don't have anyone.

I decide it's not fair and impulsively blurt out, "Because I actually might be able to help him."

I can't believe I just told her!

I hold my breath and glance around for something catastrophic to happen. If any sacred codes were violated or supernatural laws broken, there is nothing to show for it.

Bailey stares wide-eyed and says, "Uh, this is me being confused. Explain, please."

I nod and clasp my hands in my lap. "Okay, but…this is us getting on the rollercoaster, Bail. There's no turning back. We can't un-ring this bell so—"

"Yeah, yeah. I get it. So tell me already."

After another deep breath to calm my nerves, I tell Bailey about my potential to be a spirit walker. I omit the part about how I had to die to get this info, but I say Mom visited me in a dream and explained that I was supposed to be a spiritual warrior. I describe my visions—particularly that car accident on the notorious stretch of road called the S Curves. Everybody was talking about it for days afterward, so she remembers. I tell her Colin Firth picked me out as someone who could help him. I try my best to describe the visceral anguish I feel for failing him. He is in terrible danger roaming the spirit world alone. I don't know what will happen to him if another spirit walker doesn't hear his call for help.

I can't reveal much more, certainly anything about the Patronus family. Or what Dante and his fake family are. I hate omitting that part because I know how much she liked Vaughn. She has a right to know he is a demon. But they're gone now, and the less said about them, the better.

I pretend I'm not freaked by the whole thing and finish getting ready. I comb out my damp hair while Bailey stammers expletives and follows me in and out of the bathroom. I dry my hair upside-down while she pelts me with questions, most of which I can't answer. I don't know who is supposed to train me. Or why they haven't yet. I don't know why my Awakening hasn't progressed beyond visions. I don't know why I have this ability in the first place. And I don't know why it probably isn't going to happen after all.

We're crouched down, digging through a pile of clothes on the floor, when Bailey gasps with an epiphany.

"That night at the haunted mansion! Vaughn pushed you too far, and you went all *Hunger Games* and threw that knife. You almost hit Dante!" I nod, and she sits back on her heels, stunned for the second time. "Weird, I can't remember much more of that night," she murmurs. I don't explain that everyone was compelled to forget the nightmare they went through.

We haven't spoken about Psycho Steve since the night we tried to put a hex on him. Now seems the perfect time to unload, so I give details of what happened when he attacked me in Los Angeles.

"I threw a paring knife at him. Sundance attacked Steve at the same time, so it didn't actually hit him. But it landed right where his head had been. That was the first time I'd ever thrown a knife, and I swear, Bailey, I wasn't myself. In that moment, when I was pushed too far, I felt like someone else. Someone I think I'm supposed to be. Which is frustrating. I have some serious fighting skills somewhere inside me, but I just can't tap into them."

I feel myself choking up but force it down. This only makes my chest hurt, and I grimace and try to keep it together.

"So, why do you suck at paintball?" she asks, and I laugh and wipe my eyes.

"That's a mighty fine question." She's joking, but I mull it over. "Bailey, I must've done something wrong. Or maybe they decided I wasn't good enough. Or maybe it was all a mistake. Or maybe—"

"Maybe schmaybe," she says. "Listen, tchotchke, if they don't want you, it's their loss. Now—" I start crying, and Bailey wraps her arms around me. "C'mon, Soph, don't cry. I can't stand when people cry."

She rocks me for a while, and I feel pretty pathetic. Michael talks about how tough his Halo Masters are. How impressive and disciplined and demanding. As scary as they sound, I still want to be trained. I still want to be a spiritual warrior.

"Tears and mascara don't play well together," Bailey says, wiping my cheeks. "Now, listen. It's all gonna work out. I promise. In the meantime, let's take your mind off things with some tedious education. I don't know about you, but I need my caffeine hit before our daily incarceration." She offers a smile, and I reluctantly accept it.

Thank God for Bailey. Sometimes we're as different as night and day, but at least she gets me.

Once Bailey and I stuff ourselves into the appropriate amount of winter paraphernalia—boots, coats, scarves, and beanies—we clomp downstairs. Dad is still in the kitchen, waxing nostalgic with "Real Wild Child" by Iggy Pop. I smile wistfully.

Times are indeed a'changin' if I'm happy to hear Iggy's Blah Blah Blah *album again.*

After yelling adios to *ser* papa, we head out and make straight for the town square. It's hectic with people and snow machines pumping out fresh snow. Bailey tells me the snow-making gods will continue for days because the carnival booths and decorations are constructed mainly from snow and ice. We need more than our fair share from Mother Nature or Jack Frost or whomever.

I can already see the faint impressions of distinctive Slavic architecture, an eclectic display of Romanesque, neo-gothic, and renaissance with a touch of neo-baroque. Onion-shaped rooftops, small domes, and jagged spires are coming to life. The gazebo is being modified with sculpted pillars and a round tentlike roof. Mostly, it's a mishmash of blocks of ice. The towering Christmas tree has not been fully decorated, but the scaffolding around it looks promising. An ice rink is in the works across the courthouse's frosty lawn.

We veer toward our friends, huddled around a makeshift refreshment stand. They are resplendent in their winter attire of *valenkis* and *ushankas*. I realize I'll have to conform to this seasonal European influence or risk feeling like an outsider all over again.

Bailey waves and calls, "Comrades! I bring you the reluctant neophyte: Little tchotchke Sophia!" She presents me as though I haven't been living here for the past few months. But with all this Slavic persuasion, I kind of feel like the lost Anastasia, where everything seems vaguely familiar.

Everybody lifts their steaming Styrofoam cups. Rachel says, "Cheers!"

Milvi says, "Skol!"

I swipe her cup and say, "Down the hatch!"

And then Bailey swipes it from me, says, "Chin-Chin!" and takes a big drink. "*Usch,* Milvi!" Bailey grimaces and hands it back. It's hot herbal tea, not coffee, and she has an aversion to anything healthy. She spots a fresh plate of honey bread to sample, so we do.

"So, why is everybody *Stalin* around here?" Bailey asks, laughing at her own joke. She means, why is everyone out here and not in the café? Rachel explains that the Klondike Klub, the professional dogsledders, has hijacked our usual stomping grounds. They can't get into Mr. James's barn, where they usually hold meetings. I ask why, and we all look at Casey. It's the family barn, but Duffy answers for him.

"Well, it *could* have something to do with last night." He grins, and the guys start laughing and doing that guy thing where they playfully smack each other around, but it actually hurts. The Homo sapiens have just invented the wheel.

"Anyway, someone *might* have confiscated one or *possibly* two of the snow machines and *could* have aimed them at the barn. They *may* have made enough snow to cover the barn if anyone wanted to…say…snowboard off the roof?" Everybody laughs, and Duffy shrugs. "Now, I'm not saying I know for *sure* or anything, but yeah, it's *possible*."

Bailey rolls her eyes and mumbles, "*Durachit,*" which I'm guessing translates to something along the lines of "idiot."

The jig is up, and the guys can't hold back any longer. They start bragging about their supreme talents in the art of barn snowboarding. I smile, remembering Michael lifting me up and over the frozen river. I've spent some quality time surfing, but I've never been in snow until now. I finally get what all the snowboarding fuss is about. It's freaking awesome.

Just when I'm feeling all warm and fuzzy about it, my second heartbeat springs to life, and I could almost believe my memories have conjured Michael out of thin air. I spot him walking through the park with his parents. Bailey notices where my attention has gone and tells me Michael's parents are very involved in the Winter Carnival. Dimitri is something of a Slavic history buff, and Katarina ensures all food recipes are authentic.

Michael looks over when his parents become preoccupied with the mayor. I smile, but he just stares. First at me, then at Bailey, then back at me. I can't read his expression, and this worries me.

He can't possibly know I revealed my secret to Bailey. Right?

The moment Bailey becomes distracted by something else, Michael winks, and I feel a hot rush of excitement flood my system. God, what is it about a wink that can make a girl weak in the knees, literally? No matter when or where, if a guy winks and grins, all bets are off. I wonder if guys know how sexy it is? Probably not, or they'd be winking all day.

I try not to give myself away to Michael or anyone else who might be paying attention, so I lower my eyes. But I can't hide the smile tugging at my lips, I mean, damn.

"Would you get a load of him," Bailey says.

I look up quickly, thinking she means Michael, but her attention is in the opposite direction.

Over by a snow machine is that odd tourist I saw the other day. The one who borrowed Jason Momoa's hairstylist. The one who looks like he's rolled around Waikiki Beach one too many times.

"Accessory man," I say. "He's got everything but the board."

"Wrong accessories," she mumbles. "But he's kinda hot. For an old guy. He's got to be…what…at least thirty, right?"

We stand there gawking and discussing why his feet aren't freezing in his sandals. Or maybe they are, and he just can't feel them anymore. He seems fascinated by the snow machine and darts his hand into the stream of snow and laughs. Then he looks at me and holds up the snowball he has constructed. His face is alight with pride because it's a job well done. I am to show my approval, but I don't know what to do, so I just watch.

My second heartbeat accelerates as Michael casually strolls over. His parents have gone, and he is free to join us. We make the usual polite chitchat when in the company of others. And then Bailey is lured away by Duffy, who is finally ready to unload his complaints and excuses for his moodiness. They pair off while everybody migrates up the street toward the school. There is too much snow on the roads to bother driving.

Michael and I follow the others and eventually lag behind until we have privacy to talk. But we don't. He seems engrossed in his thoughts. I expect he is deciding how best to tell me what happened after he left me at the waterfall. I'll wait for him to explain. So, I match his casual stride, appreciating his hard thighs and tight torso with a certain amount of awe. He is engineered for power and love.

I wish I could slide my hand into his where it belongs. That way, I could be sure to go wherever he goes. Loving a guardian angel, I often feel like a forgotten grace note. An ornamental afterthought, hovering shadow-like until I can steal his time. I am living two lives: one in which I crave to be useful and one in which I crave to be filled with all things Michael. Top to bottom. Without his touch, my body feels denied its nourishment.

I can't risk touching him now, so I peer at him through my lashes. Like always, Michael's beauty is distracting. High cheekbones. Angled jawline. A sensual mouth that fits perfectly into the grooves of my own. His eyes are focused ahead, and I wonder what he's thinking.

Michael sighs. "I wish the cold didn't affect you," he

says. "Wouldn't mind rolling around in the snow for a while."

"If that's your way of avoiding a much-needed conversation, you can—"

"It's not. It's just what I've been thinking about. A lot."

"What?"

"Things I'd like to do with you." He grins down at me, and I blush despite myself. "I wonder if I could apply a Sigil of Heat on you," he says thoughtfully. "That way, we could roll around in the snow. With or without clothes."

I giggle and elbow him, and he breaks up laughing. His teasing is infectious, but I have serious issues to discuss.

"Stop," I say, laughing. "I mean it. You're just trying to distract me."

"From what?"

"From telling me what happened that night at the waterfall. I understand you had a call and had to leave me. I get it. But I have to know, Michael...did you almost lose a soul because of *me*? Like Raph said?"

His demeanor shifts, and the muscle in his jaw flexes. Michael can get angry all he wants, but we're in this together. I have a right to know if what we're doing is putting lives at risk.

We keep walking with only the crunching snow making conversation. I'll wait him out if it comes to that. Thankfully it doesn't. Michael takes a deep breath and then glances around before speaking.

"I'm sorry about leaving you alone at the waterfall. And I almost lost a soul because *I* was careless. But I'm handling it. Dad says no lines were crossed or rules broken at the accident.

Technically, speaking. But it wasn't an ideal situation. I'm not sure he fully believed my excuse for being late."

"Which was what?"

"That I was watching over another soul, making sure it was safe to leave unattended." We stop on the sidewalk while the others head inside.

"Me," I say.

"Yes, and it wasn't a lie." We stare at each other for a moment, and I imagine we're sharing the same thought—*it wasn't exactly the truth either.*

"What else?" I say.

"Nothing. We're leaving things alone for now. But I'll have to be especially careful in the future."

"I'm so sorry, Michael. I can't image what it's like, having someone's life in your hands."

"It's fine. We're fine. And Dad doesn't know anything about us or what really happened."

"It's not fine, Michael. You were late because I fainted. Because we were—"

"I couldn't leave, babe. Not like that."

He sounds tortured, and I feel awful. "We've made such a mess of things," I say softly. "We were careless. But, Michael, I have to know why you didn't stop kissing me. *Why you ignored the warning signs." Why you put my life in danger.*

The bell rings, and I think he isn't going to answer, but he says, "I would think that was obvious," and walks away.

* * *

Throughout my classes, I'm distracted by Michael's

answer. It's not obvious to *me* why he ignored the warning signs. He's the one who has always been overly cautious where I'm concerned. And it's not obvious to me why he's been acting strange lately. The Winter Trials can't be the reason because it started before that.

If I'm being honest, this change in Michael has people talking. I've heard comments about how intense he's been. How short-tempered and aloof. It's so unlike him. And even Raph and Gabe seem unsettled by his shifting moods. I haven't dared to mention that one of Michael's eyes turned brown the other night, and he looked like that Armaros guy. Michael didn't like that I saw Armaros in the library basement the night I was hypnotized, so I'm sure the comparison would go over like a lead balloon.

By the end of school, I realize I'm simply wandering around the edges of Michael's life. Glimpsing what is possible in his secret world but denied full access. It's a sweet, torturous existence.

I wish I had been Born of Light.

* * *

Bailey and I are walking through the square, and it's the first opportunity for her to vent about Duffy since their talk this morning. I listen with concerted effort. It keeps me from wallowing in my own troubles.

"So, in the middle of apologizing for being an idiot," she says while foraging for licorice whips in her backpack, "he starts bragging about some hookup in the city last month. When he almost got his man vegetables pureed in some chick's blender.

Like I wanna hear all the whorey details."

"So, what'd you say?"

"So, I said, 'Hey, say less. I got it. But that's no excuse for being King of the Assholes.'"

"So, what'd he say?"

"So, he said, 'That's funny comin' from the Queen of Over-a-cheaters Anonymous.' Can you believe that? He gets caught by some chick's dad while *in flagrante delicto*, and *I'm* the over-a-cheater? Pffft."

"Well, there was all that time you spent with Vaughn Raider. It kind of put Duffy's man panties in a bunch."

Bailey grins. "Yeah, Vaughn." Her voice is low and sultry, and she glances around the square like she might spot him. I don't have the heart to tell her it isn't going to happen. "Anyway, I told Duffy to be nicer to you, too. He's been quite the busy little turd."

We stop outside the café. "You guys okay now?" I ask.

She shrugs. "We're cool. Hey, you're not gonna work all day, right? You're meeting me later?"

"Yup."

We part ways, and I'm off to work at the *Gazette*, just around the corner. It's a short walk but long enough to contemplate Michael. I wonder if I could ask his family about his moodiness. It's a tricky slope because I can't give anything away. Maybe if I go around the backway and talk to Raph about the Winter Trials, I might get some info without raising suspicions.

I'm not inside the *Gazette*'s door but thirty seconds and

Miss Minnie is dictating a list of photos I can expect to take in the next few weeks.

"Aside from the customary basketball games," she says as I scribble, "there will be the *troika* rides, the ice-skating follies, the *pastila* contest, the *syrniki* breakfast, the—"

"You lost me."

"Best pastry contest and the pancake breakfast."

"And the *troika* rides I've been hearing about?"

"Sleighs drawn by three horses."

This makes me think of Michael and our sleigh ride, and I'm hit with a pang of regret. I wish we could return to our romantic interlude and undo the ending. I wish my tongue was made of honey and only said sweet things. I wish Michael could feel with *my* heart and understand that I long to do something meaningful with my life.

I wonder if I'll disappear if I ever stop wishing.

I reach for my cell phone to text Michael and then stop. I have no reason to lure him here, and he has no excuse to drop by. It wouldn't be wise, anyway. As far as I can tell, Miss Minnie notices everything. Gossip in a small town like Haven Hurst could get back to Michael's parents. It's not worth the risk, so I swallow my wishes and wait.

An hour later, I have finished my uploads and edits from the last basketball game. I offer to fetch something warm to drink.

"No, thank you, child. LeRoy left a fresh jug of homemade cider in the back." Miss Minnie smiles that crinkly old smile I've come to love. "You best get to the café. I'm sure

Bailey has reached her caffeine limit by now."

I laugh and stuff my camera into my backpack and then sling it over my shoulder. I'm halfway out the door when it hits me. *How did she know Bailey was waiting for me at the café?* I look back, but Miss Minnie has disappeared into the supply room.

Her prediction is accurate. Bailey is in the back of the café, sloshing the contents of java number four while reciting Dorothy Parker in a spontaneous poetry slam that she is forcing on others. With the blazing fireplace for a backdrop and the hearth for a stage, she is the center of everyone's attention.

Bailey sees me and hollers with unnecessary gusto. "Comrade tchotchke! Why so late?"

"I was dawdling. Why so loud?"

"She's over-coffeedent about her oration skills," Casey calls out through cupped hands. He is sitting with Lizzanne, Sarah, and Harper Rose, who are none too pleased to be subjected to Bailey's caffeine rants. "Please stop her before she hurts somebody."

I drag Bailey down as she begins singing, "Saaanta Stalin's comin' to town!"

I have too much homework for this nonsense, so I lead her toward the door. We stumble upon the tourist in funky surfer garb ordering coffee at the counter. He shifts from foot to foot, laughing as though embarrassed about something. Up close, I can confirm my take on his Aloha shirt. It's as legit as vintage can get. His boardshorts are hanging in there while his huarache sandals are living on a prayer—black tire soles and old rope that spirals around his ankles. He is smiling and staring at the blackboard menu above Mollie the Coffee Whisperer's head.

"Dude, I'll have a latte. No, wait! A chai tea—no, wait!"

He laughs at himself, mystified at the wide variety available. Mollie's hair is bright pink today, and she is sporting an exasperated frown. The guy seems oblivious to it. He reads aloud while his finger points at each option because there are too many, and he just can't keep track.

"Pumpkin spice! Dude, no—wait—you got anything coconut? No? Okay then, let's go with...no...wait, yes! Yes! Pumpkin spice! Dude, spice that pumpkin!" He heaves a sigh and settles down, happy with his final selection.

"Talk about counter-terrorism," Baily mumbles, and the guy swings around and gives us a big, toothy smile.

"Aloha, *wahines!*" He opens his arms like he's welcoming us to an enchanted island. Like we haven't seen each other for ages. "Don't mind me." He laughs again and continues in a slow rolling cadence as though his words are riding waves. "I tell you what, I haven't been back in ages, and man, oh, man! This place is off the Richter! It's got primo selections."

Bailey and I frown. This guy couldn't be farther from a local if he'd come from mars. Regardless, she asks if he's from around here. He snickers.

"Naw, dude, I'm feelin' like the *ha'ole* at *this* clambake."

Okay, this guy is weird. Ha'ole basically means white foreigner in Hawaiian. He is seriously lost without direction. I turn to leave, but what he says next stops me in my tracks.

"Hey, no worries, Sophia. She already knows." He nods

toward Bailey and cops a cool attitude. I stare openmouthed. I must've heard wrong.

"Excuse me?"

He gives me a free-spirited smile. "One ding won't make me cut out. Especially on a cruncher like this." He steps closer and lowers his voice. "I know you told Bailey all about me, so...you know...it's cool. I don't toss gremmies that easily. Just don't do it again. Yeah?"

Oh. No.

A bad feeling is knocking on my door, but I seriously don't want to answer it. I'm as stiff as a surfboard because I understood exactly what he said. And what it means. Bailey, on the other hand, is stumped.

"Okay, w*ho* are you? And *what* did you just say?" she asks.

The guy fiddles with his shirt, trying to make himself presentable all of a sudden. Then he extends his hand to me.

"Totally stoked to meet you, Sophia St. James. I'm Rama Kuan, your Ascended Master. Bitchin' cool, right?"

Chapter 9

Surfer Dude vs Comrade Tchotchke

"Holy mother of *Point Break* posers!" Bailey says, while I pace and gnaw on my fingernail. We are in my living room and surfer dude, Rama Kuan, sits on the edge of the sofa, watching me. His head is nodding like he's grooving to his own beat. I'm in a state.

"Are you telling me that you—*you, Mr. Cowabunga Dude*—are here to train me to be a spirit walker?"

The insult rolls right off him, and he breaks into a wide smile. "It's just like that, dude. Like I told you on the way over here. Name's Rama Kuan, and I'm yours for the duration."

I scrutinize him, from beach-blown hair and colored braids to saltwater sandals. He looks outdated and lost. Finally, I ask if he's sure he's in the right place.

"Dude! Last I heard you were in SoCal! I was totally stoked, so I took an early road trip back to the gold coast. You know, missing my brahs and whatnot. Had to shoot the curl till I was called up." He bobs his head, and I feel sick to my stomach.

"And just how long have you been at this?"

"Ridin' waves? Uh, for about—"

"Ohmygod! Not riding waves! Training. How long have you been training spirit walkers?"

He leans back with his hands up in surrender. "Whoa, *wahine*. Don't beat the *pahu*. Here, have a seat." He gets up and guides me into Dad's chair like I'm delirious, which I suppose I am.

He returns to his seat and rests forward on his elbows. He speaks slowly, calmly. "I dig your concerns. Really. It's cool if you wanna know my pedigree. Hey, I leave everything on the board."

He explains that he ascended around the turn of the century and that his soul is "totally enlightened," so I should have no worries about his "level of wisdom." I don't know what any of this means. I ask how many spirit walkers he has trained. He says "twenty," and I look at Bailey. She shrugs. We have no measuring stick to go by.

"Who was your first?" Bailey asks, hoping that will fill in some blanks.

He relaxes into the sofa, drapes an arm across the back, and rests his ankle across his knee. He cocks his head thinking.

"Hmm…probably shouldn't say but dude's honorable. He wouldn't mind." He smiles nostalgically at some memory. "Brah's name is Duke. Duke Kahanamoku."

The name sounds familiar, so I strain to remember where I've heard it. A visual memory pops up. Huntington Beach. My old stomping grounds. There is a restaurant at the pier named Dukes, in honor of the famous Hawaiian surfer. My face lights up, and I spring forward.

"*That* Duke! You're saying the most famous surfer in the

history of surfing is a spirit walker?" Rama Kuan grins, and I get it. "Okay, that's pretty cool. But, you have to stop the surfer speak. I mean, you do you, and all, but can we ease back on—"

"Dude!" he wails, overly offended.

"Dude!" Bailey laughs, pretending to be overly offended.

"Seriously, I don't think I can be trained by someone who sounds like the guys I used to hang with at the Wedge."

"Ah, the Wedge." Rama Kuan sighs with longing.

"What's the Wedge?" Bailey asks.

I shake my head impatiently and wave her off. "This surfing place. Balboa peninsula. Newport Beach. Never mind. Point is, we need ground rules. No surfer speak."

He looks doubtful. "Well, my first Awakening was in Hawaii, and it was totally righteous. Kinda solidified me, yeah? 'Sides, I make the ground rules at this clambake, and…the speak is what it is."

The speak is what it is?

I slump in my chair and consider the turn of events. I can't help feeling disappointed. Especially after Michael described his Halo Masters as elite warriors. I remember seeing that band of Halo warriors at the Borderlands with Mom. They looked ruthless. I don't know what that makes my Ascended Master, but I'm feeling supremely gypped. Dude.

"We cool?" he asks, and I shrug because I don't seem to have a choice. Then he stands and fills his lungs. Once he has emptied them, he turns to Bailey. "Sorry, sister, private party for the next hour. And we gotta kick-start it before the Pops gets home."

The realization hits me. *I'm finally starting my training!* I quickly walk Bailey to the door, eager to get started.

"You think he's gotta girlfriend?" she asks. We look back at Rama Kuan, shaking sand out of his sandals and laughing.

"Not in this realm," I mutter, and we giggle.

"Find out," she says.

"Nope," I say.

"But he's so hot. He looks just like—"

"I know, but this one's off-limits."

She pouts and says it's not fair that I have all the fun. I roll my eyes and open the door. I promise to call her the exact minute I'm done; then we say good-bye, and I close the door.

Honestly, I'm more excited to tell Michael. I wonder what his reaction will be. He's got to be excited for me. Now that it's finally happening. Right?

We head upstairs for privacy because Rama Kuan says it's best if Dad doesn't know about my training. I agree. Dad is happy now. I don't want him worrying. About anything.

As I change into comfy sweats behind the closet door, Rama Kuan tells me to call him Rama, or Ra if I'm in the mood to "totally nick his name."

Once ready, I ponytail my hair and start limbering up. "I've been doing some Pilates and running on the treadmill at the gym," I say. I want to be clear that I'm taking this seriously. He cocks his head and gives me a goofy smile.

"Uh, that's cool." It sounds like a question.

I jog in place and punch the air, ready for some serious kick-ass fighting pointers. Michael said his first day of training was grueling and painful. I'm gearing up, but Rama frowns.

"What?" I ask, stopping. "I can do the downward-facing dog, if you wanna start there."

He laughs and says, "Take a load off," and we arrange ourselves on the floor. He sits in the lotus style, so I do, too. "Listen, I don't wanna eighty-six your enthusiasm. I dig it. Truly. But you can't expect to barrel roll the first time out. You'd go aerial and ragdoll it, yeah?" I frown, so he holds up a hand. "Hey, no worries, but the lesson is this: baby steps. Dig the philosophy, and the rest will follow, yeah?"

"Yeah," I say, not liking the sound of things.

"Sweet, now let's angle off the expectations and clear your mind. Accept the speak, and the path will be revealed. It's like blasting the pylons. You'll get shredded if you're not prepared. So now, dig this: There are three trials you gotta pass to get you there. First: Purification of the Soul. Gotta get your head right, dude, or it stops there. Second: Illuminative Way. Once the mind is stoked, you'll see the way. Seriously. Your vision goes off the Richter. And Third: Empowerment of the Physical Form. Kinda like that barrel roll you were trying to ride. It comes in time. When the mind is ready, the body will follow."

I nod and clasp my hands in my lap. I'm so excited. I want it to all happen. Now. At once. Instant gratification is my new addiction.

"Naw, dude, you gotta chill." He reaches over and opens my hands, placing them palms up on my knees. "Don't hang on to what you think you know. Open up. Receive your gifts."

I relax my hands and leave them open. He sits back and

copies my posture. He tells me to close my eyes and breathe evenly. He tells me there is an individual mystery inside me. We can unravel the mystery only with a clear mind. I am to let go. To move past all definitions that I have given myself or that have been given to me. I have to touch the deepest level of purity within myself. To recognize the truth within me.

There are some things not made for words. There is knowing—what was known at the spark of creation, the moment of existence. The feeling of certainty. When my mind is clear of all distractions, labels, and expectations, I will face the light within.

I inhale with my eyes closed and concentrate. This is hard. There is always something in my mind. I can't clean my slate without something taking its place. Without realizing it, my hands have closed again, and I feel Rama's warm fingers prying them open. I refocus and listen to his deep, smooth voice.

"Hear the sound of water rushing through your mind. The water takes with it all the loose thoughts and fragments left behind. Let them go…let them go…let them wash through the channels of your mind until the walls are bare. Release them… release them…"

It doesn't sound like him anymore. No surfer lingo or annoying Valley twang to distract me. It seems to be the voice of another. He has gone somewhere inside himself and pulled out his inner guru.

I frown, distracted by the change in his voice and my analysis of it. I hear him sigh, so I open my eyes. He shakes his head, and I close them again, trying hard to focus.

"Stop trying so hard," he says. "Unclench your thoughts. Concentrate on each inhalation and each exhalation. Listen only to the rhythm of your breathing. Place yourself in the direct center of your being. Feel the love that lives in the center of you. Visualize a ball of white light. The light of love that lives within yourself. Feel the love spread throughout your body, filling up the empty places. But always, the ball of white light pulsating within you.

"Now, touch each finger to your thumbs and breathe evenly. Visualize the ball of white light. It grows stronger as you touch each finger to your thumb. Breathe through the mouth, not the nose. This will access the spine. Move the fingers, one by one, and breathe. Move the oxygen up and down the spine. Watch the ball of white light."

I do as I am told, visualizing a ball of white light, breathing through my mouth, feeling the oxygen up and down my spine. I'm shocked to discover that I can feel it. I can see the light as clearly as if my eyes were open. But the light is pale blue now and reconfigures as though wanting to take shape. I hear a faint ringing in my ears.

"Your spine will reveal your destiny," Rama says, his voice so soft I can barely hear it. "You must access your own soul, Sophia. It's there, within the light. Do not look for it but *feel* for it. It's the flower of life within you. Formless. Free. Glowing with emotion. Feel for it..." His voice trails off into a chant that I can't discern.

My mind is numb and active at the same time. I feel something swelling inside me. The ringing is louder, and the light is no longer pale blue but swirling with every shade of blue imaginable. I sense that it's a powerful energy force. Its movement is making my heart race. My arms are trembling, and my hands have curled into fists again.

My head snaps back, and my mouth opens as I exhale a strange breath that seems to come from the deepest part of me, well beyond my lungs. "Ahhhh!" A rush of sound comes out without my permission, and my eyes fly open. My chest is pumping furiously. My body is shaking, and I am staring at the ceiling.

It takes a moment to regain my senses, but I eventually close my mouth and lower my chin. I look at Rama. He has scooted back and is gaping in dumbfounded silence. We stare until my breathing returns to normal.

"Wow," I say, forcing a dry swallow. "Hope that was normal. Was that normal?" I'm starting to feel concerned. Rama's eyes are huge. He looks a bit confused, like he was on a bender and doesn't know where he woke up.

"Uh, yeah for sure, dude. I mean, no…not really. It's like you jumped ahead fifty steps. How ya feel?"

I consider and shrug. "Okay." I have a dull headache but nothing worth complaining about.

He seems a bit flustered and scratches his head. "You ever, I mean, um…how's your heart?"

"How's my heart?" My eyebrows rise because it's my head that aches.

"Yeah, I mean, for sure your heart's normal, right? You've never had any funky business with your heart? Transplant or anything?"

Uh-oh. I think of Michael and my two heartbeats. No, that's definitely not normal. I don't want to explain things and risk Rama telling me we can't continue.

"I'm cool," I lie.

He gives me a skeptical look, and I wonder if he can sense my emotions the way Michael can.

Luckily, he moves on, and we discuss everything I felt. He listens patiently. I can't tell if he's impressed or alarmed. He tells me that I'm on a good path. That I'm headed to the natural state of being. That once I find the soul within myself, I will experience a feeling of great perfection. I will reach the highest path.

"And what's the highest path?"

"Definitive enlightenment," he says, nodding as though it's the newest thing all the cool kids are doing.

"So how am I doing so far?" I ask, stretching my legs. They ache something awful, like I've been sitting in the funky flower position for days. I glance at the clock. "Holy crap! It's seven o'clock! I thought you said it would only take an hour!"

We climb to our feet. "Dude," he says, "you were totally immersed. I've never had anybody go three hours the first time out. Usually, my gremmies, I mean…my first timers, can only sustain an hour. Tops. Your concentration skills are off the Richter."

"Yeah, well, I've had plenty of practice thanks to the SATs and college essays." He shakes his head as though it's not the same thing. I can't get into it now. "That being said, I don't wanna sound too normal here, but…I do have a ton of homework so…"

"Naw, man, it's cool. I dig it. You have to keep up the normality. And the Pops just got home. So I gotta bail. But listen, hate to add to your load and whatnot, but you got some home schooling for me, too."

"Oh."

"Yeah, but don't freak. I'm keeping you in the shallows for a while. First off, you gotta find a word, you know, your mantra word. Then you gotta repeat this word when you hoof it to school. Do it over and over till your breathing matches your word. You dig?"

"I dig," I mumble. Already, I'm imagining what everyone will think, hearing me talking to myself.

"Cool. Then you gotta name your days. Say, like, tomorrow. You're gonna say tomorrow is your day of happiness. Or tolerance. Or whatever. Make that day true to the word. See, we gotta build up your spiritual maturity, yeah?"

"Will we train again tomorrow?" I ask, but he becomes harried, looking around and checking pockets he doesn't have.

"Aznuts! The Pops is coming up the stairs. I gotta bail but I'll be in touch." He backs into the closet and shuts the door. I roll my eyes. I have an Ascended Master hiding in the closet, and it should be funny, but I'm still feeling slightly gypped.

"Sophia?" Dad calls from the hallway. "I got takeout."

"Be down in a minute," I holler. I wait a beat or two and then open the closet door. Rama Kuan is gone.

* * *

It's a school day like any other of late.

I play subway salmon against the current, hand in

assignments at the last minute, download an empty memory card for the school paper, which prompts a sternly worded lecture from Mrs. Cooley, gobble down food I barely taste, stare across the table at Michael's empty chair, race back to my last class where I have left my jump drive, then rush into astronomy and throw myself into a seat just as the bell rings.

Only nobody is here, and I'm officially confused.

Then I see the note written across the grease board in Mr. Cummings's scrawl: *If you can read this, you're too close...to being a moron. You have forgotten that we are meeting in the gym today. See you there, Sophia.*

Son de la bitch.

I haul my assets back out of the chair and remind myself, *This is a day of tolerance. This is a day of tolerance. This is a day—*

Christmas music crackles over the school intercom system. It's Lynyrd Skynyrd's rendition of "Run Run Rudolph." I take the advice and make a mad dash back out the door.

As I head down the hall, Willa Brown, the admin's secretary, makes an announcement over the music. Whoever has parked their snowmobile on top of Principal Davis's car kindly remove it. Her voice is slurred, and I'm guessing the guys spiked her afternoon tea. Again. It might also explain why her elf shoes are on the wrong feet.

I crash to a stop at my locker, dump my armload of books, and then run to the double doors at the end of the hall. I walk into mass confusion and stop at the top of the stairs. I try to locate my class somewhere in the gym below. Our next basketball game has been cancelled due to bad weather, so every conceivable committee, club, or anything resembling a group has claimed eminent domain on the gym.

Aside from cheerleaders getting tossed around in a corner, everyone is working on decorations for the Winter Carnival.

The chess club is constructing life-size chess pieces in turn-of-the-century Russian uniforms. They look more like angry nutcrackers. The art club is painting nesting dolls, also life-size. They have celluloid smiles that give me the creeps. There is a stage at one end of the gym, where Duffy has taken over the glee club and now has them singing "I Won't Be Home for Christmas" by Blink 182. It's very un-Christmasy, and people are staring and slowing down production. Principal Davis and Mr. Cummings are yelling and pushing their way toward the stage.

I feel eyes on me, so I turn back to the right. There is Michael, the only one standing perfectly still among the bustling crowd. He's too far away, so I'm lacking the necessary second heartbeat that makes me feel whole. Sometimes, I wish I was one of those autonomous girls who excel in their oneness. Those girls who don't need anyone else to fill their void. Independent and free, without the nutritional value of romantic love and the nourishment it provides. And then I see Michael and everything inside me yearns for him. He is my heart's mate.

Michael is wearing jeans and an ice blue shirt that makes his eyes glow without effort. He has just come from outside, and his hair is windblown and sexy. He lifts his chin, wanting me to come down and join him. I make a quick sweep of the room before landing back on him. Michael shakes his head. He knows I'm searching for his family. His seductive grin tells me not to worry so much. We are alone in the crowd.

Excitement blooms in me. I've been waiting all day to tell Michael about Rama Kuan. I know he's been against the idea of my Awakening, but I'm sure he'll change his tune now that my training has finally begun. He'll see how happy I am.

Principal Davis has chased Duffy from the stage. Mr. Cummings has switched the sound system to the school's holiday playlist, and "Stay a Little Longer, Santa" by Shemekia Copeland begins. The sultry, jazzy vibe seems to unify the entire student body. Everyone starts nodding and grooving as the song takes off.

"You look so handsome in that bright red suit...For a man your age you sure look cute...Smile brighter than a Christmas tree...All the girls want to sit on your knee..."

It's infectious, and I feel myself swaying along. Then I lock eyes with Michael and descend the stairs, one...slow... step...at a time. I have an idea, so I pause at the bottom. Michael blinks slowly and gives me that sexy sideways grin. I wiggle my eyebrows and turn in the opposite direction, laughing as his grin fades.

I ease into the crowd, sashaying to the music in a wide circle around him. I catch glimpses of his tan face and blond hair. He is tracking me. Measure for measure.

I tap out the beat on my thighs, leisurely strolling without a care in the world. Fifty feet away, Michael is walking parallel to me, watching my every move. I peek around the tallest nesting doll. Michael hesitates and then comes at me. I turn and look over my shoulder, giving him a *Catch me if you can* grin.

I feel a sharp tug on my heart that knocks me into the

geek squad. They're working on drones loaded with snowflakes and tiny sleighs flitting overhead. Michael is making himself clear—he can control me whenever he chooses. I laugh an apology to the guys and saunter away. My second heartbeat sparks to life. Michael is closing in, but I move out of range. I won't make this easy for him.

Near the old-world Santas, with their Slovak coats and long beards, I pause and feel the gentle thrum of Michael's heartbeat in my chest again. I giggle and glance around. He is leaning against a giant sleigh with his arms crossed. His eyes are cobalt, so I wag my finger and click my tongue. Michael cocks an eyebrow and gives me that heated look that makes my tummy clench. He's getting impatient with my games. He beckons me with a finger. I shake my head, playing hard to get.

As the song grooves on with Shemekia begging Santa to stay a little longer, I head for the crystal Christmas tree forest. I weave in and around until I am good and lost. Michael is suddenly standing before me as though he's been waiting there all along. I gasp and look around. Students and teachers are milling close by. We can't be caught hiding in here.

"Have you been a naughty girl this year?" Michael asks, grinning. "If not, we can certainly change that." He snags my shirt and pulls me closer.

"Why, Santa Claus, are you stalking me?" I laugh.

Michael's face lights up, and he nods emphatically.

"I want to see you tonight," he whispers as he slides his fingers into my hair and caresses my cheek with his thumb. I lean into his hand, smiling.

"I want to see you, too. I mean, I have something to tell you. But…" There's too much chaos and noise, and I decide this isn't the time or place to explain about Rama Kuan.

Michael loses his patience and pulls me against him, crushing his mouth onto mine in a demanding kiss. I'm so surprised that I stiffen. Then I melt against him and slide my arms around his neck. We haven't kissed since the night at the frozen waterfall. The idea that he might not stop again flits through my mind.

The sparks are quick and painful in the dry winter air. I flinch. Michael growls deep in his throat and tears his mouth away. We're panting and trembling. I'm reluctant to let go but he removes my arms and steps back just as Jordan the Leerer crashes the party.

"Hey!" he says in an abrupt sort of way. He stares at Michael and then at me.

I take a step back and post an innocent look: *I'm just a casual bystander out inspecting the quality of our fake crystal trees. Completely legit.*

This is awkward. Jordan is assessing the situation. Michael is assessing Jordan's emotions. Jordan must think it strange to find Michael and me alone in the trees. We are never seen talking privately during school. I expect Michael to toss out some excuse. He's pretty quick on his feet. But he doesn't, which only adds to the awkwardness.

"We need everybody helping with the chess club," Jordan says. It sounded more like a demand than a request.

Michael regards him coldly. Jordan makes way for me to leave first and then follows close behind. I get the feeling I've been deliberately searched for, found, and escorted across the gym.

By the time we reach the chess club, the entire astronomy class is there. It seems we have been loaned out to help assemble the angry nutcrackers.

JD and Holden attach a giant wooden head to a soldier's body. Then they stand back, and we all wait for it to topple forward. It doesn't. To test its stability, Casey starts dancing with it, moving its arms up and down. He declares it fit. And this leads to talk about the Winter Carnival dance.

Michael has been watching Jordan, but at the mention of the dance his eyes cut to mine. He catches me smiling and smiles back. I can't wait to dance with him. It will be our first public display of covert affection.

While I'm preoccupied with fantasies of dancing with Michael, my friends are up to something. Bailey, Duffy, Rachel, JD, and Holden have been whispering off to the side. Then Bailey maneuvers JD to stand next to me. She is sporting her Cheshire cat grin, and I get suspicious. She nods at JD, who then becomes shifty and bashful. Everyone goes quiet.

"Um, so, hey, Sophia? I was wondering if, you know..." He flushes pink and glances around, and I realize they've sent him to ask me to the dance.

My second heartbeat accelerates, and I feel a painful tug that nearly pulls me sideways. I flick a pleading glance at Michael just as I hear,

"So how 'bout it? Wanna go to the dance?"

Sweet, shy, linebacker JD is looking at me with all the embarrassment and hope I have ever seen plastered on a face. A billboard sign screaming, *Dear God, Please Don't Shoot Me Down in Front of Everyone!*

I bite my lip and stuff my hands into my pockets. *I hate this. How do I say no?*

Or do I?

Didn't I joke to Michael that if I danced with him, I would have to dance with other guys, too? To keep up our secret charade? What better charade than having an actual date?

"C'mon, Sophia," Rachel says brightly. "It'll be fun! And JD is a great dancer, right, J?" He turns a shade darker and shrugs.

Duffy starts gyrating against Bailey. "The place'll be packed, nuts to butts. Maybe she's too shy to twerk."

"Oh, it's not that," I say, scrambling to think. "It's just that—"

"Well, don't say you're not going!" Rachel wails. "You *have* to go! It's our *senior* year! You have to do *everything*! For the *last* time!"

"*Da,* comrade tchotchke. You have to do everything. *Il grand finale.*" Bailey knocks me into JD, who catches me by wrapping an arm around my back. It feels like a hug, and I wiggle free and mutter an apology.

Everybody laughs like we're two pathetic wallflowers fumbling through the awkward stages of pubescence. My face is hot with embarrassment. I flick my eyes toward Michael. He is ridged and impassive. But I see a storm gathering in his eyes.

"So, it's settled then," Bailey says. I exhale and nod.

Michael will eventually see it's the perfect cover. Right?

Michael steps back from the group. His face is stoic, and his eyes are hard on me.

"Sophia, I have that book you wanted to borrow," he says flatly. "I'll be home later. Come by at eight to get it…or…not at all." He turns and walks out.

Chapter 10

I'll See Your
Half-Wit and Raise You
Two Demon Hunters

Because the roads are still heavy with snow, I follow the snowplow pushing its way west out of town toward Michael's house. Dad balked at the idea of me going out this evening, but I insisted. My excuse—I'm in desperate need of homework help.

I hate lying to him, and his concern brought me to another decision. I want to be completely honest about everything going on with me. The moment my training is over and I'm officially a spirit walker, I'll explain things to Dad. But not before.

I won't burden him with worrying about me, which I know he will. Plus, I won't risk him telling me not to do it, which he is likely to do. Things will be tricky because I still have to keep Michael's family secret. Besides, it's not like I planned to keep my spirit walking thing a secret from Dad forever.

In the meantime, I get to tell Michael and the Patronus family. I'm so excited I can hardly sit still. As I plod along, I rehearse various dialogues to an audience of red taillights.

"Hey everybody, guess what? I'm on my way to becoming a spirit walker!" *Yea! And the crowd goes wild!*

Or.

"Good evening, dear friends and colleagues…you are now in the presence of a future spirit walker." *Hmm.*

How about, "Dude, I'm totally stoked to be a righteous spirit walker. Azright!"

I laugh and take a deep nervous breath. I've got to calm down. I want this to come out halfway intelligent.

I park on the street and grab my astronomy book, otherwise called my cover story. Several times a week, Michael and I meet on the pretext of studying. I've gotten over the humiliation that his family must think I can't make the grade. Spending time with Michael has been worth falling on the intellectual sword.

I'm greeted at the door by Milvi, who is always so friendly. We hug hello, and then I shrug out of my coat and hang it on a hook. She is here tonight because it's the monthly extended-family dinner night. They're just finishing with dessert and drinks in the living room. Milvi invites me to join them, but I tell her I'm here to study with Michael.

"Oh, sorry. He's out on a call," she says so casually he could be out delivering pizza. I used to wrestle with envy whenever Michael or his brothers were called to save souls. Now I'm swimming with excitement because it's almost my turn to help.

Milvi leads the way into the living room. It's a cozy, no-nonsense space with throw pillows on a comfy couch, a crackling fire, and framed family photos. Simply ordinary.

Michael's mother, Katarina, and his Aunt Sasha are ensconced in a cutthroat chess match by the fireplace. Raph is watching football; Gabe is lost in a book; and Uriel is feeding a delicate bird perched on his finger. Michael's father, Dimitri, and his Uncle Pavvo are serving trays laden with coffee, tea, and pumpkin pie à la mode. When he sees me standing in the doorway, Dimitri's face lights up.

"Sophia!" He sets his tray on the coffee table. "Glad to see you again. Please, come join us."

"Hi, everybody." I raise my textbook by way of explanation for intruding. "Test coming up so…"

I say this casually enough, but I notice a few secretive smiles and fleeting glances. Surely, they're not suspicious. Or maybe they think I'm crushing on Michael, and they find it amusing? Maybe they feel sorry for me because there is a long line of girls crushing on Michael, and he is obligated to be friends with them?

I perch on the edge of the sofa and wonder if there will ever be a time when Michael and I can reveal our real feelings. Will our love always be in hiding?

Dimitri offers a slice of pie and a cup of tea. I accept and place them on the tea table. While everyone returns to their previous distractions, my mind runs over the last time Michael and I were together in front of the family. I can't think of anything we did to draw suspicion. Maybe I'm just being paranoid.

Dimitri and Uncle Pavvo discuss mundane things from their respective jobs while my attention drifts in and out. Eventually, my secret takes front and center, and I'm suddenly edgy.

Being patient has never been my specialty, so I dig into the pie for something to do. It's amazingly delicious. I try to eat slowly, biding time until Michael returns and I can spring my news. I'm nervous and jumpy—a kid with a secret too big to hold.

My knee vibrates, and my eyes drift to the doorway where I hope to see Michael walking in.

Uriel laughs lightly. "Somebody dose her tea with sugar? 'Cause Sophia's ready to bounce out of her seat."

I look back to the room. Everyone is staring and assessing my full range of emotions now that they've made eye contact. I stop my knee and blush.

"Sorry." I bite into a smile because I can feel my secret rising to the surface. *I don't know how much longer I can wait.*

"What's up?" Raph asks. He pauses the game and gives me his full attention.

I want to wait for Michael, but everyone is staring and it's obvious I'm hiding something. It's awkward and weird… so I go for it.

"Well, I…wanted to tell you all that…I've started my training. To be a spirit walker. It's official. I have an Ascended Master."

They react just as I had hoped. With wild cries of joy. Then they jump up and pull me into hugs. I am bombarded with congratulations.

"I'm so happy for you!" Katarina says, her bright blue eyes glowing with pride and something akin to relief. "I know you'll be a wonderful spirit walker!" She hugs me twice before stepping aside. There is a line, and I feel like a bride who's taken the big plunge and is ready to embark on a whirl-wind honeymoon.

I wish Michael was here!

Dimitri and then Uncle Pavvo hug me tightly with vig-orous pats on the back. Milvi won't let go until Gabe pries her loose. Then he tells her not to get carried away because I haven't actually become a spirit walker yet. He is forever practical. His hug is firm and official. Uriel, beet-red and suddenly shy, offers a quick one-arm hug.

And then Raph steps up, playing it cool to hide his ex-citement. "What'd I say? All that worrying for nothing." He hugs me and whispers, "You're gonna do great, Sophia. Wel-come to our *spiritual* family."

My second heartbeat starts at the same instant I hear Mi-chael's voice. "What's going on?"

Raph and I spring apart, and Milvi says, "Did you hear the news? *Sophia*'s started her training! She has an As-cended Master!"

Everyone is elated all over again, but Michael has gone pale and still. I suddenly feel guilty. I should've controlled my impulsiveness. I should've waited and told him privately like he told me about his news at the waterfall. I should've given him a heads-up so he could manage his emotions in front of everyone. They shouldn't wonder why he is against me becom-ing a spirit walker. It's supposed to be a great thing. A gift or a calling to the spirit world that few would refuse. They wouldn't understand why Michael doesn't want me involved. *I* don't understand.

Michael's nostrils flare as he inhales and lowers his eyes, deadening his feelings with great effort. I chew my lip and wait for him to look at me again. My heart aches for him to be happy for me.

Please, Michael. You know how much I've wanted this. Please, please be happy for me.

"Let's have a toast!" Katarina declares, raising her tea.

Cups are in the air, and one is shoved into Michael's stiff hand. He moves into the room and stands with his back to the fireplace. His face is thrown into shadows, but his aquamarine eyes glow with a faint light. Michael doesn't lift his cup.

"To the newest member of our spiritual family!" Katarina calls out. "Sophia St. James! She is welcomed with open hearts!"

There is a round of "Here! Here!" and then everyone clinks and drinks. The chatter escalates while I peer over my teacup. Michael is studying me with that blank expression he always used before we knew each other. The one that masked his emotions while he analyzed me for secrets and deceit. I hope he'll forgive my impulsiveness. I hope he'll find a way to accept the inevitable.

I offer a tentative smile.

"Who is your Ascended Master?" he asks.

"Rama Kuan."

"Are you kidding me?" he yells, and the celebration crashes to a halt.

Michael's family turns in shock. It's too soon to determine if it's because he yelled or because of my answer. I'm hoping it's the former. I've had my own concerns about Rama, and the last thing I want to be is right.

Michael's face is steadily growing red. He shoves his cup at Uriel and then marches up to Dimitri.

"Rama Kuan!" he shouts in his father's face. Then he points at me as though Messengers for The Council were in charge of appointing my Ascended Master and made a mistake. "Did you hear what she said? Her Ascended Master is Rama Kuan! That half-wit, lazy, good-for-nothing beach bum who—"

"Hey, wait a minute," I jump in. "Rama may be laid back but he's not a half-wit."

Please don't let him be a half-wit.

"Michael, please," Katarina says. "He is an Ascended Master, after all."

"I don't care if he's an archangel. He's not good enough to train her. She...she shouldn't even be..." He looks around, stricken. "You all think it's safe for her? Out there, in the spirit world? Fighting for lost souls? To be trained by Rama Kuan? He thinks Yoda is a prophet, for chrissake!"

The room falls silent while I wait for someone to contradict Michael, to rectify his anger. Or at least to answer his questions and defend me. But no one does, and my worry quadruples. Michael is seething and out of patience. He walks away, and five seconds later, we hear his bedroom door slam on the second floor above us.

Katarina quietly apologizes for Michael's behavior. She doesn't know what's gotten into him. Dimitri comes over and lays a hand on my shoulder, trying to ease my mind.

"Sophia, if Rama Kuan were unqualified, he would have been removed from his position. And Michael knows that. He just hasn't been himself since the Halo trials started. Perhaps a bit overprotective. Which is usually an added benefit for a guardian. Please, don't take it personally."

He smiles warmly, and I nod to show agreement. But I know a different truth; it is very personal. Michael doesn't want me to fulfill my Awakening, and no Ascended Master will be good enough. And poor Rama Kuan is taking the brunt of his frustration. I can't help but stubbornly dig my heels in a little deeper. I don't care if my Ascended Master is a half-wit. He's *my* half-wit—my only hope of becoming a spirit walker.

The mood is shattered, and I need time to think. So I thank the family for the dessert and warm wishes. Then I head to the foyer to fetch my coat. I'm nearly out the door when Raph and Milvi catch me. They're tugging along a very reluctant Gabe. Usually, Gabe keeps to himself and his books, so his face is pinched with annoyance.

"Gabe has an idea," Raph says, nudging his brother to speak.

"I didn't say it was a *good* idea," Gabe complains. "I said it was an option. If someone cared to bend the rules."

"Oh, don't be so pedantic," Milvi whispers. "It's perfectly fine."

"Then why are you whispering?" Gabe retorts.

Milvi rolls her eyes and turns her back on him. "Look," she says to me. "Gabe thinks you could use some real tutoring with your training."

I don't like the way she says *real* tutoring.

"It's like this." Raph pulls us deeper into the alcove and whispers. "Rama Kuan is kinda lax in the self-defense area. It's probably why Michael overreacted. We all care about you, Sophia. And safety *is* a big issue for spirit walkers. I'm sure you get how dangerous it is? Rama Kuan explained all that, right?"

Uh, no, but Michael has. Repeatedly. At the top of his lungs.

"Actually, we haven't gotten that far yet," I say with a sinking feeling. They look worried. "Should I have been told?"

"First thing out the gate," Gabe says, sighing heavily. "He was supposed to explain the process and give you a choice. It's a little thing we like to call *free will*. You may have heard of it?"

"He only told me about the three trials I must master to achieve enlightenment. Besides, I would've accepted anyway."

"Atta girl," Milvi says.

"Even so," Gabe continues, "you must understand what you're getting involved in. As your process continues and you pass through one level and into another, your Chelsea Light will take shape in your hand." He gathers my hands in his, and we peer into my palms. "Nothing so far, but it's too early. Anyway, as the light grows within you, it will manifest in one of your palms. Then, when you have reached definitive enlightenment, it will be like a beacon. Meaning, lost souls within the area will be drawn to it. As will demons, reapers, soul seekers, and any other vile creature from below. They'll want your light."

I withdraw my hands and curl them into fists. "I won't give it to them," I say, but they don't look convinced.

"They won't be asking politely, Sophia," Raph says.

"They'll take it. First chance they get."

"Take it how?"

"They'll fight for it," Milvi states matter-of-factly. "If they can't bargain it away from you or lure you into a trap. They're likely to chop off your hand to get it."

Okay, nobody told me that little tidbit.

"That's where we come in," Raph says. He rubs his hands together, ready to spill the beans. "We have an idea, but you have to keep it secret. No telling the parents. Anyway, we have some good friends—Demon hunters. If we explain the situation, I'm betting they'll agree to come hang with us for a while."

"And by that you mean teach me some fighting skills?"

"Kick-ass fighting skills," Raph says, and my face lights up.

Now we're talking!

"Okay, when?"

They confer, toss around a few names, and nix a few others. Eventually, they settle on something, so Milvi hurries into the living room and returns with a picture frame. It looks like a vacation photo—the entire Patronus family plus several others I don't know. Maybe somewhere in Europe during the winter?

"Estonia," Milvi says.

Three of their friends in the photo are demon hunters. I peer closer. They look awfully young, but what do I know?

"How old are they?"

"Mid-twenties, but don't let that worry you. They're legit."

I tell them I won't worry. Privately, I think they can't be worse than Rama Kuan. Raph says not to misunderstand my Ascended Master. He *is* qualified to train me. He just focuses more on the spiritual side of things. Besides, it never hurts to train with professionals.

"We only need two hunters," he continues. "I'll hit up Kanati. Milvi, you've got Chang`e. I'll let you know when we hear from them. We'll probably have to train at the barn." He looks at the others for confirmation, and they nod.

"But why don't you want your parents to know? How could this be breaking any rules?"

"It's not our place to interfere," Gabe says. "It's a bit unusual for guardians to be so closely involved with an individual human. Other than maintaining our daily lives here, of course. But your unique connection to Michael, that peculiar second heartbeat, has intertwined you into our family. Incidentally, I've been doing some research on the subject of your second heartbeat."

Oh, I don't think I like this.

"Really? What'd you find out?" I say without a care in the world. I want them to think I hardly notice it anymore. That it doesn't give me the slightest bit of comfort or make me feel whole when it's beating softly beneath my breast.

I avert my eyes so he can't read me.

"Well, nothing. So far."

Yippee!

"Oh, bummer."

Ahem, and now I'll be performing Act II, "The Innocent Expression of a Well-Mannered Preacher's Kid.

"So, about these demon hunters…we have to keep my training a secret? Well, I don't know. I wouldn't feel right about keeping things from your parents."

"You let us worry about that," Raph says. "It's more important that you get the training you need." He smiles, and I nod because I like the way he thinks.

They tell me Rama Kuan probably won't care if I'm trained by demon hunters. As long as it doesn't interfere with his sessions. I agree to fill him in.

I thank them for their help and say good-night. Raph walks me onto the porch anyway. I have a feeling he wants to say something but is hesitant.

"Well, thanks again for helping," I say, hedging toward the steps. He wraps his arms around me, hugging me tighter than necessary. I stand there stiffly and eventually pat him on the back. He smells nice, a mix of cologne and rainwater. It's chilly out, and I shiver.

He strokes my back, whispering, "I just don't...you've become very special to the family. We just don't want anything to happen to you." I nod, feeling like an awkward burrito. Raph eventually unwraps himself and looks down at me. I avert my eyes out of habit, but he guides my chin up, forcing me to look him in the eyes. I steel myself as he assesses me.

Think of something funny! Stupid! Quickly!

I think of Dad dancing in the kitchen. Raph's eyes narrow suspiciously, and then I laugh and punch him playfully in the arm. Just two buddies horsing around.

"I'm holding you to those kick-ass fighting skills. Maybe I'll even learn to kick *your* ass."

Raph laughs. "Game on, spirit walker."

I take my out and rush down the steps to the jeep. Raph's

odd behavior takes a backseat because all the way home, I beg the higher-ups to have Michael waiting in my room. He must be there. Why else would he walk out and not return so we could talk about this?

* * *

Michael wasn't waiting in my room, and he wasn't at school the next day. I'm sick with disappointment. I wonder at what point Michael and I stepped aboard the relationship rollercoaster. For weeks now, we've had incredible highs and nauseating lows. It's wreaking havoc on my stomach. Not to mention my concentration skills.

Rama Kuan is having a fit, trying to harness my attention and help me reach a new level of awareness. We've been training for two solid hours and have gotten nowhere.

I finally give up and flop back onto the floor, unraveling from the lotus position. "Well, this gives new meaning to did-dly-squat. I got nothing. Nada. Bubkes." I stretch my aching knees and then look over at Rama. His long hair is wrapped in a tight bun at the back of his head today, and he is eyeing me thoughtfully while stroking his goatee.

"You come in like a *hodad*. A wannabe. All goofy foot and off balance. Can't take the ride like that." His high-arched eyebrow lifts in question because he wants an explanation.

I sigh and stare at the ceiling. He's right. I didn't put my best foot forward because my mind split, worrying about Michael and calculating the time required to finish reading the biography of Dostoyevsky. Plus, I have to PowerPoint my fake stock account and illustrate the inflammatory tissues of a dead body. *Ah, the joys of youth.*

"Dude, you gotta show up. Attend your own party. You're so busy *doin'*, you forgot to show up."

"Right here."

"Naw, dude. In the righteous sense. You gotta find your oneness. You went straight to it the first time. I've never seen such powerful insight in a gremmie before. But now? Dude, I don't know. Where'd you go this time?"

To Michael. I went straight to Michael and filled myself like a bucket of extra crispy anxiety.

"It's just…I don't know. I think—"

"Aw, no, dude. Don't think. Leave that space. You gotta unwrap your thoughts. Go into your body and search for yourself. Expand the heart. Open yourself up. Welcome the power of *being*. Allow it in. You gotta let it come. It's gonna erupt and flow like lava. I know. And it's righteous and pure."

Don't think. Unwrap your thoughts. Expand the heart.

It sounds wonderful and exactly how I feel when I'm with Michael. Everything makes sense when we're together. My heart expands with love. But I can't tell Rama the source of *me* begins in another. He wouldn't understand a love like ours. He wouldn't understand that Michael's heart beats inside my chest, too. And when we're at odds, nothing feels righteous or pure.

My cell phone pings, jerking me out of my head. I roll over and search for it. It's under the desk where I flung it earlier, so I crawl over and tap the screen. It's a text from Raph, and I spring up.

"Ow!" I hit my head on the desk and scoot out. I stare at

the screen while Rama tells me to return to my position. I can't. I'm too excited. I tap the screen, bringing up the message.

Meet me at the barn

"Holy crap!" I look at Rama, my eyes bugging out. "They're here. I mean, I think the demon hunters have arrived." I show him the text. He reads and then frowns.

"Gotta lot to do here," he says firmly.

"Please! I should at least go and meet them. It'd be rude if I didn't. Please!"

He shakes his head. He is stubborn. Absolutely unmoving.

"You can come, too."

"Cool." He spins around on his butt and climbs to his feet. "Heard a lot about the *Sanctus Horreum*. Totally stoked to take a tour."

And just like that, we're on our way. I pack on the winter paraphernalia and then sneak downstairs, while Rama steps into the closet and reappears in the passenger seat of my jeep. He is a big shaggy dog ready for the park well ahead of time.

The only way I know to get to the barn is through Michael's property. I take extra precautions to avoid being spotted by his parents, parking down a side road in the woods. I bundle up and off we go, plodding along and making tracks in the deep snow.

Before long, I see the red barn in the dim light. I was here with Michael on our sleigh ride but didn't bother much with the barn. It's ancient. No windows and only one door. Light glows around the doorframe, and I wonder who's waiting inside. I'm a little disappointed to be trained in a crappy old wood heap like this. I was hoping for something a bit more modern and, well, sturdy. *Please let it be warm inside.*

"Hey there." Raph steps from the shadows, and I startle.

"Hey," I say and then quickly introduce them.

"Heard a lot about you," Raph says, scrutinizing Rama's wardrobe.

"Off the Richter to be here." Rama nods.

We go to the door, where Raph gives me a serious look. "Tell me what you see the moment you step inside. Okay?" I wring my hands and nod. I'm so cold and excited that I can't unclench my jaw.

He opens the door, we walk inside, and I immediately feel like Dorothy, stepping from her old house and into the Land of Oz. Spread before me is a sprawling meadow, glorious trees, a rushing waterfall, and a bubbling stream—a combination of brilliant colors and soothing scents. It's awe-inspiring and wholly impossible. It smells of rich earth and honeysuckle, and I take a deep breath, trying to absorb it all.

Finally, I exhale and grin. "Well, Toto, we're not in Kansas anymore."

Raph breaks into a huge smile. He is pleased by something, but I don't have time to ask what. I see Milvi at the same time I hear her squeal with delight. She rushes across a bridge and envelopes me as though we were separated at birth. We almost fall over laughing.

"I'm so glad you're here!" she cries. "You don't know what it's like to have someone else here. I mean, someone outside the family. And you can see it? Can't you?" We turn and gaze across the vast, picturesque countryside.

"Of course. It's breathtaking."

Raph and Milvi seem relieved but not altogether surprised that I can see the barn's secret, mystical nature. We take
a moment to watch Rama meander around with a satiated grin.
He mumbles and picks flowers.

"He's not going to try to smoke those, is he?" Milvi asks,
and we laugh.

After a quick tour of the glorious meadow—Milvi pointing out a stone balcony and private rooms beyond that lead to
hidden chambers behind draping vines—I become aware that
we are not alone. Gabe and the demon hunters emerge from
another hidden room behind the waterfall. Raph identifies it as
the weapon's chamber. We walk across the bridge to meet them
in a grassy area beneath a sprawling tree.

The guy called Kanati seems to fit right in, a native of
the raw countryside. He is tall and tan with high cheekbones
that could have been cut from glass. He has long black hair tied
with a piece of leather from which dangles an eagle feather. His
brown eyes are hawkish and alert. He wears soft leather pants
and a matching ribbon shirt with the image of a deer branded
over his heart. A flat, clublike weapon rests in his hand, and
a knife on his hip. Kanati is barefoot and moves with a lithe,
airless quality. He is a warrior through and through.

Chang`e is a stunning contrast of colors, sporting a long,
high-collared cape, red shorts, and a white shirt. The cape is
brilliant hues of blues, pinks, purples, and golds—suitable for
a festival or palace. Her pale face is made more beautiful by her

serene expression, which is set off by shiny black hair swept into a spiral bun and impaled with two dangerous-looking chopsticks. I can just make out the emblem across her shirt beneath the cape—a long, narrow rabbit stretched as though running. As far as I can see, her weapons include a long dagger on one hip and a coil of silk ribbon on the other. She is tall, graceful, and confident.

Gabe makes the introductions while I smile nervously.

Kanati says, *"O si yo,"* and I blink.

"Uh…" I'm lost in translation.

He laughs, his voice warm and smooth like the suede he wears. "Means hello," he explains, and I blush.

"Oh. Hello."

Chang`e gives a slight bow and says, *"Nǐ hǎo."*

"Oh, I know that one." I perk up because there is hope for me yet. I return the gesture and say, *"Nǐ hǎo.* Hello. That's right, isn't it?"

She smiles and nods. *"Tā hěn kù.* It's cool." She shrugs casually, and I instantly like her. *Tā hěn kù,"* I repeat, filing that one away for Bailey.

Kanati and Chang`e start talking about exercise and strategies, but all I can think is—demon hunters. They are skilled at tracking down and killing demons. If Dante was here, they would be compelled to kill him. Somehow, the idea is unsettling.

A few months ago, I watched Michael and his brothers destroy Dante, Vaughn, and Wolfgang, but I've come to understand the difference. Guardians are not made to hunt demons.

When they fight, it's in defense of a soul. Otherwise, guardians cannot attack. They don't have first strike. But if they do kill a demon, it's a temporary death. Demons can regenerate, in time.

On the other hand, demon hunters are made for it. Their kills last longer. They can and will attack without provocation. They are the real deal.

"Thanks for coming. For helping me," I say as we stroll around the meadow, chatting and getting to know each other.

Kanati smiles. "Anything for our Patronus brothers."

"Yes," Chang`e agrees, nodding thoughtfully. She smells of something light and airy. Moonlight and powder? Whatever it is, it's comforting. She asks me personal questions in a voice made of satin. She sounds too sweet and young to be lethal. To be a killer.

"Yes, I lost my mother several years ago. It's just Dad and me."

I wait for the customary condolences, but she just nods. Perhaps she lives too close to death to feel the loss. Kanati asks what training I've had so far, and we stop and look over at Rama. I'm not sure, but I think he's engrossed in a deep conversation with a tree.

"Nothing in the self-defense area," I admit with a heavy sigh. Kanati tells me not to worry. We'll start from the beginning.

And so, we do.

We take a moment to shed the fifty extra pounds I'm wearing until I'm down to my sweats, hoodie, and bare feet. Kanati removes his shirt and Chang`e her lovely cape-like thingy. We move into the grassy area beneath the tree. Raph, Milvi, and Gabe step away to watch at a distance. Milvi sees I'm nervous and taps an electronic screen on a shelf. As my instructions begin, soothing music rises from hidden speakers. Or maybe it's coming straight from Heaven. I relax and maintain a clear focus.

For two hours, I watch their examples and follow as best as I can. The demon hunters are true masters of their art—their bodies quick and efficient. Responsive. I struggle with my own, wishing I'd spent more time on kickboxing and less on homework.

We work without weapons, but after a while, I'm given a long cane pole to whirl over my head. It's heavy and slick from my sweaty palms. Two minutes of spinning it in one direction and then two minutes in the opposite, and my arms ache and tremble. When I grow tired, the cane dips and knocks me in the head. I howl, dropping it and rubbing the spot.

Chang'e corrects my stance and helps me maintain balance. It's hard because these are not muscles I'm used to exploiting. My muscle group is of the sit, stand, and lay down variety.

At Kanati's command, I whip the cane pole down and jab hard at imaginary evil. I forget to extend my right foot, stumble, and pitch forward, almost falling.

I'm as bad as I feared, and all I can do is apologize.

"Sorry, but as you can see, I suck at this kind of stuff." I hope they aren't too disappointed. I hope they don't find me a lost cause and go back to wherever they came from.

Kanati hasn't broken a sweat in the three hours of

working out. He is methodical and patient.

"Never apologize for what you do not know. It's called an Awakening for a reason. The spirit, as well as the body, will be brought to life. You are as a newborn who must learn everything for the first time."

This makes sense because that's exactly how I feel. New and ungainly.

Chang`e provides new instructions—pushing and testing me. They are relentless, but this is what I wanted, right?

She demonstrates climbing a tree in swift, nimble motions, up and over. She dances along thin branches to the top, where she plucks a red ribbon. Then she sails down, grazing along the boughs, barely disturbing leaves.

My turn.

Hoisting the cane pole over my head again, I continue, spinning it and gaining speed. It teeters, and I labor to hold it up. Then Chang`e yells a command, and I'm off and running.

I drop the cane and climb the tree. I would like to think I scamper along like a sure-footed monkey, but I don't. I'm awkward and exhausted, grunting and lumbering up without direction. My stupid foot breaks through a thin branch, and I flop down, roll forward, and fall. But I'm caught, hanging upside down by the aforementioned stupid foot. All the blood rushes to my head. And then a burst of frigid air hits me in the face. The barn door is thrown open, and Michael stands in the doorway. He is upside down in my skewed vision, but it's him. And a blast of fresh excitement hits me because I decided that when I saw him again, I would demand he be happy for me. I found a way to convince him to change his mind. And I don't plan on taking no for an answer.

"Michael!" I wave frantically and then slip and fall on my head. *Owe! That seriously hurt!* I roll over, groaning but eventually sit up. The blood rushing to my head takes an immediate U-turn, and I'm light-headed with a pounding headache.

Michael looks confused. This was the last place he expected to find me. So Raph, Gabe, and Milvi explain things while Michael takes in the scene—Kanati and Chang`e standing by with arms akimbo, and Rama lounging in a flower bed, making a daisy chain.

"*That's* your brilliant plan?" Michael says. "You said you found a way to keep her from getting hurt. I thought you were stopping her from becoming a spirit walker. Not bringing in demon hunters to train her."

I close my eyes with crushing disappointment. It was too much to hope for. Bringing in reinforcements to help prepare me to defend myself should be enough. It should alleviate his concerns, but now I understand nothing will. Nothing short of me stopping altogether.

Once my head clears, my temper rises. If Michael won't let us talk this out privately, we'll take it public. So I climb to my feet, unwilling to give him the satisfaction of rubbing my aching head, which I really want to do.

"I think it *is* a brilliant plan. Unless you don't think Kanati and Chang`e are good enough to help me?" I cross my arms.

"Of course, they're good enough. They're the best. That's not the point."

"We all want to make sure she's safe," Raph says. "That *is* your main concern, right?" The question is heavy with hostility and makes Michael's face darken.

"It is," he says tightly. He takes another minute to assess the situation and then forces down the anger simmering below the surface. I wonder how long he can control things before he explodes all over someone.

Without looking in my direction, he walks to greet Kanati and Chang`e. They are friendly enough, but their voices drop to quiet undertones, and I'm dying to know what they're saying. I look desperately at Raph.

Michael won't talk them out of helping, right?

Raph wraps an arm around my shoulders and tells me not to worry. We wait while Michael confers with the demon hunters. Meanwhile, I feel sick. This is dividing the family I've come to love. I don't want to cause trouble between Michael and Raph.

The demon hunters gather their things and wave goodbye. We watch in silence as they stroll into the trees and disappear. My second heartbeat flutters like a trapped bat as Michael slowly turns to face us. There is a minuscule shift in his expression when he sees Raph's arm around me. A tightness that I don't like. Then his eyes shift from Raph to me and pause. I hold my breath, waiting.

"You have to go," Michael says, and all the air leaves me.

Chapter 11
Michael

"I can't believe you sent her away," Raph said, following Michael into the weapon's chamber. Michael's controlling and callous behavior demanded an explanation, so Raph wouldn't back down. "Tell me why you don't want Sophia to be a spirit walker. Why you're so possessive of her."

Michael whipped around. "Why I'm *what?*" he yelled in Raph's face.

Raph flinched and recalculated his assessment. It was a bold accusation and not something guardians tossed around lightly. Michael's temper was flammable these days, and the topic of Sophia St. James seemed to be an accelerant. But why?

Michael's trials were grueling and should be occupying all his concentration—all his thoughts. He should be happy that Sophia had her own destiny to fulfill. Everyone in the family knew how much she wanted this, so why couldn't Michael support her?

Raph regained his foothold because he knew something wasn't right with his brother. Something hadn't been right for weeks now.

"You heard me," he said tightly. "We all know how

Sophia feels about her Awakening. How she feels about *you*. *That's* been obvious for weeks. Months, even. And as far as I can tell, you haven't done anything to discourage her. Like you should have. You're still helping her with homework when you *know* you could compel someone else at school to step in. But here's the thing I really don't get…why you're acting like the overprotective boyfriend. You know your guardian vow and the cost of breaking it more than anyone. You know what's at stake here, Michael, so why—" He stopped as something occurred to him. "Dude, you…you haven't *touched* her, have you?"

Michael clenched his jaw and glared at his brother. He was suddenly tempted to confess his feelings for Sophia. He was sick of the games. Sick of the walls they'd built and sick of hiding his love for her. He wanted everyone to know, to understand, that she was part of him and that her safety was the most important thing to him.

But it was too much to risk. Now anyway. He still had time to convince her to give up becoming a spirit walker. If not for her sake, then for his and their relationship. Sophia had to understand that he wouldn't be able to protect her. Not like he could now. Not if she became a full-fledged spirit walker. Somehow, he had to *make* her understand.

Raph was getting too suspicious and aggressive for answers. He seemed to be purposely injecting himself into their business.

"If I'm not mistaken, *brother*, the last few times I've seen Sophia, *you* were the one *touching* her. Hugging her. Comforting her. Not me." Michael's voice was bitter and deadly, so unlike him. He and Raph had been at odds for a while now. Arguing with a brother guardian felt unnatural. But then, a lot of things had felt unnatural lately.

"That's not what I meant. I've been trying to…reassure her." Raph stepped back. "She's worried about becoming a spirit walker. For some reason, she believes she might not be good enough. *You* tell her that?"

"I have *never* told Sophia she wasn't good enough," Michael ground out. "Now, correct me if I'm wrong, but didn't she just fall out of a tree? On her head?"

"She's learning and—"

"She's too delicate!" Michael yelled. "She's not made for this kind of work, and you know it!"

"What I know is that she needs help! She needs the kind of training only demon hunters can give her. So why did you send her away?"

Michael stepped closer and lowered his voice. "I sent her away because the Halos are due here any minute. We need the barn." He jabbed his finger into Raph's chest. "And I'm sending *you* away, too. Leave. Before I throw you out myself."

* * *

Every day, Michael had waited anxiously for his training to begin. He was overflowing with energy, and the trials were the ideal way to release the excess without giving himself away. Without attacking Sophia—the source of his excess—with affection.

As far as the trials went, he was excelling. Far beyond his fellow candidates. More than just impressing the Halo Masters, they had begun to regard him with quiet admiration. The other candidates could sense the Masters' wonder in the unique angel. Michael Patronus was living up to his reputation as a lethal guardian. And then some.

This had once been a point of pride for Michael. In the beginning. Now, it was a mere afterthought because the pull he had felt for the Halos had changed shape. It was still there underneath it all, but his central focus—his central pull—drew him directly to Sophia.

Finding her in the barn with demon hunters had overtaken any training strategies he had been contemplating. Of course, the whole thing had been his brothers' idea. Sophia wouldn't have known to ask Kanati and Chang`e for help. She wouldn't have known to train in the barn. But why hadn't she shared her plans with him? He'd made himself scarce only because he needed time to think. But why hadn't she reached out? Texted or called? Was he losing her?

As he changed into his training garb, Michael allowed a seed of fear to grow and spread tentacles. He had been secretly worrying that he was too different for Sophia. Fear said the novelty would wear off, and she would realize their lives were too incompatible. She would be deprived of normal human things he couldn't provide. He always sensed her disappointment when he was called away. He recognized her feelings of guilt tangling with loneliness. She often felt abandoned by unfinished conversations or deserted with empty hands.

If his random departures weren't bad enough, his reckless mood swings weren't helping. He was all over the map with his affection, teasing her one minute and keeping her at arm's length the next. And then he would take his affection too far and put her life at risk.

The incident at the frozen waterfall still haunted him. How could he have lost control of his emotions? How could he have ignored Sophia's escalating fear? Somehow, he'd allowed himself to push past it because his physical needs were intensifying. His insatiable craving to touch her had nearly overpowered him, and he'd gotten reckless. Too damned close to killing her.

Aside from that, another familiar energy plagued him—jealousy.

Michael shook his head, unable to understand it. Jealousy was a shit emotion, like a disgusting habit, and he hated the thought of it. The first time he'd felt the unnatural reaction, Dante had been stalking Sophia. But hadn't jealousy been a justifiable need to protect Sophia from a dangerous Demon Knight?

Probably not, but that's how he'd explained it. So why did he feel something similar when JD asked Sophia to the dance? The guy was harmless, and Michael actually liked JD. Feeling jealous was illogical because he *knew* her reasoning— she accepted to keep up appearances and divert his family's suspicions. Sophia had no idea they already knew she was in love with him. It was *his* feelings they hadn't identified yet, although Raph was getting dangerously close.

So accepting JD's invitation was a good move. Michael acknowledged that after he'd calmed down. And then jealousy crept back in like a black cloud with teeth. The idea of JD's hands on Sophia had conjured visions of Dante touching her. Kissing her. Killing her.

Michael's head hummed with restless energy. The raw truth was that Sophia had consumed him *and* his thoughts. Everything boiled down to a simple fact—he couldn't look at her without seeing himself, without seeing her beside him. It was a feeling as strong as his love for humanity—a feeling as natural as breathing.

But were his feelings too much for Sophia? Had Raph accurately identified another raw truth? One that Michael had been avoiding? Had he become *too* possessive?

Was Sophia feeling confined by their secret relationship? Had they built their walls too high? Had they painted themselves in a corner with no room to move forward? Had everything come to a paralyzing halt?

Maybe it was too much for her. Not that he could blame her. Sophia had so much energy for life that sometimes Michael felt like it was *he* who couldn't keep up with *her*. It was another thing he loved about her, but was he stifling her?

Maybe he wasn't good for Sophia. Maybe she was better off without him. Maybe their love wasn't enough to satisfy her.

The Halo Masters talked about the "exceptional things within us" and how they tended to dominate. While Michael should have identified this as his strength and ability to protect souls, he'd thought only of Sophia. He had known instantly that she was the exceptional dominant thing within him. As proof, he was no longer eager for tonight's lesson. He wanted it over quickly because he needed to see Sophia. He needed to beg forgiveness for his behavior—apologies long overdue. Tonight's training was simply getting in the way.

By the time his fellow candidates arrived, Michael had powered down the unwanted emotions, leaving a cold void. They assessed his mood and kept to themselves. But he could hear their grumbling tributes, "Michael's superior strength" and "Unshakable concentration." He also sensed and heard their concerns, "Too much power for one angel?" and "What is the real source of his aggressiveness?"

He scoffed when candidate Zack claimed to have cherry-picked his emotions and declared, "Michael has an overwhelming love to kill evil."

He wondered what they would think of the truth. That he had redirected his cravings and sexual frustrations for a human girl into deadly energy.

When the Halo Masters finally arrived, they were in no mood for chitchat and got down to business. Because the first trial was over, they were well into the second trial: becoming combat-ready. This constituted daily bouts through solids and liquids while constrained and bombarded with obstacles that would dim any sane guardian's light.

"Tonight begins the waterworks," Chief Master Sachiel announced as he paced in front of the candidates. "We like to call it drown-proofing in a high-threat environment. If you have any internal defenses, I suggest you tap into them." He stepped back, allowing Squad Master Camael to provide the details.

"Your flight wings will be bound by guardian ties," he said. "Hands and feet also bound, and a guardian sword strapped to your back. Then, you will drop into the brook, which, as you can see, has transformed to extend several hundred fathoms into a swirling black hole—an individual abyss for each of you. At the bottom is a golden treasure box. Each of you must free yourselves of all constraints, fetch the box, and return safely to the surface. Oh, and there is the annoying distraction of Rahab, a demonic sea monster that would rather die than lose his golden box."

Camael gave them a severe look. "A word to the wise… blood in the water attracts Rahab's evil little bastards whose only purpose is to gnaw the meat off your bones. Good luck, candidates. Now light 'em up!"

Once each candidate was bound, they dropped into their personal black abyss. The water was as frigid as the atmosphere and stung on impact. Michael immediately began writhing inside the tight guardian ties, trying to loosen his feet and wrists. It was useless. Guardian ties could not be broken, only severed with a spiritual weapon.

The abyss spun him in a tornado atmosphere while disturbing shadows tried to distract him. Rahab was close, his repugnant fishy smell as strong as the water he inhabited. When its tail connected with Michael's torso, it sliced him open with spine-jolting pain. A red cloud of blood poured from the wound but quickly dissipated in the vicious swirling current. Michael doubled over in agony. Teeth clenching, he scrambled for an idea. The water was too powerful to fight—the restraints too solid to break. His back wings whipped in turmoil, feathers ripping away with excruciating pain.

The blood brought the minions, those swarming, piranha-like creatures that darted around, tearing chunks of his flesh. Michael flailed wildly, shedding more feathers, and adding more pain. Then the water rippled in a long shadow as Rahab circled and snapped its teeth. Michael saw it as a Chinese dragonhead, except more hideous. It was bloodthirsty for more. Always more.

Instinct kicked in, and Michael spun with the swirling water instead of against it, becoming a whirlwind too fast for the minions to bite. They lost their hold, giving him the sliver of time he needed. He activated the fetching along his forearms, bent backward, and brought up his feet to cut the ties around his ankles. Once freed, he flipped himself over, going against the swirling abyss. The force was strong enough to move the ties along his back wings. Now that he'd lost a considerable amount of feathers, the bands were no longer tight. The water worked with him, loosening them even further. Eventually, his back wings slipped free.

The minions returned, biting his flesh, and forcing Michael to cocoon himself inside his wings. Then Rahab dove from above, mouth open to consume its prey. Michael's only option was to retract his back wings and roll, barely escaping the snapping jaws. Rahab's long, scaly body circled for another strike.

With his hands still bound behind him, Michael lifted his arms as high as possible, running the ties against the sword fastened to his back. The ties eventually snapped apart, and in one swift motion, he drew the sword, swung around, and met the attack. The blade sliced wide and deep across the serpent's underbelly. Immediately, a shrilled, deviant sound reverberated through the water. Michael spun away, covering his ears. It was the most ungodly sound he had ever heard. When it was over, Rahab floated in a bloody haze, the minions devouring him in a feeding frenzy.

Michael secured the sword and dove for the golden box. He grabbed it just as another pack of minions swarmed him. Without hesitating, he shot straight up to the surface, out of the water, and high into the air. His back wings snapped open and held him aloft, where he looked down at the Halo Masters gazing up in surprise.

Michael's chest heaved, and his vision sparkled with blue light. A combination of water and blood dripped from his body. Rivulets like open veins pooled on the ground below. Slowly, he eased down until his feet touched the soft, grassy bank, and his wings retracted. He handed the golden box to Chief Master Sachiel and walked away.

"Don't you want to know what's inside?" the Halo Master called.

Michael paused across the meadow. It was probably customary for candidates to acknowledge the treasure they'd just risked their lives for, but he felt no curiosity whatsoever. He knew where his treasure awaited. And it wasn't in a box at the bottom of an abyss.

"No," he said over his shoulder and then ducked inside the weapon's chamber.

Chapter 12

Fighting the Hands That Hold Me

I dream of Michael. We are standing in the barn with the meadow stretching in every direction, farther than our imaginations. Harmony lingers in the flowers, and the bees take it with them, spreading peace from bud to bud. Michael smiles down at me and holds my hand for a walk. He is tucked safely beside me, and I am happy. Michael is happy.

My second heartbeat is a hummingbird, dancing in my chest and accompanying me wherever I go. The thought satiates me, and I feel myself smiling as the smooth, slick sheet and heavy covers slowly slide across my waist.

"Hmm," I sigh dreamily, content.

Cool air tickles my bare arms and legs, rousing me to grope around blindly. I'm wearing a T-shirt and sleep boxies from PINK. I want to nestle under the weight and warmth of my bedding, but I find nothing within reach, not even Sundance, who usually takes up most of the bed.

I blink, fully awake now, and look down at the foot of the bed. My covers are bunched around the end, so I reach forward, but they mysteriously move away and fall out of sight. I catch my breath and take stock of things. The second heartbeat from my dream thumps steady and sure, so I look around in the dim light. No Michael, and yet I know he's here, somewhere.

My phone lights up, and our song, "Electric Love" by Børns, fills the room with soft music. As the song builds, I feel myself slowly rising off the bed, so I give an excited sort of yelp.

Michael, where are you?

I am lifted and turned until I'm facing the wall, where a pale blue light begins to glow. Michael walks through it as though it was an open door. He smiles without a word but hesitates, leaning against the wall. His hands slide into his pockets. I am gently set on my feet across the room while he watches. Michael won't fly me to him this time because he is giving me a choice, waiting for me to decide. Am I angry? Do I want him?

The soft music gradually rises, the sweet lyrics filling me with everything I know to be true. I run across the room and throw myself at him. I see a flash of relief across his face as he catches me in his arms. I cling to him, wrapping my legs around his waist as he holds me tight, spinning us around the room. I inhale his soft, ethereal scent, taking everything I am given deep inside me. After a moment, I lean back and look at him.

"Um, do I know you?" I tease.

"Let's find out," he says.

He turns back to the wall and lifts my arms over my head, pinning me like a butterfly. I feel exposed and vulnerable, so I hold my breath. Michael presses against me, snuggling into my neck and making me smile inside and out.

I wiggle my hands free and wrap myself around him. I lace my fingers through his hair and guide his head up for a kiss. Michael groans and blinks slowly, brushing his lips softly across mine. The sparks are sharper and more brutal than usual, and we jerk apart in surprise.

"Sorry, that one was a zinger," I say, touching my lips and finding them tingling with heat.

"Well, you *are* one hot tchotchke," he laughs.

I smack his shoulder. "Seriously, that one hurt. It feels like you're supercharged or something."

I grow still because one of his eyes has turned dark brown again. It's happening more often, and I wonder if it has something to do with his training. It started about the same time. I also notice a deep laceration under his left eye. So I tip his chin and find more across his cheekbone and a few down his neck.

"Babe! What happened?"

He cocks his head, wrestling with an answer or whether to answer at all. I imagine he was attacked by some sadistic reaper or soul seeker fighting for a soul.

"Tell me. Please?" I pull his collar aside and find scratches as red as blood across his chest. I'm shocked. This is the first time he has ever shown visible signs of his work, and they look painful. "Tell me!"

"Nothing to tell," he says.

I lift his shirt to look for more evidence that he's been attacked. His torso is covered with jagged cuts, strange bites, and severe lacerations that need stitches. Michael sees my horrified expression and pulls away.

"Don't freak out," he says, lowering his shirt. "They're healing already. Look." He shows me his cheek, and it's true. The cuts are much improved in the span of mere moments.

I turn away, considering things. Music is a distraction now, so I go to the desk and tap my phone until the room is quiet. "Wanna tell me about it?" I ask, not meeting his eyes. Instead, I pick up my blankets and dump them on the bed.

"There's nothing to tell," he says quietly. "I've had worse. You just never saw it before."

"You hid it from me?" I ask, facing him. Michael shrugs, so I answer for him. "You were shielding me from it. From the dangers of your work."

"You know how dangerous my work is," he says, growing uncomfortable. I can see a struggle in him, so I tell myself to be patient, to let him start the conversation we've yet to have. I plop down on the bed and lean against the headboard.

Michael sits on the edge of the bed, not looking at me. The cut on his cheek is gone, but it was fresh, telling me he got it just hours ago.

Patience was never my strength.

"Did you get a call after I left the barn?" I ask.

"No," he says without hesitation.

Michael won't lie, but he will evade to protect me. This, I have learned even before tonight. I have to be specific in my questions.

"So...you were training then? With the Halos? That's how you got injured?"

"I'm not injured."

"Were you training?"

Silence.

Silence.

Silence.

"Yes. I was training. Yes, I was hurt because it's a brutal, unbearable process with a dual purpose—to punish and diminish me and my light."

I wait, hoping he'll add more. Michael looks up in question, having read my emotions.

"I'm sorry about earlier at the barn," he says. "I should have handled that better. Differently. I just didn't expect to find you there."

I nod, waiting.

"I've been thinking about us a lot lately," he says, and for some reason this puts me in a panic. I don't like his somber expression or his voice laden with sadness.

"I've been thinking about what my life has done to you. My life is what it is, and I can't stop answering the calls to help people. I can't stop leaving you. I knew I would change you if we got involved, but I never fully understood until we got deeper into our relationship. I didn't anticipate how sad it would make you feel when I leave."

"I'm not sad," I say too quickly, so he gives me his skeptical frown. "I mean, it is hard. But it's an adjustment I'm willing to make. I understand why you're called away, Michael, and I would never want you to stay when others need you. You understand that, right?"

"I do. And I appreciate you saying that. Every time I

mention it. Honestly. But what you sacrifice doesn't always make you happy, does it?"

I look away and think about it. I've never considered Michael leaving me to be a sacrifice. I'm not sure I would categorize it that way. His purpose is so much greater than me—than us. And I can't put them together. Not like a puzzle to fit snuggly and make a picture. His work outshines us in the same way my work will—when the time comes. And the best, most important thing we can do is to acknowledge our callings and let our love move silently beneath it all.

"What makes me happy, Michael, is you coming back. For me, the best part of your leaving is the coming back. That's what I live for. That's all that matters."

Michael smiles, and I can practically feel the liberation of worry from across the space between us. We move toward each other, wrapping ourselves so tightly in love we can hardly breathe.

"Mmm," Michael sighs heavily, contented, and then leans back. He is at peace but also a little secretive. "You still fascinate me," he says softly, cupping my cheek and tracing his thumb across my bottom lip just like he did that first time on the hill under the stars. "You are what I live for, Sophia. You know that, right?"

"Yes, Michael."

"And you understand that I love you more than anything?"

"Yes, Michael."

"I want to be with you. Forever."

"We *will* be together forever," I say with blind, youthful optimism. I try to kiss him, but Michael is serious, holding me at arm's length.

I say, "Kiss me."

And he says, "Marry me."

And I say, "What?"

I stare openmouthed.

"..."

"..."

I'm not sure I heard right. I'm not sure he meant to say—

"Don't doubt me, babe; I meant what I said. Marry me, Sophia. Please?"

I cover my mouth, grinning and holding back a tsunami of nervous laughter. *Holy mother of matrimony! Michael asked me to marry him! And he's serious!*

I stand and back away, stunned. Michael just smiles, so cool and collected. I have to turn away and think. I start pacing, trying to absorb what's happening. I throw sporadic glances his way to find his eyes narrowed in thought, watching my every move. Finally, I stop and gush out,

"Michael! We've only known each other for four months!"

"Feels like a lifetime for me," he says simply. I'm pretty sure he's enjoying my reaction to this little life-altering surprise he's dropped into my lap.

"But we didn't even like each other half the time!" I say.

He laughs. "Oh, I wouldn't agree with that."

I stare like I don't speak his language. And then my mind starts swimming with possibilities and impossibilities and the general outrageousness of it all. Love wants me to shout YES from the rooftops. Common Sense wants me to launch reason at him.

"Babe, you *do* know I'm only seventeen, right?"

"You have a birthday coming up after Christmas. We'll wait until you're eighteen if it makes you feel better," he says with a shrug like it's no biggie.

I scoff and start pacing again. I can't fully absorb what he's asking. So Michael stands and holds my shoulders to settle my nerves. His touch is a wonderful balm that works every time, so I draw in a deep calming breath. Michael lowers his chin and looks deep into my eyes, assessing me.

"Babe, do you *want* to marry me?"

"Of course I do. It's just that... I never thought... I'm only—"

"Seventeen," he says with that sexy sideways grin. "And eighteen is still too young for you?"

"You're only eighteen, too," I say, but he gives me a look, so I frown. "What? You're not eighteen?"

Michael inhales and contemplates. "Well, I was Born of Light, remember? So, it's not the same. In earth time, I have eighteen years of experience, but in spiritual time I have experience and understanding far beyond that. It's not something I can calculate for a calendar. In a sense, I feel as though I have been around for ages. I suppose my origin and the *Knowing* of spiritual things could account for it. But I do understand how different it is for you. I just thought...I mean, I was hoping with the way you feel about me there wouldn't be any reason to wait to be together."

I chew my lip, taking a moment to untangle his logic. What *is* the reason to wait? My second heartbeat drums steadily because it is home and satisfied. It says, *Let there be love, and there is love. There is Michael.* He is the beginning, middle, and end of me. As I am of him. What more is there to understand?

I try to imagine telling Dad that I want to get married. I know exactly what he'll say. Exactly what *I* have said—all the rational, human excuses. But I'll make him understand. I'll make him see that—I suddenly feel my chest constricting. I'm arguing as if I've decided. And it's overwhelming. *I have decided.* Tears spike my eyes, and I look at Michael, patiently watching and waiting for my scattered emotions to come back to center. Now that they have, he smiles.

I reach up and lay my hand on the smooth plane of his cheek. Michael has a peaceful look that makes my heart swell.

There is not enough room inside me for all the love.

"Yes," I whisper. "I will—"

Before I can finish, he wraps himself around me like the air I breathe. I am bathed in his supernatural tranquility, his angelic happiness. It's a powerful force that hums in the air and radiates into my body. It's a heady, potent emotion, and I have a heightened sense of enlightenment that Rama Kuan would not believe. The thought makes me giggle.

"What?" Michael whispers across my ear.

"I'm totally stoked to feel so righteous and pure," I say. He leans back and frowns at me, so I explain. "Oh, it's just something Rama Kuan always says. He's gonna freak when I tell him."

"I'm sure he'll understand."

"Understand what?"

"Well, about your training."

"What about my training?" I wiggle out of his embrace and step back. A couple of new vibrations are worming their way past my peace and happiness. Suspicion, with a heavy dose of disbelief.

Michael's smile falters, and he cocks his head. He has picked up on it, too. "I'm sure Rama Kuan will understand why you're withdrawing from the Awakening. I mean, I know this is new territory, and it'll take some explaining to convince him—"

He stops because I am shaking my head. Because he detects the rising anger in me, as if the look of utter disbelief on my face isn't enough.

"I'm not stopping my training. What are you talking about?"

"Oh."

Michael recalculates things with a deep frown. He goes to my desk and props a hip on the edge and crosses his arms. I can't tell if he is evaluating his mistake on a human level, as a boyfriend, or on a spiritual level. When he speaks, he has that aged authority in his voice.

"I assumed that if we were married you wouldn't feel the need to continue. I thought you'd want to make a home with me."

I sink down on the bed and stare at my hands. Things are starting to make sense. His proposal was so out of the blue because it was a desperate attempt to stop me from becoming a spirit walker. It was an ultimatum, a calculated maneuver that suddenly sickens me. I never thought Michael would—

"Don't," he says, and I look up. Now he is the one shaking his head. "Please, don't attach an ulterior motive to my proposal. And don't deny that you are. I can feel it all the way over here. That's not what this is."

"But you're assuming I'll quit."

"I thought you would want to. I thought…" Michael looks away because there is hurt in his eyes. He's trying to hide himself from me as he works out how to walk this delicate tightrope. I honestly can't believe he thought I would give up my calling so easily.

"I thought," he tries again, and this time looks at me with a tortured but brave expression. "I thought I would be enough for you. Why am I not enough?"

"You *are* enough, babe. That's not what this is about. I love you. Beyond reason. And you know that. You can *feel* it. But I also have a calling. Just like you do."

"It's a choice."

"What is?"

"Our callings are a choice, babe. You understand that, right? Rama explained that part, didn't he? You don't have to accept. You have free will. Same as I do."

"But I want to accept."

"That's because you don't fully understand how dangerous—"

"I do understand!" I jump up because I don't want to repeat this argument. It's a vicious circle that gets us nowhere. Fast.

"Babe, please. The danger you'll face isn't of the earthly and mundane. I'm sure Raph and Kanati and Chang`e, *everyone,* has told you. Walking in the spirit world is one of the most dangerous things a human can do. Spirit walkers are killed all the time. Killed or dismembered. Their bodies sold for parts."

"Oh, please." I cross my arms over my chest. I think he's exaggerating just to scare me—but probably not. "You're right, everyone has told me the dangers. And I still want to be one."

"It's an admirable dream, but you don't have to accept the calling just because your mom wants you too."

"You think I'm doing this for my *mom?*"

"I know you've wondered how she knew about the Awakening process. You understand that your mother wasn't like other mothers. That she had a different perception of life. You've even wondered if *she* was supposed to be a spirit walker and somehow failed. You think you have something to prove. Well, babe, I've asked around, and no one can verify that your mother had an unfulfilled Awakening. No one knows anything about her, so it's safe to assume she wasn't meant to be a spirit walker. And you shouldn't be one either."

"I'm not trying to live my mom's life. I'm trying to live mine."

"And I'm trying to keep you safe."

"Then help me train."

"Tell me why it's so important for you to become something else. What are you searching for? Why am I not enough?"

"Please stop asking that. You know you are enough. But there is more to me than the love I can give you. You remember the night you took me flying for the first time? Back in October? I said you were changing me. Making me want things beyond myself. Remember? Well, that night I discovered I was meant for something more. It came to me while drifting quietly with you in the clouds. I felt it in my bones. There was a *reason* for my visions. I'm supposed to be a spirit walker. But that doesn't mean we can't do this together. Does it?"

Michael lowers his head and closes his eyes with a defeated look that shreds my heart. I go to him and take his hands in mine. "Babe, if I asked you to stop training with the Halos, would you?"

His head snaps up with fresh eagerness that we have found an option. That we have found a path that can easily be cleared by brushing aside everything important.

"Yes. I would stop. If you asked. I would stop *everything* and lead a normal human life with you."

"And I would *never* ask you to stop. You see? I accept your calling. Can you please accept mine?"

The flash of happy anticipation evaporates. "Babe, you've opened me up to more love than I thought possible. It's been overwhelming at times. Completely unnatural to me and beyond my comprehension to experience this particular type of love for a human. You have changed me, too. I want things I never thought possible. I want to be by your side, always. I want to protect you from harm. And I can. Here. And now. But you know even I have limitations. If you become a spirit walker, it will not be within my power to protect you in the spirit world. Do you understand what I'm saying? You will go where

I can't follow. Please, *please*, babe, don't go where I can't follow."

I drop my head in my hands and burst into tears. It's too much, listening to Michael explain, watching blue tears spill from his eyes.

I rush back to the bed and throw myself down, sobbing at the impossible situation. We have tangled things too tightly, and it's choking the life out of us. My second heartbeat is raging out of control, and then—nothing. It's as if Love has lain down its sword—there is nothing. I feel nothing.

A breeze whispers across my skin, and I know I am alone.

Chapter 13

The Vacant Space Within

Emptiness knows how I feel. *How I feel. How do I feel?* Numb doesn't have a feeling, does it?

It's after noon, and I assume it's bright and chilly out, but I wouldn't know because my internal clock has stopped. Because my curtains have been drawn for two days, and my room is dark. My phone has one job, to play "Stars" by Grace Potter and the Nocturnals. I am drowning in stars, lyrics, and tears. Just drowning and drowning, over and over again. My internal organs have been systematically ripped away. There is nothing left but shredded seams and the rattling echoes of each breath.

Michael never came back.

I haven't moved from my bed except to pee and bring in water and a box of dry cereal. The bed sheets and pillowcases are soaked with tears and sweat from restless nightmares. There is a funky aroma that will make hair stand on end, but I am beyond caring. I am in mourning. Or shock. Or just dead, for all intents and purposes.

I have sent Rama away each day, and he is worried. I can hardly explain my broken heart, even when he reminds me that we are far behind schedule. It doesn't register. The side effects of being dead, I suppose.

But it's more than a broken heart, isn't it? That first moment in the courthouse when Michael and I acknowledged our second heartbeats, we acknowledged our unique connection. We are drawn to each other. Michael is my magnetic North. Just as I am his. No need for any other compass.

There was never indecision between us, only a *knowing* of things—knowing we were meant to be together. Even with the threat of discovery by his family, I never felt it could divide us. I assumed we would find a way to outmaneuver them. *Love* would find a way. I never dreamt it would be Michael and me who ruined us.

I ruined us.

What is this obsession with becoming a spirit walker? Why can't I be happy with a simple quiet life, married to a gorgeous spiritual warrior? I could still graduate and shuffle off to college. Higher education has challenges aplenty, right? Death by Comparative Literature doesn't sound so bad.

Because it would never satisfy. Because Mom said I come from a long line of spiritual warriors. Because I have an unquenchable desire that no amount of arguing, compromising, or dismissing will fade. It is another kind of *knowing of things.*

But I love Michael! I need Michael! I don't want to go where he can't follow!

And so goes the merry-go-round in my head. Forty-eight hours of this, and it's no wonder I have a raging headache.

There is whispering in the hallway and Sundance's tail tapping on the wood floor. He, like everyone else, has been shunned and none too happy about it. Dad never believed I had a head cold the first day I skipped school. Now I'm afraid he has brought in reinforcements.

The door creaks open, and Sundance charges in, jumping on the bed. I'm attacked on all fronts, so I curl into a hedgehog and clasp the pillow over my head.

"And here I was, hoping you were spelunking in a cool blanket fort," Bailey says, strolling, uninvited, into the room. "Or at least a sheet cave."

"Go away!" I yell from under the pillow.

She exaggerates sniffing around. "Ooo, comrade tchotchke. I am suspect-ink that you've been sneak-ink the wad-ka." I don't laugh. I'm not in the mood.

"I said go away."

She slunks down onto the mattress, making it bounce. "Sorry, no can do. *Ser* papa is worried. And so am I." She tugs at the blankets and reveals my hiding spot. "Seriously, Soph, you've missed a few key deadlines in astronomy and bio. And an essay in English lit. But what about your PowerPoint in foreign gov, you ask? Well, yours truly worked a little midnight magic, courtesy of the Internet and a trolling business major from Yale, and *voilà,* you downloaded a presentation you never wrote. Just under the deadline. Stock portfolio is tanking, by the way. Plus, you owe me a fitty for Yale boy."

"In what language should I translate, *go away!*"

Bailey huffs and looks around and then gets up and throws open the curtains. I cringe like Dracula. *"Quit that!"* The window slides up, and a blast of cold shoots across the room, freezing me in an instant. *"Quit that, too!"*

Now I can hear people down in the square, bells ringing, holiday music, kids squealing, the low hum of the snow makers doing their thing. I haven't seen the progress in days, and for the first time, I wonder what the decorations look like. What life has looked like without me cavorting around. Has anyone been taking photos in my place? Has Michael been at school? Is he carrying on without me as though he didn't leave his footprints all over my life?

"C'mon, Soph. I'm starting to seriously worry. You gonna tell me what's going on? I mean, if I didn't know better, I'd say you had your heart broken. But since I *do* know better and you *don't* have a plus one, I'm left to imagine all sorts of things. And we know what happens when comrade sister starts imagining things."

"Shut the window," I grumble and wait until I hear it slide down before kicking my way out of the sheet cocoon I've been living in for two days. I sit up. My hair is in shambles and falls across my face.

Bailey gives me a startled look and says, "Hurricane Sandy strikes again," and I *pffft* hair out of my eyes.

"I don't wanna talk about it."

"Rama Kuan said something about demon hunters helping you train. Said you had a pretty rough time of it. Is that why you're going all Hobbit in a hole?"

Oh, Lord! Is that what he thinks?

"Got your butt kicked, huh?" Bailey nods with complete understanding and then starts mining through her pockets for some variety of cavity maker.

"No! I did not get my butt kicked!" I bark out and then reconsider. "Well…maybe." I suppose it *is* the truth. And it's better to let them believe I've run away with my tail between my legs. *Who cares anyway?*

I want to crawl back into my burrow, but Bailey won't have it. She reminds me that it's Friday and the roads are open. The basketball game is back on. I'm expected to take photos. Apparently, Miss Minnie and Mrs. Cooley requested that Bailey remind me of my pictographic obligations. *Dang it.* I have zero desire to stand among cheering fans and snap photos of sweating athletes trying to pulverize each other in a pointless game.

"Don't shoot the messenger," Bailey says against my scowl.

She guides me into the bathroom, where I am ordered to get reacquainted with my shampoo. She sits on the bathroom counter while I shower and shave the forest that is my legs. All the while, she peppers me with questions about the demon hunters. I explain as much as I can. I can't tell her where we train, only that it involves cane poles and trees and pain. Lots of pain.

"So, is this Kanati guy hot?" she asks.

I hear a scratching noise, so I peek around the shower curtain. She is filing her nails with gusto. "Yeah, but you won't be meeting him, so dial down your hormones. Besides, he's way off limits."

"Why is everyone involved with your training off limits, Dear Prudence?"

I snap the curtain back in place. "They just are," I say, raising my voice and rinsing my hair. "Besides, I thought you and Duffy signed a new and improved Magna Carta."

"I suppose we did. Now that he's promised to stop all jackassery." She groans and tells me the steam is futzing with her hair and that she'll wait downstairs.

I take a few minutes to finish up and then head back to my room. I stop in the doorway and peer around. The window is open again, making me shiver in my towel and turban. I hurry over, slam it shut, and lock it. Then I move through the motions of drying my hair and applying makeup. It's hard to reconstruct my face when I don't care. And I keep crying. Nothing seems to stop the avalanche of sadness and self-pity heaped on me. Except for a few brief moments when I zone out and replay Michael's sweet proposal. This is immediately followed by our tortured but stubborn confessions and resulting stalemate. Then I snap out of it and continue on autopilot. By the time I trudge downstairs, I have no idea what time it is or what I'm wearing.

We have an early dinner with Dad, who is brooding and watchful. He is wearing his old worried expression like it was the only thing he could find in the closet. I know he wants the truth about whatever tragedy had me locked away for two days. I feel bad for worrying him, so I fabricate some lie I hope he'll believe. And then Bailey, who probably sympathizes with him, adds another lie to match mine. And then I add another one to match hers. And then she adds another one, and pretty soon we're racking up lies like matching Mah-jongg tiles.

"Typical teenage drama," I finally say, kicking Bailey under the table. I want her to stop. I want it all to stop.

Then we put on our best industrial-strength smiles and wait until Dad's worried expression changes to relief.

Bailey and I clear the dishes, say *adios* to *ser* Papa, and then head out. It's chilly, and I huddle in my coat as we walk around the park. The snow shepherds are busy corralling a manmade blizzard. They are packing great mounds for the sculptures and ice architects. Our quaint little town is gradually becoming the North Pole.

* * *

Haven Hurst's basketball team is slightly better than our football team but less destructive than our hockey team. I strategically plant myself courtside for the best shots while inconspicuously looking for Michael. No second heartbeat. No Michael. I do spot Raph, Milvi, and Uriel in the stands but try not to make eye contact. Still marinating in misery, I don't want their company or their overattentive radar anywhere near me. I'm successful in my action shots and my autonomy—until halftime.

"Sophia, where've you been?" Raph says striding over. He sounds urgent and worried. I fiddle with my camera, deleting missed shots and clicking the keepable ones into separate files, one for the *Gazette* and one for the school newsletter. Pretending I'm busy doesn't detour him because Raph wants answers, so he pulls me aside and lowers his voice.

"Kanati and Chang`e said you haven't shown up in two days." He waits for me to explain myself, but I just shrug. "Hey, you know Michael only sent you out of the barn that day because the Halos were coming. Right? He can't stop you from training there."

Oh, I didn't know that, but I nod like I did.

"Well, what's wrong then? Something else happen?"

My emotions are so close to the surface that I'm tempted to let them boil over, spill everything and not worry about the mess. I know I've ruined things between Michael and me, but even on my worst day, I would never intentionally ruin things between Michael and his family. So when Raph tips my chin up, and I meet his bright blue eyes flicking back and forth in question, I conjure up my best fake smile. It's beginning to feel like a parlor trick.

"Sorry," I say with pseudo cheerfulness. "Just having a bad couple of days."

Raph tells me I shouldn't be discouraged with my training. It's normal to feel inadequate the first few sessions.

"But, Sophia, you have to show up. Demon hunters aren't used to waiting around. I'll stall them for as long as I can. But...you gotta pull yourself together."

I nod but don't make any promises. The buzzer sounds, and the third quarter gets underway.

* * *

I'm sitting in my academic advisor's office after school. Mrs. Cunningham is expounding on the reckless disregard for my grades and college potential. I stare blankly. Nod occasionally. She asks a question, and I snap to.

"Yes, I still plan to go to college," I say on reflex.

"You don't sound very convincing. Perhaps I should send you to see Mrs. Patronus?"

She means Dr. Sasha Patronus, Milvi's mother and

Michael's aunt. Dr. Patronus has recently been hired as the interim school psychologist because our regular one has gone on maternity leave. She's very nice, but I have no desire to have my emotions analyzed by a member of Michael's family. Time for another parlor trick.

"Not necessary," I say with a winning smile. "Just got a little overwhelmed trying to conquer the world. I'll be fine." I stand up to put an end to the session because my parlor trick has an expiration date. Mrs. Cunningham quickly jots down a follow-up session that I'm not to miss, and I slip out the door.

I walk through the town square as though I'm in a trance. Now that I have cried myself empty, the numb realization of things has settled in. Despite my calling and spiritual connection to a guardian angel, I am no different than anyone else. I fell in love. I had my heart broken. And the pain is worse than anything I could have imagined. It feels wrong. It feels as though I am losing something I was meant to have. It's like losing Mom all over again.

I bypass the café and head straight for work, where I upload and edit my photos from the game. Miss Minnie is hovering. I have apologized three times for ditching work, but she's worried, watching me like an egg ready to hatch. It's stifling, so I cut out the moment I can. When I reach my house, Dad is waiting at the door because news travels fast. He wants to know what my advisor had to say.

"I just have some catching up to do," I mumble, brushing past him and heading for the stairs. I feel like a recurring guest star on *The Walking Dead*. He tells me to eat something;

I'm looking thin. I smile vaguely. "Later. Gotta get to it."

Sundance follows me up and around the staircase and then stops outside my open bedroom door. He won't go in, and that's fine. I have a serious amount of homework to do before Rama arrives. I can't get distracted.

I hoist my backpack onto the bed and pause. I look around. Something's not right. My window is open again, so I walk over, close it, and lock it. Then I hear a faint *ping* sound and freeze. Another ping followed by a tinkle and very slowly a soft lullaby fills the air. The song is familiar and drains the blood from my face.

I whip around to my desk and gasp. There sits the small antique music box that Dante gave me in the pretty pink bedroom on Halloween night—right before he set the place on fire. I slam it shut, trembling. Then my door gently closes and a deep voice says,

"*Ciao, cara mia.*"

I turn.

Dante leans against the door. He pauses, making time for me to absorb my shock, and then he walks over, his light green eyes dancing with mischief. I backpedal until I hit the window and run out of room.

"Dante," I breathe out, trying to process the new and not-improved feelings surging through me. If I didn't have full faith in my eyes at this point in my life, I would never believe what I'm *seeing*.

Dante looks exactly the same: tall, lean, and devilishly handsome—black hair brushed back, and that tantalizing grin, so telling of what he's thinking. He is savoring my surprise as though he is the best Christmas present I could have wished for.

I wouldn't go that far, but a small—and I mean minuscule—part of me *is* relieved to know he isn't suffering somewhere in Hell. Acknowledging this irritates me because I shouldn't have *any* sympathy for him. Which is why another part of me—larger and more visceral—is afraid. He is a demon, f'chrissakes! The demon who brought out the darkest thoughts in me. The demon who stood by while his friends tried to Take my dad's soul. The one who eagerly killed me without remorse.

And here he stands, in his fine, hand-tailored white-linen shirt and dark Italian pants as though he's been on holiday. As though he didn't put me through my own personal Hell. It all comes back in a tidal wave, and I feel that small part of compassion eroding into hatred.

Trust but verify is a good adage, so I approach him cautiously, lifting my hand to touch his face. Yes, it is him. He is here. And his skin is as hot as I remember. Dante grins, and then I haul back and slap him across the face. His head nudges sideways, and hair falls across his forehead. My chest is heaving, and my whole body is trembling. I can't believe I just hit him. It wasn't a thought or a conscious decision—it just happened. And I'm shocked. I've never hit anyone in my life.

What the hell is wrong with me?

I struggle to find the anger that prompted me to lash out while Dante lifts his face, beautifully calm. Always so calm, as though nothing could ever surprise him because he has seen too much of life. Of death.

"Why, *amore mio,* are you not happy to see me?"

"You killed me, Dante. And I'm not particularly fond of people who kill me." I hold up a trembling finger. "Correction: of *demons* who kill me."

A small smile lifts the corners of his mouth. He steps closer. I stiffen but willfully meet his gaze. There will be no backing down on my part, and the sooner he understands, the better.

Dante caresses my cheek with the back of his fingers. His touch heats my skin, and I fight the urge to flinch.

"But you begged me to take your life, didn't you?" he croons, cupping my cheek and holding me in place. "You said you belonged to me. And then you begged me to Take you home."

"I was trapped."

"But you did not ask to bargain with Wolfgang, did you, Sophia? He held your father, not I. And yet, you came to me, *amore mio.* Just as you should have because we belong together. And you know it."

I don't know what to make of his logic. It's true that I didn't even consider bargaining with Wolfgang. It was Dante. Always Dante. He sees my confusion and tilts his head in question.

"Would you have me apologize?" he asks. "Would you like to hear me say I am sorry for doing as you asked?"

I swallow and look away. I've always hated when his twisted reasoning makes sense. But yes, he did as I asked. That doesn't mean I shouldn't be upset for being put in the position in the first place. I know that wasn't Dante's fault, either. My mistakes made Dad vulnerable to the demons. My mistakes demanded sacrifice. But it was Dante's so-called pack who provoked Dad into slipping the noose around his neck, into committing suicide.

And even if Dante took advantage, I can't say I'm sorry he did as I asked. It saved Dad's life; it brought me to Mom and took my life in a new direction.

But couldn't Dante have stopped Wolfgang without my death? It's a question I have torn apart a thousand times since that night. Did I have to die?

I feel myself wavering because I am admittedly not as cold-blooded as I need to be. It has always been an effort to be strong around Dante. My insides have gone wrong side up, and I feel unsettled. He always has a way of unnerving me, of setting my blood on fire with just a look. His touch magnifies that effect and makes my thoughts scatter.

"I don't...I'm not asking for an apology," I say, my voice thin and unsure. "That's not exactly the way I remember it."

"Wolfgang wanted the pastor. I only wanted you," he says gently, as though his confession of endless love is all that is needed. As though it has never been complicated.

I look back at his handsome face so full of longing, and I remember. Dante's love for me was as overwhelming as it was ancient. He is certain that my soul belongs to him. Even now, I can see his conviction has not faltered. He has not accepted the truth. No matter what past life we may or may not have shared, it is Michael I love.

And Dante has come back...

Reality jolts me wide awake as though I've been asleep for the last several minutes. I knock his hand down because

Sympathy and Nostalgia have melted like the fire in my blood.

"Have *you* come back for my dad? Because if you have, I'll fight you with everything I have and—" I head for the door, but he grabs my arm.

"*Per favore, ti prego.* I only want to talk." He tries to lead me to the bed, but I jerk free.

"Are you guys back for my dad or not?" I repeat stubbornly.

Dante holds his hands up in surrender. I am not the same girl he could so easily manipulate like before. Yes, he can sense my weaknesses, but he takes my concerns and threats seriously.

"Wolfgang did not resurface. Only Vaughn and me. And the kid, Santiago. But we are not here for your father. It is my understanding that Pastor St. James is *al sicuro dal male.* Safe. Considered untouchable. Does that satisfy you? May we sit and talk? Or would you like to strike me again?" He lowers his chin and gives me that luring smile, ideal for reeling me in and seducing a life-altering kiss from me.

Not anymore.

I cock my head and recalculate all things Dante. His return is alarming, to say the least, and I'm guessing the Patronus family doesn't know. Raph would have mentioned it on Friday. With Dad on the sidelines, I play out various scenarios that make a concert of noise in my head. If this were a chess match, I would say I have been ambushed by a crafty opponent. My only option is to do some luring of my own. I need to coax out Dante's next move.

So, I acquiesce with a wave, indicating Dante should

take a seat on the bed. I follow and sit four feet away, which he quickly rectifies by scooting closer. Too close, so I give him a perturbed look. He is unfazed and reaches for my hands, but I cross my arms and get to the point.

"Why are you here, Dante? And where *is* Vaughn?" I glance around in case I've missed him. I learned the hard way that demons move silently, like shadows.

"He is at home. He was attempting to educate me on the current street dialect and media distractions this time. I am afraid it is a hopeless cause. I left him to salvage the mansion."

"You're calling the Hardgrave mansion home again?"

"It is temporary, of course." He sighs heavily and shrugs.

Temporary. He doesn't plan to stay long. But he does have a plan. Dante always has a plan. But to what end this time? He must know I am no longer naïve when it comes to him. He has taught me to be cautious and skeptical.

I watch him thoughtfully. He seems subdued and strangely tired all of a sudden, as though he has gone to a great effort that has drained him.

"How did you get in here anyway? The window?"

"I would rather use the front door, but your father is home. I thought perhaps you would prefer that he and I not cross paths again." He smiles congenially, ever the thoughtful little demon.

"Oh, I would most definitely prefer that. Besides, I'd love to see you shimmy up the trellis in those clothes."

He laughs and takes advantage of our light mood by moving closer again. This is my fault. I shouldn't have joked so casually. I don't want him to think he is welcome here.

Dante pries my arms apart and holds my hand in his. Then he gazes into my eyes. "I am always happy to please you, *cara mia*. But, unfortunately, I do not shimmy up trellises. In these clothes or any others. Those days are far behind us, no? Besides, I have access to your home because you invited me in, remember? Our date to the Harvest Festival dance?"

I don't know what he means about those days being far behind us, but I do remember the night of the dance. He wouldn't come inside until invited.

Dante grins, a chess master enjoying the fruits of a well-played move. "I can come and go as I please now. Undetected." His eyes flash, and I feel myself blush.

"Oh." I look down and squirm on the inside. "And... just how long have you been coming and going as you please?"

I hope he hasn't witnessed anything embarrassing. Especially my breakup with Michael or the self-deprecating aftermath. Surely not. Wouldn't Michael have known if a demon was skulking in the shadows?

Dante tips his head back and laughs. I hate to admit it, but I actually missed that laugh. It haunted me for a year before I even met Dante. He was in my head, and I felt an intimate connection with his deep, devilish laughter.

"Not to worry, *amore mio*. I have been the consummate gentleman. Oh, I was tempted to peek in the shower; *mio Dio!* How I was tempted! But no. I was a good boy." He leans forward and cups my face, caressing my cheeks with his thumbs. "God, how I have missed you, Sophia. You don't know what I went through to get here."

He wraps his arms around my shoulders, and I sit very still, tense and guarded. Caution wants me to bolt. Empathy feels a stab of sadness. It's as if no time has passed for Dante. He is picking up where he left off when so much has changed for me.

With the full spectrum of emotions ebbing and flowing through me, I'm surprised to feel a measure of comfort with Dante. We were always able to talk. I mean, really talk— about multiple subjects. We had some fantastical conversations that now make perfect sense, considering what he is.

I find myself wanting to tell him about my Awakening and my training to become a spirit walker. I wonder what his reaction would be. But then the faint aromas of cinnamon and clove tickle my nose, and I push him away. It was an old trick, lacing his breath with spicey toxins to control me. I know better now.

"What are you doing here?" I stand and move away, angry with myself. Dante can make it hard for me to remember just what he is and what he is capable of. So I go to the window and look outside, just for something to do. He doesn't answer.

"Well?" I ask, turning back. I find him grimacing and tugging at his shirt. "What's the matter with you?" He shakes his head, but I can see he's in pain. I retrace my steps and stand over him. "Tell me. And this had better not be a trick."

"Nothing. It is nothing." His voice is thick and strained. "Perhaps I should go. For now." He squirms in his shirt and then I see it, something black spreading along his left sleeve. I touch it, and he flinches.

"What is it?" My fingertips are greenish black and sticky, and I wipe them on my jeans. Dante shifts uncomfortably as sweat appears across his forehead. Something is seriously wrong.

"Lay down," I say and then sit, trying to ease him back, but he won't go.

Dante clenches his jaw and leans his head heavily on my shoulder. I have to brace myself so we don't fall over. Whatever he has been silently enduring has overtaken him. And I'm at a loss. More black lines gradually appear like a roadmap across his shoulder, trailing down his back. A black, crisscrossed pattern stains the soft, white linen shirt.

"Oh, God," I whisper and start unbuttoning his shirt.

Dante forces a quick laugh. "Wrong deity."

"Don't. This isn't funny."

He groans and fights me, but I swat his fumbling fingers. "Stop it." I open his shirt and gingerly peel it over his shoulders. I am shocked and appalled by what I see.

Dante's entire back is flayed with horrible lashes. They are seeping fresh, black blood. A green chain tattoo circles his bicep and trails down his arm. It's new, too, still red around the edges. But this is no ordinary human tattoo. It was branded into his skin. The lashes across his back are struggling to close. Just like Michael, Dante will regenerate and heal. But these wounds are especially deep and gruesome. Just coming here today has reopened the worst of them.

I cradle him against my neck and stroke his head. Dante doesn't shed a tear, but he does give me his weight as he gives his stern, male ego a moment's reprieve. He must have suffered horribly, but he won't complain.

Tears sting my eyes as memories rise from the darkness—Dante being dragged down the black funnel at the Borderlands. Dante shouting my name, already mourning the loss of me before he is even gone. He must have been tortured repeatedly for returning to Hell without a soul. Tormented while I was out galivanting around and worrying about myself.

I suddenly feel awful for slapping him.

Dante is quiet and tense, his breathing coming in fitful waves. The bleeding has abated, and after a few more minutes, he gains some composure and withdraws. Hair has fallen across his forehead, and he runs his fingers through it, embarrassed by his disheveled appearance. Dante is always so formal—so proper. He must be in great pain to break down in front of me like this.

He carefully slides into his shirt and adjusts the cuffs. When he speaks again, his voice is low and husky with shame. "My apologies, *cara mia*. You were never meant to see that."

I pinch my eyes closed and reopen them, taking a deep breath. "I'm so sorry I slapped you," I say with all sincerity.

He laughs lightly. "Did you? I hadn't noticed."

After what he's been through, my outburst must have been nothing but a pathetic human afterthought.

"Dante, please tell me who did this to you. Were you beaten because of me? Because you returned to Hell without a soul?"

He smiles softly, reverently. "There is nothing I would not endure to be with you, *amore mio*. You know that. I never intended to Take your soul in the traditional sense. I wanted you for myself. I wanted you to live below with me. And for that, I was punished."

My stomach spasms as though I've been hit—a visceral reaction to things my mind cannot accept. I can't hear him say such things. They are as painful and as impossible as his confessions of love.

I'm not sure what I thought would happen when Dante was dragged below. I guess I never really believed he could be hurt. Certainly not to this degree. He always seemed so strong. Indestructible. Even after Michael decapitated him in the courthouse, Dante simply faded and disappeared. I never saw him suffer.

He notices my distress and tries to move on, telling me how Vaughn almost faded into oblivion, Santiago was spared, and Wolfgang was still locked away. He took the brunt of the blame and endured a unique brand of punishment. Wolfgang has become The Order's whipping boy. I feel terrible until I remember how evil he is.

"I'm so sorry you were tortured. I can't imagine what you've been through. But, Dante, why have you come back?"

He frowns and cocks his head. "I...thought you would understand, Sophia. I told you at the Borderlands. We are not finished. That was *not* the end. It is not an easy thing to do, tracking your soul over the years. Now that I have found you, I am not giving up. We are destined to be together. You declared this to me in our past life, remember?"

Remember? *Remember?* No! Of course, I don't remember!

And now I'm overwhelmed all over again. Stupefied, actually. And I have a million things to launch at him, but the closet door flies open, and Dante and I spring up.

Rama steps into the room with his usual, dramatic flair— hand raised and smile wide; he thinks I'm still moping about and wants to reenergize me. But before he sings out his greeting *aloha, wahine,* he sees Dante and stops cold. His hand drops, and his mouth clamps shut. The color drains from his face.

Uh-oh.

I rush over because he looks like he might faint.

"What's going on?" Rama's voice is surprisingly crisp and clear. He might have been shocked, but he is no wilting flower. He glares at Dante.

"Oh, well, this is my...um..." I don't know how to explain what Dante is, so I look to him for help.

Dante slides his hands into his pockets and smirks with an amused glint in his eye. "Well, if it isn't Obi-Wannabe-Kenobi."

Rama scoffs. "Hello, Darth Faker."

Chapter 14

Bats in the Belfry, Demons in the Bedroom

"**D**o you two know each other?" I ask, dragging my eyes from one to the other. Dante chuckles and crosses his arms. He's well adept at masking the pain still radiating through him.

"You're Rama Kuan," he says casually. "A somewhat newly minted Ascended Master, if I've heard right."

"And I've heard plenty about you, Demon Knight Dante. Your reputation is...appropriate." Rama is not happy, and he turns his back on Dante to face me. He scowls through the hair framing his eyes. "Well, *wahine,* mind telling me why you have a demon in your bedroom?"

"Well, gosh, that's not something a girl hears every day," I tease, but he doesn't think I'm the least bit funny, so I straighten up. "A few months ago, we kinda went out, and I kinda invited him in, so..."

I fade off as his expression drops with understanding. I have never seen Rama angry or upset, only mellow. I wouldn't blame him for blowing a gasket. Finding a notorious demon keeping company with a spirit walker trainee could certainly harsh anyone's mellow. If people still do that these days.

Rama smooths down his funky beach shirt and straightens his spine. He speaks to Dante from a higher authority. "Chill someplace else. Sophia and I have some training to do."

"Yes, about that," Dante says dismissively. He walks over, and they stand toe-to-huarache-sandal. "I think you've done all the training you're going to do here. So, why don't you meditate or levitate or remediate yourself back to wherever you came from."

Dante's eyes are swirling, trying to coerce Rama to comply. I have no idea if Persuasion is powerful enough to control an Ascended Master, but I don't want to find out.

"Hey!" I say, wedging myself between them. "For your information, I'm experiencing an Awakening. I'm on my way to becoming a spirit walker."

"I think he's already hip to that," Rama says, his eyes hooked to Dante's. He is not compelled, just supremely annoyed. Neither one of them backs down, despite my involvement. "Is that why you've come? To stop her Awakening? Or maybe turn her dark at the last moment?"

Dante's eyes stop swirling and turn cold, deadly. I'm racing to catch up.

"Wait, you *know*?" I tug on his arm, but his eyes remain locked with Rama's. "How do you know? Is that why you're here? Are you trying to turn me dark? Dante! Answer me!"

I wait an eternity, but he won't speak to me, so I turn away and plop down into the desk chair. I fume while they quietly threaten each other. I hear vague Italian and then something about lesser demons and Rama not being qualified to train a dog. They are ignoring me altogether.

"It's *my* job to train her," Rama says.

"Talk her out of it," Dante says through clenched teeth.

"Hey!" I yell. "Nobody is talking me out of anything. Dante, look at me!" He finally turns. "I want this!" I say, but he shakes his head. Then he says what everyone else has said. That I don't know what I'm asking for. That it's too dangerous. That I will be killed.

I deadbolt my arms across my chest, feeling everything inside me lock up. "I'm sick of people telling me I can't do this. Rama is my Ascended Master, and he thinks I can. Don't you?" I toss the opportunity into his lap, but he fumbles for the truth, so I say, "I know, I know, we're behind schedule, but I did really well the first day, right?" This, he agrees with, and I smile smugly.

Dante pulls me to my feet and takes me by the shoulders. Rama makes a weird whimpering sound and starts pacing because he doesn't like a demon touching me. I don't, either. But Dante has a point to make, evident by his grave look.

"Sophia, I came here for the reason I told you in the beginning. You belong to me, and I will do everything in my power to convince you or *remind* you. That has not changed."

"And I told you months ago that I don't believe you. You tricked me with your hoodoo voodoo and gave me strange memories that don't mean anything."

"My 'hoodoo voodoo'?" his eyebrows shoot up, and he laughs.

I roll my eyes. "Whatever."

"Not whatever. And it was not a trick. But I now understand why your memories are buried so deep. This Awakening
has taken over and replaced your common sense."

"My common sense is just fine, thank you very much!
Now, if you'll excuse me, Rama and I have to get started. We're
behind. And I have a lot of homework and...stuff."

I open the window and wave a clear path for Dante to
climb out. Instead, he gives me a sardonic look and strolls to
the closet. He steps inside and then looks back.

"*Ciao, cara mia*. It was so good to see you again." His eyes
drift down my body, deliberately displaying his carnal desires.
"I look forward to our next visit, where I will come and go as
I please." He laughs at my mortified expression and quietly
closes the door.

* * *

I bend myself into the lotus position across from Rama.
The realization that Dante has come for me again is settling
onto the highest shelf in my mind. It sits there alone because
everything else has been pushed aside. The fact that he didn't
try to drag me off to his cave by my hair is both comforting
and unnerving.

Dante is cunning and calculating. Whatever moves he
is planning, I'm sure he won't be repeating any mistakes. He
won't strike until all the pieces are in place—all guards down.
No loopholes *this* time. We have entered into a Master Class of
Manipulations, and I have to be ready for anything.

Rama asks that I unwrap my thoughts and relax, but

I can't. Neither can he. Finding a demon in my bedroom has unnerved us. He tells me he already knows about Dante, having been updated on my past transgressions when he was assigned to me. But neither of us expected Dante to show up again.

"Don't know why your demon dude would've been released. Word up the spirit chain says he and Vaughn Raider were in the Death Bunker. Can't figure why they're free to roam." We fall silent to contemplate things.

"I don't know the inner workings of Hell, so it never occurred to me to ask," I say. He nods.

"Yeah, gotta keep him outta your green room. Need your head free and clear of all debris."

The green room. That sweet space inside the tube, where every surfer likes to linger and be one with nature. To be free of life's troubles. Yeah, well, easier said than done.

I couldn't have been more prophetic. An hour later, Rama and I have made little progress on my journey to enlightenment. Seeing Dante again has affected me more than I care to admit. Concentrating is impossible, so we give up and head to the barn. I'm becoming rather adept at sneaking out of the house. Bailey would be proud.

When we arrive, Raph is waiting with Kanati and Chang`e. I'm grateful they stuck around to give me a second chance.

I walk over and say, "Hiya" and *"O si yo"* and *"Nǐ hǎo."* They return the greetings.

"So, how are you?" Raph asks.

"Defiantly optimistic, and you?"

He smiles and backs off, giving us room to work. I face Kanati and Chang`e.

"Look, I'm really sorry for bailing like I did. I was going through something, and...well, I understand your time is valuable. It won't happen again."

They are apprehensive but willing to stay if I am *truly* committed. I reaffirm that I am. No more doubts. No more delays. They agree to pick up where we left off.

The physical training is punishing. If the wear-and-tear on my body alone isn't enough, Chang`e snaps her silk whip each time my pushups lag or pull-ups falter. I do the plank, burpees, and a variation on the Insanity Workout I've seen on infomercials.

Up a tree and down again. And again. And again. Chang`e is a graceful drill sergeant, telling me my body must be transformed into a weapon. I must think I am lethal. Deadly. I must kill without hesitation.

I agree on a basic level, but since I've never actually engaged in hand-to-hand combat with a demon, reaper, or soul seeker, it's hard to rouse those killer instincts.

When jumping rope becomes routine, I get distracted by thoughts of Dante. As far as I know, he hasn't made an appearance in town, so nobody knows he's back. And Vaughn is chilling at the mansion. Dante admitted his reason for returning was purely for me. He has no plans to stalk anyone, so the good people of Haven Hurst should be safe. I certainly feel safe. I'm in control and won't be taken in by Dante's ultra-smooth Italian seduction techniques like before.

Besides, the last thing I want to do is run to Michael and ask for protection. I *have* to prove to him that I can take care of myself. And what better way than to deal with a couple of notorious demons on my own?

My internal pep talk does little good when my muscles are ripping and my legs are crying uncle. I finally tap out near midnight and crawl into bed.

* * *

I just set my alarm for five o'clock—as in the *a.m.* Ugh. My training is not only sucking the life out of me but also cutting my homework time in half. I need to snag a few hours for my most immediate assignments before school starts.

As I lie in bed, I contemplate quitting my job at the *Gazette.* I'm still responsible for taking photos for the school newsletter, so a few extra shots for the local paper aren't a big deal. Besides, I love my job. I love walking into the shop and seeing Miss Minnie and LeRoy. I'm not a fan of attending *every* athletic event, but I do love photography. I do love the creative outlet. It's one of the highlights of my day.

It also helps to stay busy, so I'm not constantly thinking about Michael. There were a few moments the other day when I was so deep into an assignment that I forgot my second heartbeat was missing. I forgot that the heart left behind was shattered. And then I took a breath, and the shards cut me all over again.

I roll over and cry myself to sleep.

When I wake hours later, it's not to the church bell alarm on my cell phone but to the familiar twinkling lullaby from Dante's music box. I sit up with a start, and there he is, a shadow reclined in my desk chair with his legs stretched out and ankles crossed. He is wearing fresh, unbloodied clothes and a lazy smile.

"*Buongiorno, cara mia.*"

"What are you doing here?" I demand. The room is dim because it's early, but I catch the flash of white teeth as he laughs.

"I am waiting for you to wake up," he says cheerfully. He comes over and sits on the bed. I look around for Sundance, but he has bailed because he doesn't like demons in my bedroom any more than I do.

"You can't be here," I say, nudging him with my foot beneath the blankets.

He slips a hand underneath and captures my ankle. I stop. We stare while he gently massages my foot, his hot hand working to relax the muscles. It's far too intimate, and I remember I'm wearing only a skimpy tank top and panties. I clutch the blanket over my chest.

His eyes stay with mine while his hand glides up my leg. His heat stirs my blood, and I feel it rushing through my veins. I hate that he provokes such a physical reaction in me. My head is perfectly clear and focused, and my body betrays me like an addict.

"Dante, don't," I murmur with a catch in my voice. He laughs quietly and withdraws, seemingly satisfied with his effect on me. I breathe out with relief. "A little too early in the morning for smoldering Italians, don't you think?" I pull my knees up and wrap the blankets around me.

"'Smoldering'?" Dante repeats in pleasant surprise. "Am I a smoldering Italian, Sophia?"

Oh, we are so not going there.

I clear my throat. "Anyway, why are you waiting for me to wake up?"

He grins, letting me off the hook. Then he moves around the room, opening dresser drawers and rifling through my clothes. "Well, I was anxious to get started. So what shall we do today? And what is *this* torturous device?" He dangles my bra from his fingertips.

I give him a sarcastic look, but he is serious. Dante's knowledge of intimate apparel is right up there with technology. I shake my head dismissively. "It's just my bra. And what do you mean, *we?*'" I tap my cell phone to wake it up. The clock reads 5:45, and I explode. "Dang it, Dante! Did you cancel my alarm?"

All modesty forgotten, I whip the blankets away and swing out of bed. I stomp to my desk and slam the music box shut. Then I check the clock on my laptop to verify the time. I'm almost an hour late. I turn around, furious.

"How could you do that? I have things to do. And now I don't have time to—What?"

Dante is flushed, and his eyes are wide. His arms drop to his sides because he is staring down at my—

Ah, crap!

I march over and grab the sweats from his hands. He grins and hangs on, so we tug back and forth.

"Stop it," I say. He eventually releases them, laughing at my embarrassment. "And please stop laughing. You've messed everything up today by canceling my alarm."

"I wish I could take credit," he murmurs, craning his neck to watch me get dressed. "Unfortunately, I have no idea how to navigate your cellular machinery."

I consider him with a critical eye while cinching the drawstring around my waist tighter than necessary. I tie a bow in quick, vicious movements. He is probably telling the truth. Dante was lucky to handle the Lamborghini that Wolfgang insisted they buy. He never seemed interested in technology.

"Well, anyway, I have an essay I should've been working on and a test this morning. Now I don't have time to work on either."

"Why are you bothering with all these mundane lessons? Come away with me. I am sure I could educate you on a thing or two."

"I don't want to go off with you, Dante. I want to graduate."

"Then you have taken my advice? You are no longer training to become a spirit walker?"

"No, I did *not* take your advice, which wasn't advice at the time, as I recall. More like a demand or threat. Anyway, I am *still* training to become a spirit walker. And if you're here to tell me, again, that I can't do it, you can leave. I mean, you should leave anyway. It's not right that you're here. I don't want Dad to find you."

"He is still asleep. And I don't want you to complete your Awakening. It's far too dangerous."

"So I've been told. Repeatedly." I search the room for fresh clothes, bumping him out of the way and loading my arms.

"Sophia, how do you think I knew about your Awakening?" he says, following me. I stop and think but come up empty.

"Good question. I have no idea." I dive into my drawer, but he pulls me around, forcing my attention. He is suddenly angry.

"The moment I was dragged back to Hell, I was locked in the Death Bunker," he says. "I had no contact from anyone on the surface. So, how do you think I learned about your Awakening? *How?*" He shakes me, but it doesn't produce an answer because I don't know how his world operates. "The Order, Sophia. The Order of Reapers knows about your Awakening. Lord Brutus is the highest member of The Order, and he made a point of telling me himself. They have already sent demons to turn you dark the moment you reach your enlightened state."

I stare, dumbfounded. The idea that evil entities from below know my personal business is unnerving and as frightening as…well, hell. The idea that more demons are roaming my peaceful little haven is unacceptable.

"And how did The Order find out about me?" I ask, watching the wheels of his mind go to work. Dante deliberates but decides not to make his next move. Not yet anyway.

My next move is to let anger simmer just below the surface. "So let me get this straight. You won't tell me how The Order found out about my Awakening, only that they've sent demons to turn me dark? Demons like…*you,* Dante?" I sound accusing, and Dante steps back. He doesn't like the implication.

"No, Sophia. Not like me. As far as I know, there is not another demon in the world who is in love with you."

"Oh," I say quietly. I'm embarrassed because that's not

what I meant, and he knows it. There is no escape from the uncomfortable side effects of someone casually reminding you of their undying love. Especially when you can't reciprocate the sentiment. I absently pull a sock from the drawer and add it to my pile. He's watching, waiting for me to respond.

"What kind of demons, then?"

"Lesser demons. Not Knights. They are ruthless and unpredictable. Without the scruples of demons from the Royal Court."

"Scruples!" I scoff. "You're telling me demons have scruples?"

"Some do. As hard as it is to believe. Yes. Some have a code of honor."

I suppose he wants to be included in that category, but I'm not so sure. I study him with unconditional skepticism.

According to Rama and our little chat yesterday, no one escapes the Death Bunker. For all I know, Lord Brutus sent Dante here to pretend to be in love with me. Just to get close and turn me dark the moment my Chelsea Light begins to glow. Apparently, it is a valuable currency down below.

"What, *exactly,* do you want with me, Dante? Tell me why you're *really* here."

He lowers his voice and speaks slowly, methodically. "I am here to stop you from fulfilling your Awakening. I am here to protect you from any lesser demons who try to harm you. And I am here to ensure you remember our past life."

Hmm. He might be telling the truth. But it hardly matters. I don't trust him.

"And I won't stop my Awakening. I'll defend myself against these so-called lesser demons, and I...don't want or have your memories. I'm sorry, Dante, but it's my decision." I go to the door, where I hope to escape to the bathroom for a quick shower that'll clean away all these negative feelings.

"And what does Michael Patronus have to say about your Awakening?" he asks.

I stop with my hand on the doorknob. I won't turn around. I won't let him provoke me.

"Don't be here when I come back," I say and walk out.

* * *

It's too late to gain any traction on homework this morning, so I take a long shower. The water is scorching hot and punishing, but somehow the pain feels deserved. My conversation with Dante is on a loop in my head. The most disturbing part is learning that lesser demons are roaming Haven Hurst undetected.

How do you recognize a lesser demon?

Are they like normal people but with cheap cologne? Bad comb-overs? Eighties fashion sense? Is there an age limit or health restriction? I really don't know what I'm working with here.

As I towel off and pull on jeans and a sweatshirt, I realize I should've pumped Dante for information before kicking him out. I should have used him like a cheat sheet—anything to stay alive and off the demonic radar, right?

I dry my hair and then pad down the hallway in my socks. When I open the bedroom door, I halt. Dante is still here, lounging across my bed and propped up on his elbow. And he is not alone.

Bailey is sitting next to him with wide doe eyes. If a picture paints a thousand words, Bailey's face is the unabridged edition. She has a look of sheer wonder, that fresh *I just hit the lottery* expression.

Crap!

I shut the door and glare at Dante. "What did you do?" I demand. Bailey jumps up and rushes over.

"Is it true?" she bursts out. "What he told me? Is it true, Soph? Tell me!"

I look around her to catch Dante's crafty smile. "What did he say?"

She spills the secret of the millennium. Dante and Vaughn are demons, and Dante and I share a past life.

"That's not true," I say, and Bailey frowns, looking back at Dante. He is still sporting his crafty smile but effortlessly makes his eyes glow yellow. Bailey gasps and Dante breaks out laughing. "Yeah, well, I meant the part about a past life." I plop down at my desk while Bailey dances around the room like it's a *Wiccan* festival. I brush my hair and then stop and yell at him. "I thought it was forbidden to tell people!"

"I escaped from the Death Bunker, Sophia. There's not much more they can do to me."

Oh.

I slump and chew my lip, working out the mechanics of the situation. Then I remember that I might need information from Dante. I probably shouldn't upset him too much.

Bailey throws herself across the bed and stares dreamily at the ceiling. She babbles on about Vaughn being back in town and how she can't wait to see him again and tell him she knows about his evil little society.

Leave it to Bailey to equate demons and Hell to some exclusive fraternity.

"Did you compel her to behave like that?" I ask.

Dante laughs. "No, that's all her."

He gives me a magnanimous smile, and I get the distinct feeling he's made his next move. The chess board is becoming overcrowded, and I've been outmaneuvered. Again. Then he makes another move by inviting us to spend the day in New York City. "Whatever you two would like to do. I am happy to please you."

Bailey bolts upright, jazzed at the idea. "Yes! As long as Vaughn goes, too, right?"

"Of course," Dante says.

"No thanks," I say. "I'm behind on my classes. And you guys *both* know I'm training with Rama Kuan. I'm not missing another session."

Dante and I stare off. I won't back down, so he speaks to Bailey instead. "You should not let Sophia miss out on her last year of high school with all this Awakening business."

Now I understand why he revealed his identity. He's using Bailey to tag-team me into quitting. I squint at him and smile.

"Look at you, getting all sneaky and human."

Dante posts an innocent look. "I just don't know how you will manage it, Sophia. Graduate high school *and* complete your Awakening. There doesn't seem to be enough hours in the day. Too bad you can't be in two places at one time."

"Yeah, too bad."

Actually, he has a point, and I'm starting to feel the academic pressure boiling inside me. We're going to be late if we don't leave now. Bailey seems lost in thought for once, and I doubt she's been listening. So, I grab my phone, my backpack, and my Bailey, and we leave Dante alone in the room. Then I poke my head back inside.

"By the way, if you talk to my Dad, like, *ever,* I will never speak to you again. *Capisce?*"

Dante nods respectfully. "I understand, Sophia."

Chapter 15
A Mad Russian's Roulette

All throughout school, Bailey is hyper beyond her normal sugar high but won't divvy out details. I suspect she's overjoyed to learn that her dark love interest, Vaughn Raider, really is hotter than hell.

"Au contraire," she says, dumping seventy-five pounds of knowledge into her locker and giving me her Cheshire cat grin. "You don't think you're the only one good at keeping secrets, do you?"

Oh, Lord. Do I want to know?

Michael hasn't been at school all day, and I feel more alone inside myself than I care to admit. All extracurricular activities, including Dante, haven't been enough of a distraction. I am officially a walking basketcase.

I wish I could tell Bailey how I feel about Michael. I'm so tempted, but I wouldn't expect her to take it well. Especially when I didn't tell her about Dante and Vaughn. Another secret of this magnitude might make her feel like we aren't the friends she thought we were.

Besides, she probably wouldn't even believe that Michael and I were a thing. I mean, nobody in their right mind would.

Michael and I were so careful not to draw attention when we were together. So even if I did tell Bailey, I'd have to explain why it was a secret. And there ends the temptation.

By the time the last bell rings, Bailey has miraculously kept her secret. But she continues to tease me with cryptic remarks all the way to the square. We stop outside the café, make plans to meet later, and say good-bye. Bailey disappears inside while I head to the *Gazette*.

I only plan to give an hour because I'm up to my eyeballs with homework and training. Holiday music drifts around the square, but it's not enough to cheer me up. I'm hardly paying attention when the speakers crackle, the song stutters to a halt, and a new song begins. It's devastatingly familiar and stops me in my tracks.

The beautiful, swirling, synthesized notes of "Electric Love" by Børns dance through the air and find my heart. Our song, the one Michael insisted was written for us. The one he loved to sing when we slow danced in my bedroom. The one I haven't been able to listen to since he left and never came back. It plunges deep inside me because it is heavy with memories. So many feelings are tied to those notes, those lyrics. It's a bittersweet weight, a reminder of all things lost.

I gaze across the square, face by face. But there is no Michael and no second heartbeat. Which doesn't mean he isn't out there, somewhere. Just too far away.

Too far away.

My eyes burn with tears, a feeling I am well acquainted with when I can't pretend things are normal. I thought I was dried up, having cried myself numb for days. But I underestimated my heart. It can still release pain when squeezed too tightly. The last thing I need is to come undone, so I draw in a ragged breath and tell myself I'm fine. It's all fine.

It's not the biggest lie I have told myself, but it is the most necessary at the moment.

My desk is a chaotic, semi-organized mess, so it takes a minute to get my bearings. Then Miss Minnie reminds me of tonight's assignment, which I have forgotten.

"The first event of the season," she says with a crunchy frown. I know what she's thinking—Between the two of us, it's odd that *I* am the one forgetting things. "The tree-lighting ceremony and the Turn On Your Santa show."

Ah, it's all coming back to me now.

I bring up the calendar on my phone, checking the long list of assignments. It's going to be a tight fit to make this work. I calculate how much time I can allot for each homework assignment between my sessions with Rama and the demon hunters. Not much. But I'm determined to keep busy and stem the tears still threatening to fall, so I dive in.

Miss Minnie has extended my duties of photographer to include copyediting. It seems I'm not the only one with a faulty memory. LeRoy, Miss Minnie's brother, has become rather creative in the spelling department. He refuses to touch a computer since he lost a slew of files a few months ago. He now writes his column of historical tidbits in longhand. I do my best to translate and have become fluent in gibberish. It takes a good forty-five minutes before I'm done and dismissed.

Rama is waiting in my room when I get home. He has lit soothing candles, softened the lights, and arranged pillows on the floor. We're free of demon intrusions and get right to work.

As we settle into a peaceful state of meditation, he tells me to search for my soul. Within me is the soul and within the soul is all the wisdom of the world. The spiritual realm I'm seeking is the inner life of my soul. Everything I need to know and use on my journey is within me. I must not fear it or the power it brings. I must embrace the light radiating behind my closed eyelids and let it expand within me.

The ball of light is swirling shades of blue again. The ringing in my ears is familiar now and growing stronger, pleasant. I have the sense of seeing as though my eyes are open. I have the sense of knowing as though the secret knowledge I was born with is gently rising to the surface. My heartbeat is strong and decisive. I feel an escalating sense of awareness. The ball of light is expanding, making my arms feel weightless. The feeling travels throughout me, extending into my torso and legs. I inhale a deep, soothing breath and hear Rama whisper.

"Yes. Yes." He sounds happy and far away. I wonder why this should be, so I open my eyes. I startle in surprise and look down. I'm levitating.

"Aaagh!" I immediately fall on the pillows. "Oomph!"

Rama is staring, speechless but with a huge, toothy grin. He nods like a pigeon. "It is righteous and pure. Yeah?"

"Yeah," I grumble, rubbing my sore butt. Then I laugh. "I can't believe I did that. Was that supposed to happen?"

"Oh, yeah, dude. For sure. Only...not quite so early. It

was awesome though. Like your body has already had the privilege, you know?"

I do. The memories of Michael levitating me hit hard—
like a sucker punch right to the gut. I won't allow them to bring
me down, literally, so I stand up and shake off the stiffness.

"What's next?" I'm feeling restless, impatient. He wants
to know what I experienced. What I felt and saw, so I tell him
everything. He sits quietly, assessing me.

"I believe you have accomplished the first trial, my little
wahine: the purification of the soul. I mean, anyone who can
levitate without the full vision yet is totally purified."

I smile with excitement. *I have passed the first trial! Maybe
I can do this, after all.*

"And now?"

"We chug on. The second trial: the illuminative way.
Gotta light it up and see where it takes us."

I'm not sure I like the sound of that but as I don't have
options, I decide to trust him. "Tomorrow then? We gotta hit
the barn now. Unless you have somewhere else to be?"

I laugh as he scrambles to his feet. Rama loves going to
the barn. He says it helps him rebalance and totally chill.

We have an arrangement so Rama can stay in the room
while I change clothes. He faces the corner like a troublemaker,
and I strip down, digging through the closet. He tells me what
to expect about the next trial while I select something more
suitable for a rigorous workout. I've learned that yoga pants
and sweats do not fare well through the boughs of an angry
tree. So beneath my running suit, I wear dark blue shorts and

a white tank top. Once I am presentable, he moves into the closet, and I head downstairs.

I hear Dad in the kitchen, cooking and singing "Henrietta" by The Fratellis. He's hooked, and I stand in the doorway, smiling. He sees me and presents a plate of fresh goodies.

"Chak-chak?" he asks.

"Those for tonight?" I take one. It's piping hot, and I stuff it into my mouth and lick honey from my fingers.

"Yup," he says, taking one, too. "I think I've got the hang of these." We smile and watch each other chewing. He does have the hang of these. They're scrumptious.

Dad sees my gym bag and asks where I'm headed. I tell him I'm working off stress. He considers me with a side-eye look but eventually nods. I say I'll probably see him later at the ceremony and then leave.

* * *

Because I've passed my first spiritual trial, I'm energized and eager to train with the demon hunters. I have a renewed sense of purpose that is struggling for release. Basically, I want to beat the crap out of something. So I'm hoping for some kickboxing. Or at least a round on the punching bag.

But Chang`e introduces a new method of training—slow movements, gentle side steps, easing the air back and forth around me with my hands. Because I'm so restless and impatient, it's challenging to calm my body, breathing, and arms. I'm moving in *slow*, slow motion, and I quickly realize it's a discipline. I mustn't rush or force my movements. I must control every inhalation. Every exhalation. Every aspect of myself.

Whirling the cane pole over my head has strengthened my muscles, and I feel them engaged, working with me for once instead of against me.

Kanati paces silently, his long black hair glistening in the light. He plays a soothing song on an ancient wooden flute that seeps inside me. I feel an internal peace similar to my meditation but with eyes wide open.

After a while, we take a break, where I ply myself with water and air. I stand apart, watching Kanati and Chang`e whispering. They are forever discussing me. I hear strange words: *Okichitaw, Shaolin, Wudang.* They're agreeing or disagreeing about something; it's hard to tell.

Eventually, we continue with Kanati guiding me through a series of movements. I'm to use my hands to simulate weapons: a knife, a spear, or some hatchet-like thing. I'm not sure, but I copy his movements, slicing, jabbing, and hacking high and low. We practice for another hour, moving at a medium speed which is more to my liking. I feel nimble but not yet graceful. The muscle memory is not automatic, but I'm on the cusp of things.

Kanati demonstrates a defensive move that I am to duplicate. And then he comes at me, thrusting an imaginary knife. I deflect his arm and whirl around, but we get tangled and have to start again. This time, I deflect his fake attack, hit, spin, and come around as I should. I've got it down, so we repeat things. Each time, I respond efficiently, if not automatically, hitting and spinning, and then...my second heartbeat springs to life, and I stumble over Kanati's foot and fall to my knees.

"What happened to your focus?" he asks.

I slump onto the grass and look around. Michael and Milvi have walked through the barn door. They stop and stare, and where am I? On the ground with Kanati leaning over me.

Michael doesn't look pleased, so I'm guessing he has no intention of making things right between us. I lower my head and sigh into my lap.

Why play our song in the square, then? Just to torture me? To remind me of what I am giving up?

Milvi asks if she can approach, and Chang'e says it's time for another break anyway. I climb to my feet and brush myself off.

"How's it going?" Milvi asks cheerfully. I think she's trying to be funny, but she's not. Milvi has been genuinely happy for me from the start.

Why can't Michael be happy?

I watch him disappear into a chamber behind the waterfall. I've wondered how it would feel to see him again and now I know—excruciating. If we were not made to be together, why does it hurt so much to be apart?

I gaze across the big beautiful meadow and force everything painful down into the deepest part of me. If there is a pocket or a box or a footlocker somewhere inside me, that's where I want to stuff all this hurt and self-pity.

I can't get overwhelmed. I can't burst into tears. Not here.

This is, by far, the most difficult discipline I must master. If I can't have Michael, I must fill the vacant space inside me with something else. Anger? Determination?

There is nothing I can say to change his mind, but maybe

I can *show* him. Maybe, if Michael sees that I'm progressing and learning to defend myself, he won't worry so much. Maybe, he'll even change his mind and support me like his family does.

I face Milvi with a tentative smile. "Things are great. I'm getting there. No, seriously. I am. Come on, let's spar."

I pick up two cane fighting sticks and toss one to her. Seeing Michael again has shaken my emotions loose. I feel reckless, so I grip the stick and assume the position. Milvi stares.

"Come on, nothing too aggressive." I goad her, but she's hesitant to take the bait. She glances at the demon hunters for permission. "Let's go," I yell and take the first swing, spinning the long stick over my head.

Milvi reacts on instinct, raising her stick to stop mine. And so we're off, lunging and clacking back and forth. Milvi is sprightly and confident, with far more training under her belt. But we're having fun, dancing across the grass in mock battle with my ponytail whipping around, slapping my face. The exercise is exhilarating and pumps my blood. This is what I need to release stress. Blood and sweat—not tears.

Milvi and I get tangled and start horsing around. We trip and fall, laughing and blaming each other.

"Are you *trying* to get yourself killed!" Michael yells.

We immediately stop the shenanigans and roll apart. Michael is wearing training gear and a mask of fury. He marches over and snatches the cane from my hands, glaring at me and then at Milvi.

"We were only fooling around," Milvi says casually as she flips up to her feet. She smiles at me and then strolls to the shelves stocked with towels and water bottles.

I stare up at Michael and brace myself against the burn-ing emotions threatening to take over. Being so close to him, feeling my second heartbeat after such a long time, is shaking my confidence.

This is the guy I love. This is the guy I can't have.

"It's not a game," Michael says through clenched teeth.

For a moment, I wonder if he's referring to our relation-ship or my training. I know he is reading my emotions; I can see *my* pain registering in *his* eyes. It hurts to look at him. It hurts to face the wall of stubbornness we have built.

So I look away and mumble, "I never thought it was."

Michael considers for a moment and then addresses the demon hunters. "Is *this* how you've been training her?" He sounds accusatory and rude.

Kanati's chin goes up. He is proud and doesn't like to be questioned on such matters. "She is doing very well," he says with enough force to make me believe it.

Michael's eyes snap back to mine. He looks me up and down, appraising me like a cheap suit. "Well, let's see then." He throws the cane stick to the ground next to me. I grab it and climb to my feet.

"What do you mean?"

"Let me give you a real taste of what you'll face."

Michael steps back and takes up his position. Kana-ti starts to protest. I may be improving, but he knows this isn't fair. Even at my best, a spirit walker's training could never match a Halo warrior's. Chang è throws out a hand to stop

Kanati. She accepts the challenge for me. Milvi also wants to grow my training at every opportunity; apparently, mood music is required. So she taps her phone, and "Russian Roulette" by Rihanna rises in the meadow. I think it's rather appropriate.

Michael and I stare each other down like two gunslingers at high noon. I am the awkward one trying to limber up at the last minute. The one who is too stupid to back down when she knows she's outgunned and outsmarted.

My heartbeats race. I grip the cane pole, rethinking things. *I don't really want to be doing this.*

And yet, we circle each other slowly, cautiously. I'm trembling and working to hide my fear. I wonder what Michael is thinking, seeing me again and feeling my heartbeat inside his chest. Does it infuriate him? Does it make him feel whole like it used to? Does he care that he is provoking me when I'm not ready? He knows I can't win at this. *I* know I can't win.

Michael is shaking his head. He won't go easy on me. He has read my emotions like a playbook and sensed my fear and helplessness. But he won't withdraw, and neither will I. We are too stubborn for our own good.

The lyrics rise and bathe the scene with blatant honesty.

And you can see my heart beating...Oh, you can see it through my chest...Said I'm terrified, but I'm not leaving...Know that I must pass the test...

I spread my arms and open myself up for whatever Michael has in store. His eyes flare with anger, but I'm not sure who or what it's directed at. Perhaps he thought I would slink off and hide. Instead, I am inviting him to *pull the trigger.*

Michael stretches a hand toward me, lifting me high into the air. I wobble and use the pole for balance. Then he rotates me just as he did at the frozen waterfall. The music swells as I watch everything slide by. The peaceful countryside that doesn't exist outside this barn. The lush green trees and white columns hidden beneath honeysuckle vines. The stone balcony and cascading waterfall. And then I stop and hover.

I gaze down at everyone gaping, even Rama, who has stumbled from a cluster of fragrant plumeria. And then I look at Michael, calm but intense. He is making his point loud and clear. I am the puppet he can control at will. But I smile softly and give him a look that says *Come on, I can take it.*

His eyes narrow in a challenge, and then he flings me to the left, where I crash into a tree and almost fall. I use the pole and push away, floating back to where I started.

Michael flips me backward, and I flail around, trying to find balance in the air. Then he pitches me toward a stone pillar, where I raise my feet just in time to save myself from a crushing blow. I push back with no time to recover as I slingshot across the meadow. Back and forth and then up and down, I am tossed like a sadistic yoyo. Finally, I am dropped without care. I hit the ground hard, rolling and groaning. I've lost the cane, so I scramble, pounce on it, and spring up to face him.

Michael holds his cane lightly in his fingers, spinning it like a pinwheel. He is toying with me. He sent me into the air to disorient me because he knows I'm always light-headed after he levitates me. But I recover quickly this time; my training with Rama showing some useful benefits already. I attack by whirling my cane sharply across Michael's. It's a good, solid hit that should have knocked his loose, but all I do is trigger his next move. In one fluid motion, his cane changes direction, hitting the tip of mine and sending it flying high into the air.

I startle and look up, watching it spin far out of reach. I'm disarmed, and then my knees buckle to Michael's cane swept behind me. I am flat on my back in less than two seconds, with Michael standing over me. His eyes are hard and piercing. But for a brief moment, they soften, and I think he might offer to help me up. I think he might smile and wink. My whole world could change from the flutter of an eyelid. How absurd. How wonderful. How disappointing.

Without breaking his gaze, Michael snags the whirling cane out of the air before it impales the ground next to my head.

I exhale a deep, sad breath and close my eyes. I give myself another moment before rolling away and climbing to my feet. Kanati and Chang`e are walking over, and I clench my jaw to mask my humiliation. I'm panting and trembling, but I'm not leaving. I lift my chin and await their instructions.

"That is enough for today," Kanati says. He gives a curt nod, dismissing me.

I don't allow myself to exhale the relief I feel. Or to cringe or limp. Instead, I grab my gym bag and march across the meadow. I just reach the door when I think I feel a single tug on my heart. I grip the handle and pause...

I must have been mistaken.

* * *

An hour later, I am still upset. All the way home, in

and out of the shower, dressed and changed into something warm, and then meeting up with Bailey, my mind replayed my embarrassment like a bad episode of *Jackass*. Well, what did I expect, leniency?

"Ha!" I scoff.

Bailey says, "What?" and looks around.

We're walking from my house to the square, where I've been instructed to keep an eye out for Vaughn. She is desperate to see him and hopes he'll show up tonight. Unfortunately, I've been preoccupied, so I tell her I didn't see Vaughn and that she shouldn't hold her breath. Winter carnivals seem an unlikely stomping ground for Demon Knights.

The courthouse bells chime as we plunge into the chaos of the park. The school choir is set up in the newly winterized gazebo and begins singing "Carol of the Bells." It's lovely and soothing, so we stop and listen. Like everyone else, Bailey wears warm *valenki* boots and an *ushanka* hat. Except for Duffy, who opted for a furry aviator hat that barely contains his wild dreads. I am without a hat because I vetoed the urge to wear my favorite beanie with Mickey Mouse ears. But, in a sea of Cossacks, I'm glad I did.

The towering Christmas tree is decorated with brilliant purples and reds. No surprise since Abigail Monroe and the McCarthy twins are heavy hitters on the town council *and* members of the Red Hat Society. Everyone is gathered around it, chatting, sipping hot refreshments, and nibbling treats. Dad's *chak-chak* is a big hit.

Bailey gets me up to speed with the local traditions—at

precisely ten o'clock, the tree will be illuminated, at which time everyone will applaud as though this is a wonderful thing, and I'll take the required photos. Then the lights around the square will spring to life in a domino effect, one shop after another. All Santas will be appropriately turned on, so to speak.

The frosty decorations will follow until every onion-shaped dome, giant ice sculpture, and life-size gingerbread house is glowing. We have several minutes before things get underway, so Bailey leads me to the refreshment stand. Principal Davis is behind the ice block counter in his Slovak attire and a fake frosted wig with an icicle beard. He looks as cold as Jack Frost.

Bailey says, "Two wad-kas, please," and he points across the way to another ice block stand.

"Hot tea or cocoa," he says. She rolls her eyes, and we leave.

I look at her. "Did you think he might—"

"Not for a minute."

We mosey down narrow, snowy walkways and around the humanized chess game in progress. I pull Bailey to a stop as a towering figure walks our way. He is dressed in royal finery—a full-length cornflower blue cape decorated with elaborate blue, black, and white swirls. It's lined with thick white fur that I'd love to sink my fingers into. His white hair brings to mind an old wizard and is covered with a matching blue hood with two great horns rising out and up to meet three feet over his head. Between the horns is an ornate blue crown. He has twinkling eyes and a long frosty beard and carries a white, crystallized staff that looks like a giant icicle. He is breathtaking.

Bailey identifies him as *Ded Moroz*, Father Frost, or Grandfather Frost—take your pick. Trailing behind him is *Snegurochka,* his granddaughter, the Snow Maiden. She wears a royal blue silk cape with delicate white fur trim. Her hood is down, displaying yellow hair in braids and a face as perfect as porcelain. She has a dazzling smile and pink lips and waves to the crowd.

When the parade of frosty royals moves along, what's left is a guy standing directly across from us on the sidewalk. He has dark, shoulder-length hair and wears a leather jacket and jeans. I'm guessing he's somewhere in the mid-twenties range. He has a mildly attractive face that is grinning at me.

I elbow Bailey. "You know him?"

"Who?"

"That guy right there, standing across from us."

Bailey looks around, but her eyes slide past him. "Comrade tchotchke has been sipping the wad-ka after all?"

I don't get it. The guy is only ten yards away. Then I narrow my concentration, and sure enough, I can see the faint outline of the café right through him. He shrugs and lifts his hands with a look that says, *Yeah, it's just me.* I frown because I'm sure I've never seen this guy before.

He steps forward like he's coming over, but a dark, hooded figure strolls up next to him. Santiago. He snags the guy's attention, and they start chatting like old friends.

People walk by and throw funny looks at Santiago because he is laughing and mumbling to himself. It occurs to me that I'm not sure who or what Santiago is. A demon? Lesser demon? Soul seeker? Some underworld flunky? That sounds about right.

When the stranger nods toward me, Santiago looks, and our eyes clash for the first time in months. For the first time since he evaporated into thin air along with the rest of the demons. But now that I look at him with fresh eyes, I see what I missed or misunderstood. His blatant contempt for humanity. His smug arrogance in knowing things beyond his measly pay grade. With that condescending smirk living on his face, Santiago now makes sense.

We stare for a long moment while I contemplate him. Then he crooks his finger, beckoning me to join them.

Dante's warnings about lesser demons unfold in the space between us like the proverbial red flag. I don't believe Santiago to be a direct threat; otherwise, Dante would have warned me. But I don't know who his friend is. I don't know what I don't know.

I lift my chin with a look that says *I will not be beckoned like a dog.*

"Here they come," Bailey says.

She's on her tiptoes, craning to see over the crowd as some of our classmates stroll up the street: Rachel, Holden, Lizzanne, Sarah, Harper Rose, JD, and Casey. They are dressed in colorful, elaborate Slavic costumes and hold torches to symbolize lighting the tree. Of course, it's all ceremonial. Behind the scenes, a switch will be flipped, and *voilà*, illumination.

Bailey tugs my sleeve and drags me into the crowd. "C'mon. Get your photos."

I fiddle with the camera settings, find a clear spot, and go to work. The school choir has been replaced by a large ensemble—a Bavarian Oompa band on steroids. And now Mayor Jones calls for attention at the microphone. He welcomes all guests to the start of Haven Hurst's annual Winter Carnival. It will continue each weekend, concluding with the dance on Christmas Eve. Then he gives Vern Warner the signal, and the old-fashioned streetlights around the square extinguish. The town falls quiet as though darkness is a blanket that muffles sound. Time stretches until I wonder if Vern has done something wrong.

The gentle plinking of piano keys eventually breaks the silence. Soft but sure, the tinkling expands with cords, cymbals, drums, and then a burst of electric guitars. The music swells, evolving into "A Mad Russian's Christmas" before it explodes with bombastic energy. The Christmas tree bursts to life with a blast of colors as though the song has resurrected it like Frankenstein, only a stunning tower of glory.

A multitude of languages fills their air with cheers. Muffled, mittened hands clap furiously. The tree flickers in rhythm to the aggressive music while storefronts follow suit as Santas, elves, and reindeer pop alive in glowing bright whites. Ice palaces that have transformed the town into a winter wonderland shimmer in green, red, purple, gold, and blue hues.

I shoulder my way through the masses, capturing shots of the Christmas tree, the lights, and the elaborate ice sculptures of ancient mythical creatures. I frame up the creepy nesting dolls, the Nutcracker soldiers, and the people—everyone enjoying their annual traditions. I even shoot Abigail chatting with the McCarthy twins. *And is that Bailey?*

I adjust the setting again, panning over happy faces for a nice panoramic shot. This is going to look so cool—but then I stop at Santiago, the only person standing rigid and sour-faced in the lively crowd, the only person staring straight at me. I lower the camera and frown. He has ruined my shot. He must have been following me or waiting for me to finish my job but grew impatient. Santiago moves aggressively through the crowd. So I clutch the camera and brace myself on the off-chance that he is someone Lord Brutus sent to harass me. To turn me dark.

"Relax," he says, his mouth hooking into a dark grin, and his eyes falling to my hands like a guillotine. "Nothing to worry about until one of *those* starts glowing." I shove my right hand into my pocket, making him laugh. "Yeah, like that'll do any good."

"What do you mean?"

"You won't be hiding it from them." He jerks his chin over my shoulder, so I turn and look up. Along the rooftops are men and women in long black coats and pale, grim faces. They are pacing and staring into the crowd like lions on the prowl. "Lesser demons," he says.

I turn my back on them and clutch the camera. Santiago has answered the question of what they look like; now I need to know what they can do.

"Do they know it's me? Even without the light?"

"Like I said, you're nothing but an annoying Forgiven

soul at the moment. A human with the potential to sin, like everyone else around here. But I'm sure Dante has told you they're not hunting the morally corrupt on this trip. They're here for you. So when your hand starts glowing, game on."

I reexamine Santiago and his blasé attitude. He is a follower, not a leader. He obviously doesn't have the authority to out me so early in my Awakening. But I wonder if he has the ability or courage to take my light—to chop off my hand to get it, if given the opportunity. More than likely his fear of Dante would override such impulses. Santiago probably values self-preservation above all. Luckily, this works in my favor and provides a tiny measure of comfort.

"So, what about them? What do they see?" I indicate the crowd around us, everyone enjoying the festivities. If any harm came to them because of me, I would never forgive myself.

"They can't see into the spirit world so…" He shrugs.

"Is that it? You came over to point out your creepy little flunkies? To get me all worked up for nothing?"

His nostrils flare because he is sensitive, and I have insulted him. Santiago never seemed to understand that he died and was sent to Hell. The last time he was here, he behaved like he messed up and got grounded. Was it a byproduct of his youth, or was he just dense? I don't know what got him sent below, but I'm sure he would say it wasn't his fault.

"Dante wants to see you," he says hotly.

I scrutinize him for deceit. If he's lying or trying to trap me, he'll have to do better than that.

"I don't answer to his beck and call," I say, turning away.

"Yeah, well, I do. Besides, you're gonna wanna see who he has. Trust me." He cups my elbow and leads me through the park. He walks fast, and I can hardly keep up. I ask what he's talking about, but he just says I'll have blood on my hands if I refuse. I can't imagine this to be true.

We skirt around the giant Christmas tree and leave the park. Past the ice rink packed with people, we head around the back of the courthouse and into the parking lot shared with the high school. It's overflowing with cars and dirty piles of snow, so we pick our way through. Because it's pretty dark here, I keep my eyes peeled for the freaks in long black coats. But, as far as I can tell, no one is following.

We squeeze between two SUVs, then round on a white van and stop. Several people are waiting on the snow-packed school lawn: Dante, the guy in the leather jacket I noticed earlier, a woman I've never seen before, and—

Colin Firth!

I gasp, and Colin lifts his head with terror swimming in his eyes. He is traumatized and trembling in his burgundy smoking jacket and silk slippers. I don't know what to think. I don't know how or why he is here.

"Bonasera, cara—"

"Dante!" I yell and clomp over, trying not to slip in the snow. "What's going on? Why is *he* here?"

I point to Colin Firth, but the woman throws out a sultry laugh, so I look at her. She has long black hair, red lips, and dresses like an expensive hooker in thigh-high Jimmy Choo boots that Bailey would donate a kidney to have. The diamond-studded belt buckle around her black miniskirt says GRIM. I swallow a bad feeling that tastes like blood.

Dante inclines his head and speaks formally like he was raised on a rich diet of confidence and etiquette. A tone that doesn't belong in a high school parking lot.

"Sophia, may I present Teriza, a...colleague of mine." He pauses and adds a touch of pride to his voice as he presents me. "Teriza, *this*...is Sophia."

She smiles, slow and catlike, while her dark eyes flicker with amusement. Even though I feel she's laughing at me, she gives off a deadly vibe, a threat to anyone she dislikes. There is probably a long list, which I've been added to by simply existing.

Her movements are fluid and flawless as she strolls toward me, not the clunky, chunky footfalls I'm prone to. She smells of burnt ashes and death and emanates a faint purring sound that puts me on guard. I don't want to turn my back on her, so I turn in sync, scrutinizing her as she scrutinizes me. We are doing the dance of distrust and suspicion.

"Ooh, she is quite the defiant little minx, isn't she, Dante? To speak to a member of the Royal Court with such disrespect." She clicks her tongue reproachfully, so I shift my attention back to Dante.

It occurs to me that I don't really know him at all, not layers deep like I do Michael. I know what little Dante has told me of himself and what little Michael's parents have shared. Dante was human. He committed suicide and has been in Hell ever since. Haven Hurst is the only context in which I know him. Up here, he was playing games and attending school to fit in. Not unlike Michael and his family.

But unlike Michael, Dante lives on the surface as though walking in a dream where I am still sleeping, and he is the prince charming who has come to wake me. Come to wake my memories and see him for the first time in *this* lifetime. In this dreamlike existence, Dante is a Demon Knight who proved his authority over Vaughn Raider, Wolfgang, and Santiago—on more than one occasion. But I never considered how that authority translated to other entities below. So this Teriza chick is implying he has extensive power. More than I gave him credit for.

Dante tilts his head, smiling softly. He has watched patiently while this newest information opens like a book inside me. It opens so wide I can leaf through the pages and learn more about him. Dante would have me believe our story has a fairytale ending, where the characters find their rightful places in the world. I want to tell him *I* am the author of *my* story, not him. But now is hardly the time or place.

I focus on the guy in the leather jacket—another question mark. By his casual appearance, I'm guessing he's not a lesser demon, ranking somewhere else on the evil food chain. A quick assessment says he is not in Dante's league. No powerful vibe. Nothing nefarious lurking behind his eyes.

Dante tracks my attention. "Yes," he says. "It is my understanding that you are already acquainted with Degan."

Degan laughs at my surprised reaction. "Yeah, it's me. I got new threads after Raph snapped my neck." He shows off the rich leather jacket. "Pretty sweet, right? Man, I hated those grungy clothes. Didn't you?"

He sounds casual and cool, like someone I would hang with. Raph killed Degan at the car accident but said it was temporary and he could pop up in a new body later on. Now that I think about it, I never saw Degan after that.

And now I remember what he is—a soul seeker. *And this Teriza chick must be a reaper.* I'm finally up to speed on who's who or, more accurately, what's what. So I plant myself between Colin and the others, glaring at Dante.

"What have you done?" I demand.

"Ah, I see that you recognize Mr. Firth. He told me he met a young girl who wanted to help him cross over but was not yet a spirit walker. I could only assume it was you. And now that we are all acquainted, let me explain. Since you stubbornly refused to stop your Awakening, you left me no choice but to help you out."

"Help me how?"

"No, Sophia, help you *out,*" he repeats sternly, so I don't misunderstand. He wants to help me get out of my Awakening. *Just like Michael.* "I thought you should experience firsthand the impracticalities of trying to save a lost soul. I suppose there is a romanticized aspect to things, but the reality is quite different. As our lucky lost soul here will demonstrate in a moment. Isn't that right, Mr. Firth?"

Colin shakes his head vigorously with his lips clamped shut. He is trying to be invisible by staying quiet. Santiago laughs. "He thinks if he talks, he'll alert the lesser demons."

"And why is that funny?" I ask hotly as Santiago solidifies my assessment of him. He hasn't an ounce of compassion for anyone.

"Uh, 'cause he's already surrounded by a Demon Knight, a smokin' hot reaper, and a soul seeker who could Take him in a second."

"Thanks, kid." Teriza smiles smugly, flipping hair over her shoulder.

"And why *haven't* you Taken him?"

Teriza sets her black eyes on me and puckers her red lips. "Well, Precious, I suppose it's because you and I are going to fight for him."

Crap.

Chapter 16
Blood On My Hands

rap. Crap. Crap. Reality dawns, and it's like drinking poison. It spreads, nauseates, and corrupts my insides. The realization of how far Dante will go to manipulate my life and my wishes is outside my belief system. It's crystal clear that he knows me about as well as I know him. If he knew me at all, he would know I find this reprehensible—sacrificing a lost soul to prove how dangerous my Awakening can be. It is unforgivable.

I scan the parking lot, hoping Rama didn't take my advice. I asked him to leave me to my own devices tonight because I was sulking after Michael humiliated me in the barn. It's obvious that I *have* no devices, and poor Colin Firth is going to suffer for it.

"There is no one to help you," Dante says, easing the camera from my hands. He casually leans against the van like an innocent bystander. We both know differently. "This is what you wanted so badly, Sophia, so have at it." He gestures toward Colin.

"This isn't fair to Colin. I'm not ready, and you know it."

Teriza strolls closer and uncoils her whip. "Oh, Precious wants life to be fair. How utterly adorable."

"Stop calling me that."

"Okay. Precious." She fakes a pout, and I curl my fists so I don't scratch her eyes out. I take in a deep breath and focus on Dante.

"If by some fluke, I'm able to stop Cat Woman over here, I don't know how to help Colin cross over. I can't keep him safe. So, this little exercise in humility isn't going to bring about the outcome you hoped."

"Your loss," Teriza says, reaching for Colin. He cowers and lets out a wail, and I lunge between them.

"Stop it! Leave him alone!"

Her red lips curl into a cold smile. "You can't have it both ways, Precious. Casper may not be a serial killer, but he *is* dead. Not *my* fault that he didn't take the safe elevator to the top floor. I'm here to drag him down to the basement. So, you'd better stop toying with him. Why…that's just cruel."

"Shut up!" I yell, and she backhands me across the face. My head snaps sideways as pain explodes across my mouth and cheek. I double over, cupping my face as it throbs. Now I do taste blood. I touch my lip and grimace; it's stinging and wet. I straighten up and look at Dante. He has taken a step forward and is scowling at Teriza.

I grit my teeth and face the reaper. Something is churning inside me, working its way to the surface. Something similar to those dark thoughts Dante triggered in me months ago. I immediately suffocate them, pushing them back down; I don't believe I can be turned dark so easily—or at all.

I close my eyes and take a deep, measured breath. I hear Rama's voice telling me to find my calm center, and I am there.

Calm. Centered. I smile, then I open my eyes, haul back, and punch Teriza right in the face. Her head flies back, and she staggers sideways while I step forward because I put all my weight into it. My heart pounds, and my knuckles throb. I have never hit an actual person before, and it's a far cry from a punching bag. I felt soft flesh and bones snapping. I hadn't expected that because she's in spirit form. I hadn't time to expect anything.

Teriza clutches her nose in stunned silence, then her eyes flare, and she screeches, coming at me with claws out. She grabs me by the coat and hurls me against the white van like a ragdoll. It's bone-crunching, and I drop hard, holding my ribs and moaning.

Before I can assess the damage, she picks me up and throws me at a car. I slide across the hood, wailing, "Mother fuuuuu—" over the edge and into the snow. I land on my side with a hard grunt. My ribs feel broken or at least cracked. All the air has left me, and I struggle to breathe.

This is too much. I am failing, me and Colin. I knew I wasn't ready, and I find myself hoping for Michael. Hoping he'll appear and help. Can't he sense my pain? Can't he sense that I'm in trouble?

Why doesn't he come?

And then I remember, and another truth becomes crystal clear. Michael warned me that he couldn't help. He told me repeatedly, '*You will go where I can't follow.*'

Aside from failing Colin, the worst part is realizing I haven't even left yet, and I already want Michael's help.

I'm so disgusted with myself that I don't want to think about it. So I push to my hands and knees, gingerly standing up. I limp precariously—pathetically—around the car. Teriza has lost her cool and is pissed that I've mussed her hair, nose, or whatever. She wipes black blood from her nose and glares while I stumble through the snow, unable to take a full breath. My lip burns and my whole face throbs like it's swollen. I stumble and fall to my knees, cradling my rib cage. Colin whimpers a wretched sound, and I don't know if it's for himself, for me, or for the inevitable.

Teriza cracks her whip around Colin's neck, sealing the deal. His eyes bulge, and he wails mournfully, but she has recovered, laughing that foul sultry sound. She relishes his fear, his pain, just like Wolfgang relished mine. Teriza loves the agony she creates. And she especially loves that I am forced to watch.

Colin's pleading eyes turn on me as he vibrates and smokes. All theatrical training discarded, he screams with pure unadulterated terror. He reaches out desperately. So I throw myself at him and catch his hand, but Teriza drags him away. Inch by inch, his fingers fade through mine, and I sag to the ground, sobbing with blood on my hands.

* * *

Bailey hands me a steaming cup of tea. Trembling, I wrap my hands around it and set it on my knees. I'm under a throw blanket on a couch in the café, and she is nursing me into feeling better. I can't go home yet because Dad might be awake, and he would demand an explanation for my swollen lip and inability to breathe. Besides, I still feel emotionally sick to my stomach. The moment Colin disappeared with Teriza, I fled and puked in the bushes.

I will never forgive Dante. Or myself for failing Colin Firth.

Bailey knows what happened and sits quietly while I sniffle and wipe my tears. I suspect she's imagining ways to cheer me up, but it's no use. I lost a soul that I shouldn't have tried to save in the first place. What else is there to say?

"Listen," she finally says. "You know I'm sorry about what you went through, right? You've got some chutzpah, I'll say that. But I'm not one to piss and moan when life takes a dump on me, and I don't think you are, either. So…" She throws a look around and then scoots closer and lowers her voice. "I've been cooking up a little something that might help. See, as far as I can tell, you've been running around playing Whack-A-Mole. Trying to hit every obligation only to have another one pop up. And then Dante said something the other day that got me thinking."

"Bailey, I don't want to talk about Dante. Ever. Don't mention him. Ever. I am never, *ever* going to see him again. Got it?"

"Wow, don't go all Taylor Swift on me; just hear me out. It's important. So anyway, the *demon who can't be named* said it was too bad you couldn't be in two places at once. Remember? Good. Well…he was wrong."

She gives me a crafty smile, and I recall how sneaky she's been lately. "This have anything to do with that secret you've been hoarding?"

"Oh yeah. Now brace yourself 'cause this will totally rock your boat." She takes a deep, excitable breath and begins. "You know how the McCarthy twins are exactly the same?"

"Hence the word *twins*," I grumble.

"Yeah, well, they weren't always."

"Always what?"

"Twins. See, several years ago, Gracie McCarthy's husband died. She was really distraught. Devastated, actually. She was deep into a depression when she was approached by a witch who offered to help her out. Well, the witch was kinda new and subpar with the process and screwed the whole thing up. And then—"

"Screwed what up?" I ask, bypassing my shock that she would speak so casually about a witch.

"Bringing the dead Mr. McCarthy back to life. And stop interrupting—"

"But why—"

"Because shut up. So, anyway, Mr. McCarthy actually came back as a duck. You know, you've met him. Romeo?"

I sit very still and stare at her. Bailey's blatant calmness and frank expression speak volumes. She is telling the truth and fully expects me to believe her. Anything short of that is unacceptable. Because I have nothing better to do and I'm curious to see where she's heading, I go where I'm led.

"Okay. Let's say Romeo...the *duck*...is Mr. McCarthy," I say.

"He is—"

"I know. Just...can I let it sink in for a minute? Sheesh." I sigh and then frown. "But wait, there's two—"

"I'm getting to that part!" she says, all snippy because I can't keep my mouth shut. "So there's Gracie with Mr. Mc-Carthy, who is now a very crabby old duck. Gracie is none too

happy about the situation, so she and the witch repeat the process and create a pal for Daffy, and . . . presto change-o, Juliet
is born. More or less."

*"Romeo and Juliet," I say, nodding and playing along. I mean,
I just got my butt kicked by a hookery reaper, so yeah, I'm on the cusp
of believing anything.*

"Now then," she continues. "All is well for Mr. McCar-
thy. He's got someone to futz around with, but Gracie is lonely.
Her depression nosedives. So, the witch takes it to the next
level. They get help from a friend willing to make an avatar for
Gracie. I'm fuzzy on the details, but whatever they did worked.
Because out of nowhere, Gracie's long-lost sister shows up.
Only she doesn't have a long-lost sister. They created a double
for her. And that's what we're gonna do for you."

There is a band setting up in the corner and doing a sound
check. They begin their first cover song, "Bohemian Like You"
by the Dandy Warhols. I gaze absently at them, feeling numbed
from top to bottom. Then I slowly drift back to Bailey. She is
waiting to see if the verbal lobotomy has affected my speech.

"You...can't be serious," I say, but she nods, so I sit back
and consider. With everything I've seen since moving here and
being forcibly educated on demonic activity beyond my comfort zone, Bailey's idea isn't that far-fetched.

"But...who's the witch?" I ask, and she leans closer and
whispers, "Abigail Monroe," and I nearly drop my teacup. "Are
you freaking kidding me?" I yell, and she laughs.

"Why do you think I got her and the twins together to
put a hex on your ex-boyfriend?"

"Yeah, look how well that turned out. But…how do *you* know all this?"

"Well, it just so happened to be my best friend they went to for help. Her Christian name is Alice White. Her street name is High Alice. She's clairvoyant, among other things. Seriously gifted. She was the school photographer last year and worked for the *Gazette*. But she graduated and moved away."

"What do you mean her 'street name'?"

She shrugs. "Just how everybody knows her. Most people thought she was a stoner, but she really had visions. Serious shit. Without chemical enhancements."

I think about my own visions—without chemical enhancements. Then I think about the McCarthy twins, who always seem happy as clams. They may tease and squabble like siblings, but they're always in sync. Always together. The idea of having another *me* running around might give me the willies, but I consider the logistics. *If* I have a double to do the academic heavy lifting so I can concentrate on Rama and the demon hunters, I could complete my Awakening soon. Maybe even be a spirit walker by Christmas. Then I could be ready the next time a lost soul asks me for help.

I'm warming to the idea, but why does it feel like cheating? I don't want to break any rules, so maybe I can bend them just enough to squeeze through unaffected. What I'm doing is overcoming, adapting, and improvising. I know there are others like me experiencing an Awakening and training to achieve total enlightenment. But how many have a notorious demon knight and a guardian angel trying to stop them? How many have Lord Brutus and his lesser demons trying to steal their Chelsea Light the moment it ignites?

No, it's not cheating. It's waging war against enemies, foreign and domestic.

"So, what's your plan?" I ask.

"First step is to talk to Abigail and the twins, which I already did tonight. They said we definitely need High Alice, or we're risking a duck infestation. They don't know where to find her, but her great-aunt might know."

I sit back, fearing the impending voice of doom. Just when I was getting my hopes up. Just when my mind was blossoming with sweet anticipation.

"And where in the world would we find the great-aunt of High Alice?" I ask, thinking we might as well be searching for the Wizard of Oz.

"You tell me. You work for her." Bailey grins because she is playing with me.

"Are you joking? Miss Minnie is High Alice's great-aunt? Well, that's convenient. So, will Miss Minnie know where she is?"

"Uh, yeah. Miss Minnie's clairvoyant, too."

I scoff. Now I know she's joking. But wait—I suddenly remember all those odd comments Miss Minnie has made over the last few months. How she seemed to know things she shouldn't. Even my first day in Haven Hurst when she knew me before I introduced myself. Another thought occurs to me, so I ask Bailey if Alice White is related to Officer White.

"She's only his daughter."

"Wait—did High Alice tell him I was coming to town the night he pulled me over and gave me that bogus ticket?" Bailey grins, and I say, "Are you freaking kidding me?"

"High Alice told me she had a replacement coming for her old job. Said she was leaving Miss Minnie and the *Gazette* in good hands. I guess she knew about you well ahead of time. She must've told her dad before she left town." Bailey shrugs like it's easily believable.

The night Officer White pulled me over, I wasn't speeding. So, he told me to buckle up my dog. I always thought it was a pretty flimsy excuse for stopping someone. But if he hadn't stopped me, I wouldn't have reached that car accident when I did. I wouldn't have seen Michael in spirit form.

Hmm.

Bailey plops her feet onto the coffee table and crosses her ankles. "Look, I know it's a lot to swallow, but let's not overthink it. We've got the perfect opportunity to help you become a spirit walker. And the next time you see a lost soul, you'll be ready, right?"

We are of like minds.

Dante and Michael have gone out of their way to stop me from becoming a spirit walker.

Well, boys, comrade tchotchke has a plan of her own.

* * *

Bailey and I take my tea on the road and shuffle to the *Gazette*. It's slow going because I have copious amounts of pain to deal with. The first night of Winter Carnival is winding down, and almost everyone has gone. We don't expect the office to be open, but Bailey wants to leave a note on the door for Miss

Minnie, saying we need to talk first thing in the morning.

To our surprise, the lights are on, and she is waiting behind the counter. Bailey makes a face that says *Fah-reeeee-ky,* and we step inside.

"You okay?" Miss Minnie asks, eyeing my swollen lip.

"I'm fine," I say dismissively, although standing upright hurts like hell.

"And now you want to find Alice."

"Oh." I throw Bailey a look to see if she has set this up already, but she shakes her head. "Yeah, we need—"

Miss Minnie holds up a hand. "I understand. That's not the issue. You see, Alice has gotten herself into a sticky situation. She…" Miss Minnie frowns and rubs her fingers over her arthritic knuckles. She pulls a tissue from her sweater sleeve, dabbing her eyes. "It's *La Croix.*"

"What's *La Croix?*" Bailey asks.

"A nightclub. In New York. And Alice…well, I suppose she has her reasons for being there. If you want to find her, I would look there, except…"

"Except what?" I ask, stepping to the counter. I'm determined not to let anything interfere now that we have a plan. It may be whacked, but it's our only plan.

Miss Minnie fidgets, clearly uncomfortable with whatever she's wrestling with. When she makes her decision and turns away, I clutch her forearm.

"Please, Miss Minnie! This is important. The most important thing I've ever done." I look down at my hand on her arm. It's the first time I've ever touched her, and a strange warmth flutters through me—something is passing from her into me. I pull away but it doesn't break the sensation; it continues to spiral inside me until it swirls into my thoughts, into my consciousness. I feel a tranquil sense of awareness.

"You know what I mean," I state flatly. "You've known all along. You know why I came to this town. And you know why I have to find Alice."

Resignation passes over her features, and I realize she has known *everything*. Officer White pulled me over because she told him to, not High Alice. Miss Minnie told him to send me here for work. She wanted to keep an eye on me. She sent me to take photos in the courthouse the night Michael saved my life. Everything changed that night. I don't know how or why, only that Miss Minnie has known.

"I trust you, Miss Minnie. So please, *please* trust me."

She blinks and nods, acknowledging that I've put things together. But not everything.

"You don't understand, child. Things have changed unexpectedly. *Alice* has changed. She might not be able to help in the way you want. But she does have the book you need. I suppose if you were to get the book, you could…it's just that… Alice lives in the backroom of *La Croix*. You can't get inside. It's a nightclub that—"

"We'll get fake IDs," Bailey says as though we're picking up milk from the store. Miss Minnie shakes her head.

"That'll do no good. They don't check IDs. It's invitation only. Girls, *La Croix* is a private nightclub for demons."

Chapter 17

The Future Perfect
Past Tense of Me

I am sitting on the edge of my bed feeling like someone dropped an anvil on my head. *A private club for demons? Of course, why didn't I think of that?*

According to Miss Minnie, we need High Alice. Or at least we need her book to make me a temporary two. *La Croix* is invitation only, and we either have to be demons or be invited by demons to enter.

I yanked Bailey out of the office before she shot off her big mouth. I knew exactly where her mind went, and she confirmed it the minute we stepped onto the sidewalk.

"The solution is obvious—we have to ask Dante and Vaughn to get us in."

"I'm not speaking to Dante, so—solution not obvious."

In fact, we have no solution. Our plan has hit the proverbial brick wall. So now, I am sitting here pondering ways to summon Rama. He wasn't here when I got home, and I desperately needed to talk to him. I have to tell him I lost Colin Firth and, oh, by the way, I really, *really* need to sneak into a den of demons, find a spellbook, and make another me. I'll use simple words. Short sentences. Don't want the gnarly onshore to make him perl or bail altogether.

How does one summon an Ascended Master anyway?

I open and close the closet door a million times, but he doesn't appear, so I give up. Luckily, Dad was in bed when I snuck in and covered my face with icepacks. He'd freak if he saw my fat lip, and I hope the swelling is gone by morning. I doubt I have the appropriate camouflage makeup to hide the bruising, though.

I toss the icepack to the floor and ready for bed, moving cautiously with significant pain. Then I shoo Sundance out, afraid he'll bump me in the night. Finally, I ease between the sheets and lay back. It's been a grueling day, and I gradually decompress, exhausted. Even my bones ache. I gather my scattered thoughts and manage a few minutes of peaceful, wholesome meditation. I balance on the edge of sleep and then fall. Deep, deep, down into a blissful abyss.

The blissful part doesn't last long, but the abyss part is accurate. Dreamy images fade in and out, mostly disturbing, and painful. Mostly of Colin Firth, standing alone on a stage, crying. The audience beyond the floodlights are dark grinning faces with jagged teeth. They are eager to devour him, but his eyes flit around, desperate for help—down in the orchestra pit, up to the balcony. He finds nothing but more devilish faces. I am there, waiting in the wings, so I raise my arms, beckoning him. But I have no hands and blood drips from my open wrists. And then the audience rushes the stage, devouring Colin in chunks while he cries out and blames me.

Guilt is a sharp, tangible thing; even to the subconscious mind, it cuts and slices deep wounds. It wreaks havoc on the psyche. I twitch and toss in my sleep, desperation clawing at my insides.

I want to help! Let me help! Don't go!

And then a warm hand smooths the creases in my brow, chasing away the disturbing visions. It brushes my hair aside and cups my cheek, bringing out a forgiving sigh. *I like this hand. It's comforting.* The bed shifts, and the hand leaves, replaced by soft kisses. They trail down my face, producing a moan. "Mmm." I turn toward the affection—a flower to the sun. *This is a dream more to my liking.*

The kisses dance along my cheek, drifting whisper-soft over my mouth. Warm lips linger and tingle, and my mouth opens on its own, asking for more. The kisses are light and delicious. Soft, caressing lips. Then I feel a weight on me, and I grimace. A sharp pain shoots through my rib cage, rousing me. I blink quickly and open my eyes.

Green eyes shine in the dim light as Dante grins down at me. He shifts his weight, so I can breathe easier, but it hardly matters. I've caught my breath in shock.

Oh, my God! Dante was kissing me! How could I have been so careless?

The last time he kissed me, fire rolled through my body and destroyed everything it touched. The last time he kissed me, Dante happily killed me.

A moment is all it takes to assess the effects this time.

Thankfully, I feel nothing burning or eroding, no organs dying out and shriveling. Instead, I feel heat from his body. And outrage.

"Get off," I demand. I struggle, but my arms are pinned beneath the blanket. Dante lowers his chin, giving me his concentrated attention.

Are his eyes swirling?

No.

Wait, are they?

I don't know if Dante has ever used his demon on me. The only time I saw Persuasion surface, Dante's eyes split into snake eyes. I can't be sure if that is the only visible sign, and I don't want to find out. So I try to turn away, but those light green eyes have hooks that hold me in place. I couldn't look away if I were dragged from the room. This is the moment the toxic spices should flood my senses and anesthetize my system. But there is nothing stirring the air between us. There is nothing between us at all.

Dante speaks with his eyes, telling me the raw truth of what he wants. Blood thumps at the base of my throat as though demanding my attention. Dante's fire passes into me like forging another connection. He is dangerously handsome, making the sensible as soft as clay. Making a moment feel like an eternity when he looks at me in a way that only he can. As though he is not in the present but back in time, lost in the life before this one—before many other lives. His soft gaze says he is my love, and I am his. His smile says I am not running *from* him but *to* him, with tenderness and affection. With shared desire.

Familiarity swirls around me, thick as fireflies—Dante

above me, smiling down with all his love laid bare. Far in the distance, I hear the music box chime. *Our song.* I blink lethargically, my eyelids drooping, and my body relaxing beneath his. I feel strangely sedated after all.

Dante shifts to lay next to me, propped on his elbow. He holds a steady gaze while sliding the covers down my chest and stomach. He lifts my right hand like it's something to cherish and brings it to his soft warm lips. Gentle kisses on my bruised knuckles send tingles up my arm and a surge of adrenaline to my heart. I feel it quickening beneath my shirt. He carefully replaces my hand, and hesitates, awaiting my response. I frown because he is asking permission for something.

Then he slowly lifts the hem of my T-shirt and pauses when I catch my breath. I shake my head against his grin but he leans over, placing a tender kiss on my bruised ribs. The tickling heat dances across my skin, a disturbing mixture of pain and pleasure. I fight the urge to touch where his lips have been.

Dante lifts his head, assessing my reaction to his intimate touch. His eyes are pale as the Caribbean Sea and tell me he knows something I don't. His tantalizing smile speaks to me again, saying he wants more now. So he slides out of his shirt and lays across my stomach, skin against skin. I tremble from the surge of heat while he snuggles against me as though it's the most natural thing in the world. Dante shares his fire with the understanding that we cannot be parted. Without speaking a word, he lures me into confusion, summoning unwanted thoughts and desires. I doubt what I know to be true. Something hidden in the dark moves into the light and brings deep cravings to touch and be touched. To feel his familiar weight on me. Again.

Arms that aren't mine ache to hold him. Lips that don't belong to me part with need. Ancient longing drifts from the farthest corners of my body, guiding my hands to him. Blindly, my fingers dive through his hair, down his neck to rake my nails across his shoulders.

"Please," I slur, begging for something familiar, feeling tortured and outside myself.

Dante moans and slides on top of me, burying his face in my neck. "Yes, Lovaria, yes."

My eyes spring open, and I'm startled to find myself panting and trembling with need. Weight on my chest brings my mind back to center, and I realize what's happening.

"Dante! Stop!"

I push against him until he eventually lifts his head. His hair is tousled and sexy, his eyes wide with confusion. They race across mine, and for a moment, he seems as displaced as I am. Then he frowns and rolls onto his back. His rapid breathing suggests he was lost in the same otherworldly madness that had consumed me. So we lie quietly and stare at the dark ceiling, trying to calm our breathing—to gather our thoughts. I don't understand how this could have happened. There were no spices, no Persuasion manipulating my thoughts. So how did I fall under the influence of his...of his...

Nothing. There was nothing, only Dante and his love for me. Can his love be so powerful that it can reach inside me without supernatural aid? Does it go that deep?

No, it has to be a demonic trick. Dante changed tactics this time around. That has to be it. Maybe he thought saying her name would convince my subconscious that I was her. But who is she? Why did he look startled when he saw *me* beneath him, not *her*? Why was he disappointed?

And why do I feel strangely irritated knowing how much he loves her? *I mean, what in the actual hell?*

"Who is Lovaria?" I say, then grit my teeth, embarrassed that it came out so aggressively. Dante sighs heavily because I am the stubborn voice of reality. I turn and look at him. He takes a moment before speaking.

"You tell me, *amore mio.*" His voice is laced with such heavy sadness that it chips away at my anger and embarrassment. How can he keep doing this? Sometimes it seems like he is drowning in pain, which only magnifies my guilt for adding to it. Dante's heartbreak goes so devastatingly deep, as though he carries all the sorrow of the world within him. I recently lost Michael, so I know a fraction of what Dante feels. But my heartbreak is fresh, whereas his seems as old as time. And still, he fights for it.

"She was the one you loved. The one you lost," I say, reaching over and squeezing his hand. Although I'm not convinced I'm the one he wants me to be, I'm not without compassion. I hate to see anyone suffer.

To my surprise, Dante laughs. "It is strange to hear you speak of yourself in the third person. In the past tense." He rises on his elbow and smiles down at me. His eyes dance with amusement before becoming somber again. Then he gently cups my cheek. "But I know you are in there. Somewhere. You have a very old soul that belongs to me—so many lives to sift through. But when you return, all will be as it should be."

"Will you tell me about her?" I ask, hoping he'll see how different we are if he remembers the details. How impossible it is.

"No, *amore mio*. I will not tell you what you already know. When your memories return, they will come from you. Not me. And in the meantime, I will continue to be patient."

"You call this being patient?" I say, pulling the covers over me. He tugs them back down, and I smack his hand because I'm not being playful. I haven't forgotten about Colin Firth. So I clear my throat and say what I should have already said. What I would have said if I hadn't been under his—well, whatever influence he had over me.

"Dante, I want you out. Now. I'll never forgive what you did tonight."

"Forgive *me*?" He sounds genuinely bewildered. "For what, *now*, may I ask?"

"For the death of Colin Firth."

Ah, now he remembers. But he looks dubious as he fiddles with the sheet.

"Poor choice of words, I should think. I did not kill nor cause the death of *Signor* Firth. Remember? He was already dead."

"But you set him up to be Taken to Hell. And that's almost the same thing."

"Actually, you should thank me."

I scoff. "How do you figure that?"

"Earlier this evening, Santiago and I came upon Degan,

who had cornered a lost soul outside your high school. It seems that *Signor* Firth came to Haven Hurst in search of some mysterious girl who claimed she might be able to help him cross over." He gives me a reprimanding look as though I've been caught telling fibs. "Being the soul seeker that he is, Degan had Firth dead-to-rights, so to speak. But I had the brilliant idea to give the old man a fighting chance. I sent Degan and Santi to find you while I summoned Teriza."

"So, you thought I could save him?"

He shrugs. "I thought you would like to try. Am I wrong? Did you not want to try to save him?"

I exhale a heavy sigh as the tables slowly turn. So here I was, thinking Dante had been cruel and vindictive when all he was trying to do was help me. Sure, he said he wanted to help me 'out' of becoming a spirit walker, but at least he was giving Colin Firth a fighting chance. Sort of.

"Then why summon a reaper? Why not let me fight Degan for Colin's soul? Seems to me that soul seekers are far less skilled and lethal than reapers."

"This is true. But Degan refused to fight you. I believe the fool is infatuated with you. You haven't been leading on poor, unassuming soul seekers, now have you, *cara mia*?"

I roll my eyes. "So, you call in a skilled reaper, and I get my butt kicked. That sounds completely fair."

"I knew she would not hurt you."

"How did you know?"

"Because I would not have allowed it," he says firmly. We fall silent and watch each other, contemplating things.

"But she did, Dante. She threw me around like a ragdoll."

"Well, you did strike her in the face, Sophia. Shocked the hell out of her, too." He smiles affectionately, and I squint at him.

"I think you secretly enjoyed my debut beatdown, didn't you?"

"I don't know what that means, but if you are asking if I enjoyed seeing you flung about then, no, Sophia. I did not enjoy it. At all." With a wicked grin, he trails his fingers lightly over my stomach and across my rib cage. His touch gives me goosebumps, but he is communicating something else, something I don't—

I push him away and quickly sit up. I touch the places Dante kissed me, first my mouth and then my ribs. There is no cut lip. No swelling. No pain. My knuckles are also scratch-free and completely healed. I scoot back and fall against the headboard.

"What in the name of Dr. Strange have you done?" I say, but he cocks his head and frowns; I've gone beyond the scope of his late-night media education. "You *healed* me," I clarify, and he smiles.

"Yes."

"*You* healed *me*."

"Sophia," he says in warning because he hates when I do this repeating thing.

"So, that's why you came here tonight? To heal me?"

"Please do not look so surprised. You are breaking my heart if you think I would leave you to suffer."

I won't admit it, but it never occurred to me that Dante was capable of helping people—of easing pain or doing good. His skills have more layers than I imagined, and I'm starting to see him in a whole new light. Not that I'll get carried away here. Dante is still a demon who wants to Take me to Hell.

"But how can *you* heal *me?* Or anyone, for that matter?"

He shrugs. "A privilege of being a Demon Knight," he says vaguely. His mind is wandering, and his hand is tugging the covers back down. He is relentless, so I clutch the sheet to my chest with one hand and grab his discarded shirt with the other.

"Put that back on." I toss it at him, and he catches it in his smile. Then he exaggerates frustration and sits up. "Wait— what's that?"

I roll his forearm over and reveal an exquisite-looking dagger tattoo. It's both ancient and futuristic, and I'm astounded he would have something like this. Dante seems so traditional, so formal and proper. And this is deviant art at its finest.

"You like?" he asks and holds out his other arm.

"Two? Seriously? This is kinda badass for you, isn't it?"

He looks at them through my eyes but shrugs. "They serve a purpose."

"What do you mean? They're just tattoos."

Instead of answering, he lays his head in my lap again, making himself right at home. Shirt forgotten, he doesn't seem to be leaving anytime soon.

I sigh and rest my head against the headboard. It's late, and I'm tired, but my mind wants to unpack the night. Dante is a lesson in complexities and patience—in dogged perseverance and longing. And yet, he remains a complete mystery to me. Teriza spoke of him as royalty, as someone with immense power below. So I study Dante more closely—the long, sculpted muscles of his back and shoulders as they curl around my legs. Even in the dim light, I can see he is stunning, a real work of art. But this artwork is damaged with more scars than a single lifetime should provide.

"Oh, Dante," I murmur, running my fingertips over the whipping lines across his soft skin. They have regenerated but are not entirely gone. Some are long and twisted, more than an inch wide, and pulsate beneath my fingertips. Such angry scars. Such pain he has endured for…me?

How can he put himself through so much suffering? How can he be so sure I am the one? And how can I be so sure he is wrong when he is willing to risk everything to find me?

I close my eyes, feeling myself unravel. My emotions have long since stopped obeying me, evident by the unwanted tears burning my eyes. Control is something I have to work at these days, so I go to my training and repeat my mantra in a slow, meditative rhythm until I find the calm within. *Deep breaths.*

After a moment, I open my eyes, letting them fall on the strange, green chain tattoo wrapped around his bicep. I saw it the first day he showed up when it was fresh and painful.

"What's this?" I whisper, inching my fingers toward it.

He snuggles his head against my stomach and mumbles, "Not for you to worry about."

It must be bad. He would tell me if it wasn't bad, so I know it was another torture he endured because of me. It's too much, and everything rushes back to the surface, and I drop my face into my hands and cry. I cry for Dante and all he has suffered. I cry for all he *will* suffer when the end finally comes and he doesn't get what he wants.

Dante sits up and wraps his arms around me, cradling my head into his neck. "Hush, *cara mia*. I cannot bear it. You are breaking my heart."

"I'm forever breaking your heart, aren't I?"

"No, *amore mio*. There was a time when we were happy as children—our love as powerful as the sun. And you loved me above all things."

I look at his blurry image, drowning in my tears. "You said I have an old soul. That it has been through many lives. If that's true, have you considered that the life you're trying to bring back won't come? It had its time. And the life I'm living now has a greater purpose than the one you're looking for?"

"No," he says bluntly. "There is no greater purpose than our love. It is not complicated, Sophia. I still have the memories, and I know for sure. This would not be a discussion if you had them, too."

"My mom told me I come from a long line of spiritual warriors. In this lifetime, I'm meant to be one again."

Dante shakes his head. "Let me bring up your memories, and then you may choose which life you want."

"You make it sound so easy."

"If it were easy, we would not be debating this." He smiles apologetically. "But you are very stubborn in this life. You have been fighting me."

"And what if I don't fight anymore? The memories would come easily?"

Dante becomes very still because he thinks I'm considering it.

"Yes, I believe so," he says with mounting excitement. I realize his body temperature spikes dramatically when he is emotional. With the idea of freely resurrecting my memories, he is practically a furnace. "Are you willing to try? Are you willing to stop fighting me?"

I gaze around the room, stalling for time while I work out the scheme unfolding in my mind. Dante needs something from me. And I need something from him.

Well, here goes nothing.

"Dante, what do you know about quid pro quo?"

Chapter 18

Occult Supervision

Rama is pacing the length of my bedroom while I sit on the bed and watch. I have explained the situation: the loss of Colin Firth's soul, my humiliation at failing, and the plan to enter a private demon nightclub to get a spellbook and make me a twin.

He is distraught, but I've been arguing my point like a death row attorney. It's necessary to save the lives of my flailing academic and spiritual careers. He's been grumbling reservations.

"Should stay in the ankle snappers where it's safe, *wahine.*"

"I have to do it. It's the only way. You see that I need help, right?"

"I see a brave *ha'ole* with too many distractions."

"Then you'll help? When we get the book, you'll help cast the spell?"

"*If* you get the book," he points out.

Yeah, okay, there's a snag. It seems that *La Croix* is so secretive that no one knows where it is. I asked Dante to help find it *and* get us inside. I omitted the part about making me a double, knowing Dante would never agree to help me become a spirit walker. He thinks I need a spellbook to tap into my former lives and memories. That way, I can decide for myself what life I will choose. This was, of course, a bold-faced lie.

Dante agreed to search for *La Croix* but refused to succumb to the contemporary trappings of a materialistic society and buy a stupid cell phone. Instead, he made Santiago sacrifice one of his phones to Vaughn. I gave out Bailey's number, and we've been waiting on pins and needles to hear from Vaughn.

"I have someone tracking down the club's location," I tell Rama. "If we get inside, will you help?"

"Dante?" he asks, and I nod.

"He and Vaughn will escort us there. Keep us safe."

"You trust him?"

"I do."

He wrinkles his nose and scratches his head. Then he holds out his hand. "Lemme see the name of that book." I hand him the paper with Miss Minnie's scrawl. It's gibberish to me, but Rama nods as he reads. *"Reu Nu Per Em Hru.* Means The Chapters of Coming Forth by Day. You got some serious connections here, *wahine."*

"What do you mean? I thought it was just a book of spells or something."

"This is Egyptian text. You're diving into a den of demons to find the Egyptian *Book of the Dead."*

My face drops, and I rethink my plan while he continues, "It's no good without the supplement. Gotta have the Papyrus of Ani inside. Whole thing is eighty-sixed if you don't have it. You dig?"

"Uh-huh," I mumble. I'm glad Rama agreed to help, but

why do I feel blindsided, like things just got more complicated?

With business out of the way, we finally begin our next session. But I feel rushed and disjointed. The idea of crashing a demon nightclub weighs heavily on me. So we make little progress and call it quits to head to the barn. On the way over, I beg Rama not to divulge our plans to Kanati or Chang`e for fear they'll stop me from going—or tell Michael, Raph, or Milvi. I can't possibly sneak into a horde of demons with guardians on my back.

The barn is warm and inviting, but I'm still too distracted to follow instructions. I go through the motions with my mind on Dante and my eyes on the door. I'm hoping Michael stays away. I can't face him again after being humiliated.

When I drop a cane pole for the fifth time, I turn and hurl a second one across the meadow. "Holy shiiiiit!" I yell to the vast, open sky with my hands on my hips and my chest pumping furiously. Anxiety and anger have overtaken my discipline—my self-control.

"What is the matter with you?" Kanati asks. "And why do you keep saying 'Holy shit'? You *do* know there is no such thing, right?"

I whirl around and glare at him, and then burst out laughing. I am so beyond myself right now that it's funny. I lean over and brace my hands on my knees, stress laughing. Really hard. I think I've alarmed them. Neither Kanati nor Chang`e seems to get my outburst. They withdraw to the sidelines, where they scowl and discuss my lack of focus as though I'm not here.

About that time, my phone vibrates, and I pounce on it.

It's a text from Bailey. Vaughn says the target is located, so the plan is a go. Tonight.

I grip the phone and hold back a maniacal laugh. *It's happening!*

I race over to Rama, who reads the text and then abruptly announces that today's lesson is over. Kanati is furious.

"We have much more to cover tonight," he argues, following us to the door. Rama lays a hand on his shoulder.

"No worries, my warrior brah. We'll come early tomorrow, and all will be righteous and pure." He offers a genial smile, but Kanati is not pacified. I duck out before any more can be said.

* * *

Step one of the plan: Set up a fictitious all-night study session with Bailey so Dad won't bother us. I tell him we have plenty of nutritional supplies and will be up late. We'll do our best to hold down the noise.

Step two: Bailey arrives with an overstuffed backpack for the aforementioned all-nighter. She doesn't bring books but appropriate clubbing apparel that I am sorely lacking. So while Bailey and I change clothes, Rama faces the corner and doles out his parental warnings.

"Don't drink anything. Don't smoke anything..." Bailey and I smirk at each other and roll our eyes. "Don't bargain with anyone. Don't make promises to anyone. Don't trade any body parts under any circumstances." *Okay, now we're listening.* "Don't leave with anyone. Don't be alone with anyone. Don't take anything anyone wants to give you. Don't touch anyone whose eyes are swirling."

"I think we get the idea, Rama. You can turn around now."

Bailey and I scrutinize each other in the mirror. She's wearing black leather pants, a white satin halter top, and red stilettos. She looks smoking hot and about twenty-five. I'm wearing her black leather mini skirt, tall boots, and a silver sequined top. I'm reminded of Teriza and have to look away. Bailey says my normal daywear makeup is not hip enough for the ultra-secret, über-exclusive, demonic nightclub. So I apply smokey eyeshadow, a dramatic swath of liquid eyeliner, and enough black mascara to pave every road in Haven Hurst.

Bailey sits on the bed with her feet in Rama's lap so he can touch up her glittery silver toenails. "Hold still, *ha'ole,* gonna muss the artwork."

Bailey is nervous. She hasn't seen Vaughn since he came back and is practically hyperventilating. Vaughn nearly faded into nothing in the Death Bunker and needed more recovery time. I suspect he knew he needed his strength fully regenerated, if only to handle Bailey's demanding needs. When I asked about Duffy, Bailey shrugged and said he was trying too hard to domesticate her, and she wasn't having it.

Bailey's phone goes off, and she taps the screen.

"He's here!" She jumps to her feet.

"You mean, *they're* here, right?" I look at her in the mirror. Yup, she is hyperventilating.

"Yeah, yeah. They're here. C'mon." She grabs her coat and creeps out the door without me.

I stand up, gather my coat and purse, and face Rama, who's looking pretty grim. I know he doesn't like what we're doing, but when he pouts, I get all mushy and maternal.

"Come on, give me a hug good-bye," I say, opening my arms. He sniffles and plops his forehead onto my shoulder without lifting his arms. I pat him on the back.

"You're gonna remember what I said?" he mumbles, and I nod. "Got something for you." He pulls a necklace from around his neck—a thin leather strap with a pale stone at the end. It was hidden beneath layers of puka shells, so I never noticed it. The stone is small and rectangular, reminding me of the statue heads from Easter Island, except it has a hawk where the lips should be.

"*Aumakua.* Guardian spirit to rest against your heart."

He places it around my neck and drops it inside my top. I feel the cold lump directly above my heart. Then Rama holds my shoulders and closes his eyes, chanting something I can't translate. At the end, he opens his eyes and exhales in my face with a deep *haaah* sound. I stiffen and blink rapidly. It's a weird sensation, as though a thousand words of sand have scattered across my face. When he releases me, I touch my cheek, expecting to feel tiny grains on my skin.

"You take the word of protection with you." He smiles with satisfaction and walks me to the door.

"You okay?" I ask.

"Naw, totally beat. Think I'll chill here till you get back if that's cool?"

"Of course." I give him a reassuring smile that says, *Please don't worry.*

Finally, I sneak out the back door and wobble through the snow on my tiptoes. I tread carefully because I'm inexperienced in the high-heel department. We agreed to meet in the alley behind the Cut 'N Dye hair salon, so I head straight there. It's dark, but I see exhaust floating from a large black vehicle with red taillights.

Dante stands by the open door, his hands folded and eyes on me like a patient chauffeur. I slow my steps, taking in his appearance—charcoal pants, a black collared shirt, and a silver-gray jacket. His hair is swept away from his forehead, and a dark scruff frames his sharp jawline. One dark eyebrow lifts as his eyes leave mine and trail down my body. Why do the words *violently handsome* come to mind? How can someone look violently handsome? I don't even know what that means, but it seems appropriate for Dante.

"*Buonasera, il mia amore.* You look ravishing." He bites his bottom lip as he grins, which produces an unwanted rush of heat to my cheeks, and I know I'm blushing. I've been so worried about staying safe and hiding my true motive for getting the book that I didn't prepare myself for the full effect of Dante. His raw desire devastates my focus, and I remind myself that he has his own motivation—to kill me. That should be enough to scare me straight. It would scare any reasonably sane person, but Dante's unbending love is so consuming that I sometimes feel compelled to surrender just to make him happy. Just to see the pure joy on his face and know I put it there. I suspect this is what worries Rama the most—my lack of strength around Dante. I can't image how I would resist if he used Persuasion to manipulate me. I only hope I never have to find out.

I finally pull my eyes from his and force myself to look around. I need to recenter my thoughts and calm my racing heart. "A Cadillac Escalade? Really?" I say nervously. I don't like the sound of my voice, but I have to continue and pretend he hasn't uprooted my common sense. "And here I thought you loathed the materialistic trappings of modern society."

Dante laughs and takes my hand. "This is true. But I also insist on the finest things for my lady." He looks deep into my eyes while kissing the back of my hand. A fresh sensation shoots through me, and I tremble. When my pulse jumps at the base of my throat, Dante's eyes flicker with excitement, and I wonder if this is a good idea after all.

A squeal of laughter from inside the truck breaks the moment, and I withdraw and pull my coat around me. Then Bailey yelps to a slapping sound.

"They wanted a private moment," Dante says, guiding me to the door. "Apparently, your friend has missed my friend very much."

I brace myself and then peer inside. This is no ordinary Escalade but a luxury stretch SUV. Dante holds my arm so I can duck inside and take a seat in the back, facing the front. The door closes quietly, and dim lights illuminate my surroundings. The interior is a soothing shade of cream with shiny wood accents. Four luxurious leather seats face each other, but Bailey has opted for Vaughn's lap. They snuggle around each other, smiling at me. I can't bring myself to reciprocate.

The last time I saw Vaughn Raider, he was helping my dad place a noose around his neck to commit suicide. I understand Wolfgang took Dad to the courthouse that night, but Vaughn guided him toward death. Dante never touched my dad, so I found it easier to forgive him. I found it easier to forgive him for killing me, too. Which should not make sense under any circumstances, but given the options, he did as I asked.

Since their return, Dante has repeatedly assured me that Vaughn is not here to Take any souls, including Bailey's. But I can't forget his part in all this. Vaughn must realize where my mind is at because his playful look dissolves into a blank stare.

Dante slides in next to me from the other side and shuts the door. He takes in the awkward scene and then reaches over and holds my hand.

Bailey sits up. "What gives?" she asks, frowning.

I never told her about Dad killing Steve or anything that happened in the courthouse, so she knows nothing about Vaughn's involvement. She understands he has a "fetish" for pain, but that's it. Telling her would serve no purpose, so I shake my head and look away.

Vaughn clears his throat and speaks quietly to me as though softening his words will ease their impact. "What I attempted to do for *him* was a much gentler option than what Wolfgang had planned. Believe me."

My eyes snap to his, and I clench my jaw, holding back everything I want to scream at him. They scared the hell out of my dad. If Michael hadn't compelled Dad to forget what he saw, he would have had a nervous breakdown. So, I don't want to hear any justifications for what Vaugh and Wolfgang put my dad through. I shake my head, and Vaughn nods with understanding.

"What are we talking about?" Bailey asks.

"Nothing," I say abruptly. "Forget it."

"Sophia?" Dante pries my fingers loose because I've been digging my nails into his hand. I didn't hurt him, but he wants me to relax. He wants me to move on.

"Sorry," I murmur.

"You are okay, yes?" He looks at Vaughn. "We are good?"

To his credit, Vaughn looks genuinely remorseful. He waits for me to answer, to decide if I can move on. I wonder if he'll leave if I insist. Of course, it would irritate Bailey, so I don't seriously consider it.

I nod. "Yeah, I'm okay. Just nervous."

Vaughn exhales and offers a brief smile. "Nothing to be nervous about," he says, trying to overcome the awkwardness and get on my good side. "Dante and I've got this covered. No demon will lay a hand on you guys if you're with us."

Bailey basks in his promise and snuggles against his neck. He slides one hand up the back of her shirt while pulling her leg over his lap. She has no shame about devouring him like a starved woman while Vaughn chats away.

"And Dante insisted on rolling in style. Only the best for you." He nods behind us, and I turn to a flat-screen TV where the back window should be. "We have custom sound, security cameras, hand-crafted wood lacquer finish, custom wool carpet, brushed metal knobs, and aviation-grade interior lighting."

I gaze around, taking it all in. The ceiling is gorgeous suede punctuated by soft lights. The whole thing is beyond impressive, and I look over at Dante.

"We have internet, a monitor, and cutting-edge infotainment—whatever that means. Plus, it's armored with maximum ballistic protection." He smiles proudly, and I have to laugh. He's trying so hard to catch up with the times.

"It's amazing, Dante. Really." I hope to sound impressed, but I wonder why we need such protection if they're with us.

"I am happy to please you, *cara mia*." He gives me a look that makes me squirm, so I scramble for something else to say.

"Um, so who's driving?"

He taps a blue button on the electronic panel at his side. A small window behind Vaughn and Bailey slides open, and Santiago's face appears. "Hey guys. I'm driving, and Degan is navigating."

"Hey, Sophia. How's it going?" Degan says like we're old friends.

"What's he doing here?" I whisper to Dante. Thankfully, Bailey is preoccupied with Vaughn and doesn't hear Santiago or Degan. She can't see Degan because he's in spirit form, and I don't want to explain. Besides, I'm not in the mood to be friendly with the soul seeker who wanted to drag poor Colin Firth to Hell. Dante pats my knee in answer, telling me not to worry. I'm not worried, just uncomfortable.

"You guys ready?" Santiago asks. "This is gonna take a while."

"Yes," Dante says. "Get us there as quickly as possible." He taps the button again, closing the window. Then he lowers his voice and leans closer. "It seems Santiago and Degan pooled their resources to found *La Croix*. The directions are a bit complicated, so I'm leaving it to them. Besides, I would rather give you all my attention." He nuzzles against my neck, brushing his lips across my ear. "You look so beautiful, *amore mio*."

When he tries to kiss me, I lean away because I didn't imagine this night to be a romantic interlude. We aren't on a double date, even though that's exactly what it feels like. Bailey and Vaughn aren't making it easy with the way they're moaning and making out in front of us.

Then Bailey yelps and clutches her mouth. "Ohmygod, you really bit me."

Vaughn looks drowsy with lust from the pain he caused, and I'm ready to lunge at him and drag Bailey away. But Dante grabs my arm and holds me back. We watch as Bailey's stunned expression melts into a naughty grin. She throws her arms around Vaughn's neck, attacking him until they're rolling sideways in the seat, clinging to each other. Their groaning and smacking elevates, and I fall back against the seat.

"I can't take this. Got any music?"

Dante's face lights up as though he's forgotten a surprise. He hits a button, and our seats expand into recliners. Then he taps the monitor and pulls up a screen with a list of songs.

"Always happy to please you, *Sophia*." He touches his selection, and the upbeat groove of Blue Öyster Cult comes on. I relax but roll my head sideways and look at him when I recognize the song. Dante is grinning in anticipation.

"*That's* your choice? "Don't Fear the Reaper"? Look at you, being all ironic."

He laughs lightly and holds my hand. "You have nothing

to fear. I will always protect you."

I smile but think, *No, Dante, I will learn to protect myself. That's what tonight is really about.* I have to look away before he sees my regret. Dante was ecstatic when I told him about a spell that could revive past life memories. It never occurred to him that I was lying. And then I stacked another lie on top of that one when I said Rama insisted on performing the spell, so Bailey and I didn't screw it up. Dante's unshakable faith in me was the only reason he didn't question Rama agreeing to something that had the potential to stop my Awakening.

Bailey is busy devouring Vaughn, and I don't know where to look, so I shift sideways and face Dante. I lower my voice so Bailey can't hear, and I ask him what it means to be a Demon Knight in the Royal Court of Hell.

Dante is surprised by my question but seems happy that I asked. He turns sideways until we're facing each other. "Well, I suppose it means the same thing below as on the surface. It is reminiscent of those glory days of ancient times. Strangely enough, earthly traditions are highly coveted in Hell. But because no one is born to a title, they must be earned by deeds and obedience. The more earned, the higher one advances up the royal chain of nobility. I became one of the Chosen or a Demon Knight because I displayed unique abilities that The Order found useful."

"What kind of abilities?"

He pauses to contemplate. "My family called me *testardo come un mulo*, stubborn as a mule. But The Order called me *resiliente*, resilient. I could withstand anything The Order did to me. I had steadfast patience and tolerance. Basically, I am unbreakable." He gives me a knowing look, and I have no doubt. Not only has he spent ages searching for his lover's soul, but he has also endured unspeakable pain. Even if his body were to break under horrendous torture, his spirit and determination seem unwavering. Indestructible.

I don't know where to put this knowledge. It hurts everywhere I try to hide it. I don't want to imagine adding to the pain he has suffered. I don't want to give him anything more to overcome or tolerate. The ending that I know is coming will destroy him. It is as inevitable as the sunrise. The least I can do is give him tonight. Give him my attention and interest.

"So, go on. Tell me what happens in this Royal Court? Do you have a king and queen? Ceremonies and stuff?"

He laughs warmly. "It is indescribably boring to me, but I suppose it does pass the time. And yes, there is a king and queen of Hell, and I am sure they will adore you as I do."

He rambles on, but I've stopped listening, paralyzed by his casual reference to me being in Hell. A chill creeps up my spine, and I'm reminded of the seriousness of what I'm doing. At some point, Dante will discover I have lied, that I have no intention of reviving any past life memories—if they even exist. He'll be furious, and I don't know what it will lead him to do. Hopefully, I'll already be a spirit walker and out of his reach when that time comes.

Good Lord, but there is an awful lot riding on hope.

Dante chuckles at some story he's been telling, and I tune back in. He's talking about the different kingdoms in Hell and how each kingdom has its own Royal Court and noble demonic lineage. He is part of the Royal Court of the Fifth Kingdom.

I throw out a question, pretending I'm listening and not stewing in fear. "Oh, and so what does everybody do all day?"

He gives me a dubious look. "You mean apart from reaping souls?"

"Um, yeah. Besides that."

"They plan wars against other kingdoms, devise ways to kill angels, perfect their weapons against demon hunters, work on new techniques for possessing Forgiven souls. You know, the usual." He sounds far too casual for my taste.

"That does sound boring," I murmur.

"Oh, but there are festivals, ceremonies, and the Demonic Games. Remember that I said Hell is steeped in tradition? There is a deliberate mirror effect of life below to life on the surface. Of course, Hell is behind the times in most regards. Only recently have I discovered they are making technological strides regarding surveillance. In the old days, we could return to Hell through any gate. Now it seems that you and I must reenter through gate five because that is the gate I left from."

I feel my jaw slacken and my joints loosen. My head is suddenly swimming because all the blood has drained into my toes. An odd whimpering sound escapes me, and Dante leans closer.

"Sophia?" He cups my cheek. "What is it? Are you ill?"

I shiver like I've got chills, and I think I'm going to be sick. I can't handle any more talk of Hell. Dante pulls me into his arms, and I can't resist. I feel pliable and suddenly exhausted. Bailey asks what's wrong as Dante rubs my arms.

"She is feeling faint. When did she last eat?"

Bailey unwinds from Vaughn and squints at me. "Uh, I'm not sure. Think she had a bag of Cheetos a couple of hours ago. No, wait, that was me."

"I'm okay," I murmur and squirm because I don't want to be wrapped in Dante's heat, even though it helped stimulate my insides. My blood is moving again, churning in my stomach, and pounding through my veins. I try to withdraw, but he snuggles close.

"Stay with me, *cara,*" he whispers. "Relax in my arms. We do not want you light-headed when we get to the club."

I can't agree more, so I relax and use his body heat to my benefit. Bailey returns to Vaughn, and they're back at it. The music has graduated several songs down the playlist and rises to soft instrumental tunes. It's classically cool and seems a more appropriate vibe for Dante. I stare out the window, noticing we have left Connecticut and entered New York. We're flying and making amazing time. I ask Dante where we're going, and he drags his lips across my ear, whispering,

"Some place called Manhattan, I believe." He sounds sexy and sedated, so I look at him. His eyes are hooded as he stares at my mouth. He wants to kiss me, so I think fast.

"Why won't you tell me about her? About Lovaria?"

His eyes flick to mine, and for a moment, I think I've upset him. He hesitates and then frowns. "I told you, *amore mio,* I am willing to wait and let *you* tell me about her. That is what we are after this evening, is it not?" There is a challenge in his question that worries me. Everything will be lost if he suspects I've lied.

"Yes," I answer abruptly and turn away. I can't look him in the eye, so he nuzzles against my cheek.

"When your memories return, I know you will be angry that I did not force this sooner. But be gentle with me, *cara mia*." His chest vibrates with silent laughter. "And remember that I have kept my promise. I never gave up; I never stopped searching for you. Just as you asked."

* * *

It's well over an hour later when Santiago finally pulls to a curb and cuts the engine. We gather our coats, slide out, and stand on the sidewalk at Pelham Bay Park. Bailey and I shiver and huddle close. Santiago explains that he and Degan will stay behind while we take the 6 train south. Several minutes later, I'm off on my first subway ride.

Aside from the funky smell, it's not too bad. I'm mostly amused that Dante seems so out of place riding a subway. He claims to abhor modern conveniences but has exceptional taste for the finer things in life. Over his expensive Italian clothes, he wears a rich black leather coat that's as soft as silk and falls to his knees. He sits upright with an aristocratic air, which is strange considering he's been in Hell for...well, I don't know how long.

The other passengers ignore us while Bailey resumes her position on Vaughn's lap. She whispers things that bring a flush to his cheeks. I lower my voice, leaning toward Dante.

"Will you at least tell me how long you've been in Hell? How long you've been a Demon Knight?"

"I'll give nothing away, only that I was below for quite

some time before being knighted. Like everyone else, I had to earn my station."

"But what were you like before you died?"

"Sophia, as much as I would love to reminisce with you, I'll refrain. Not with the conversation so one-sided. Besides, you are not asking anything you don't already know."

I mull this over, thinking back to October when Michael's mother told me Dante had committed suicide. I can't image what would cause a guy so confident and proud to take his own life. Our conversation isn't as one-sided as he believes. I know circumstances—because others have told me—but not details. Because I want to keep my own secrets, I pretend ignorance.

"Will you at least tell me how you died?"

He slowly turns and looks at me, driving his eyes into mine. He is as serious as I have ever seen. "*That* is a memory we will discuss at length. When the time comes."

I swallow and turn away. I hit a nerve, and I don't like that I hit a nerve. Something rancid settles in my stomach. Dread. Deep, unnatural dread. Dread for the eventual outcome Dante won't like and dread for the moment that I fully understand the details of his death. To think this Lovaria girl wasn't involved would be naïve and foolish. He obviously loves her, but I wonder if he blames her for something. For his death? For his horrendous afterlife? Has Dante transferred that blame to me? Is that why he's determined to drag me to Hell?

The train car jerks as we begin to slow down. I can barely make out an announcement over the speakers. We are approaching the last downtown stop, Brooklyn Bridge–City Hall, but I don't know if we have to transfer. When I ask Dante, he shrugs and shakes his head like he's sulking. I slump, cross my arms and my legs, and then uncross my legs; I'm antsy from all the new things I get to worry about.

Once the car stops and the doors open, I start to rise, but Dante holds my arm. He shakes his head again; we're not exiting. Vaughn won't let Bailey up either, so we sit back and watch the passengers shuffle out. I'm confused. This was the last stop, so why aren't we leaving?

The doors close, and the car moves forward. We are the only ones left. Dante and Vaughn stare at each other, and I get the feeling something is about to happen. We ride on in silence as the long subway eases into a curve. I look ahead. Nothing to see but empty seats, metal poles, and the number 6 illuminated in the station-stop panel. Then the car shudders, and the lights flicker before snapping off, throwing us into darkness. I hear Bailey gasp as I reach for Dante in alarm. I catch his arm, but he quickly takes my hand, giving me a reassuring squeeze. I easily find his face in the dark because his eyes give off a faint glow. They watch me intently before crinkling at the corners. He is smiling, happy that I sought him out for protection.

The lights flicker, eventually blinking back on. Now Bailey and I both gasp in surprise. We're no longer alone. Two people have appeared out of nowhere. A guy and a girl are sitting near the front. The guy wears a long dark coat and looks sinister, like the lesser demons prowling Haven Hurst. The girl is about our age, scantily dressed without a coat. A black manacle circles her throat with a chain leading to her companion's hand. She is pale with an uneventful expression, teetering on boredom.

Or perhaps she was compelled into submission. The guy's solid black eyes stare down the aisle at us with keen interest.

A shiver of fear tears through me. This trip is starting to feel very real, and I wonder what I have gotten Bailey into. I'll never forgive myself if she gets hurt.

I tug Dante's sleeve, wanting to ask for some kind of reassurance that the guy up front can't hurt us. If he is a lesser demon, I want to know why Bailey can see him. But I don't have to voice my concerns. Dante knows, and he puts a finger to his lips for quiet. He isn't worried, although he doesn't want to invite trouble either. A sentiment I appreciate. So I sit back, clenching and unclenching my hands.

I do this for a while, but when I can't stand another minute, I peer at the lesser demon again to find him looking ahead. And then I notice that the number 6 in the illuminated panel now reads 666.

My heart jolts simultaneously with the subway car. Then sparks fly across the windows as we enter a large loop and gradually roll to a stop. The car shimmies just as the doors slam open. Dante and Vaughn stand up, pulling Bailey and me to our feet. Dante takes my hand, but we wait while the lesser demon tugs the girl out by her chain. When we step outside, I realize this is not an active station. We stopped in the middle of a dark, abandoned cavern.

The doors close, and the subway lurches forward, leaving us in a hazy light. The lesser demon is striding off with the girl like he's walking a dog. We move in their direction, following at a slower pace.

Since this is my first subway experience, I don't know what to think, but I suspect what I'm seeing is not the norm. The deserted platform has an antique quality, as though we have stepped back in time. Stunning tile artwork woven into patterns of brown and gold runs along the barreled ceilings. Further on are glorious Romanesque arches with stained glass windows that must shine blue during the day. They are currently black but reflect light from brass sconces. The entire aesthetic effect is unexpected, and Bailey and I stare openmouthed.

We follow an intricate cobblestoned walkway that eventually brings us to a hole in the ground—the entrance to a spiraling staircase. There is no option but down, so Vaughn goes first, then Bailey, me, and Dante. It's not bad except for the rustling chains echoing off the walls from the lesser demon and the girl just ahead.

The lower level is the opposite of the abandoned station, reminding me that we are deep in the underbelly of New York. The tunnels are gray corrugated concrete with those familiar brass sconces. We stroll on to fiendish displays of urban artwork along the walls: giant rats with hollow eyes and morbid blue skulls with huge black antlers. Finally, we reach the end to find a warning across the back wall that Dante says is written in chalk made of ground bones: WE OWN THE NIGHT.

"Do not take this lightly," he advises. "Whatever lies beyond that door, most assuredly, *owns the night*." We turn to a brown door where the lesser demon and the chained girl wait to be admitted. "Bailey, do not leave Vaughn's side unless instructed. Is that understood? Good. And Sophia..." He takes my hand. "We will not part without my permission. Yes?"

"Uh-huh," I say, my eyes glued to the door. Music pounds behind it and matches the erratic beating in my chest. I'm trembling because I know I've gotten us into something horrific.

The brown door doesn't open. Instead, a decrepit old man peels himself away from it like a carved relief. He is tall but slightly stooped now that he stands on his own, and his skin appears dried and crackled. He wears the ancient brown cloak of a monk, but the hood is down, revealing a bald head with bulging veins that give the impression of an exposed brain. I swallow hard and squeeze Dante's hand.

The old man scrutinizes the girl while talking quietly to her captor. He eventually stuffs her through a side entrance as though accepting her as payment. Then he opens the brown door, allowing the lesser demon to enter. I dig my nails into Dante's hand, horrified by what I have witnessed—*human payment to enter a private demon club.*

I look up at Dante to gauge his reaction. I wonder if this is worse than he anticipated. If it's bad enough to turn back. Will he risk my life to find the book? To get what he wants?

But he is too hard to read. His eyes are hooked in place as he studies the old man. And then I see that air of authority Teriza mentioned—Dante's elevated station in Hell settles in his tight shoulders and hard jaw. It rises behind his eyes as they slide to Vaughn, who is also watching him. Vaughn gives a quick nod, accepting some unspoken command. Then Dante pulls me forward, moving in hard, determined strides. He is a man of authority while I practically drag my feet. I'm putting so much trust in him. Trust that he could use to his benefit in ways I can't imagine. What if I've misjudged something? What if he has made his next move, and I've been outmaneuvered?

I glance at Bailey, who smiles tentatively. Then I see fear in her face, so I shake my head to let her know she can change her mind; she doesn't have to go if it's too much. But she nods and hugs Vaughn's arm. She trusts him and wants to continue.

We stop before the door, and the old man gives us his full attention, which is scary enough. He is not just old but petrified. As in *made of freaking wood*. Those bulging veins on his head are gnarled roots trying to poke through, and he is lopsided and slightly grotesque. His eyes are deep hollows shrouded with gray, weed-like eyebrows. Thin, cracked lips curl back to expose a jumble of teeth like weathered gravestones. I wait for him to speak, but he doesn't. I'm afraid he expects Dante to offer Bailey or me as payment.

The old man's eyes fix on Dante, so I look up at him. His eyes are black and yellow, splitting into snake eyes. I'm seized with panic and try to withdraw my hand from his. I don't want to touch him while he brings his demon to the surface. But Dante tightens his grip, and I have no choice but to feel the unwelcomed vibration passing through him. I only hope there is no lasting effect.

Persuasion has dilated Dante's eyes like a visual calling card, and the old man flinches in recognition. He becomes noticeably uncomfortable.

"My apology, sir," he says in a deep, brittle voice. He bows stiffly. "I did not...it is an honor to have a Demon

Knight"—he glances erratically at Vaughn—"er, *two* Demon Knights, with us this evening. If I had only...well...I should've expected...it's always a special occasion when Baron Samedi and his wife perform."

"Your name," Dante demands.

"I am PaPa Bois."

Dante nods. "We will require an escort this evening."

"But of course. Anything you ask. Right this way." He swings the door open, giving us free access.

I take a deep breath and then step inside the private demon nightclub.

Chapter 19
Not for the Folks at Home

We enter the vestibule of *La Croix* where our escort, a demon named Kappas, greets us with a respectful bow. Kappas appears to have walked straight from the rice paddies. His conical hat, thin shirt, and short pants are forever dripping wet. He has webbed hands and feet and smells of fish. His eyes float like buoys in water.

"Welcome to *La Croix*," he says. "My apologies, please, but no weapons." He pulls a couple of repulsive tarantula-like spiders from his pockets and tosses them onto Vaughn's shoulders. As Bailey and I recoil in fear, the spiders clack up and down Vaughn, checking him for weapons. They find something strapped to his ankle and emit an ear-piercing squeal that makes us cringe.

Vaughn slips a knife from the hidden sheath and tosses it to Kappas. "Gonna need that back soon." He grins and winks at Bailey, who has the audacity to blush.

The spiders leap onto Dante and repeat the process. He is weapon free. Nobody seems bothered by this arachnid-pat-down, but Baily and I are not having it. We back away and shake our heads.

"They have no weapons," Dante says firmly, making it clear that he won't allow us to be searched.

Kappas bows and pockets the spiders. "Very good. This way, please." He throws open the doors to the private entrance, and my eyes and ears are immediately assaulted. The club is a wild concoction of blaring music, blazing fires, and writhing bodies. Dante seems desensitized to the hedonistic display, but I grimace in open disgust.

La Croix is everything I imagined. And worse. I feel like I've stepped into Hell's basement—dark, smoky, and teeming with exotic demons. It's a deep cave hollowed out by giant claws, and we're standing on the walkway that runs around the cavern with a view of the pit below. The barrel ceiling is close and oppressive just above our heads and lacks the old-world charm of the 666 platform.

Bowls of fire cast the room in a smoky red haze. Black iron cages hang throughout the room, packed with people. Their arms reach desperately through the bars while their incoherent cries die under the weight of grinding guitars and violent acoustics. Long tethers fall between the cages where some combination of man and ape swing up and down in *Cirque du Soleil* fashion. The creatures are painted in wild, eclectic patterns with neon colors that glow in the hazy light. If a creature should slip during the acrobatic routine, the noose around its neck will break its fall.

From this angle we can see the stage, marked by four pillars of fire at each corner, and the band, which consists of the repulsive and bizarre. Some members have shrunken heads, gnarled and dented heads, liquid or smoke-filled heads, or no heads at all. Some are half-man, half-goat; some with mouths stitched shut; and others with alligator skin. The lead singer has the face of a Picasso painting, both eyes on the same side and giant, perverted lips.

Despite the fantastical appearance, the band is good and plays a wildly rambunctious song I don't recognize. The dance floor is full of lesser demon types and an occasional human with a manacle chain. A quick survey tells me it's the hired help who are diabolical, not the demons in civilian clothes like Dante and Vaughn. The abhorrent clearly stand out.

Across from the stage is the bar. It takes up the entire wall and consists of a series of conjoined coffins with glass tops where pale bodies lay interred. Shiny copper pennies adorn the eyes. The more sophisticated demons hover there, chatting and sipping drinks as though this were any other private underground club in New York. I imagine Teriza partying here and find it even more repulsive.

"Drink from the bar?" Kappas yells over the blaring music. "Rum and hot pepper! The house favorite!"

Bailey and I share a look. Hers says *Maybe just one*, and mine says, *No way in Hell's basement are we drinking anything*. Dante tells him we are here to see a friend.

"High Alice!" I holler, and Kappas startles as though I said something outlandish. As though I'm not allowed to speak. Which turns out to be accurate because he looks up at Dante and yells,

"It speaks!"

Dante shoves him in the chest, sending him stumbling backward. "She is my guest!" he yells, abruptly furious. The man cowers.

"Forgive! Forgive! It is not usually permitted to speak! Only the one It speaks *of*!"

"High Alice?" Dante shouts, and Kappas nods. "Where is she?"

The song we've been trying to outmatch dies out, and the low rumble of applause takes its place.

"She is special," Kappas says. "Kept in the back. No one sees her. Without Baron Samedi's permission."

"And where is Baron?"

"Preparing to entertain. He loves to entertain." Kappas points to the stage where band members are rearranging the set for something big. "It is too late. You will speak after the show. In the meantime, a table?" He gestures toward a balcony above the bar. It's for the elite demons, the private club within the private club; no manacled humans allowed.

The furniture is a conglomeration of modern meets Baroque, lavish red-velvet sofas and high-back chairs that rise at least seven feet overhead and come to a point. The tables are rectangular glass filled with green smoke. Several people lounge on the sofas while others mingle in groups of five or six. There are more people seated at gaming tables in the back, with a small crowd gathered around the craps table. Men and women in formal suits and expensive furs throw their heads back, laughing and enjoying a night out on the town. It looks relatively normal and elegant until a fox stole wrapped around a woman's shoulders snaps at a passing waiter.

As we follow Kappas around the walkway, he points out people of interest to Dante and Vaughn. "Marquis Naberius. You want, I can escort you over."

The marquis, seated on a sofa with friends, sports a sophisticated Dracula vibe complete with a widow's peak and a black cape and cane. But when he laughs, his face vibrates unnaturally, and for a moment, I think he has the head of a raven. It happens so quickly that I'm not sure I can believe my eyes.

"And there, Count Halphas with Knight Furcas." Kappas indicates two men standing at the rail. The count resembles a skeletal stork in a long coat, and the knight is smoking a pipe made from a human jawbone—teeth intact. He is educating the birdman on something important, and flames shoot out of the molars every time he takes a pull from his pipe.

Vaughn says, "Hey, look, there's ol' Chax. Didn't know he was back on the surface." He points out some guy covered in silver jewelry: necklaces, earrings, bracelets. He even has silver chains hanging from his pockets. He's talking earnestly to a woman with a green Mohawk and angry red eyes.

"Why all the silver?" Bailey asks.

"And why is he standing in the middle of a triangle?" I ask.

"He has a fetish for silver, and when he's confined inside a triangle, Chax is forced to tell nothing but the truth." About this time, the girl punches Chax in the face, and Vaughn bursts out laughing.

"Is this satisfactory?" Kappas indicates a table by the rail, and Bailey and I hurry over. We want nothing to do with the freaks.

"At least the Mohawk girl seemed normal," Bailey says from across the table. And then the girl storms off, and we notice her head is divided down the middle, with the left side facing forward and the right side facing backward. Bailey and I lock eyes; we are so tempted to crack stupid jokes about being two-faced but are too scared.

Vaughn wants to order drinks, but Dante won't allow it. I'm grateful he is being careful with us. It eases my fears that he might take advantage of the situation.

"Thank you," I say.

"For what?"

"Bringing us here. Protecting us." I watch him closely, trying to read any signs of deceit. But he wraps an arm around my shoulders, pulling me against him.

"It's for *us,* that I do this, yes? When we find the book and have the spell, we will be ourselves again. Just you and me. As we were before."

I nod and smile tightly. "But it may take some time, Dante. You realize that? It probably won't be all, abracadabra, and *poof,* I'll remember."

"And perhaps it will."

"But…if it doesn't, you'll be patient, right?"

Dante's eyes narrow playfully. "I have all the time in the world, *cara mia*. But perhaps we can prompt certain memories along? Hmm?" His hand caresses my cheek and then trails along my throat and atop my breastbone. He suddenly jerks back in anger, his fingers smoking. I gasp and clutch my sequined shirt-front because something white-hot is sparking against my skin.

"What do you have?" he demands, pulling my hands away and groping between my breasts.

"Hey!" I yell and slap at him, but he knocks my hands away and brings up the necklace with the smooth gray stone. Dante's eyes widen in shock, and then he quickly returns the stone without touching it and throws a panicked look around.

Vaughn leans over the table, whispering aggressively. "How did she get in here with that?"

Dante regains his composure and nods toward the marquis and his guests. They are glancing around, sensing something odd all of a sudden.

"What's the matter?" I whisper. "Rama gave me an *Aumakua* for added protection."

Vaughn scowls. "And did he mention that your lucky charm is magically delicious to almost everything in here? You'd better keep your head down, or we'll have unwanted attention."

I tell Dante I'm sorry and that I had no idea. His smile is rigid as he pretends nothing is amiss to anyone who might be watching. "I assume your Ascended Master did not have confidence that I would protect you as we agreed. But he was a fool to let you walk in here with a holy relic. Perhaps I should remind him of who you truly are and that your soul belongs to me. Not him."

"No, that's not necessary," I mumble. I catch Bailey giving me her *What the hell you doing?* look, and I feel awful. I didn't mean to put us at greater risk. "Why would anyone in here want a holy relic anyway? I'd think demons would despise them."

"They do not despise them," Dante says. "It is more a

lurid fascination. Most damned souls regret their sins. Too late, of course, but they crave what they know they have lost. Acquiring a holy relic would give them a distorted sense of redemption. Others accept their fate and make the best of it. Some mimic the Forgiven as a desperate show of similarity, but nothing could be farther from the truth. They are all slaves to their fear."

"But the *Aumakua* burnt your fingers. How can they acquire it if they can't touch it?"

"Most relics are worthless imitations and have no spiritual powers whatsoever. They are purely symbolic. Your Ascended Master added a Sigil of Protection to yours. And that is why I reacted to it. But that will not prohibit another from trying to take it. And it has most likely made you a target of their curiosity. My plan of keeping you off the demonic radar is compromised."

More than a few demons have taken notice of us in the past few minutes; Dante is right to be concerned. Luckily, things on the stage are about to take attention away from us.

A loud gong reverberates throughout the cavern, bringing a fresh wave of excitement rippling through the crowd below. The cages filled with people are removed, and we suddenly have an open view of the stage. We're not close enough to get burned by the flames that are now shooting high from all four corners, but near enough to feel the scorching heat. The crowd doesn't seem to mind; they're shuffling closer, packed tightly in great anticipation. Dante explains that Baron Samedi and his wife, Maman Brigitte, are famous for their parties and entertainment. A very jovial couple that loves extravagant displays of showmanship.

"They don't sound so bad," I say.

"He is the Loa of the Dead who escorts souls to the Cross-roads. She is the Death Loa who distracts unsuspecting humans with her laughter and playfulness while luring them to Hell."

"Oh, that figures," I mumble. "Loa means spirit?"

"Yes. And Samedi means Saturday. Evidently, Baron prefers to *raise the roof* on weekends." Dante smiles because he thinks he is being current. He is also trying to salvage the evening with humor, but it's not enough.

Down below, the mob swarms the stage with a zombie-like frenzy. They are starved hostiles, begging for what is coming. Not unlike Bailey, who is jumpy and nearly speechless, her eyes whipping around and her mouth hanging open. I ask if she has spotted High Alice, but she shakes her head.

The four fire towers around the stage slowly extinguish, and then everything goes dark. My knee vibrates with fear and anticipation. I just want to get the book and get out of this nightmare. Dante lays a hand on my knee, forcing me to sit still. Then red bolts of lightning flash across the stage. Thunder booms, and more lightning zaps over the dome ceiling. Jagged spears of electricity dance around us, so close we can hear the hiss and snap. The music rises to a Middle Eastern flavor but gradually builds with thumping percussion and voices. It's a familiar tune that has Bailey and me exchanging bewildered looks. Then we grab the rail and peer down.

The stage is lit up, and a new band sings "Catchafire" by TobyMac. It's one of my favorite songs, and I got Bailey hooked on it a while back. The lead singer is dressed in a black suit and a white fedora with a red feather that matches the red socks peeking above his black shoes. He struts across the stage, singing and whipping around with his dance crew. They dig into the song, swaying and grooving.

I shout over the music, "But this is a religious song!"

Dante shrugs and leans over, shouting back. "It is mockery or foolishness! Too late for a Sinner's fate!"

The song continues with the lead singer wailing about catching a fire for God. Every time he sings the word *fire,* the four corners of the stage explode with towers of yellow flames. If the lead singer is Baron, he's not what I expected, less flamboyant and more regular. And where is his wife, Brigitte?

The lyrics eventually give way to a female rapper, and that's when Maman Brigitte struts onto the stage to a deafening roar. She's a stunning beauty, tall and dark—the perfect blend of Cleopatra and Beyoncé—with a wedding veil over the famous Egyptian, blunt-cut hairstyle. She is a perpetual bride with a curvaceous body covered in a strapless, emerald-green bikini top and long, sheer, matching panels of material meant to be a skirt. It rides dangerously low on her round hips. The open skirt reveals her shapely legs as she sashays around. When the music takes off, she belts out a wicked rap, taking command of the stage. The crowd goes insane, reaching out to touch her. Maman Brigitte has long, thin arms decorated with lace tattoo sleeves like green netting. She waves her arms while ripping through her rap, sending the mob over the edge.

"Spark to a flame, I'm flipping up my game...I caught the fire, and I'll never be the same."

The lead singer pumps it up, and the noise escalates. He draws the crowd in with his smooth voice and luring lyrics. Words are a drug that gets them high, tempting them with the promise of a better life they can never have. Then he slows the tempo, settling the throng while rocking to the groove as one massive beast. Heads sway, anticipation builds, and he starts all over again,

"Here come that boy from Kingston town...Ooh ah ooh, Jamaica bound...here come that boy, boy...Papa San..."

The fans know what's coming, and in a flash of blinding light, the stage explodes, and there he is, the king of the nightclub, Baron Samedi.

He is a towering figure, wearing a tophat, black tails, black-and-white-striped pants, and a black cane. He is new-age formal but for an indecipherable tattoo branded across his bare chest and painted face. The upper half of his face is stark white, while the lower half has a gruesome black jawbone with white teeth. He wears black sunglasses and walks out stiff-legged and rapping into a mic. He is accompanied by a line of lesser demons dressed in black military garb. The four flaming towers turn dark red and shoot higher into the cavern, while his deep, angry voice growls out the song.

"They're digging on the Spirit just the way they were told...And your mind's in the run if it make it flow..."

It's a visual feast that should fill a stadium, not a dark, evil underground cavern. And then Baron and Brigitte join the lead singer, working the crowd into a heightened frenzy—arms waving and bodies crawling over one another. They seem desperate for a last chance to catch a fire for God. As if Baron and

Brigitte had the power to forgive their sins. As if their tortured cries of agony could raise Hope from the dead. It's a sickening display that I don't want inside my head. Then, just when I've had enough, the song ends with a spectacular detonation of sparks and raining fire. Bailey and I cover our heads as glowing embers fall like dying stars.

There's no time to discuss the freak show because Kappas has returned. "Up," he says. "We will go now."

Finally! I'm ready to end this shitshow.

He leads us through a maze of energetic demons that I hope are too busy with their demonic glorification to sense my lucky charm—which now feels like a noose around my neck. Along the metal walkway and down the stairs, we dump into the chaos, where Dante grabs my hand. I grab Bailey's, and she grabs Vaughn's. We snake our way toward the back, following a line of fans clustering around a black metal door wedged into the craggy wall. Everyone wants backstage, and I feel like a hedonistic groupie.

Kappas worms his way up front, irritating the already hostile mob. He beats on the door, where a giant red eye appears behind a peephole. He says he wants High Alice, and the eye disappears. We wait. I clutch my shirt and the lucky charm beneath it. The lesser demons are too anxious to see Baron and Brigitte to notice anything out of the ordinary. But I'm jumpy again because I have too much pent-up anticipation. It's been a long night already, and I just want the book. Then I want out. So I fast-forward, imagining Rama working the spell and making another me. As bizarre as it sounds, I'm excited. *I always wanted a sister.*

AWAKEN

Suddenly, out of nowhere, I feel three distinct tugs on my heart.

I gasp, and Dante looks down at me. We're all waiting patiently, so there's no cause for alarm. Then Bailey looks over and frowns. I scowl at myself and lower my eyes. I must be mistaken. I couldn't possibly feel Michael tugging on my heart. Even if he still loved me, I would never feel it here. I haven't felt it since we broke up. So how in the world—there it is again, and I lift my head in alarm. I glance around, and so does Dante. But no one is paying attention to us. Well, no one but some lesser demons eyeing Dante. They smile coyly and try to catch his eye. I don't know if it's because he's so hot or because they know he's a Demon Knight.

Dante asks what's wrong, and I scramble for an excuse. "Uh, uh…I need to use the restroom."

"Now?" he cries, and I grimace helplessly.

Kappas points out a single door at the end of the hallway marked INCUBUS or SUCCUBUS.

Eww. No.

I shake my head and tell Dante I'll hold it. The black door we've been watching opens to the sound of metal scraping on stone. The groupies shift restively, calling out to Baron and Brigitte while craning their necks to see inside. Everyone wants an audience with the famous couple, but a burly refrigerator-of-a-man steps into the doorway. Charred black and extra crispy, his top layer of skin looks to be perpetually shedding and exposing the pinkish-white subdermal layer. He regards us with glowing red eyes that seem to strip me bare.

"Enter," he orders. "Do not speak until spoken to." He steps aside while we file through to wails of protest from the adoring fans. Then he slams the door in their faces.

We're now in a dressing room-cum-entertainment-lounge with glowing red lanterns and a black thurible hanging overhead like a light fixture. Clouds of incense drift down, the fragrance earthy and dry. Black roosters and polluted symbols of hearts, crosses, and coffins decorate the walls. I tug on Dante's hand, nodding at the walls. He tells me they are *Veve*, religious symbols or beacons for the Loa.

Baron Samedi and Maman Brigitte are seated on a red sofa facing guests in a grouping of chairs. They are laughing and joking, having a pleasant evening. The Extra Crispy bouncer dude leans over and speaks quietly to Baron, and his eyes shift to us. He has ditched the sunglasses but remains in his stage clothes and makeup. Then I realize it's not black and white paint but real—his actual face. My skin prickles when his eyes land on me, hollow eyes that I imagine collect souls at a glance. Instinct wants me to shield Bailey, but she is preoccupied, gazing around the room.

Baron and Brigitte take their time studying us. We are uninvited guests, so worry gnaws at me. I wonder what we'll do if they deny our request to see High Alice. What Dante will do. Then Bailey slips her hand in mine, and I turn to her. She has gone pale and is as stiff as a board. I squeeze her hand with a firm look of confidence—no point in letting on that I feel exactly the same.

Suddenly, Baron and Brigitte break into smiles and

robust laughter; they rise and graciously welcome us with open arms. We're old friends that they just can't believe dropped in to say hello. It's unnerving as hell.

Dante leads us over and inclines his head respectfully. Baron and Brigitte reciprocate with a slight bow.

"Demon Knight Dante Dannoso!" Baron bellows jovially. "It is truly an honor. Please come. Sit." He wants the chairs vacated, but Dante holds up his hand.

"My guests and I thoroughly enjoyed your performance, Baron Samedi, Maman Brigitte, but I am afraid we cannot stay. I am in need of High Alice."

Brigitte's chin goes up. She doesn't look hostile but is not happy, either—more on the suspicious side. "High Alice does not leave *La Croix*," she says in a deep, sultry voice.

Dante faces her with a pleasant smile. I can tell he is making an effort to be polite but is in no mood for games or complications. He tilts his head as though amused by her comment. Brigitte's eyes flutter, and she grows nervous having Dante's full attention. Baron looks sharply at his wife as though she is causing trouble.

Wait—this powerful couple that monitors the Crossroads to and from Hell is intimidated by Dante?

He seems to have some unspoken authority over them— even without the use of Persuasion. This is impressive and frightening. Once again, I wonder who he is and how I'll outmaneuver him to get my way.

"Of course! High Alice would love to visit!" Baron says overdramatically, trying to recover the mood and his wife's mistake of countering Dante. "This way, if you please." He gestures toward Extra Crispy, standing by. The demon opens the door to another cavernous hallway.

Dante thanks them and guides us toward the hallway, but I pull him aside at the last minute. "Listen," I whisper nervously. "High Alice is an old friend of Bailey's, so if you don't mind, it'll just be us girls? Some quick catching up and stuff. You know? And then we'll get the book and leave."

I put on my best smile, but Dante eyes me warily. He doesn't like my request. He doesn't want to leave my side. His eyes flick down the hallway and then to Vaughn in a silent command. Vaughn walks the length of the hallway and back again. He finds nothing worrisome and nods. Everything is copacetic, so Dante reluctantly steps back.

"Five minutes, Sophia. That is all." He gives me a stern look, so I grab Bailey, and we go.

Extra Crispy escorts us to a door and then leaves. Bailey knocks, slowly opens it, and we step inside a small room crammed with hundreds of books. Everywhere are books and oversized scrolls. Volumes, all ancient and fat and brown, line the shelves. Some are crumbling, while others are held together by crystal ball bookends. Bailey sees High Alice perched on a ledge, reading a manuscript, and squeals with delight. They throw themselves together, hugging and rocking side-to-side. I stand aside, gawking. I didn't know what to expect from High Alice, but she surprises me.

She is dungeon pale with long, lean muscles beneath a black T-shirt and red skinny – jeans. Her hairstyle is a tight fade about two inches above each ear with a thick black and white mop across her forehead. She has several bolts through her left eyebrow and a red nose ring. Only one of her eyes is lined with kohl, giving the appearance that the other one is dead and not worth the effort. When she and Bailey finally pull apart, High Alice smiles knowingly because I am no surprise.

"Hey, Sophia, how's it going?"

I shift uneasily because this is awkward. She seems to know me without effort, and I don't know where to start. "Hey, Alice. Nice to meet you."

She laughs. "So, you want a do-over, huh?"

"It was my idea," Bailey says. "Pretty sweet, huh? But listen, Alice, do you really wanna stay here? I mean, that Brigitte chick said you couldn't leave. You want us to get you out?"

"No, I'm cool."

"Miss Minnie is really worried," I say. "Can't you come home? Just for a while?" I would love to show up with High Alice in tow. It would make Miss Minnie feel better. She's done so much for me; I feel I owe her. Even though Michael and I didn't work out, I'm grateful she guided me to the courthouse that night.

High Alice tilts her head and gives me a funny look like she's sifting through my thoughts. But she frowns, so maybe she can't read minds. I guess being clairvoyant has its limits. "I'm here 'cause I wanna be," she finally says.

"Why?" Bailey asks, but High Alice stays focused on me when she answers.

"Because I've got a purpose here." Her statement is

flat and telling, and I'm supposed to understand. We are the same—with a purpose to fulfill. Bailey asks what her purpose is, but High Alice doesn't answer.

"We don't have much time," she says instead. "And I believe I know what you're after. I'm cool with you using the book, but here's the deal—this edition of the *Book of the Dead* is attached to me. It's important to what I do, so I made a binding spell. It goes where I go. Of course, I can modify it because I'm the one who made the spell. I'll release it to you, Sophia, but once you complete the spell, the book will dissolve and return to me."

I nod, considering options. "Does it matter which spell? I mean, is there a spell to, say, bring up memories from a past life?"

Bailey has been poking around the room but looks up at my question. We stare, and I know what she's thinking—I believe I have the soul of Dante's lost lover. *Not quite.*

High Alice assesses our visual conversation with a scowl. This isn't something she has foreseen, and she doesn't like it. "Yes, there is," she says with a warning. "But the book is only good for *one* spell before it dissolves. So if you're choosing between spells, do so wisely. I won't part with it again."

"I understand," I say and then take a deep breath, expelling Dante from my thoughts. "Now, what can you tell me about this doubling spell?"

We take a seat on a stack of books, and High Alice explains what Rama has told me. We need the book for the general spell and the supplement the Papyrus of Ani, for some essential details. Since we are using the Egyptian *Book of the Dead* to cast the spell, we'll create a Ka or a double. She tells me to be cautious with the process. The incantation must be clearly enunciated and at a methodical tempo. Never interrupted. Creating a Ka is a delicate procedure. When the time comes, I must be sure to stay completely still. Doubles do not split evenly, and we don't want the Ka to have too many vital elements. We'll share memories of past events and people so that the Ka may integrate smoothly into my life. But we should stay relatively close. Ka should never be too far away, or we'll risk breaking the connection.

"And what happens if the connection is broken?"

"Then you'll have a rough time returning to *whole* during the Apocatastasis—the process that reverses the doubling spell. Both forms, meaning you and your Ka, must be present to reconstitute to the primordial state." She looks grim and serious. "Some people may have a Ka for a lifetime. *If* they abide by the basic binary laws. Like the McCarthy twins have done. For what you're trying to achieve—becoming a spirit walker—you may split your elements, giving part of yourself to your Ka so you can complete your training. But it's best if you are *whole* in the spirit world. Sophia, you understand it's extremely dangerous to walk among the dead? Good. And you'll need every one of your vital elements functioning. It's that simple. Stay close to your Ka."

"I will."

"But I doubt you can explain to everyone you have a long-lost twin like Gracie McCarthy got away with. So, you and your Ka must come and go separately."

"I'm helping with that," Bailey pipes up.

"But what about this Apocatastasis thing? Is that a spell

we'll need from the book?"

"Once the doubling spell is cast, and the book has dissolved, what remains in the ash is a fragile slip of parchment with the Apocatastasis incantation. Like I said, you'll need it to return to your original state. So keep it safe until you're ready to use it. Then it will be spoken only by you in the presence of your Ka. I suggest you lay down for both spells. Makes the transition easier, and nobody falls." She smiles, and I nod. "And now, we'd better do this before your demon friends bust in on us. The one called Dante is very protective of you, huh?"

Bailey and I look at each other, not surprised High Alice would know about Dante and Vaughn. Still, her accurate assessment of Dante is unsettling.

High Alice disappears behind a wall of books and rummages around. She returns with a large, flat book. It's aged with brushed gold, a copper spine, and leather straps with brass buckles. She holds it out so I can place my hand next to hers on the cover. When she intertwines our fingers, tiny electric vibrations pass between us. My eyes snap to hers, but she is chanting with her eyes closed. The vibrations travel up my arm until they dissolve, and we are done. Then she steps back, and I take the book. It's heavy, so I hold it against my stomach, wrapping my coat around it. She walks us to the door where she hugs Bailey good-bye.

"Tell Dad hey, and Aunt Minnie hello and that I'm fine here. She's got to stop worrying." She turns and gives me a quick, awkward hug because my arms are full. "And you...be careful with yourself, Sophia. Your soulmate is eager to have things settled between you."

"What?" I say, but she opens the door and shoves us out just as Dante and Vaughn appear in the hallway.

"Let's go," Dante says, taking my elbow and pulling me away. I go without a word because I'm reeling from High Alice's parting words.

We return to the main room, which has reverted to its previous state with human chandeliers, the dangling demented, and the morbid musicians. The dance floor is packed, so Dante pushes toward a stairwell on the far side that leads up to the main exit. We're nearly there when Marquis Naberius walks down the metal mesh steps and stops at the bottom. His pale face and black hair give him a translucent, Transylvanian effect. His cold dead eyes settle on Dante.

"*Ciao*, Dante. I'm sorry we could not visit earlier. I was entertaining guests." He takes a deliberate look at me and then Bailey. I feel her grip the back of my coat. She is unnerved like I am.

"*Ciao*, Naberius. It has been a long time. Now, if you will excuse us, we have another engagement." Dante is cool but tense, waiting for the marquis to step aside. But he doesn't. He is anticipating something or someone. And then Chax, the guy obsessed with silver, walks over and targets me.

"This the one?" he asks the marquis while reaching for my throat. Dante reacts in a swift, unseen flash that knocks Chax backward. I clutch the lucky charm beneath my shirt while fumbling to keep the book hidden inside my coat.

I hear Vaughn's low, tense voice say, "Do not speak." Then he steps between us and the other demons.

The marquis moves in, and the four demons square off.

They want my lucky charm, with or without my throat attached. The marquis tries to convince Dante to give it up in exchange for something else he might want. Dante warns him to move aside or risk losing a hand. Or something of greater value.

The marquis is not persuaded and pulls a sword from inside his cane. Chax yanks a large silver cross from his neck and unsheathes a hidden dagger. Dante and Vaughn are suddenly at a disadvantage. I glance around for an escape, but there's nowhere to go. Amused lesser demons gather behind us to watch because it's entertaining when royal demons go bad.

The only time I saw Dante and Vaughn fight was in the courthouse when Michael and Gabe killed them. But even then, they had weapons.

Vaughn starts toying with Chax, almost begging to be cut. I see Affliction swirling in his eyes and know things could get bloody. I worry about Bailey, but her face is alive with terror and fascination as she watches Vaughn taunt Chax into attacking. Dante moves slowly, keeping his focus on the marquis and the sword. I can't see his face, but I imagine that Persuasion is in control.

"You may choose to reconsider, Naberius," Dante says. "Now is your last chance. You will not get what you are after. And you will leave here minus *both* hands."

"Your arrogance has exceeded your ability, Demon Knight. I do not succumb to compulsion. And you are not armed." He smiles coldly.

Dante raises his hands as though planning to surrender but then whips them down as daggers slide into his palms. Vaughn does the same, and they are suddenly armed with ancient weapons. Dante moves with unnatural speed as he spins and slashes, catching the marquis unaware. A bloody black X appears across the demon's chest while he staggers in shock.

Dante and Vaughn go to work, the blades ripping through the air and leaving a fiery green comet-like tail in their wake. The supernatural weapons slice through the demons with the efficiency of samurai swords. Vaughn cuts Chax in half, his upper body slowly sliding off and flopping to the floor. The Demon of Affliction tips his head back and howls with pleasure. His eyes roll in his head while a smile breaks across his face.

The marquis stares in horror and then whirls around to raise his sword against Dante. A green streak reflects in the demon's eyes at the same moment the sword and hand are severed. He cries in sudden anguish, reaching for his wounded arm. A second green flash takes his other hand. Both lay on the floor, and the marquis stumbles away, yelling obscenities.

Dante and Vaughn swing around, challenging the crowd, but no one wants to continue what the marquis and Chax started. So they turn their backs and leave us alone. With no more threats, Dante and Vaughn retract their weapons. Then Dante walks to me, his eyes blazing yellow and black with exhilaration and his chest pumping feverishly. He has a fierce, deadly expression that I have never seen before, not even when he fought Michael.

Dante's eyes dance across mine, searching for signs of what I'm thinking. What I'm feeling about his violent behavior. Honestly, my mind is numb, and I'm waiting for his eyes to return to soft green. I want to know that when I speak, I'm talking to Dante, not Persuasion. But he reaches for me with his demon still visible in his eyes, and I instinctively flinch out of reach.

Dante's jaw tightens, and his nostrils flare with displeasure. He never liked my fear, especially when I feared Wolfgang, who loved to scare me. Dante doesn't want me to be afraid of him. But I'm not looking at Dante; I'm looking at Persuasion. I want to say that I'm grateful for the protection, but I won't speak to Persuasion—only to Dante. His demon scares the hell out of me. Those mystical weapons scare the hell out of me. I've never seen anything like them, not even training with the demon hunters. But I don't have time to wonder what effect they might have on anyone from the upper realms because Dante takes my hand, squeezing hard and forcing me to endure his scorching heat. I grit my teeth and take it. He doesn't apologize. He doesn't try to mask his dark energy and the demon front and center, looking down at me. For the first time, I can truly appreciate how dangerous and deadly Dante can be.

I try to hold my own, but I worry that Persuasion is testing me, trying to manipulate something. I don't know how it feels to be compelled by a powerful Demon Knight, and I don't want to find out. So I blink hard against his aggressive stare, suddenly wanting the calm, aristocratic Dante back. The one who shies away from cell phones and laptops. The one who used to blush when we took awkward selfies, and the one who used to kiss my hand every morning. As much as I hate having this thought, I want *my* Dante back.

Maybe I can help him return. Maybe he's waiting for me to ask for him. I don't know how long Persuasion can stay once he's risen. I don't know how any of it works, only that I'm not leaving here with Persuasion. So, in a pathetic attempt to find Dante again, I break my word and speak to his demon.

"I want Dante," I say stubbornly. His brow twitches, and his eyes narrow. He's wondering if he heard right or if I've lost my mind.

"Right here," he says tightly, but I know it can't be him. It can't be—

His eyes sizzle until they're soft, Caribbean green again—those gorgeous eyes that strip me bare. But they still glare at me. Changing the color did not change the intensity, and I wonder who is in charge when Persuasion rises in Dante? Who is in control all the time?

My thoughts stall as I stumble over unwanted questions. I need to lighten the mood, so I try to think of something playful. Something the old Dante, *my* Dante, will appreciate.

"Wow, I didn't know you were such a badass." My voice trembles and kills my forced smile. A shadow flickers across his face, and Dante grasps my chin with his free hand, leaning close to my face.

"Yes, you do," he says, but it doesn't sound like him. It doesn't look like him. Even with soft green eyes, Dante wears a hard, unreadable mask. Then he pulls me up the stairs, just as I feel three tugs on my heart.

Chapter 20

Michael

Two Halo candidates surrendered during the final days of the second trial. That left Michael, Zack, and Viola to endure the brutal, physical punishment dubbed red week, named for the journey through fire and molten lava but also the copious amount of bloodshed.

Michael performed well, despite his distracting thoughts of Sophia. He was plagued with guilt over their last encounter when he'd humiliated her at the barn. He'd only meant to teach her a lesson—that playing around with Milvi was no indication of the evil she would face in the spirit world. It was no laughing matter, and seeing her so careless had sent him over the edge.

Chief Master Sachiel, with his red beard and sharp eyes, called for attention, pulling Michael from his thoughts. He stood erect, tucked his hands behind his back, and deadened his emotions.

"We begin the final trial: battle strategies and weapon warfare," he announced. Michael immediately felt his fellow candidates' flood of emotions. They were relieved the second trial was over. It was by far the most physically grueling trial they've had to endure. Everyone looked forward to arming themselves and discovering the Halo secret to permanently killing demons. Decapitating demons was fine if you were in a hurry, but it only sent them below where they could regenerate. There was a better way—the death kill—and the candidates were eager to learn.

Squad Master Camael took over, leading each candidate to a sitting area. He began his lecture on the basic understanding of Halo warfare and battle configurations, specifically the tortoise formation, which the Halos often used. It was effective when combating legions of demons that attempted to advance on a particular territory. On occasion, one of the Five Kingdoms of Hell warred with another—their legions ambushing each other in the Borderlands. Most often, the Halos were waiting with their own ambush, destroying as many demons as possible.

The candidates also learned the silent signals to switch from fight formation to flight formation without missing a beat. They discussed standard rescue operations, demonic removal in high target areas, and shock force, where bands of Halos attacked from above or launched balls of light to sweep an area clear of all demonic activity. The no slash, just burn policy.

When a battle concluded, Halo warriors rotated out of their band so that anyone who had a permanent kill could cleanse their light for seven days. Then, once the warrior had balanced his energy, he could reenter the squad for duty.

"And now, we have one last technique to learn." Camael's expression grew cold and deadly. He knew what the candidates wanted and was happy to provide it—the secret to a permanent kill. "Complete and final destruction of a demon requires a highly specialized skillset some of you may never possess. In combination: timing, accuracy, and speed. Do not be discouraged. It may come in time. A critical point to remember—if you think you can achieve a permanent kill, do *not* decapitate the demon. Understand? The head must remain intact during the process."

He raised his hand, clawing two fingers and a thumb. "And *this* is your weapon of choice. Your bare hand. Once you have incapacitated the demon with your dagger or sword, you will penetrate the back of the neck and yank out the spine. Your target is less than five inches wide, so you must be accurate on the take. When your fingers reach bone, the demon, which may be struggling like hell, will instantly yield. One hard yank and the demon is forever severed. Obviously, you gotta get close. And they know what you're up to. So they're likely to throw their heads back, making it impossible to dig into the neck. It's the coward's way out because they can expel themselves through the mouth, usually a green smoke. Or yellow vapor. Or red fog. Depending on what kind of miscreant you've gotten hold of. Once they're airborne, they get a free ride, and you got nothing.

"So let me make myself clear, it's no parlor trick to yank out their spines—it's timing, aiming, speed. More than likely, they'll take off. Or take off your head and then gut you while lying on the ground. You can regenerate only so fast. And they can do all kinds of freaky to you while you're out. There's not a demon weapon yet that can kill an angel. But they're getting close. They'll anesthetize you and then put abnormal urges in your head till you don't know your own name.

"And it goes without saying they're always after your weapons. You don't want your own blade used against you. If they get into your head, and you find the only blood you're spilling is your own, power down and stop fighting. One of us will find you. Just don't give in to the urges." He gave them a stiff look, assessing each candidate individually. Then he nodded, satisfied that his message was made loud and clear. "Now, first lesson in the final trial is close-quarter hand-to-hand combat. Gear up."

They headed to a table laden with equipment: swords, daggers, body armor, shields, and helmets. It was practice quality, but they suited up with everything available: chest and back plates, arm and leg armor, and open helmets. Sachiel stepped up to explain the rules of engagement during close quarter combat.

"Each candidate will enter a separate series of tunnels and chambers beneath the barn. You must clear each chamber of demons and return within twenty minutes or less. This is actual combat, people—a real taste of everything you'll encounter. So don't trust anything you see down there. Keep 'em out of your head. Now let's hit it."

One by one, the candidates disappeared down separate stairwells. Michael armed himself with a shield and sword and then entered a tunnel below the waterfall. Dark and damp, the stone walls smelled of rich earth. His eyes immediately adjusted and swept the area. He moved in short, quick steps, on alert. The first chamber door was ajar, so he kicked it off the hinges, then rounded into the chamber.

The first demon came at him from behind, red eyes flaring and sword flaming. Michael ducked, spun around, slammed it with his boot, and sent it reeling. Then, knowing that demons liked to attack in pairs, he flipped his sword and thrust it behind him, catching another one in the gut. The demon exploded into a cloud of dust that burned his eyes. He coughed and momentarily lost his bearings. Then the first demon returned, wielding its sword again. Michael deflected it with his shield and then cut a clean path across its torso. Only then did it shatter into dust.

Michael scanned the chamber. No red eyes remained, so he moved on, and the scene repeated in the next chamber and the next, down twisting tunnels with ledges where more red-eyed demons attacked high and low. They were getting craftier, harder to kill. The floor was uneven and treacherous, making progress slow. Wild screams exploded around him, the sounds of Forgiven souls being attacked. It wreaked havoc on a guardian's emotions. Michael had to work to maintain control. He was flooded with memories from Halloween night when Sophia and her friends—*his* friends—had been trapped in Dante's haunted mansion. They had been so close to death that he and his brothers had barely arrived in time to save them.

Michael allowed the memories to distract him, so the next attack caught him off guard. Searing pain scored his arm as the blade made contact. He hissed and lunged for the demon, smacking it senseless with his shield before slicing off its head. More came, some wielding ancient maces and others with long spears. Some were misshapen forms dripping ectoplasm with fangs and horns. Their red eyes churned like blazing furnaces. Some were charred, grotesque lumps pieced together by a madman. Their hideousness was disturbing, but Michael killed them as quickly as possible and moved on.

Before he reached the next chamber, a delicate, familiar scent caught his attention— Sophia's perfume. It teased his senses as though she stood with her arms wrapped around his neck. But how? He examined the shadowy tunnel. It wasn't possible, and yet there was no mistaking—

Demons poured out of the next chamber like ants fleeing a burning house. They scurried along the walls and ceiling, clacking their jaws. Some were skinned to the bone. Some had black wings and swooped down with their talons raking the air. But Michael beat them down as they came. Then he tossed a ball of light into the tunnel, where it exploded in a silent burst of white energy. The demons were sucked into the light while ash shot into the air, filling the tunnel with their dusty remains. Before it settled, the second onslaught came, and Michael wielded his sword in great sweeping arcs. He hurled his shield, taking down the handful attacking his flank. Then, unsheathing a second sword, he spun and swung, cutting down demons while their thin, fiery blades beat against his body armor.

Every so often, a burning blade connected with skin, and he seized in pain. But he was destroying them faster than they could come. He was going to make it. The last chamber was straight ahead.

Michael raced forward, bounded off the wall, and came down hard on a particularly tall demon. He sliced it open, but something hit his head on the way down. Another demon lurking in the shadows had hurled a hammer that glanced off Michael's temple, knocking him to the ground. He fell to his knees but quickly sprang up, both swords impaling two demons falling from the ceiling. And then he heard Sophia calling his name.

Michael jolted to a stop and squinted in the gray haze. She was just ahead. He knew it. He could smell her perfume. *"Michael! Please!"* she called, and he took off running, only to clash with more demons. They threw knives and spears, but Michael spun away, cutting them down from behind.

"Please! Michael! This hurts too much! I miss you! Please come back!"

He was filled with sudden rage because he couldn't go to her. Rage that she was in pain. She was sad and crying, and it was his fault. He never wanted to hurt her. He wanted her to feel love. Only love. So, as the next wave of demons attacked, he narrowed his focus and tugged three times on her heart. I. Love. You.

She had to know he still loved her. She had to know. Didn't she?

Two blazing whips snapped around Michael's wrists as the demons took advantage of his distraction. Then they slashed and stabbed any exposed flesh. Michael's head flew back, and his body arched in pain. His helmet was ripped away, and two more fire whips wrapped around his ankles, stopping his struggle. Michael was jerked to his knees, his arms stretching wide and painful. The armor was torn from his chest and legs, and a thousand knives pierced his skin. He shuddered as pain enveloped him. And then her sweet cries reached him again.

"Michael! Please! This is unbearable! I can't take anymore! Please come back! Come back to me, Michael!"

His head slumped in surrender. The torture continued while he drowned in Sophia's pleas. He missed her so much. He was so sorry he had left her. He wanted her back.

I. Love. You. I. Love. You. I. Lov—

Michael's head snapped sideways as a demon struck him in the face. He offered no resistance as they beat him. His body was pulverized, but he welcomed the pain. It was due. He should never have hurt her. If Sophia still wanted him—still loved him—that's all that mattered.

"Please, Michael! Give up. Stop the trials! Come back! Please, stop the trials!"

Michael's eyes sprang open. *Something wasn't right.*

Warm blood pooled around his knees while his arms stretched beyond their limits, muscles shredding inch by inch. The pain hardly registered now because he knew instinctively that *something wasn't right.*

Sophia would never ask him to quit the trials. She told him repeatedly that she would *never* ask him to deny his calling.

Michael ground his teeth and curled his arms inward. He strained and shook as he slowly forced them together, bringing the demons down beside him. Then he clawed his fingers and thumbs and plunged them into their necks, ripping out their spines like yanking off a belt. They shrieked as their bodies shriveled into ashes. Then Michael lunged for the third demon, yanking out its spine before it expelled itself through the mouth. And he couldn't stop now that he realized it had been a mind game. Somehow, the demons had penetrated his most private thoughts, tapped into his deepest fears, and used them against him. Michael was on a rampage.

By the time he had torn through the last chamber, every demon was destroyed—either piles of ashes or sagging, spineless skins on the ground. Then he gathered six dripping spines and walked calmly up the steps.

Chief Master Sachiel and Squad Master Camael stood in the meadow with stunned expressions as Michael approached. Never in all the trials had a candidate made a permanent kill, let alone six in one day. No one else had emerged from the tunnels yet; certainly, no one else was expected to carry demon spines.

Michael threw the bones at their feet. His body was bloody, torn, and trembled with exhaustion, but he lifted his chin. "Tell me what you know about Sophia St. James," he demanded.

The Halo Masters shared a look of silent conference. They seemed reluctant to kowtow to the whims of a candidate. But with six demon spines at their feet and time left on the clock, they capitulated.

"I have seen the girl called Sophia St. James at the Borderlands," Sachiel said. "I was with a band of Halos returning from battle when we came upon her and her mother. Sophia is the one you and your brothers saved from the bargain with Demon Knight Dante, is she not?"

"She is."

He nodded thoughtfully. "And the demons in the tunnels used her image to distract you?"

"Her voice," Michael ground out, remembering Sophia's heartbreaking pleas, an agonizing sound he feared would live inside him forever.

"It's not uncommon for guardians to form attachments to souls they have saved. The demons looked for your weakness, Michael Patronus. Did they find it? Have you a weakness for this soul?"

His gut reaction was to deny a weakness, to play it off as nothing but a trivial diversion, but he changed his mind at the last second. It might have been a demonic ploy, but he couldn't help wondering if Sophia really did miss him as much as he missed her. Had she changed her mind? Would she refuse her calling if he refused his? How had the demons known to say such things? Had they tapped into her thoughts or feelings? Did Sophia want a normal human life with him after all?

The Halos were waiting, and Michael needed more time to think, so he relented and threw out the answer they wanted to hear. "I don't have a weakness." He walked away and headed for the armory.

Michael tossed his weapons aside and removed the remains of his armor. His hands trembled, and his eyes swam with tears. He staggered to a bench and slumped down with his head in his hands. He squeezed his eyes shut as pain worse than anything the demons could inflict burned through him.

What had he done? How was he supposed to live without her?

Pale blue tears streamed down his cheeks.

Chapter 21

Dante

It had been a successful evening, and Dante was restless with arrogance. His date with Sophia had gone perfectly. They had secured the spellbook she needed to bring out her memories, and he had demonstrated that he was more than capable of protecting her. The tattoo blades had proved far more useful than he had imagined.

There was nothing left to interfere. He only wished he could see Michael Patronus's face when Sophia was reborn to her old life—when she remembered who she was and what she wanted most. *Who she wanted most.*

It was only a matter of time now. Sophia had asked to be alone with Rama when he performed the spell. Evidently, there were restrictions; only one spell could be cast, and Sophia would not risk contaminating the process. She had called it a *one-and-done kind of thing.* He liked that she was being cautious, but he hadn't liked being excluded. So he told himself it would be worth it in the end. He wouldn't be there when the spell was cast, but he would be when her memories returned. It could take some time for the spell to fully bloom inside her, and he was willing to wait. In fact, since he didn't have a death contract,

Dante had all the time in the world. Sophia would be his.

"And very soon, she will answer to the name, Lovaria. Again," he murmured into the fire.

"How's that?" Vaughn asked, throwing himself into a tall wingback chair.

The sitting area had been reestablished since the haunted house party, and the mansion had also been made over to appease their needs. The giant hearth blazed continuously, but the flat-screen TVs in the entertainment room were new and without Wolfgang's destructive accents.

Dante turned to answer and then scoffed, shaking his head. Vaughn's neck was covered with deep bite marks, and his arms were scored with black lines. "You look like a succubus's teething toy."

Vaughn broke into an evil grin. "My girl likes to play rough. What can I say, I'm a lucky guy."

"Undoubtedly. And will you follow the young lady through the halls of education as she asked?"

Vaughn cocked his head and gave it some thought. "Seriously, I think I'd follow that chick anywhere."

"Within range," Dante reminded him. Their chain tattoos extended only so far, but neither knew the effects if they reached their limit. They had taken a risk going to New York. No telling how the night might have gone had they reached the end of their tethers and left the girls at *La Croix* without them.

"You think the marquis or Chax will report back to The Order?" Vaughn asked. He didn't like the idea of Lord Brutus discovering their whereabouts so soon. Especially now that

Sophia's memories might be restored and he'd gotten to see Bailey. He hadn't realized just how much he missed her, how much he wanted her, until tonight. Bailey was unlike anyone he'd ever known. She had gotten under his skin—in more ways than one.

"I am sure they will avoid telling anyone how and where we dismembered them. Unfortunately, we had an audience of lesser demons who like to gossip. I suspect Lord Brutus will eventually hear about it. By then, Sophia will have her memories, and I'll have her in Hell with me. Where she belongs."

Santiago strolled into the room but stopped when he heard Dante's remark. He'd just unloaded his backpack from the Escalade and checked his phone for messages. While the Demon Knights had been clubbing it up at *La Croix*, he'd been scouring the city for the items on Julian Wexler's list. What he didn't expect to find was a text message from him.

"What is it?" Dante asked because he didn't like the look on Santiago's face. The kid was more nervous than usual.

"Well, uh, I just got this text from Wexler and—"

"Wexler?" Vaughn hollered. "The gatekeeper? How can he text you from Hell?"

Santiago shrugged. "I dunno. Dude's got mad skills. Anyway, he says Lord Brutus already knows where you guys are. I mean specifically. And he went ballistic. When you escaped the Death Bunker, he assumed you were bound to Hell. You know, 'cause of the friendship bracelets that witch left on your arms? He's had his men scouring the Five Kingdoms looking for you."

"Who informed him?" Dante demanded.

"You guys did when you used the daggers. They have a

supernatural connection to the underground, and bam—Lord Brutus was alerted."

"Don't you have any good news?" Vaughn grumbled, and Santiago grimaced.

"Actually, that was the only thing close to good news. I guess Wexler forgot to mention that your tethers come with an expiration date. We don't get to roam the land of the free forever. When time is up, no matter where you are, you'll be yanked back down."

"How much time do we have left?" Dante asked tightly. He was simmering with rage because this was vital information he should have been told earlier.

"Uh, 'bout a week. Maybe less."

Dante growled and hurled a tumbler of amber liquid into the fireplace. He took a moment to simmer and reconfigure his thoughts. "It might be enough time. *If* her memories return quickly. Perhaps some coaxing would spur the process along."

"There's more," Santiago said tentatively, stepping back should Dante decide to throw the decanter next. "Well, I guess Lord Brutus was on the warpath after he learned you guys got all the way to Haven Hurst. He punished Isatou for tricking him with the tattoos, and then he…released Wolfgang."

"So?"

"You guys know how Wolf was tortured and all? Well, I heard Lord Brutus went psycho on him. Wexler said he heard Wolfgang is part demon and part monster, like those creatures he faces in the Demonic Games. The gossipmongers say chains can barely hold him."

"And now he's on the loose," Vaughn said, flicking open his switchblade and slicing it across his thigh.

"Not on the loose," Santiago said. "On the prowl. Lord Brutus is sending Wolfgang up to...kill Sophia. You guys just put a larger target on her back. Like a neon sign. Like one of those giant arrows—"

"That's enough!" Dante yelled, his demonic rage bursting at the seams. He flew out of the chair and hurled the tea table against the fireplace. More tables, chairs, and lamps followed, and then he tore down pictures, curtains, and doors, ripping apart anything his hands touched. When the room was in shambles, he went after Santiago, clutching him by the throat and crushing him into the wall. The kid's eyes bulged as he flailed and grasped at the hand crushing his neck. Vaughn jumped on Dante, trying to tear him away before he severed Santiago's head.

"Stop! Dante! We need the kid! And we need a plan! Now back off!"

Dante shook with fury, his snake eyes glowing wildly in his head. It took several long minutes for Vaughn's soothing voice of reason to reach him. Gradually, Dante recovered control and lowered the kid, who slid to the floor, clutching his throat and gasping for air.

"We need a plan," Vaughn repeated calmly. He held Dante by the shoulders, working to bring him back down with something he could understand—a rational game plan.

"Yes," Dante murmured, forcing his demon down and regaining himself. He shoved Vaughn away and then ran a hand through his hair. "We know Wolfgang better than anyone. We know his tactics, his ploys, and preferences."

"But what about Sophia? You have to tell her. She'll have to be ready if he finds her without us."

"He won't."

"You willing to risk that?"

Dante contemplated, his mind frantic for a way to keep Sophia out of Wolfgang's reach. "I'll have to stay with her. Never leave her side."

"You have to *teach* her to defend herself, Dante. If she's still training to become a spirit walker, she'll have access to supernatural weapons, right?"

"You want *me* to teach *Sophia* how to kill a *demon?*" Dante's eyebrows rose at the ridiculousness of it.

"Yeah, well, you'll just have to make sure she doesn't kill *you*. Unless you're into that kinda thing."

"She has been training with her own personal Jedis," Dante grumbled, and Vaughn laughed, knocking him in the shoulder.

"Look who's been watching the movie channel."

Dante gave him a cynical look and then kicked a path through the debris until he stood before the fireplace. The heat stirred his blood and calmed his nerves. He closed his eyes, thinking. "Two demon hunters have been teaching Sophia how to defend herself. And we need her capable of killing a monster."

"She'd have to be a spirit walker."

"Not necessarily. She would only need access to spiritual weapons. I haven't sensed them in her room, so I suspect she's not in possession of them yet. But if Sophia can get her holy weapons and decapitate Wolfgang, he'll be sent below, as usual. By the time we return to Hell, Wolfgang will still be regenerating. Plenty of time to secure Sophia out of his reach and chain Wolfgang in the Death Bunker."

"And then what?"

"And then...I will kill Wolfgang. Permanently."

Santiago made a choking noise that had nothing to do with his throbbing throat. "You're gonna permanently kill a Knight of the Royal Court?" he asked in disbelief.

Dante's eyes cut to the kid. He had forgotten he was still in the room and would never have revealed his plans in the presence of an underling. Permanently killing one of the Chosen was nothing short of treason to The Order.

Santiago held up his hands. "Hey, it's cool with me. I never like the asshat. But, seriously, if you want Sophia to kill Wolfgang first, you'd better get her used to killing lesser demons. I mean, the guy was a roman gladiator back in the day, and now he's the poster child for Animal Planet."

Dante squinted at the strange reference, but Vaughn agreed. "Kid's got a point. Start off easy. She should step on some ants before she faces a charging bull."

"And who did you have in mind?" Dante asked, taking to the plan. He liked the idea of Sophia sharpening her fighting skills. It might make her easier to turn dark just as she completes her Awakening. And if he could turn her, he would create a bond that even *she* could not break.

Vaughn retrieved the switchblade he'd dropped when Dante went ballistic. He snapped it shut, considering options.

"Bailey told me about the original graveyard in Haven Hurst, how it was moved out here when they built up the town square. There are some headstones out back. I'm sure some *bodies* are pissed they got uprooted. Let me poke around and see who pokes back. We could start Sophia on a few ghoulish hors d'oeuvres and work her way up the food chain."

"Very well. I'll stay as close to her as possible. If I can time things right, she'll awaken her supernatural tendencies and her memories in the same instant. Then I will turn her, and she'll be my Lovaria again. As fate should have allowed. In the meantime, I will turn her into a lethal fighter."

"And what about that spy Lord Brutus said was in Haven Hurst? The one who told him about her Awakening? It won't be easy to lure Sophia away if one of her friends is the old man's sock puppet. Any idea who's turning tricks for him?"

"No," Dante grumbled. He had been working that angle as well, but none of Sophia's friends had shown signs of demonic possession, which was disturbing. He feared Lord Brutus had developed some new technique to keep them undetected. The spy could be anyone.

"I'll handle that end," he finally said, frustrated. "And, Santi, I want you in communication with Wexler. We need to know exactly where Wolfgang is at all times. Specifically, when he passes through the gate. I want to know what form he takes—if he changes his appearance. He could disguise himself as any number of beings. Let me know his identity and who he brings with him. We have less than a week to prepare Sophia, kill Wolfgang, and return to Hell."

Chapter 22

Once a Double
Twice the Trouble

It's late by the time we creep in. Rama is true to his word and waiting in my bedroom. He must have sensed us coming up the staircase because he is staring wide-eyed and frantic when we arrive.

"We got it," I say, heaving the book at him. He takes it in the gut and sits on the bed to unbuckle the leather straps.

"Any problems?" he asks, and Bailey and I look at each other.

"No," I answer quickly. I won't mention the nauseating hedonistic environment, the fight with the marquis and Chax, or that my lucky charm was a troll magnet. "I wanna do this tonight. Now. Just give us a minute to change."

Rama stands and walks to the corner with his nose buried in the text. He tells us there are some seriously wicked opportunities in the book. We have to be careful with the spell. Bailey and I strip and change into sweats and tees. She mouths, *You're doing the doubling spell, right?* and I wave at her to shut up.

"Uh, Ascended Master here," Rama says, flipping a page.

"Totally heard that. Everything cool?"

"Yeah, we're cool. You can turn around."

He moves across the room and then scowls at me over the edge of the book. "We got a smooth ride, *wahine*? Or you throwin' some wind on it?"

"I…uh, no, no wind. It's all smooth. We're good to go."

He considers me through narrow eyes but eventually nods. "I found the spell."

I relay the instructions from High Alice. The incantation must be read carefully. After the spell is cast, the book will dissolve and leave a small parchment. My job is to remain very still during the process. Rama tells me to lie quietly on the bed but make room for the Ka, so I scoot over and leave the right side empty. Bailey stands at the foot of the bed, and Rama is next to my head. I breathe deeply and stare at the ceiling. I nervously curl my fingers into the blanket. Then Rama places a delicate white feather on my chest, telling me that my heart must be light and without care, weighed against the feather and found equal. I release my grip and close my eyes, meditating. Before long, I sink into the mattress. The heaviness of my bones settles deep inside me, and I become lost within myself.

Rama begins the incantation—a foreign language that I can't understand. Then he tells me to enter the *Sekhet-Hetepet*—the Fields of Peace—so that I may find my spirit's double, my Ka. He is monotone and precise, and I have great faith in his ability. I remain calm inside myself, envisioning the Fields of Peace. My version has a beautiful meadow with red poppies and white and yellow broom flowers. There is a low rock wall and a bubbling brook. It seems familiar and comforting. Peaceful.

I imagine finding my double there, walking beside me. I tell her what we're doing and that I must be able to trust her. I ask her a question that I hope she'll answer when she wakes beside me. We walk on, but then she dissolves, and all I think about is Michael. I want to know how I could feel him tugging my heart at *La Croix*. And why I haven't felt anything since. I wonder if he misses me. I wonder if I'll still feel the second heartbeat when I am two.

I think I fall asleep because Bailey is telling me to wake up. I crack open my eyes, groggy. She's frowning down at me, and then I remember what we're up to and look next to me. The bed is empty. *It didn't work.*

"No," I moan with disappointment. I look at Rama, who seems a little green around the gills. "What happened?"

He shakes his head, and I sit up. Then Bailey gasps so hard her eyes bulge. She's staring at the bed beneath me, so I turn and look. There I am, still lying down, *topless,* when I'm actually sitting up. I yelp and roll onto the floor.

"Holy Godiva!" Bailey whips the blanket over the Ka, who is completely naked. I scramble to my feet, and we stare down at me, sleeping on the bed with just my head peeking out. Bailey's eyes swing back and forth between me and…me.

"Is it you?" She pokes my arm, and I smack her.

"Don't be stupid. Of course, it's me. *She's* the naked one."

Ka hasn't roused, but I see the feather on the floor, so I pick it up and hand it to Rama. He hasn't spoken and looks ill. He won't take the feather. The spellbook is gone, and his hands hold a pile of ashes with a tiny rolled parchment—the spell I'll need for the Apocatastasis. I tell him not to move while I grab an empty Cheetos bag and carefully brush the ashes and parchment inside for safekeeping.

"You okay?" I ask.

He holds his stomach. "That was a windchop for me. Reminds me of the time I hit a breaker and swallowed a Neptune cocktail. I was selling Buicks the rest of the day and—

"Okay, okay," I grumble. "I'm sure you weren't *too* traumatized by the floor show." We look at me on the bed, but none of us knows what to do now.

"Well, *wahine,* you wanted to go tandem, so wake her up."

I step over and watch Ka sleeping. It's freaky seeing a perfect rendition of me. At least from the chin up. "Should we put some clothes on her first?"

"And have her wake up to strangers hiking up her panties?" Bailey says.

"Better than waking up naked. Isn't it?" I look at her like she would know. She grins.

"Depends on who's doing the waking."

"Well, if it were me—" I stop and laugh. "I guess it is me. So, I'd just want to be woken up as is." I gently shake Ka's shoulder. Her eyes flutter and open, so I step back, holding my breath. We're *all* holding our breaths.

Ka stares at the ceiling for a moment and then slowly turns and looks at me. Something registers in her eyes, and she smiles. "Yes, you are," she says, and my stomach flips.

Bailey whispers out the side of her mouth, "What's she talking about?"

"She's just answering something from our private conversation. I wanted some verification if this worked."

"Can she read your thoughts?" she asks.

"Oh, please," Ka says, rolling her eyes.

Bailey's mouth drops. "Okay, this is freaking me out. She even sounds like you."

Ka sits up, letting the blanket fall into her lap as she stretches and arches her back like a fairytale princess finally waking from a deep sleep. We may be carbon copies, but it seems I have kept all the inhibitions.

I rush over and cover up my Ka while Rama walks to the corner and drops his head against the wall with a loud *thunk*. I'm so embarrassed. I'm sure this is not what he bargained for when he was assigned to train me to walk in the spirit world.

"Have some modesty," I say to Ka.

"Why? I don't have anything you haven't seen before."

"Because we're not alone, you idiot!" I say, but think, *This is the most bizarre conversation I have ever had.*

I ask Bailey to get some clothes and then we turn our backs while Ka slips into my pajama shorts and a T-shirt. Once dressed, we all pile onto the bed to go over the plan. Rama heads for the closet.

"Gotta shoot and scoot."

"You're leaving?" I ask.

"You and Ka got things to work out. *Carpe noctem*; seize the night. I'll cruise back in the morning."

For the next two hours, Bailey, Ka, and I explore options of how best to make this work. It's pretty easy because Ka already knows what we're up to. I need to be with Rama and the demon hunters as much as possible. Ka needs to attend every class and do all the grunt work. Basically, take up where I'm leaving off.

Bailey throws out random questions, testing Ka's memories. She nails them. Even going back to my first day in Haven Hurst—where I met Bailey and Rachel—what kind of bread the McCarthy twins baked for me. And she knows I'm going to the dance with JD.

"Just like him as a friend, though," Ka says, making a point to me. I freeze.

Ka knows about Michael and me.

Why hadn't it occurred to me that she would know my deepest secrets? I have inadvertently shared Michael's forbidden feelings and his family's identity. On the other hand, it is *me*, after all. And I've proven I can keep important, life-altering facts to myself. Still, I don't like someone else knowing what Michael is and what he means to me. Even if it is *me*.

This is so messed up.

Ka doesn't say more, so I'm assuming she understands. If she knows my secrets, she knows the importance of not sharing them. And this particular morsel is something we don't share with Bailey—with anyone. Ka seems to understand, but she has an impish grin that worries me.

Bailey starts talking about Dante and Vaughn while Ka listens patiently. I study her, trying to sense her emotions the way Michael does. I wonder if she knows something about Dante that I don't. If I did have a past life with him, I wonder if she got the memories.

"Stop it," Ka says to me, and Bailey stops talking. "You can't tell what I'm thinking or feeling any more than I can tell what you are."

"Then how did you know what I was doing?" I ask.

"'Cause that's what I would be doing if I were you. But see, I *am* you, and I'm *not*. I'm perfectly fine with what we're doing, whereas you're uptight and all"—she waves her hands—"Don't shake my Magic 8 Ball! You can't know what I'm up to."

"What the heck!" I snap, and Bailey bursts out laughing. Ka smiles. She's mocking me, and I feel like a third wheel.

"Wow, Soph," Bailey says. "Some DoOver. She nailed you."

"Oh, shut up."

Ka snuggles under the covers, so we do, too. It's late, almost four in the morning, and I'm exhausted. *We* are exhausted.

We negotiate ourselves until we're comfy. It's a tight fit with Bailey and me on the ends and Ka in the middle. Bailey tells Ka not to be late for the café in the mornings like I always am. I set the alarm, and then we drift into sleep with me occasionally mumbling comments and Ka grumbling answers.

"Don't forget to feed Sundance in the morning."

"I know."

"And don't forget to hand in the English essay."

"I won't."

"Don't wear my new running shoes 'cause I need them."

She smacks me on the head to shut me up, and I don't say another word. It's exactly what I would've done.

* * *

Rama and I stand at my bedroom window, watching

Bailey and Ka walk across the square to the café. It's cold and white out, so they're bundled up.

"Well, there I go. Off on my first day of school."

"Howzit being two?"

"Strange, but okay. I feel lighter. Less burdened."

He nods like he understands. We fall silent as Dante and Vaughn join Ka and Bailey on the sidewalk. When everyone hugs hello, I feel myself growing tense. I don't like how Ka wrapped her arms around Dante's neck. She shouldn't be doing this in public. Now that Dante and Vaughn are attending school again, Michael and his brothers will know they've returned. But Ka shouldn't be too affectionate with Dante. I have no choice but to trust her to stick to the plan. She must tell Dante we performed the memory spell and that it's slow to work. No memories have emerged yet. He must be patient.

I ask Rama if Dante will detect the difference between Ka and me. He says no. All necessary vitals function in Ka, so no one will know that she is not me or that I am not her.

Dad has some appointments today, so we wait for him to leave, and then I hurry down for a quick breakfast. I pack in some energy and protein, and then we begin my first session without the distractions of school or Dante. *Or Michael.*

I squeeze my eyes shut and force Michael from my mind. I can't let the pain of our breakup continue to haunt me. I can't let myself stumble over the broken heart he left behind. And I absolutely cannot become obsessed with wondering if I will ever feel the second heartbeat or my internal I Love You again. I just can't.

We are situated on the floor and beginning our meditation when Rama asks, "What name have you given this day?"

"Enlightenment. This is a day for true enlightenment."

He nods his approval and smiles. Then he tells me to go to the bed, so I start to unwind and get up.

"No," he says, stopping me. "Continue as you are and *go to the bed*." He gives me a meaningful look, and I frown, considering.

Ah. I get it.

I wiggle back into position, close my eyes, and focus on breathing. I settle into my sitting bones and inhale deeply, filling myself up to the collarbones. Then I expel it all in a slow, easy exhalation. Rama says to search for the light within me, and I find it quickly now. I no longer need to sift through burdens and distractions. The emotional disorder has dissipated, and I easily create harmony. I can draw from the sacred spaces between my organs, cells, muscles, and ligaments. The body's consciousness becomes the spirit's. And there is nothing but light within me—pale blue light of a higher dimension. I'm overwhelmed with compassion and wisdom. Unconditional love flows through me.

Rama says to search for the white triangles, the creational geometry that will interlock and overlap before my eyes. The moment I see them, they begin to spin, and I feel a lightness of being. The spinning morphs their shape, and they bloom into a geometric flower whose pattern makes up the patterns of my cells. We are one and the same. I rotate with the effect and hear ringing in my ears.

The spaces within me vibrate, splitting my vision into a dark place of submission against a bright, dominant force. They are opposites that push and pull within me, and I feel my consciousness elevate into another dimension and then another. An aura of colors surrounds me as I climb into the fifth dimension and out again, rising beyond what is known and understood. I am bathed in a rainbow of colors—the eyes of my imagination seeing through solids, liquids, and darkness. I am beyond the conscious self, gliding through the gateway to glimpse into the spirit realm.

It's a vaguely familiar sensation, bringing to mind my time with Mom at the Borderlands. Only now, my body is in control and not left behind. I am the master of me, and I come with the knowledge to help others. I am in a field of light when Rama appears before me. We move together on the fringe of the spirit world as he continues his teachings, guiding me toward the understanding I will need—harmonic concordance. He says, *To hear the needs of lost souls, I must absorb their vibrations and be in tune with their pleas.* I nod. I do hear their sweet cries, and it sounds like confection in the air...

Chapter 23

Smells Like Teen
Spirit Walker

Rama is so proud and tells me repeatedly on our way to the barn. I am exceeding all his expectations. Not only did I move past the fifth dimension, but we walked on the fringe of the spirit world while my body levitated over the bed—something none of his former students had achieved. Most students simply sit or lay down when walking in the spirit world. He says it's a duality of consciousness to control body and spirit. I call it multitasking.

I finally heard confection in the air, so I know I'm on my way. Perhaps the next time I hear it, it'll be real souls asking for my help. And I'll be ready.

When I tell Rama I come from a long line of spirit walkers, he doesn't doubt me. "There is greatness inside you, *wahine.* I believe you were truly born to it."

I had better be because I feel like I'm giving up a big part of my life for this.

I walk into the barn, feeling pleasantly different. I am no longer a lost girl searching for my purpose. It's an unearned sense of confidence, but every part of me is aware of certain things I must accomplish now. My muscles will no longer hesitate with indecision; they'll do what is required. The body is willing to rise to the demands of the mind. Now I must make those demands.

Kanati and Chang`e are waiting for us. As far as they know, I'm skipping school to focus on my training. Still, they don't look pleased.

"What's up?" I ask, stripping down to my blue shorts and white tank top.

"There is unbalanced energy in this town," Kanati says. "We thought perhaps you would know something about that?"

"I don't even know what that means."

"A certain measure of Forgiven souls. A certain measure of guardian energy. And an excessive amount of lesser demons in the area."

Ah.

For some reason, this doesn't bother me as it would have yesterday. Instead, I consider things with vague curiosity and then start my stretches. Chang`e approaches when I shrug without answering.

"Sophia, when last we met, Kanati and I both sensed a dis-tinct…demonic fragrance on you. Burnt spices? Cloves, perhaps?"

Ordinarily, a lie would pop into my head, anything to avoid this topic and get on with the vital task of turning me into something lethal. But things have changed, and I'm with-out concern this morning. I tell them about Dante, Vaughn, and Lord Brutus sending lesser demons to turn me dark when I fulfill my Awakening.

They are not happy. They say it's common for lesser demons to sense an Awakening if they are within range. But to have them dispatched by the leader of The Order of Reapers with the specific task of turning someone dark is rare—a first, according to them. I must have done something to anger Lord Brutus. Rather than go into details, I ask them why they haven't gone after the lesser demons? After Dante or Vaughn?

They regard me with grave expressions. Chang'e says they would be grossly outnumbered; plus, they have committed their efforts to me. "But we have alerted our fellow hunters. I wouldn't be surprised to find them in Haven Hurst before the week's end."

Kanati takes my hands, turning them palms up. There is nothing new or different, but he wraps his hands tightly around mine, bringing us palm against palm. Then he closes his eyes, concentrating. I look at Rama in question, but he shrugs and tucks a flower behind his ear. A gentle tingle begins in my right palm, fluttering with gradual strength. Soon it swirls and spreads into a warm sensation. I expect to see a pale blue light seep between our hands, but there is nothing except heat. Kanati opens his eyes and releases me.

"You have made significant progress today, haven't you? Achieved the highest level without aid from the Chelsea Light? When it comes, you must be ready. You must have every skill necessary to defend yourself and the souls you will protect. So let us begin. One-to-one combat."

I recheck my palm. Still nothing, but I could sense it rising to the surface as though Kanati was pulling it. And that alone makes my adrenaline spike. *I am so close.*

Kanati assumes the position, and I eagerly prepare for his attack. He comes at me, and I block and roll away, facing him on the turn. Again, he initiates the attack, and we grapple, and I flip him onto the ground. I have no weapons, so I brace my foot against his rib cage and twist his arm back. We begin again.

Less than an hour later, we've wrestled, flipped, tossed, and slammed until we're dripping with sweat. He is pushing me to my physical limits, but I'm not fading. I feel energized and centered. Chang`e takes her turn with the cane fighting sticks, and I spin and whip them without hesitation. I envision my movements before I act on them—mind and body in complete synchronization. Then I take a short fighting stick in each hand, sparring and driving her to the edge of the bank. The war inside me has turned, and I am balanced. I am in command of me.

"Well done!" Kanati says, beating his fist against his heart and tipping his head forward in salute. Chang`e presses her hands together and gives me a slight bow, and I blossom inside. I have impressed my demon hunters *and* myself. The girl from yesterday would have been jumping and flailing the happy dance, but I have nothing but a sense of harmony within me. I am settling into this feeling with mature confidence.

They invite me to a table with strange-looking weapons spread in neat rows. They are sleek and mystical, made of silver or crystal or gold, everything glittering with supernatural light. Chang`e says I must choose the weapons that speak to me. The ones that call to my hands. Every spirit walker selects their own weapons, and the weapons will answer their call. She gives me a meaningful look, and I lock her words inside my head. *The weapons will answer my call.*

Kanati runs down the list: the *tamahaac* or tomahawk. The stryker, much like the traditional hawk but with a smaller blade. The long knife and gunstock war club of the *Okichitaw* warrior. The *francisca,* a throwing axe that looks heavy. Silver throwing stars. A *mambele,* the South African throwing dagger with a curved blade. Long-range weapons such as the hurlbat, the sling, darts, and javelin. A crystal dagger and a pair of small pistol crossbows no bigger than handguns.

I survey them all, one by one, and then back away from the table. I close my eyes and inhale deeply, bringing my mind and body to a peaceful state. Then I narrow my thoughts and call to the first weapon. Within moments, the weapon rises from the table and flies toward me. My left hand shoots up just as it slams into my palm. I grip the hilt and open my eyes. The crystal dagger. I smile in satisfaction and hand it to Chang`e to continue.

I have my mind set on two more, and they are spinning through the air before I close my eyes. The pistol crossbows land in my hands, loaded and ready to fire. I inspect them, checking their balance and weight. They are light and graceful, the grips fitting perfectly as though made for my hands.

"Are there more arrows?" I ask, looking for a secret storage compartment inside the grips.

Chang`e smiles at my naïve question. "These are holy weapons, Sophia. The arrows will come as you need them."

Holy weapons with an endless supply of ammunition. How cool is that?

"You have chosen wisely," Kanati says, but I detect a slight disappointment that the *Okichitaw* weapons didn't call to me. He is being a good sport about it because he sees that I'm happy with my weapons. They have selected me as much as I have selected them.

"Now you must learn all they can do for you," he says, guiding me to the giant tree in the center of the meadow. Chang`e straps a belt around my hips. It's lightweight, and I hardly know it's there. I have a sheath for my dagger, and two thigh holsters for the pistol crossbows. All three weapons are within easy reach, and I adjust my stance, ready for practice.

My first target is the tree, so I throw the dagger, hitting where I aim. But I'm suddenly flooded with memories of the night Steve attacked me. Throwing a knife with my left hand felt natural then as it does now. It confirms everything I've come to understand—I was made for this.

Back and forth I go, throwing and retrieving. I hit everything I aim at, but this exercise becomes daunting; fetching is no fun. It's not until ten minutes later that I notice Chang`e and Kanati grinning with their arms crossed. What I'm doing amuses them, and I think I'm missing something. I look at the dagger in my hand, considering things. Then I haul back and throw it hard, sending it to the top of the tree. It slams into the branch and nearly severs it. *The weapons will answer my call.* I raise my hand and concentrate, willing the blade to return to me. It shakes loose and backtracks into my palm. I grasp it, smiling.

"You could've told me from the start," I say. "It would've saved a lot of time."

Chang`e laughs. "Your weapons obey you, not me."

I switch to the crossbows, wheeling them around like a kid with a new plaything. Which is exactly what I am. I pelt the tree with an endless stream of tiny arrows. They are small and lethal, and I almost feel bad for the tree, but since it's supernatural and no harm is done, I go at it. Three hours pass, and I'm in love with these things.

Kanati wants me accustomed to fighting with weapons on my hips, so I take on both demon hunters for the first time in my training. With our short fighting sticks, we clack across the meadow. The grass is cool beneath my feet, and I move swiftly, keeping up without receiving too many hits. I drop the sticks and roll when they change tactics, whipping out my crossbows. Kanati runs toward my left flank, and I fire at the moving target. He flips in the air and lands on his feet while three arrows impale his fighting stick. Chang`e charges, whirling her stick overhead, so I spin away, slicing her stick with my dagger. It strikes like lightning and splits the wood in half.

And then, out of nowhere, the sky cracks open, and a man falls through. He is backward in body armor and flailing with a sword in each hand. His blond hair dances in the wind as he sails down, kicking and jabbing like a child having a tantrum. He hits the ground with a hard *whump* and lies still. Within moments, his helmet sails down and lands next to him.

I think he must be dead, but then he grunts, rolls onto his stomach, and looks up. It's Michael! He seems disoriented until his eyes lock on mine. We stare, both in shock to see the other. Finally, he opens his mouth but doesn't have time to speak. The sky cracks again, and a grotesque creature falls through, landing a few yards behind him. It's a hairless, four-legged beast with horns and a serious overbite. Thin gray skin shows a map of black veins, but on the whole, it looks juicy with ectoplasm.

Michael scrambles up and runs at the creature just as it charges—a supernatural bull, leading with its horns. Michael drops to his knees, sliding under the creature's belly. His swords cut two swaths from neck to gut before he rolls out.

The creature wails an unearthly sound. It may be mortally wounded, but it's big and will take time to drop. Another crack from the sky produces two more like Michael, who crash down in body armor and flailing swords. A man and woman hit the ground and roll over. All three pounce on the beast, driving their swords in deep. It screams and claws the earth but eventually stumbles, collapsing onto its horrendous snout. I watch calmly, but my heart is a jackhammer. The beast reminds me of the gargoyles at the haunted mansion, only a thousand times worse.

Michael and the others climb to their feet, panting. They look exhausted, worn, bloody, and cut to shreds. And yet, their amazing beauty shines through—sharp cheekbones and chiseled jawlines, eyes that sparkle with mystical light. Angels are unmistakable, even dripping with blood and glaring at me.

I can't read Michael's expression. Nor can I feel his heartbeat inside my chest. So I don't panic—yet. He could be too far away. Not that it matters because I love Michael with or without the second heartbeat.

Even so, I can't bear the idea of never feeling his heart beating inside me again. But what if he can't feel *his* second heartbeat? Will he know something has changed in me? Will he think our unique connection has simply run its course? Will he think it means I don't love him? *Please don't let him think that!*

Michael's eyes drop to my weapons, and I hold my breath. What does he think? Does he finally approve? Will he tug on my heart to let me know? Will I feel it?

Two warriors stroll into the meadow from a copse of trees. They are dressed in black and gold armor, so I assume they are Halo Masters. Kanati lifts a hand in greeting, and the men make their way over to us. This must be Michael's Halo training, but why does he look so angry? The others are relaxed, discussing the kill. Michael is still coiled for a fight.

It's me. Michael is still upset with me. He doesn't think I belong here.

Kanati greets the men as Camael and Sachiel. To my surprise, Rama pulls himself from the flowerbed and joins them. I stand aside while they talk with their indoor voices. I can barely hear them.

Camael says, "How are things progressing?" and Rama says, "We're almost there."

I look over. *They're talking about me? The Halo Masters know about me?*

The one called Sachiel breaks from the others and comes over. He asks if I remember him from the Borderlands, and a light goes on.

"Oh, yes! I mean, I don't remember you specifically, but yes, I remember seeing a band of warriors. That was you?"

He laughs warmly and nods. He seems pleased that

I remember. But I can't share his enthusiasm because I see Michael over Sachiel's shoulder, pacing like a caged animal. He's watching us and frowning as though confused by our friendly conversation.

"And you weren't afraid of us then, were you?" Sachiel continues, pulling my attention from Michael.

I cock my head in question. "No, I never felt afraid of you guys. Should I have been?"

"No. Definitely not. I'm glad you weren't afraid. It's a good sign—the warrior in you recognized the warrior in us. A sign of trust. We sensed a strong light within you and were curious to see—" He cuts himself off, and I think he wants to say more but knows he can't. Or shouldn't. He lowers his eyes and then sheepishly offers his hand. "Welcome to the family." We shake hands, but he quickly pulls away like he's embarrassed or hesitant to touch me. As though he's not allowed. It's weird, but I smile anyway and thank him for the welcome. It means a lot. He says he understands that I'll be ready soon.

"I hope so," I say, glancing at Michael. The other candidates join him and walk over. "Are the Winter Trials winding down, too?"

"Just finishing. We have our warriors." Sachiel turns, and we watch them approach. Michael looks anywhere but at me. When he is within range, my second heartbeat springs to life, and I bite into my smile.

He's still here!

Sachiel looks sharply at me, so I avert my eyes and deaden my bursting emotions. It's difficult because my thoughts are running rampant—*I want to know what Michael feels, what he thinks. I have to go to my training to calm down. It takes a moment before Sachiel loses interest and moves back to Rama and Camael.*

I recognize the expression on Michael's face; he is deliberately masking his feelings, just like I am. Just like he does when we're together and *not* together in a crowd. The more he pretends not to feel anything, the more I know he does.

While the Masters chat about an official ceremony at the end of the trials, Michael's eyes wander around the ground and then slowly climb up my legs. He analyzes the crossbows in my thigh holsters and the crystal dagger in my hand. I see a faint smile tug at his lips before his eyes slowly lift to mine—and I know. He approves. Whether he wants to or not, Michael approves.

I wait patiently, hoping he'll say something to show he has changed his mind, that he accepts my calling and that we can fix this. We can fix us.

I feel a gentle tug at my heart and brace myself for two more. *Please let there be two more! I brush aside all my worry and planning and doing to allow my love for Michael to rise to the surface. It is front and center, unfolding as naturally as breathing. I want him to sense my love and nothing else. In this moment, there is nothing so important. Our love is strong enough to bend around our needs—our callings. But it will take both of us to hang on.*

We stare without speaking, but I know Michael can sense my love; I see it reflected in his pale blue eyes. He looks drowsy with it, as though he is swimming in my love, *drowning* in it. I have given him more than he can absorb, and he blinks heavily, slowly.

Please, Michael, tell me you'll come back. Please hang on. Don't let me go.

There is another faint tug, and then...Michael sighs, turns, and walks away.

Chapter 24
Tea with Demons

Rama and I have two more positive sessions, but he is grow-ing concerned. I've entered the rainbow aura, the pinnacle of my transcendence. And yet, I haven't tapped into something called *Kundalini*—the full release of my spiritual energy.

I worry that I've lost my focus after seeing Michael. There was so much love in his eyes, and I felt my second heart-beat, but he didn't reach out; he didn't come to my room that night. He didn't say he still loves me, and I'm reeling from the loss all over again. Michael and I were a couple before and should have worked out our differences together. But now I worry that he has made a couple's decision on his own—*he* has decided our lives are too incompatible to work. So for two days, I've struggled to regain my mental footing.

Although I've achieved a great deal, Rama says I must master the last step in the third trial—the empowerment of the physical form. Without this, I won't complete my Awakening. It's that crucial.

Kundalini, or "the coiled-up one," is the essence of my spiritual energy. It's coiled inside the deepest part of me, wait-ing for release. Once activated, it must join the spirit through an organic journey, rising and passing through every chamber of my spine in a process called *Sushumna*.

As my spiritual energy drifts upward, it opens the capacity to all intangible things: compassion, commitment, strength, confidence, and courage. It is a vital threshold I must pass through. The body is the temple of the consciousness, and no obstructions can remain in the consciousness. The mystery of myself is not from discovery but from the release of those primordial obstructions: desire and fear. As they are released from consciousness, no obstructions remain, and the body—the temple—drops off to complete the true empowerment of the physical form. *This* is the Awakening of all things possible.

"You have released the desire within you, Sophia. It is no longer a device of service but integrated within you. So, what is this *fear* you hang on to? What has you so afraid that you remain tightly coiled within yourself?"

I open my eyes and look at Rama seated across from me. He speaks from his meditative state through his Ascended Master voice.

The answer is ready on my tongue. It came without hesitation, but I'm ashamed to say it aloud. *I am afraid to kill. I am afraid of the beasts that Michael and the warriors fight. I am afraid to fail. I am afraid of the dark side that Dante brings out, and I am forever afraid of what is truly inside me.*

I stare into my lap. My hands are as tightly coiled as I imagine my spiritual energy to be. I'm furious with myself. I know I want this. I want to be a spirit walker, but I'm afraid to release the familiarity of my fear. We've been together for so long that I would feel naked without it. To surrender doesn't feel like freedom but subjugation, a terrible weakness.

Rama opens his eyes and leans back on his hands. He regards me thoughtfully and then nods. "Don't fret, *wahine*. It's not uncommon to flounder at the end of the ride. But the spirit is like steel. It's gotta be tempered with fire. And nothing takes it to the macks like spiritual warfare. Some people need slaps upside the head to get their courage. Some need to take tea with demons."

"Tea with demons?"

"Face your fears. You dig?"

"Uh-huh." I think about *La Croix*. It was crawling with evil, and I was petrified. But I felt safe because of Dante. When I watched him kill to protect me, I was scared but also excited. The fact that I felt safe with a demon is more frightening than all my primordial fears combined.

Rama tells me there is plenty of time and that I shouldn't worry. I should never rush this part of the process. It's too critical. My courage will come when all is ready within me.

"In the meantime," he says, standing up. "I've got something for you." He goes to the rucksack he's taken to carrying around and withdraws a long piece of cloth. *He lays it on the bed and gently unrolls it like an artist unraveling cherished brushes. Or a chef opening an assortment of favorite knives. Rama displays a collection of beautiful long braids. There is pride in his eyes and respect in his touch as he gently re*arranges them as though they are delicate and sacred. As though they are more than what they appear.

There are varying shades of blondish/brown that closely

matches my hair. He offers these to each student when they reach the rainbow state.

"Braiding hair is an ancient and spiritual process, *wahine*. The flow of hair has its own harmony, whereas braiding brings a sense of oneness to life. A oneness of thoughts. Of knowing. Unifying strands are like unifying thoughts. You dig? Good, now take as many as you like. As many that call to you." He bows out of the space, giving me a moment to myself.

I look them over, unable to find much difference between them. And yet, I feel drawn to four in the middle and one on each end. I gently gather them with the same reverence as Rama did while his face breaks into a huge grin. He takes them from me and lifts them like an offering to the light shade over our heads. He mumbles something and then hands them back. After a firm nod of satisfaction, he guides me into my desk chair, and we look at each other in the mirror. My hair has gotten so long it nearly reaches my waist, so he lifts it and lays it across the back of the chair. Then he eases a comb through it like a shy stylist.

"Feel the oneness of thought," he says, dragging the comb in and out again. "Feel the individuality of you and your spirit."

He continues for a while until he is satisfied with the process. Satisfied that I have complete calmness and oneness. Then he sets the comb aside, slowly takes one braid at a time, and uses some supernatural Ascended Master hairstyling technique to bond each braid to my natural hair. This holy act produces a tingling current across my scalp. Two braids are fused on each side of my head and one down the back.

"These I give with love to my *lani wahine*. My heavenly girl. And this one I accept with love, to bond with my *lani wahine*." He adds the last braid to his collection, fusing it behind his right ear, where it flows with his windblown hair. His assortment of colorful braids ranges from soft oranges, greens, reds, yellows, and pinks. What I once thought of as an interesting hairstyle I now understand to be something far better. His braids symbolize unity with each of his students—a bond I can feel in my bones. But my braid seems plain and unnoticeable by comparison.

Rama places his hands on my shoulders with a look that says *there is one more thing*. So I wait and watch him in the mirror. And then the braids in my hair and the one in his gradually begin to glow. At first, they appear as bright as lightning but quickly settle into what he calls their *lani* color—heavenly color. My *lani* color is indigo.

My eyes balloon with wonder. The braids I originally chose matched my hair, but their spiritual color has risen from somewhere inside me. Of all the options, Rama says I have chosen a very unique color.

"But I *didn't* choose this color. I didn't choose *any* color."

"You did. On some level. They spoke to you through your subconscious." He squints in thought, watching me run my fingers along a braid. "Indigo mean anything special to you?"

I drop my hand and quickly shake my head. No way I'm telling him how Michael's eyes turn this exact color when he kisses me.

Instead, I go to the practicalities of things now that I have to worry about more than just myself. "What about Ka? Won't people see the difference in us if I wear these?"

Rama says the braids will match my normal hair color until I'm infused with spiritual energy. Then their true colors will ignite. Basically, there is nothing to worry about.

Even now, the indigo is returning to blondish/brown. But the connection remains, making me suddenly feel sentimental about this bond with my Ascended Master. So I stand on my tiptoes to kiss him on the cheek.

"Thank you. I won't let you down. Promise."

* * *

The weekend is finally here, and it's the last night of Winter Carnival, time for the formal dance. Ka and I have been coming and going on different schedules, so she brings me up to speed with myself. My finals went well. My grades have been successfully resuscitated, and all college applications are in the mail, even though she was disappointed with my school selections. She believes we should've aimed higher.

She also took that follow-up meeting with the school counselor and thwarted any further concerns on that end. But she is worried about something that has plagued her for days.

"It's this feeling that I'm being watched. I mean, beyond the lesser demons pacing on the rooftops. They can't sense anything 'cause you don't have the Chelsea Light yet, but I'd swear, Sophia, someone is watching me. I feel it when I walk through the square, and it makes my skin crawl."

"Someone like who?" I ask, wrangling into a new pair

of jeans. Ka proved to be a handy personal shopper as well as a doer of all things academic and domestic. So we no longer squabble over the "good" pair of jeans.

"Someone from the spirit world. And not just one person but a few. I sense them lower to the ground. Lurking."

"It's not Dante?"

"Of course not." She laughs and opens a bottle of nail polish to touch up her toes. "I can sense Dante a mile away."

I whirl around. "What?" I snap, and she cringes.

"Jeez, Louise. It's just a figure of speech."

"But you can sense when he's around?"

She gives me a patronizing look. "You don't have to keep testing me, you know? I get it. And, of course, I can sense when he's around. It's just intuition or something, right? Isn't that what you feel?"

I turn away before she can read my face. I don't sense when Dante is around. He is forever sneaking up on me.

Because my hair has gotten so long, I gather a thin section around my face and clip it to the back of my head. The four braids on either side hang freely with the rest of my hair.

"He's so hot," Ka continues, blowing on her toenails.

"He's from Hell. They're all hot."

"Don't be obtuse. I mean, seriously hot. Especially when he does that lazy sideways grin. Mmm. He asked me to this dance thingy, but I had to tell him I was going with someone else. He didn't like it."

"Too bad, 'cause I'm not—I mean—*you're* not going with him."

"That's what I told him. But he was antsy all day. Like he was dying to tell me a secret but kept changing his mind. Oh, that reminds me. He invited me out to his place."

"What? When? What did you say?" This is unexpected, and I think maybe I need to keep an eye on her. Me. Whatever.

She gives me the pouty look that I perfected a while back when I was weaseling something out of Dad. "Well, I said I would go. After I take photos and the carnival dies down. I'll have some time before JD gets here. You still want me to go to the dance, right?"

I move into the closet, giving myself time to think. I change shirts and consider. *Why would Dante invite me to the mansion? And tonight of all nights? He knows the dance is tonight, so what is he up to?*

"Has he asked about any past life memories?"

She scoffs. "Only every freaking day. I finally told him I remembered a field with red poppies and white and yellow broom flowers. I said there was a low rock wall and a brook running alongside it."

I gape at her.

"What?" she asks. "That's what we remember, right?"

I think back to the night of the spell when Rama spoke of Fields of Peace. That was the vision that came to mind, but where had it come from? It *had* seemed familiar.

Ka comes over and holds my shoulders. "You look pale. You gonna faint?"

I turn away because it gives me the heebie-jeebies standing so close to myself. "Where'd you get that memory?" I ask.

"From that night in the haunted mansion. The music box." She picks up the box Dante left on my desk and flips it open. It starts the familiar tinkling tune while I search for the memory. There is it, just as Ka described. I don't like that she made the connection before I did.

"You can't go to Dante's tonight," I say, snapping the box shut. I drop it in a drawer and close it. "And please don't listen to that anymore. In case you've forgotten, I don't want any memories from Dante's past life."

"You're gonna break his heart all over again."

"Don't care."

She flops onto the bed and regards me curiously, probably because she knows I don't want to hurt Dante and I'm stubborn about my mission. "Are we sure about that?" she asks with a note of caution.

"I'll take photos of the carnival tonight. You can stay here and rest up for the dance. If Dad gets home before I do—"

"I know. I know. Don't let him hear me getting ready. I've kinda got this down."

* * *

I'm bundled in the new Slovak clothes Ka selected for the occasion: furry *valenki* to warm my feet and a vintage, brown suede coat with thick wool lining. It's embroidered with red, white, and yellow flowers on a green vine. The buttonholes are large, leather loops with wooden toggles for buttons that look like spikes. It's über warm.

I walk into the town square or the North Pole. Same diff. The place is packed with people in faux fur and various boots.

Everyone who is anyone is here. I heard a senator and several celebrities were expected.

All around the square, troika sleighs glide over snow-packed streets, horses trotting and bells jingling. Giant Hula-hoops of neon yellow, red, green, and orange decorate the trees. The ice palace is illuminated with exotic towers clustered like a family photo of onion-shaped domes. They radiate all the colors of the rainbow. Across the square is our version of Saint Sophia's Cathedral, which I admit is pretty incredible. The ice turrets have red and green stripes with swirling gold tops like soft-serve ice cream. The cheerful guards posted out front are old-world Santas and nesting dolls. A folk music ensemble is stuffed into the gazebo, playing a heart-pounding song. Limber dancers are bouncing, squatting, and kicking in the traditional *kozachok* dance. It makes my knees hurt just watching. So I frame up and take photos of everything.

I eventually maneuver through the crystal tree forest relocated from the gym. I'm looking for Bailey, but when I exit the other side, I crash into Duffy. He came barreling through the *trebuchet* snowball launchers, where he disrupted competition without apology. He didn't even acknowledge hitting me.

"Hey!" I say, but when he looks back, his face has a dark scowl that worries me.

"Better watch yourself, Sophia. It's almost time."

"What?" I ask, but he doesn't explain. Instead, he shoves through the crowd and disappears. I can't figure out what's gotten into him lately.

"Comrade tchotchke!" Bailey cries, clomping over in

furry Chewbacca boots. She's clutching a mug of something hot and steamy. The peppermint stick suggests it's the café's version of a white Russian mocktail. I'm so happy to see Bailey because I haven't seen her since the night we made Ka. I throw my arms around her.

"Merry Christmas, comrade!"

We hug, and I whisper that it's the *real* me, and then she raises her mug and says, "Mazel tov!"

She takes a sip and offers it to me, but I shake my head. I glance along the rooftops, where some of the lesser demons are pacing. Others are sitting and dangling their legs over the roof-line. Some are laughing and pointing at the pathetic humans romping in the snow. I suppose they're bored because comrade tchotchke is a little slow in the *Kundalini* department.

"They still there?" Bailey asks, looking up. "I can't see them, but DoOver says they're always there."

"DoOver?" I give her a look, and she laughs.

"She didn't like me calling her Comrade KaKa, so..." She shrugs.

I tell her not to worry about the lesser demons. They don't want anyone but me. And then I mention Duffy's bizarre behavior.

"*Oy vey.*" She sighs. "He's been acting so weird lately. And not just around me. I caught him following DoOver around the square the other day. Like he was stalking her. I told him that if he didn't cut it out, he was gonna have a very Police Navidad. *Durachit.*"

I match this information to what Ka said—she felt more

than one pair of supernatural eyes on her. Not human.

Hmm. Could she be mistaken? It's probably the lesser demons, right?

It's cold, so Bailey and I need to keep moving. We stroll around for a while, just taking in the sights and snapping photos. And sure enough, I start feeling like I'm being watched, too. No one in the crowd is paying attention to us, and the lesser demons are starting to fight amongst themselves.

Then why do I feel eyes on me?

Bailey is going on about what Ka has been up to at school. "Spending a lot of quality time with Dante. He's under the impression that Rama cast the memory spell. So he's expecting you, or DoOver, to remember your past life."

"I know."

"No, Soph. I don't think you do. Now, don't take this wrong, but you're not one to accessorize with a Scarlet Letter, so I'm gonna tell it straight. Your DoOver got all your sexual chutzpah. Like, she's not acquainted with Dear Prudence. She and Dante have been sneaking around for some private groping. I even caught them in the girls' bathroom. And once in his Escalade."

Crap!

Ka couldn't have gone all the way because I would know, right?

"DoOver doesn't talk to JD, so he asked me if he was still your date for the dance. I told him yeah, but…"

"Yes. I am. I mean, Ka is going with him. I need her to be at the dance so I can be elsewhere."

Or maybe just invisible. I can't let myself think about that romantic night at the waterfall when Michael asked me to the dance. I really wanted to dance with him, and now everything is ruined.

My throat tightens into a hard knot, and my eyes sting. The pain is fresh all over again, as though everything fell apart only yesterday. I blink back tears and swallow the knot, so it returns to the pit in my stomach, where it's been festering for weeks.

Bailey and I round the ice palace and enter a tunnel with looming ice sculptures. They are massive and beastly, probably a species of Frost Giants or White Walkers—very low on the evolutionary chain. The backlighting throws eerie shadows across their faces, giving me the creepy shivers—and something more. The sensation of being watched. Again. Which makes no sense because Bailey and I are alone.

Thanks to Ka, I'm becoming paranoid.

Bailey is jabbering and oblivious, so I loop my arm through hers and guide her out. I tell her that Ka will go to the dance with JD while I chat with Dante.

I never wanted to set foot back in the mansion, but I have to undo some of the damage Ka has done. She's taken my relationship with Dante in the wrong direction. I know he can be charming and seductive, and I should've warned her. I'll put a stop to it tonight.

And just like that, I am having tea with demons.

* * *

Ka bought herself a stunning red-velvet gown with a white fur wrap—something strongly resembling Judy Garland in "Meet Me in St. Louis." It was a curious choice until I remembered Ka and Dad have been waxing nostalgic with a smorgasbord of Christmas movies lately.

Her hair is piled in a lovely loose bun with tendrils framing her face, and I stare in open admiration. She has far better fashion sense than I ever did—*do*.

When she's finally ready, we stand in the middle of the room, and I take her hands. "Be careful," I say earnestly. "But have fun. JD is a nice guy, so go easy on him." We laugh and sound exactly the same. I'm almost envious, seeing her in a gorgeous gown while I'm wearing black pants, boots, and a tight black turtleneck. I could be robbing a bank, and she could be wearing a crown.

"You be careful, too," she says as we hug good-bye.

With JD waiting downstairs, she grabs her wrap and slips out the door. I listen from the hallway; there are lots of compliments and nervous laughter from the foyer. I imagine they are posing before Dad's camera, so I grab my coat, sneak out the bedroom window, and drop down the back of the house. Dad thinks I left my jeep parked at Bailey's, but it's really on the next block. I'm shivering by the time I climb in, so I blast the heater and head to the mansion. The drive seems darker than I remember. Probably because Haven Hurst is sucking up every kilowatt of electricity in the tri-state area. I wouldn't be surprised if the Winter Carnival could be seen from space.

It begins to snow as I turn down the long, narrow road to the mansion. The looming forest is white, so anything fresh settles on top and disappears. I roll into the circular drive, noticing Dante's Lamborghini and Wolfgang's Bugatti Veyron have been replaced by the black Escalade. This brings a small measure of comfort, but I have no credible verification that

Wolfgang hasn't resurfaced. Only Dante's word.

The mansion rises three stories above me, but only the bottom floor shows signs of life with glowing windows. Heat radiates ten feet deep around the perimeter, which is bone dry because the snow never stood a chance. I glance around as my nerves spring to life. I'm on alert even knowing Wolfgang isn't here.

I knock softly and barely lower my hand before Dante sweeps the door open, beaming at me. *"Buon Natale, cara mia!"*

His overexcitement makes me suspicious, and I give him a perturbed look. But then I remember how friendly Ka has been, how intimate they've been, so I adjust my attitude. I haven't spent any time with Dante since *La Croix*, so I'm taken aback by the change in him. His face is alive with eagerness and hope. He seems to have reversed aging—looking younger and energetic with a lightness to him. He is no longer burdened by the heaviness of his situation. There is brightness in his eyes. And love. Yes, I have to admit that Dante looks good in love.

I try to keep this from distracting me—from devastating me. Ka was right when she questioned my feelings for him. I don't want to hurt Dante. It's not his fault I fell in love with Michael. It's not his fault I'm called to be a spirit walker. And it's not his fault I'm willing to do anything and everything to stop him from Taking me to Hell. Perhaps the best things I can offer him are pleasant memories from his time here before I become a spirit walker and he returns to Hell without me.

"Merry Christmas to you, too, Dante!" I smile wide, hoping to match his enthusiasm.

He kisses both of my hands and pulls me inside. He

draws me into a hug, and I stiffen on reflex. Then I soften and wrap myself around him, hugging him as though it's for the last time. I want him to feel everything I feel for him, everything he imagines I feel. I'm surprised by the emotions rising in me, as though I'll miss him when he's gone. I want Dante to be happy. But mostly, I want him to be happy without me. And that's why I feel stupid tears gathering in my eyes.

"I am so glad you came," he whispers, stroking my head. He starts to withdraw, but I need a moment to collect myself, so I cling to him. He tightens his arms, and I feel him smiling against my cheek. I squeeze my eyes shut and force myself to think about what he truly is and how he wants to kill me. I need anger to replace these idiotic, sentimental feelings for him.

Finally, I suck in a deep breath and release him. He spreads my arms, grinning and looking me over. He seems pleased but slightly disappointed, as though I forgot something.

Crap, was I supposed to bring a Christmas gift?

"I, um, I can only stay a minute," I say, stepping away before he says something only Ka would understand. I glance around for anything nefarious lurking in the shadows, like Wolfgang. But there is only Vaughn, peeking around a high-backed chair before the blazing fireplace.

"Hey, Sophia! Come on in. Get comfy." He is full of holiday cheer, so I move mechanically across the room, feeling like an unassuming rook in a chess match. Dante may be in love, but he has made his next move by inviting me here. And I haven't been able to identify his strategy yet.

Dante joins me, sliding his hot hand up my shirt to rest

against the small of my back. It's such an unexpected touch that I twitch and look at him. His easy, playful grin brings a flutter of nerves to my stomach, and I wonder how intimate he's been with Ka. I should have asked her for details. I should have insisted that she keep her knees together. Not that I think they've gone that far.

Christ, I feel like I'm flying blind here.

"Care for a drink?" Vaughn asks, standing and gesturing toward a sideboard with crystal decanters. He's awfully polite for the Demon of Affliction. I don't want anything, but I use it as an excuse to step away from Dante and his hot hand.

I look things over, then shrug. "Actually, I probably shouldn't. Thanks anyway." They are watching me, so I cross my arms and look around. No holiday trimmings. No tree. "So, why are you guys in such a good mood? Dine and ditch somewhere?" I hope a joke might settle my nerves.

Dante doesn't get it, but Vaughn says, "More like cut and run." He laughs but then sees my smile drop. "Hey, that was a joke. I haven't…you know…"

"Oh, yeah. Sure. I know." I blink and look away. This is getting awkward fast, and I'm not sure how much longer I can fool them. "So, like I said, I can't stay long. You know I'm going to the dance with JD, so…"

"Yes. I remember." Dante's face grows dark, and I remind him that I accepted the invitation before he returned to Haven Hurst. He seems to understand but is not happy about it. He guides me to the fireplace. Along with the blazing heat, I feel his agitation. Something is bothering him, but he is trying to conceal it.

"Before you spend the evening with that boy, I wanted to show my appreciation for what you did."

Crap. What does that mean?

I scramble to remember everything Ka told me. And then everything she might *not* have told me. Or maybe there was something Bailey said...

While I am deliberating, Dante is fidgeting with his left arm like he did the first night in my bedroom. His chain tattoo must be bothering him again.

"I very much enjoyed your first memories, Sophia. And I'm looking forward to hearing more."

I internally sag with relief. It was just the field of flowers.

"And so, I thought perhaps I could do you a favor. To continue the *quid pro quo* you spoke of?" I step back because I am not as trusting as Ka, but Dante takes my hands again. I feel his anxiety building. He's up to something.

"I would like to help advance your training," he says simply. "Vaughn has located some *entities of a certain nature* that could help you prepare."

I take a moment to catch up. So now that Dante believes my memories are returning, he is willing to help with my Awakening? There is something fishy about this, but I'm willing to hear more.

"Monster demons?" I say, thinking of the creature Michael and his fellow candidates destroyed in the barn. It took three of them to bring it down, so I'm hoping Dante has something a little less gigantic in mind.

"They won't be too horrific. But, Sophia, if you truly

want to learn to defend yourself, you must face your enemies. And I say it should be sooner rather than later."

I couldn't agree more, but this isn't what I had in mind by coming here tonight. My version of *tea with demons* meant covertly laying down some ground rules in this sham of a rom-com between Dante and Ka. I hadn't anticipated getting help to kill *entities of a certain nature* from notorious Demon Knights.

That being said, I can see the wisdom in it. Dante is right, as is Rama, who believes the only way to uncoil my spiritual energy is to face my fears head-on.

The moment I nod, Dante breaks into a smile. Then he cups my face and kisses me hard on the mouth. I'm stunned. But there's no time to react because he turns away, pulling me with him. My mind stumbles over the significance of such a kiss. Dante is no longer trying to use his supernatural abilities to administer the kiss of death and Take me below like before. Something more important made him change his initial plans, and that can't be good.

We march down a long hallway through a vast unused kitchen to the back door where Vaughn waits. I'm shocked to see him there. *Fast little bugger.*

He looks me up and down and says, "What do you have?" and I say, "Huh?"

"She has no weapons," Dante says abruptly, and I understand his earlier disappointment. I came unarmed.

Neither one is happy about my lack of munitions, so Vaughn pulls a long knife and a large dagger from his boots. He shoves them into my hands. They are huge and heavy. Then he opens the back door, and we all walk onto the porch.

I'm wearing the new black peacoat that Ka thought I would like. I shiver because it's not nearly warm enough; I didn't expect to be outside tonight.

Dante hits the porch lights, illuminating a sea of whiteness across the yard. The falling snowflakes seem larger under the lights, and it's nearly blinding.

We take a path where someone else has gone before the last snowfall. The footprints lead us to the edge of the forest, where disheveled gray headstones rise out of the snow like rotten teeth. Dante tells me this is the cemetery that was moved from the town square several hundred years ago. I am to kill anything that rises from the graves.

"Are you serious? I thought maybe one of the lesser demons in town could—"

"You cannot make a permanent kill, and that would only risk one of them telling the horde who you are. No. I don't think so. You will learn to kill whatever is in front of you. The face hardly matters." He nods to Vaughn, who rears back and throws one of his smaller daggers at a cockeyed headstone.

The blade impales the small space between the names CHESTER and BROWN. Nothing happens at first, but then the headstone gradually splits and falls apart. Smoke rolls up the fissure, where a man claws his way out. He is stooped and demented with long raptor-like talons instead of fingers. Shredded, gray skin hangs loose on the bones. A bald, hideous head is without lips, showing black gums with jagged teeth. There is no nose left, only two holes that leak black liquid. Red unnatural eyes peer around.

Poor Chester Brown has been demonized for my benefit, but I have no room for pity. I'm freaked beyond words and flail backward in the snow. Chester's head swivels, and his eyes lock on me—the one who must have disturbed his death. He comes at me, stomping through the snow. He's faster than I expect, so I call out for Dante, but he and Vaughn are suddenly back at the mansion, watching from a distance.

Chester swings a stiff arm, knocking me to the ground. I'm still shocked by the nightmare I walked into and didn't see it coming. When he claws at my legs, I instinctively roll away, barely escaping. But I left the knife in the snow, so I scramble up, clutching the dagger with both hands. I'm scared, shaking, and forgetting everything I learned.

Chester comes at me again, and I take an awkward swipe, connecting with his left arm. It breaks off at the elbow, spinning away and spitting black blood across the snow. He's not deterred but stomps onward as I scramble and fall. I hear a zipping sound, followed by the crack of stone. Another dagger splits another headstone, and more smoke rises. This is followed by another headstone falling apart and then another. Vaughn is releasing too many corpses when I haven't destroyed the first one.

Chester swings his remaining arm, but I dive behind an upright headstone. Beyond Chester is a grotesque creature lumbering toward me. It's naked and slimy, with yellowish-green skin stretched over its bones. It has no visible ears but twitches and jerks as though listening for sounds. This makes its bulging eyes rattle in its skull. The creature rakes the air and throws itself around.

More demonic dead come at me—all hideous and spastic.

They have humped backs, skeletal wings, or dangerous claws instead of hands—a study in grotesque and deformity. I slash and run, desperate to remember my training. What little courage I have is enough to destroy the yellowish-green one and another demon that is blind altogether. Chester tears off the short stump of his left arm and hits me in the shoulder. I fly backward and land hard in the snow, stunned. I have no weapon left, so the demons pounce, and I wrap my arms over my head and scream.

I brace myself for the pain but feel nothing. No claws or bones beating me. No jagged teeth piercing my skin. I take a moment, then lower my arms.

Armaros stands over me, that frosty dude I met at the Borderlands with Mom. He is a towering gray and white figure, with shoulder-length blond hair and two small braids in his beard. He is armed like an ancient knight. Although he has a timeless and compassionate quality to his face, he is sporting a deep scowl just now.

"What is going on here?" he bellows down at me. I grimace and gingerly climb to my feet. Dante and Vaughn appear behind Armaros with grim expressions. When I don't answer, Armaros swings around, shouting at Dante. "You have risked her life for a game!"

"It was no game, I assure you," Dante says evenly. "Sophia must learn to defend herself if—"

"That is not your concern!" Armaros charges, leveling his sword at Dante. "You have overstepped your bounds, Demon Knight. You have conjured the dead for your amusement and nearly gotten her killed!"

"Hey! Wait just a damned minute!" I yell, stepping between them.

Armaros startles at my outburst or perhaps at what I've said. Maybe he expected tears? Who knows, but I'm fuming. I push his sword down with my fingertips and stare defiantly up at him.

"Dante and Vaughn are helping me learn to defend myself. And besides, why is this any of *your* business? And *where* do you come from? Are you just floating out there? Loitering in the spirit world? Popping in whenever? Wherever? Why are you watching me?" I've had enough of being watched like prey. Even though I don't sense an ounce of evil in him, I'm at my wit's end with this guy.

"Your mother asked that I keep watch over you, Sophia." His voice is gentle and devastating to my anger. I implode at the mention of Mom. I remember how she smiled at Armaros when she introduced us. Whoever he is up there, Armaros is someone Mom trusts.

Dante and Vaughn are stunned that I've spoken to Armaros like a spoiled brat, and I feel ashamed, mainly because of Mom's involvement.

"Please tell Mom I can't do this if everyone keeps trying to protect me. Dante and Vaughn were only helping me test what I've learned."

"Is this true? You are helping her complete the trials?" Armaros asks. Vaughn marches over and retrieves his daggers from the headstones.

"Yeah. But she ain't gonna ring hell's bells, I can tell you that much," he grumbles.

Dante is quiet, and I feel I've disappointed him. Again. I've disappointed everyone. Rama said I should face my fears. I did. And they kicked my butt.

Chapter 25

Dante

Dante gulped down his drink and then hurled the tumbler into the fireplace, shattering the glass. It was the last of five he'd destroyed, and Vaughn handed him another. Alcohol was liquid fire to demons and helped fuel their rage. Dante wanted the fire, wanted the rage burning in his gut. He was furious that Armaros had interfered again, but honestly, he was more furious that Sophia had failed. She wasn't ready to kill or defend herself. And she fled without trying again.

Not that Armaros would have allowed it. His presence was concerning, and Dante hadn't accepted his explanation for watching over Sophia as easily as she had. Sophia didn't know his true nature or that it was unusual for her mother—a common spiritual entity—to ask a Grigori for help. The real mystery lay with the infamous Grigori—why had he agreed? Armaros must have his own agenda, and if time allowed, Dante would find the answer.

Time. Something he had far too little of at the moment.

"It's still itching," Vaughn said, scratching his green chain tattoo. Not that he was complaining; his demon loved the irritation, but it wasn't close to satisfying his urges. It was a curious thing at best, and he lifted his sleeve to inspect it. "Does yours feel like it's shifting under the skin?"

Dante clenched his teeth and nodded. For the past few days, his tattoo tether had been writhing as though coming to life. A sign their time was running out.

"Where is the underling?" Dante asked, just as Santiago walked in from the game room. He was sweating from a twenty-four-hour nonstop gaming tournament.

"Right here," he said, thumbing his phone. "Just got a text from Wexler. Wolfgang passed through the gate three days ago."

"What!" Dante yelled, his eyes flaring yellow and black. He wanted to rip something apart. "Three days ago! He could've killed Sophia without us knowing he was here!" He started after the kid, but Vaughn grabbed him.

"Hey, it's not his fault. Intel comes when it comes. You know that. Besides, Sophia was just here. Wolfgang hasn't gotten to her. He might not even be in Haven Hurst yet."

"*We* made it here in less than three days," Dante reminded him. He pushed Vaughn away and stared into the fire, seething. "No, Wolfgang is here. And if I know him, he's been watching her, biding his time until he can kill her the moment she completes her Awakening."

"Yeah, well, he's not famous for his patience," Vaughn muttered. It was a joke, but he knew it was no laughing matter.

Dante grunted his agreement, suddenly feeling that he'd been foolish long enough—attending school just to keep an eye on Sophia. He loved that a memory had risen from the ashes and even noticed the change in her. How could he not notice her affection and undivided attention? It was a long time coming, and he had only wanted to enjoy it for a while. But now the risks were too high. Sophia was not ready to kill Wolfgang. And Dante's only recourse was to take her to Hell with him. Now. Before time ran out and he was dragged back down without her.

He left the fireplace and marched across the great room, heading toward the giant staircase.

"Where are you going?" Vaughn yelled, hard on his heels.

Dante paused halfway up. "I am changing into something more appropriate for a formal dance."

"Now?" Vaughn bellowed.

"Sophia is with that boy, and I mean to cut in on their dance."

"And then what? Boogie till the cows come home? You've got mad timing, Dante."

"Timing is the mad device pushing me right now. We will be yanked down any minute, and you know it. But I plan to be prepared. I will dance with Sophia in my arms, and when the tether is activated, it will pull *both* of us below."

"And what about Wolfgang?"

Dante's eyes narrowed. "If I spare a moment hunting Wolfgang now, as I am sure Lord Brutus would prefer, I will lose Sophia. Again. But if I can bring her to Hell without killing her, the other members of The Order will be more forgiving. Imagine their delight in having a future spirit walker safely tucked away in Hell?"

"You wanna take Sophia to Hell and *then* finish her

Awakening? Turn her dark in private so she'll bond to you indefinitely?"

Dante smiled. "And no one need kill her for her Chelsea Light. She will transfer it to The Order because I will ask her to. They may use its power however it suits them. And it will no longer concern Sophia or me. She will have her memories back, and we will be together. As we should be."

"Looks like you'll need a wingman," Vaughn said, starting up the staircase. "If Lord Brutus's spy tries to stop you from dancing with Sophia, I'll take him down."

"Yes. Take him down. Whoever he is."

Chapter 26

Psychopomp and Circumstance

I am so frustrated that I can't see straight. I completely humiliated myself at Dante's house. I mean, what was I thinking, walking into a zombie apocalypse with a couple of kitchen knives?

I drove around for an hour and ended up on the back road outside the barn. It's the only place I could think of to let off steam. I want to punch something. To beat something to a pulp.

I throw open the door and march inside but immediately realize it's not empty like I hoped. The demon hunters are sitting on rocks by the stream. Three others I don't know are with them, but also Michael and Raph. I stop, and everyone looks at me. Michael and Raph stand up, worried about the reckless emotions they can sense.

No one speaks, yet I have the feeling I was the topic of their conversation. Chang`e walks over and takes my arm, leading me closer. My second heartbeat starts with a sharp thump, a well-defined feeling that brings Michael to life inside me. It reminds me that, despite the mess we've made of our relationship, I am not alone; whether he likes it or not, Michael lives in me, and I in him. So when my eyes shift to his, I don't waver or back down. I raise my chin defiantly as if to say *I still feel you. So what are you going to do about it?*

I know I'm being careless. Raph should have no problem reading my emotions, but right now, I'm charged for a fight. And any confrontation will do.

But Raph doesn't approach me, and Michael doesn't react to my aggressive emotions. He simply frowns and watches me like a hawk.

Chang`e introduces the three strangers; Tarja from Estonia, who is very pale with white hair and a pleasant smile; Gargi from India, thin and tall with wide brown eyes that don't miss a thing; and Dubaku of West Africa, who is rather large and intense. Raph says he is built like a Nandi Bear, and everybody laughs. Dubaku flashes a broad smile with large white teeth, then drops it and looks intense again.

I don't know what to make of this, so I just say, "Hey," like I don't care.

Kanati clears his throat. "Sophia, these are the demon hunters we spoke of. Remember? We noticed too many demons in Haven Hurst?"

"Oh." Reality dawns, so I study them more closely. I wonder if they feel overburdened to have so many demons congregating in one place. They must know it's my fault. I don't know how to apologize for it, so I shift uncomfortably.

Raph thinks he is coming to my rescue by acknowledging my mood swings and failure to complete the last trial—faking a friendship with Dante and Vaughn must be difficult. Even Michael has stayed away from school. He says they now understand why I have been so agitated and distracted, why I've been *off.*

Michael's eyes drill into mine, sifting through my emotions like junk mail. He tosses aside the trivial to find the important, weightier stuff—the truth I am masking. I don't know what he'll find, exactly, but it finally makes sense *why he has stayed away. Why he hasn't spoken to me. He thinks I'm hanging out with Dante.*

He has probably seen Ka with Dante.

"You okay?" Raph asks, and I shrug. I have to let them believe my failure stems from Dante's presence. I may be angry with myself *and* Michael, but I can't tell anyone the real reason for my inability to complete the final trial. The breakup with Michael has torn me apart much worse than a doubling spell ever could.

Instead, I put on a plastic smile. *Fake it till you make it.* Isn't that a famous creed or motto, or fortune cookie proverb? Sounds like my only option.

"I didn't mean to interrupt anything," I say to Kanati and Chang`e. "Just stopped by for some extra training. I can go it alone if you're busy."

"You're not going to the dance, then?" Michael finally speaks, and I catch the question in my gut. I'm instantly back at the frozen waterfall, in his arms, where he is asking, in his shy human boyfriend voice, if I will be his secret date to the dance. A mad rush of butterflies attacks my stomach, but I force myself to turn and look at him. I try to conceal my emotions the way he does. Michael has become a master at it, whereas my eyes sting with unwanted tears. My throat closes up, trapping the answer inside. *I can't. I just can't.*

I came here to demoralize something inanimate, not to have the pieces of my broken heart kicked farther apart.

I walk toward the punching bag, but Chang`e cuts me off, suggesting we spar. So I follow her into the open meadow, grateful to put distance between Michael and me. While Chang`e straps on her weapons, I pull my hair into a high ponytail and wrap a braid around it. Then I walk to the table and buckle on my weapons. Knowing Chang`e can be rather destructive, I strap a small round shield to my forearm. We begin with hand-to-hand combat.

Chang`e uses her sword, and I unsheathe my crystal dagger. It fits comfortably in my hand, unlike Vaughn's oversized meat cleaver. But I'm stiff at first, my shoulder and back sore from being pummeled by the graveyard corpses. The memory of that humiliation rekindles the fire in me, and I become aggressive and reckless. I'm fueled by emotions, not strategy. Too many times, I fumble and leave myself vulnerable to attack. I feel the others watching, which only makes me self-conscious.

My dagger is no match for the sword, and she outmaneuvers me to no end. I'm trying my best, fully committed to the fight, but strange thoughts vie for my attention. They don't make sense, so I shake my head to stop the mental struggle, which seems to expand them into a surprising sensation.

I withdraw and step back from Chang è. She looks at me in question, but I turn away, trying to dissimilate the whirling emotions telling me something is wrong. They are quick, stabbing feelings that overtake everything else. I look around to see the others' reactions, but they're chatting amongst themselves. No one senses anything wrong. Not even Michael, who has shifted to his power stance while assessing me and my progress. Or lack thereof.

You didn't go to the dance either.

I bite at the unwanted thought. I shouldn't care right now; Michael's presence isn't helping me control my scattered thoughts. So I readjust my dagger and my focus.

Chang è and I move across the field, close to where Michael and the candidates killed that beast. She hurls herself into the air and comes down with a hard blow. It's a solid hit against my shield that sends me reeling. I roll across the meadow and skid to a stop. She is relentless, whirling end-over-end like a possessed cheerleader. I jump aside, narrowly avoiding a direct hit. Then she pounces, and we summersault twice before crashing sideways. I have lost control of my thoughts again because these damned feelings steal my focus.

"Stop!" I yell before she strikes again. But Chang è orders me to continue, to fight. Always fight.

I glance anxiously at the barn door, feeling compelled to leave because *something is seriously wrong.* Is it Bailey? I can't be sure; I can't pinpoint the exact—yes, I'm flooded with an overwhelming sensation that Bailey is in serious trouble. She needs me.

"I have to go," I say, walking away. Chang`e is on my heels.

"I thought you wanted to practice, Sophia. Whatever you're after, don't go. You're not ready."

She's right, of course. Haven't I already proven that tonight? But I can't stop. Something is propelling me to keep walking.

I pass Michael and say, "Bailey is in trouble," but he frowns and shakes his head. Michael doesn't sense anyone in trouble, so I hesitate at the door. If Michael doesn't feel it, then why do I? I look back at everyone staring at me. I'm the only one reacting to the jarring sensation that my friend is in trouble.

Michael says, "Don't go," but I walk out and slam the door.

* * *

Decorations block the roads surrounding the town square, so I park the jeep on the shoulder and climb down. My destination is the courthouse. The third floor was converted into a glamorous ballroom for the dance. If Bailey is in trouble, that's where she'll be. I'll just have to sneak in so no one recognizes me.

I pass the library and make it as far as the ice-skating rink on the courthouse lawn when I sense evil behind me. I gradually turn around, raking my eyes over the square. With the dance underway, the town is empty and quiet, like the inside of a freezer. Nothing moves.

But I'm not wrong. There is something out there. So I move cautiously across the street, making my way between the gazebo and Saint Sophia's Cathedral. The lights are on, but they cast creepy shadows all around me. Snow crunches beneath my boots, making a racket in the stillness of the night. I stop in the center of the park and try to settle my fear. Bailey is in trouble. Maybe a lesser demon got her?

I check the rooftops, but they are empty for the first time in weeks. I didn't like the demons up there, and I like it even less now that they're gone. The feeling of being watched morphs into solid understanding, so I spin around, my heart knocking in my chest, making me tremble. Something moves in the distance, and I flinch.

Don't be afraid. Not now. Not when Bailey needs me!

I imagine someone or something is holding her against her will, luring me to save her. Maybe one of the graveyard demons revealed my identity to the lesser demons. Maybe they'll kill Bailey if I don't surrender.

I walk toward the ice palace and the tunnel of ice sculptures. A dark figure emerges at the far end, and I brace myself. It lifts its head, then I hear a whinny, and my whole body relaxes.

It's a freaking horse. It probably got loose from a sleigh.

The horse tosses its head and moves on, clomping lazily through the snow. I move deeper into the tunnel as the dim backlighting begins to flicker. I stop as awareness ripples through me. This is the place where I felt someone watching Bailey and me. This is the place that now reeks of evil.

My scalp prickles with fear—that biological instinct you recognize as a gift from nature (if you're paying attention). I suddenly know I was tricked. Michael was right; Bailey is not in danger. I am.

The ice sculptures tower over me, but when I look closely, I see the horror of their true nature—dark creatures with beastly heads encased in ice. Then I hear a crackling sound that stops my blood. They are coming to life and breaking free from their constraints. I gasp and backpedal, slipping and falling against frozen benches. Then the largest sculpture grows black and forms a man in a long black coat. Throughout the tunnel, the other sculptures pulsate with red light, illuminating tiny fissures across the frost. They crack open as the beasts free themselves from their frozen coffins. They are hideous creatures with dead eyes, flat faces, and horns that curve around their jaws.

Chunks of ice tumble down, and a roar shakes the tunnel as the giant beast in the black coat is freed. He steps forward, slowly turns his head, and looks down at me.

Wolfgang!

I recognize his black, bottomless eyes, dark hair, and square jaw. But he now has two small horns protruding above his temples. He is part man, part beast. But it's Wolfgang. His eyes blaze when he sees me, and I scramble away, racing into the square.

Instinct propels me toward my house, but two lesser demons step from the shadows. Their eyes are black, and they carry battered clubs, so I spin away, running for the crystal forest. More demons emerge with daggers and swords. I look to the right, and more come. They are not attacking but herding me back to Wolfgang.

I whirl around to find him making his way from the crumbling tunnel. He and his creatures kick blocks of ice out of the way. Then Wolfgang stops and snarls at me.

"Nowhere to run this time," he says, and I stare in horror because he has fangs—long, vampire fangs that he snaps with a primeval urge. They are made to tear meat. And so is he.

Panic hits, and I look for help, but there is no one around. I stumble over the ice, desperate to reach the life-size chess game. I wrestle a spear from the Nutcracker in Russian garb. A lesser demon laughs at me as I whirl the spear with lightning speed. He lunges like he's only trying to scare me, but I knock him in the head, and he reels away, cursing at me.

Lesser demons hurl chunks of ice, taunting and hissing.

I duck and race for cover between the chess pieces. My cheekbone stings, and I touch it, finding it wet with blood. Demons surround the chessboard, trapping me. I could never fight my way out. But then Wolfgang yells orders—no one is to kill me. *He* has been granted the privilege. He stomps through the game, smashing and shoving pieces aside. I scurry next to the king, who is tall and wide. As I flatten myself against him, my hand brushes the crystal dagger at my hip. I have gotten so accustomed to the weight of my weapons that I forgot they were there. Such a rookie mistake, but I can't take time to scold myself. I'm armed.

I drop the spear and whip out the dagger with renewed confidence. Lesser demons creep along my flank, poking spears at me. They flush me out, and I take off running across the park. Wolfgang comes after me, tearing up the snow behind me. When I glance over my shoulder, I find him loping like an enraged silverback. It sends a jolt of ungodly fear through me, and I stumble over a chunk of ice, falling to my hands and knees.

A moment is all it takes, and I'm exposed—an easy target for Wolfgang to make the kill. But I scramble to my feet and face him as he slides to a stop, fog shooting from his nostrils like a wild beast. He bares his teeth again, inching forward. I'm panting and trembling, more afraid than I have ever been. With lesser demons at my back, I am facing the worst. I have no options left, no help. I can't rely on the *hope* that Armaros might appear to save me again. I don't know who he is or how his world works, but I know this is no game manufactured to teach me a lesson. This is not Dante's doing. If I can't defend myself, I will die, just as Michael feared. Just as everyone warned me. I haven't even completed my Awakening yet, and I am facing the greatest threat of my life.

Understanding rises to the surface, so I take a deep, calming breath. My shoulders ease down, and I raise my chin in defiance.

"Look at you, Wolfgang. Some great Demon Knight you are. Turned into a monster and sent to kill *me,* nothing but a small-town girl. I haven't even graduated high school yet. The Order must think I'm all you can handle these days, huh?"

He rises to the insult, roaring an unnatural sound that makes the lesser demons cower. His fingers extend into blades while his eyes—wild with rage—roll in his head and then lock on my dagger. It pulsates with blue light, a supernatural power he recognizes. This is my opening, so I haul back and throw it, hitting him just below the collarbone. Wolfgang wails in pain. His beastly body shudders, and his hands hover over the weapon like he wants to pull it out but is afraid to touch it.

With Wolfgang writhing in agony, the beasts from the tunnel attack. I whip out the pistol crossbows and fire nonstop until they stagger and fall. Lesser demons howl like sadistic wolves and race toward me, weapons raised, claws out. I turn 180 degrees, methodically firing at anything moving. I have an endless stream of arrows, but the demons hurl swords and daggers, forcing me to run. I head for cover in the crystal forest.

I weave around, firing at anything black. And then shrieks echo across the square. Kanati, Chang`e, and their friends are attacking the demons. Kanati moves with supernatural speed, wielding a gunstock war club and a tomahawk. Chang`e wields her sword and then throws a moonglow grenade that explodes with dust. It burns the demons like acid. They screech and writhe, eventually dissolving into ashes.

Demons are coming out of the woodwork, so I push through the forest to help the hunters. As I clear the trees, Wolfgang leaps through the air, knocking us to the ground. The pistol crossbows skid across the ice, out of reach. I'm stunned, with sudden pain shooting through my chest. I can't breathe. Wolfgang rakes his claws across my legs, and I cry out and roll away. Instinct kicks in, and I scramble up, holding out my left hand. The crystal dagger embedded in Wolfgang's chest flies back to me. Then I spin around, gaining momentum to send it whirling through the air and into his chest again. It slams dead center where his heart used to be. He throws his head back, roaring in disbelief.

I call to the pistol crossbows lying in the snow. Once secured in my hands, I turn and fire. Over and over, I drive arrows into his torso, arms, and legs until he stumbles for cover behind the tallest nesting doll. Lesser demons surround Wolfgang, stopping me from advancing. I lower the pistols, trembling and fighting to pull air into my lungs. My ribs throb, and my legs burn like they've been severed at the knees. I take a weak step forward, but I can't go on.

The demon hunters creep closer, crouched and ready for attack. Chang`e's beautiful face is grave as she watches me, anticipating my next move. *What is my next move?* I'm paralyzed with indecision. Do I fight my way through the barrier of lesser demons? Even with help from the hunters, I wouldn't escape without more injuries. No, it's better to cut off the head of the snake. But how?

Chang è nods encouragingly and then drops her eyes to my pistols—they can do more than I have asked.

Wolfgang is hiding, but my weapons will answer to my call. *My* call.

At this moment, I realize I have forgotten who I am. I have forgotten the girl hiding deep inside me when I defended myself against Psycho Steve. I am a spiritual warrior, made to destroy evil.

I face the lesser demons and the nesting doll standing between Wolfgang and me. I raise my crossbows without fear, and I fire. The demons duck, but the arrows sail in a wide arc around them, landing somewhere out of sight. A loud grunt indicates Wolfgang was hit; it worked, so I fire more. Up and around, the arrows bend their trajectory to find the target because that's what they are called to do. I continue to pelt him until he staggers into the open. Wolfgang has more than thirty arrows draining his blood, but his eyes blaze at me. When his demon blockade cowers in fear, I holster the pistols. Then I raise my hand, calling to the dagger in his chest.

I run at Wolfgang as my dagger flies through the air, glowing with mystical light. I spring off a nesting doll, snatch the dagger, bound off another doll, and come at him from above. I swing at his neck, the blade stuttering through gristle and bone. Then I hit the ground, roll, and slide into a crouch, ready for retaliation. But the strike is fatal. Wolfgang's head falls to the ground, his knees buckle, and his body collapses, spewing black blood. With their leader destroyed, the remaining demons slink off and fade into the shadows.

I straighten and suck in a ragged breath. My eyes won't leave Wolfgang because I can't absorb what happened. Everything unfolded faster than I could think, but also in slow motion, as though I had seen the outcome before completion. It's a surreal experience that I can't begin to pick apart now. Finally, I look up and find Kanati, Chang`e, and the hunters staring at me. They are shocked, but no more than I am. After all, I'm just a small-town girl. Who knew I could destroy a powerful Demon Knight-cum-monster like Wolfgang?

Chang`e's face breaks into a huge smile, and she points, so I look down. My left hand holds the dagger, but the center of my right hand is glowing. My Chelsea Light is vibrant indigo and the most beautiful, most powerful thing I have ever seen. I feel as though my strength and my compassion have equalized within me. In my left hand, I hold the means to defend what is righteous. In my right, I hold the purest form of love. This knowledge radiates throughout my system, and I finally understand what Rama has been trying to teach me—there is balance in the world within me, and it is *righteous* and *pure*.

I blink and discover my eyes are not my own but that of a spirit warrior, the one I had glimpsed in the past. She is here. And I am her.

I turn, gazing at my surroundings as though seeing for the first time—I see light in the darkness. I see colors and shapes blend and then separate to form complex objects with pristine clarity. There is a splendid measure of accuracy as everything solid becomes momentarily translucent. I hear music in the silence—the faintest sounds enunciating their intentions with precision. They wash over my skin like a million feathers, surrounding me and taking flight in a swirl of rich chaos. I look to the night sky, anticipating the oncoming snowflakes I can hear gently floating from Heaven. They crash against each other, forming new shapes and sticking together where they land. I recognize the natural formation, a primordial purity of all things around me. My innocence falls away, and I am liberated from the cycle of life. I have no more lives to live but this one. It's overwhelming and far more than I expected to experience. The transcendence brings serenity and order within me. It has brought my Chelsea Light to the surface.

I lower my chin to find the demon hunters sharing expressions of shock and awe. And then I see Michael and Raph walking up behind them. Michael's pale blue eyes sparkle with diamond chips as they fall on my glowing hand. My Chelsea Light pulsates with color that once matched his eyes. Our secret color, as I think of it.

Michael lifts his eyes to mine, and then he stops abruptly. He seems confused, trying to take in the scene. Raph laughs and jogs over, wrapping me in a hug that pins my arms to my sides.

"You did it, Sophia!" he cries, shaking me. "You destroyed that fire-eating scumbag *and* got your Chelsea Light!"

I laugh lightly, too overcome to speak. Michael's dumbfounded expression is remade into a deep scowl when he sees Wolfgang's body in pieces. Raph releases me and then steps back as we study the bloody remains. I wait for Michael's reaction. Is he proud? Shocked? Happy? I'll take anything in the neighborhood of pleased.

A sizzling sound and faint green smoke rise from Wolfgang's body parts. Then the smoke dissipates as though he was never there, and all that's left is a pile of clothes. Michael steps forward like he wants to stop the process and kill Wolfgang again. I frown and tilt my head in question. Wolfgang is gone, and Michael should be happy like we all are. So why is he glaring at the pile of clothes?

"Good riddance," Raph mumbles.

"Hey, what's with your hair?" Chang è says.

All eyes shift to me, so Raph pulls my ponytail over my shoulder. The five braids are glowing bright indigo, but I'm not surprised because I felt them tingling. I grin, secretly embarrassed by their color. Then I peek at Michael, hoping he'll at least be happy about this, but his eyes are wide with wonder, and his face is flushed.

A voice behind me says, "They are special for my *lani wahine*," and I whirl around. Rama is picking his way through the snowy carnage; everywhere are piles of clothes and tendrils of green smoke. Rama has a dopey grin because he understands what has happened, or maybe he witnessed the whole thing. Who knows? All I know is that I'm overwhelmed with gratitude. And since I can't help myself, I throw my arms around him.

"Oh, Rama! I have so much to tell you! Something has changed inside me! I mean, *everything* has changed!" I choke up and can't go on.

Rama fidgets, patting my shoulders and trying to hold back his emotions. Finally, he unwinds me from his neck, sniffling and nodding. "Azright. But…save it for the ceremony."

"What ceremony?"

Raph scoffs with disbelief. "You mean you didn't tell her?" He throws his hands up and shakes his head at my incompetent Ascended Master. He has no patience and wraps an arm around my shoulders. While Raph explains about the official ceremony for spirit walkers and Halos that I'll attend later tonight, I look at Michael. Does he wonder if the worst has happened now that I'm ready to go where he can't follow?

Michael's face is finally calm and so incredibly handsome. Deep longing makes him even more beautiful than any other emotion he radiates—the delicious bodiless sensation that enters through my eyes and spreads around my heart. It's a powerful drug, making me shrug out of Raph's arm and walk toward Michael. I have to talk to him. I have my own longings—I ache to feel the second heartbeat. I have to know that I *can* feel it, now that I'm a spirit walker. But Michael sucks in a breath and takes a deliberate step back.

* * *

The spiritual ceremony for Halos and spirit walkers could be mistaken for a high school or college graduation—if held at a Renaissance Faire. The barn is resplendent with colorful tents and vibrant banners. Guests in current fashion stroll among Halo warriors in black and gold armor, as well as demon hunters and spirit walkers in various styles. A stage is set up in the center of the meadow with benches flanking the middle aisle. Every seat is taken, and the overflow gathers along the perimeter.

The Halo candidates stand below the stage, at the foot of the stairs, and will receive their honors first. Michael is joined by two survivors, Zack and Viola. Spirit walkers line up on the right side, opposite the Halos. Two other spirit walkers have joined me: Marco from Turkey and Nayelli from Spain. We face the crowd with our hands tucked behind us, waiting for things to begin.

I haven't caught Michael's eye yet because he won't look at me. But I felt my second heartbeat the minute I walked toward the stage, and I've been dying to smile. A big, stupid smile that proves I haven't messed things up too badly by making Ka and becoming a spirit walker. All my vital elements— the ones connected to Michael—are still mine to enjoy. Now, if I could only convince Michael to be happy for me. To trust that everything is going to be alright. I've made it through the most challenging parts. *I think.* Anyway, I don't need his affirmation, but I want it more than anything else. And I know he can feel it. I'm bringing all my love to the surface, putting it on display for him to interpret. Others can think I'm overjoyed by what's happening around me; Michael will know, if he cares to admit it, that everything wonderful I'm feeling is for him.

I spot Rama seated with the Patronus family. Even Uncle Pavvo, Aunt Sasha, and Milvi are here. Uriel has a bird on his shoulder and Raph a smile on his face. Michael's parents must have left the dance early because they're in a ballgown and a tux. I love seeing their proud faces, but I can't help feeling the sting of regret. I have no family here. Not even Mom, who I've been searching for without any real hope of finding. Wherever

Mom is in the spirit world, she doesn't seem to belong here.

I'm disappointed that Dad will miss out. Once I explain everything, I'm sure he'll wish he could have been here. And Bailey. I wouldn't be here if not for her. After Rama performs the Apocatastasis and I'm whole again, I'll describe everything to her. Hopefully, she's enjoying herself at the dance anyway.

Kanati and Chang`e take seats in the crowd and wave to me. Chang`e was nice enough to show me the dressing chamber, where I changed clothes and washed off the blood. I'm wearing brown ankle boots, a brown leather vest laced up the sides, two leather cuffs, and indigo shorts that match my glowing braids. My sheath and thigh holsters are empty—weapons on the ceremonial table on the stage—and my ponytail is high with the center braid wrapped around it like a royal indigo crown. I'm feeling anything but princess-like. Lethal. Ready.

Drums announce the start of the ceremony, a slow, deliberate rhythm setting a serious tone. The Halos and spirit walkers turn and face each other. Michael stands directly across from me because we're both first in line. He finally meets my eyes, and I hold a steady gaze while my second heartbeat accelerates. I'm bursting with excitement, bursting with life.

Please be happy! Please understand that I am more than the love I can give you. We *are more than our callings.*

Michael has deadened his emotions, and I could wait in vain for a sign of life. But this is the first chance I've had to visually scrutinize him, so I take advantage. Michael has changed—obvious changes and subtle differences. Physically, his shoulders seem broader, packed tighter. His thick arms are more muscular and cut deeper than I remember. But it's in his expression that I find the most difference. Wisdom and physical punishment have aged the look behind his eyes; his trials have made a man out of him. Michael seems hardened, like a seasoned warrior already—like the Halo warriors I saw at the Borderlands. He has always wanted to be a Halo, and I'm genuinely proud that he has earned the highest rank a guardian can achieve. I am just as proud to be a spirit walker—to earn the highest rank a human can achieve. So I lift my chin and hold his eyes like we're holding hands.

A procession of Halo Masters files up the center aisle and takes seats up front. Chief Master Sachiel waits on the stage. He begins by greeting the guests assembled for the special evening. He apologizes for the last-minute arrangements, but as these ceremonies are always last minute, it should be expected, and he doesn't want to hear complaints.

A smattering of polite laughter brings a smile to his rugged face before he gets down to business. He says the Halo trials and the Awakenings were especially grueling this year. The spiritual family should be very proud of those who have prevailed. He details events, but I'm drifting, wondering what will become of Michael and me now that training has finished. Will he be deployed with a squad right away? Will he stay local or be sent into other realms? There's so much we never discussed. So much I don't know about his calling, or mine, for that matter.

Squad Master Camael joins Sachiel on the stage. They call up the Halo candidates first, so Michael and the others climb the stairs and face the crowd. Camael invites them to receive the Sigil of the Halos. Michael pulls aside his shirt collar, and Camael places a hand over his heart.

"Receive the Sigil of the Halos to mark you as one of us, a spiritual warrior and a Halo of the Son." A white light glows beneath his hand, stirring Michael's spiritual energy. Michael's eyes sparkle with a prism of colors, and I think he has never looked more beautiful. Powerful yet serene in knowing he will fight a righteous fight.

Camael removes his hand, leaving behind a circular rune with ancient markings. Finally, he moves on to Zack and Viola, repeating the sacred initiation. Then Sachiel holds his hands over a table laden with armor, blessing the holy weapons.

"You may now receive your spiritual armor: the Shoes of Preparation." Each candidate takes their shoes from the table, slips them on, and stands at attention again. "The Belt of Truth," Sachiel continues, and the candidates wrap black belts around their waists. "The Breastplate of Righteousness." They strap on gold breastplates with black markings that match their sigils. "The Helmet of Salvation." The warriors tuck their helmets under their arms. "The Shield of Faith." Small and round, they look indestructible, like the warriors themselves. "And the Sword of the Spirit," Sachiel says, backing away from the table. The three warriors gather their swords and hold them across their bodies. They now look every bit as lethal as they are.

"Fully armored, do you pledge to stand against evil, protect all heavenly realms, and fight the powers of darkness?" Sachiel asks, to which each candidate replies, "I do."

A cheer goes up, and Michael's family jumps to their

feet, clapping and beaming with pride. The vast meadow fills with whistles and calls of encouragement. The warriors do not crack a smile.

Then Sachiel turns in our direction and announces the coronation of the spirit walkers. Michael and the Halos step back while Rama and two other Ascended Masters take the stage. They make their brief introductions, and then we are called up.

I take a deep breath and mount the stairs. I know I should be nervous because that's how I am, but I have a depth of calmness I've never experienced before. I have crossed the threshold and feel reborn, understanding that I have not added anything *to* myself but revealed the mystery *within* myself. I have moved beyond the functions of thought or belief and transcended to a sense of knowing certain things. With my Chelsea Light—the driving force of all good things—I have the ability to override all physical and theological laws. And this understanding settles inside me where it belongs.

I catch Michael's profile as we approach. His eyes remain fixed ahead, and I'm left to wonder how he feels. I suppose I already know; I have made my choice, and he has made his. For all my hoping and internal pleading, I've gained nothing. Michael might have changed in extraordinary ways, but he hasn't changed in the one way I needed him to.

The spirit walkers stand opposite the Halos while Rama walks to the front of the stage. He has remained in his beach attire, which stirs comments among the crowd. He glances back at me and smiles. I return the smile. I have never been prouder to have him as my Ascended Master.

Rama clears his throat and speaks in his Ascended Master voice. "This is a day of celebration for those who have fulfilled the Awakening of the Heart and embraced their Metaphysical calling. They have: Purified the Soul, Illuminated the Way of Compassion, and Empowered the Physical Form." He turns to us and recites the oath: "Do you swear to protect lost souls to the best of your ability? To defend against evil entities above and below?"

"I do," I say, along with my fellow spirit walkers. Then each Ascended Master stands before their student. Rama lays a hand above my heart, and I feel a sigil tingle beneath my vest. It's warm in a circular formation and starting to tickle.

Rama whispers, "It is totally righteous and pure," and I grin. His chin is quivering because he's holding back a flood of tears.

The Ascended Masters gather for a moment of silent meditation, and a hush falls over the meadow. Then the unexpected sound of rippling water from the brook rises. It seems to evolve into the hum of a monastic choir, growing, and building until the water practically rages into whitecaps. Then it slowly fades back into the pleasant, bubbling brook that it was. It has purified the air and stirred up the sweet fragrance of honeysuckle. With the Ascended Masters in accordance, the barn is refreshed in peace.

One of the Ascended Masters steps forward and spreads his arms over the table with our weapons. He murmurs a blessing for their undertaking. And then, one after the other, we lift our hands, calling to our weapons. We catch them and secure them in holsters, sheaths, and quivers. It's a silent, peaceful process without the fanfare of the Halos' holy weapons.

My crystal dagger and crossbow pistols almost immediately glow with a beautiful indigo light. The others startle as though this is something unique and unexpected. None of their weapons are glowing. Murmurs spread throughout the audience. Heads crane to see me, so I look quickly at Rama, worried that something is wrong. He nods at my hair, but I already know the braids are glowing—I can feel a warm tingling across my scalp, the same as in the park when my Chelsea Light first began to shine.

Rama smiles proudly, and the crowd breaks into applause; they seem to recognize me as something more than the others. Something different but wonderful. Faces alight, and smiles spread like wildfire. I have no idea, but I give a dramatic bow because it feels like the right thing to do in a situation like this. Cheers and whistles explode across the meadow, and I giggle because I never expected to feel so welcomed. So loved.

When Sachiel eventually strides across the stage, everyone settles down. He throws me a disbelieving look, so I wipe the massive smile off my face and remember this is a holy ceremony. Then he raises his hands and makes the final announcement that welcomes us into the spiritual family. The crowd gives us a standing ovation. Then Sachiel beckons the spirit walkers and the Halos to meet in the center of the stage.

It's over, and everything has gone perfectly. So I put a bounce in my step and another—bigger—smile on my face. I lift my chin against Michael's calm demeanor and start walking toward the center of the stage. I'm brimming with so much happiness that Michael can't help himself; his stoic composure shatters, and he breaks up laughing.

I laugh, too, and then I feel three gentle tugs on my heart, and I stop in my tracks. My fellow spirit walkers bump into me, but I don't care. Michael is talking to me, secretly saying he still loves me. He knows I still love him because I can see it reflected in his eyes—those pale blue eyes sparking with bursts of indigo. I bite into my smile.

Michael has stopped, too, and we stand ten feet apart before a multitude of people who have no idea we are laying bare our forbidden feelings. I can't describe how much I want to launch myself at him, to wrap myself around the source of my life. If I spoke now, Michael would hear a thousand ways I missed him, need him, and love him. He would laugh at the way I stumble over descriptions and explanations. And he would kiss me to stop my rambling nonsense. But we can't do any of those things yet. So I simply smile and flick my eyes open with a playful look. We grin like lovers, and then Michael slowly winks, and everything inside me melts.

That wink! Good lord, what is it about a wink?

Rama clears his throat, and someone shoves me in the back, so I step forward. Michael and I meet in the center, where we turn and face our spiritual family. I'm holding back a tsunami of temptations, mostly involving my mouth on Michael's and me crawling on top of him and never leaving.

"Later," Michael whispers.

I close my eyes, grinning because he knows exactly what

I want. And I know it's exactly what he wants, too.

Everything is going to be fine. Michael and I are going to be fine.

The roar of the crowd escalates with wild cheers and whistles, pulling me back to the ceremony. They call out good wishes and wave at us.

I'm laughing with nervous energy—a bubbling excitement for what comes next. I have never been happier in my entire life, but as I lift my hand to wave back, an unbearable sensation rips through me—flesh tearing away from bone, unnatural stitches snapping apart. I grunt as though I've been hit in the stomach. As though vital elements are being yanked out, and I suddenly can't catch my breath. Images of my life flash across my mind, chased by random thoughts. And then I hear the screaming. It's me, in my head, screaming, *Ka! You're too far away! Don't go! Don't go!*

Something separates inside me, and I stagger forward, clutching my heart. Spinning darkness and bolts of lightning swirl around me, producing a wave of nausea.

Michael catches me before I fall, wrapping an arm around me like a steel band. Then he tips my chin up, his eyes moving frantically against mine. A moment is all it takes before he sucks in a breath.

"Sophia! Where is your soul?"

THE END

Of

Nothing

About the Author

Lori Adams is an American author of the Avalina Jones Series, the Kate March Mysteries, and the Soulkeepers Series. She grew up in Oklahoma and now lives in California.

During her nomadic travels, she attended six colleges and universities before starting a career in writing. When she's not writing, Lori loves watching Classic Hollywood films and exploring beaches and tide pools, always on the lookout for unusual shells, rocks, or the occasional buried treasure.

The idea for the Soulkeepers trilogy: Forbidden, Awaken, and Unforgiven was born out of sheer curiosity for the invisible, that tug-of-war between good and evil. The unseen. The unimagined. And the precious, innate knowledge hidden within us.

Lori Adams can be found online at LoriAdamsBooks.com

Contact Lori at Spyhoppublishing@gmail.com

Take a sneak peek at the last book in the
Soulkeeper Series

UNFORGIVEN

Chapter 1
Taken

After all this time, I found the reason for me. I gained what I wanted most. I am Sophia St. James, and I am a spirit walker.

I am more than I once was—the procession of words and descriptions, the weight of blood and bones, the image at the end of someone's gaze. I pushed through the ordinary into the *extra*ordinary—a holy space where knowing myself requires no sound or pronunciation. My physical body has *awakened* a primal lifeforce within me and granted me the privilege of hearing lost souls begging for guidance—that sweet confection in the air. I have the means to help these souls cross over. And I have the weapons to defend them against evil. But I made a grave, *unimaginable* mistake.

Looking back, it seemed as quick as a thought, the idea and execution of making a second version of myself. Call it a double or a twin; she is a Ka conjured from an ancient Egyptian spellbook who emerged as accurately as if peeling my image from a mirror. But in my naïve innocence—my distraction in training to destroy the evil demons around me—I left my other Self vulnerable to the most dangerous demon of all. The one who loves me.

I am my own undoing.

* * *

It's midnight on Christmas Eve, and snowflakes silently drift down on Haven Hurst, Connecticut, adding another layer to the mounds of snow already blanketing the town. It's a Hallmark Christmas card, a Currier and Ives winter wonderland. Lights twinkle inside cozy homes. Tendrils of smoke drift from chimneys. Bells ring in church steeples, marking the night's celebration.

Inside the spiritual barn on the outskirts of town, a different sort of celebration has concluded on this holy night—the annual gathering of new spiritual recruits into the Fold. A cheerful crowd assembled for the mystical graduation in a green meadow that stretches farther than the eye can see. Colorful tents, reminiscent of medieval times, stand bold among natural grasses and lush foliage. Each tent displays the banner of those loyal to The Council of Guardians: Halos of the Son, Spirit Walker, Demon Hunter, Messenger, Seer, and Guardian.

Men and women in sacred armor and ceremonial garb stand among the hallowed gardens. A breeze stirs the scent of honeysuckle from vines that have wound up stone columns to a wide balcony hidden among trees. A sheer waterfall drops into a pool and adds holy water to the bubbling brook meandering around the Tree of Life.

I am standing on a stage in the meadow with two fellow spirit walkers and three new Halo warriors. The ceremony just ended, and Michael Patronus, my secret boyfriend and Halo warrior, holds me steady. I hear him speaking, but his voice sounds miles away like my ears are stuffed with beeswax. This seems appropriate since my head is buzzing.

A congregation of concerned faces stare from the audience—my new spiritual family, most of whom I don't know. But others are close friends like Michael's parents, Katarina and Dimitri; his brothers, Raph and Gabe; his Aunt Sasha and Uncle Pavvo; and cousins, Uriel and Milvi. They are worried because I gasped loudly and stumbled forward. Michael caught me before I fell, but he has no idea what's happened. As far as I know, most spiritual entities can detect my rapid adrenaline spike—a lethal dose to typical humans. But I am not typical, and they can't pinpoint the cause. No one knows the pain I'm feeling comes from my soul being ripped from my body.

I grip Michael's hand because I know the worst has happened. Ka has gone beyond our boundaries and taken the gentle vibration of my spirit with her. I don't know how it happened. All I know is that Dante, the Demon of Persuasion, has Taken Ka and my soul to Hell. The certainty of that knowledge is the most terrifying thing I have ever accepted. Hiding it from Michael and the others will be the most difficult thing I've ever had to do. I can't let anyone know what's really happened, not when I just gained everything I wanted. Michael admitted that he still loves me, even as a spirit walker. So there is no way I'll risk losing him *and* my place in this spiritual family.

The crowd is being patient, but they are due an explanation for my odd behavior. I need to think of something to say, but Michael is frantic. He is reading my emotions and fears but doesn't want to accept them.

"Sophia!" he whispers with quiet urgency. "*Where* is your soul?"

I turn away, lifting my eyes to the bright blue sky while searching within myself for what I know I won't find. I felt the tearing of stitches that bind my soul to flesh. What's left is a tender, vacant space that anyone in the spirit realm will eventually notice. I need time. If my Ascended Master, Rama Kuan, and I were alone, we could meditate and journey through my inner layers until we find the solution. But I'm not alone, and I can't face the others or allow them to look in the eyes. Not until I fix this.

Michael repeats his question over and over while sliding an arm around my waist. He's afraid I'll collapse, and so am I. Aside from feeling dizzy, I'm scared to death that he'll confirm his own fears. Michael is the only person who can sense my emotions without looking directly into my eyes, but I hope he is only guessing now. It all happened so quickly, maybe he's not sure what he's detecting. If I don't make myself whole, he will know he's right. And he will be horrified by what I've done. Honestly, I'm too ashamed to face him and confess the truth.

If Rama and I can't do this together, I'll have to go it alone. This void in me needs to be filled by something powerful. So I close my eyes, letting Michael hold me while I *feng shui* my thoughts. During my training, I learned to improvise, overcome, and adapt to any situation. But how do I put that to use now? How do I improvise a missing soul?

I need to *be* whole. I need to *try* to be whole. I need to *appear* to be whole.

I mediate until my mind's eye gradually sees a clear path, and I know what must be done. It's the only acceptable solution, so I don't waste another moment. I have an abundance of spiritual energy, but I don't know if what I'm attempting to do is actually possible. So I pull in a deep breath and hold it for as long as possible while I walk within myself. I draw upon my rainbow aura, gathering with it all the spiritual energy stored inside me. I know this to be a powerful, conscious force that moves my circuitry—the source of electricity that sparks my second heartbeat, that makes my braids and weapons glow indigo. It is the lifeforce that collects in my right palm to make my Chelsea Light.

I guide the energy and colorful aura into the void where my soul once lived. It's a poor substitute for the real thing, but the dappled light might be enough to camouflage the darkness. It might buy me time to correct my mistake. And it is my only option.

When I come back to the surface and open my eyes, I feel Michael's heartbeat inside me. It's stronger than ever, indicating that our supernatural connection hasn't been broken. I'm flooded with relief. So often, I've worried that it would disappear. That I have messed things up beyond reproach. Feeling him inside me means everything.

I look up and find his beautiful angelic face distraught, his pale blue eyes swimming in fear. He has sensed something tragic within me, so I force a smile, but it does nothing to smooth the creases in his brow.

"I'm fine, Michael. Really." I hold his gaze so he can see for himself. *Please see that I'm okay.*

"Sophia, please don't try to—"

"Hey, *wahine*, you chill?" Rama says, interrupting at the

perfect moment. He lays a hand on my shoulder, easing himself between us. Michael steps back but stays close, worry radiating off of him.

I nod and lift my voice so Michael can hear. "Yeah, just a little overwhelmed, I guess. Fighting the demons and killing Wolfgang drained me. And my Chelsea Light is pretty strong; it'll take a while to get used to it." I grimace at my lame excuses. I felt none of what I said, and it hurts to lie. It hurts to think Michael might see this as a weakness. I've lied about so much already. Not that it matters because Michael is not buying it. He sees through me like glass. But he doesn't appear to be as alarmed as he was minutes ago. Still, I have to push the narrative a little farther.

My right palm is still glowing with a faint indigo light that matches my braids. The same color that matches Michael's eyes when his affection for me changes his physical composition. So I lift my light and tell Michael I'm having trouble controlling my energy, which accounts for almost fainting.

"It's beautiful, don't you think?" I ask with a secret smile. He knows why I think it's beautiful and why I'm asking.

Michael's eyes drop to my palm. He considers it with a puzzled frown before looking back at me. Of course, that wasn't the excuse he was expecting. I can practically hear the wheels in his mind recalculating his assessment of my behavior. He's starting to doubt himself. I can almost see my Chelsea Light reflect indigo in his eyes. His special color. Our color. He doesn't say it's beautiful, but I know he thinks it is. Michael loves the meaning that accompanies that bluish-purple color;

he loves the look of wonder on my face every time I watch his eyes churning.

I see his lips twitch and know he's holding back a smile. Rama sees it, too, and makes a strange mewling sound. He doesn't like the vibe he's picking up. The other Halo warriors and spirit walkers gather around, so Rama jumps in to answer for Michael.

"Bitching cool, *wahine*. Never seen such a beautiful light."

I smile and play along. "I wasn't expecting it to be this color. Is that normal?" I feign innocence, but I'm very aware that having weapons and a Chelsea Light that pulsates with a powerful indigo light is *not* normal for a spirit walker. I'll be sure to explore that freakishness right after I take care of more critical issues. Like finding Ka and my missing soul.

"There is nothing about you that's proven normal, Sophia," Michael says quietly. He is masking his feelings, and I can't decide if it's to avoid detection from the others or me. Either way, he would be in a world of trouble if his eyes churned to indigo now. And I think we have all the trouble we can handle at the moment.

"Best take a load off," Rama says, gesturing to a nearby chair. He gives me a look that says he understands about Ka. I would hope so because he performed the ritual that made me a double. He knew the rules as much as Ka and I did. She wasn't supposed to travel too far away and risk taking my vital elements with her. I don't think any of us imagined that included my soul.

While Michael guides me to a chair on the stage, Rama addresses the curious crowd and explains why I nearly fainted at the end of the ceremony.

"My *wahine* went overboard today. Nothing to worry about. As most of you know, Sophia destroyed a Demon Knight from the fifth kingdom. Took a lot out of her. She needs time to rebalance her energy."

The guests nod knowingly. Luckily, his excuses made perfect sense. Destroying a Demon Knight is no easy task, especially for someone as young and inexperienced as I am. Rama smiles and urges them to carry on with the celebration. The annual graduation for Halos of the Son and spirit walkers is usually a festive, if not reverent, affair. He wants everyone to enjoy themselves. Raph and Milvi shoulder their way through the masses, eager to reach me. They have supported me every step of the way during my Awakening, so I'm grateful for them. But I need time to recover and speak privately with Rama.

"Please tell them I'm fine," I say to Michael. He drops to one knee beside my chair and deliberately looks me in the eye. He is dressed in ceremonial clothes of black and gold armor, a sword, and a black cape. He looks every bit like a Roman soldier, like the other Halos. I wish I had time to congratulate and compliment him on everything he's achieved. But he tries to ask me what happened, and I can't let him voice his fears, so I cut him off.

"Michael, please. Tell your family I just need to catch my breath. I'm good. Everything is good." I put up my best smile against his suspicious scowl. I hate that my words are made of lies. I hate that the lies are necessary, like the air I breathe. But filling Michael's head with lies is better than filling it with the truth.

Moments before my soul was ripped away, Michael

tugged on my heart three times—his supernatural way of saying, I love you. He knows I feel the same way because he can feel my love. Even through all the chaos swirling inside me, Michael can find my feelings for him. But I always want to say it back to him. One of my favorite things is seeing the excitement on his face when I tell him how much I love him. I think it makes him feel more human—more like me.

But there wasn't time to say it on the stage. And we shouldn't even be this close right now. Ours is not a relationship to share with others. No one can know Michael and I are in love. Maybe later, when this mess is sorted out, I'll tell him how much I've missed him and how much I absolutely love him.

Michael reluctantly agrees to do as I ask, but he is pacifying me. I'll have to try harder to convince him that I'm fine. He jumps from the stage and catches Raph and Milvi before they mount the stairs. Rama quickly pulls up a chair, sits, and grabs my hand. Panic rises in me all over again.

"What's happened?" I whisper. "What went wrong?"

He shakes his head. "Don't know. Gotta ride this into the shallows, and then we'll see."

"I have to talk to Bailey. Last I knew, she was at the dance in the courthouse, keeping an eye on Ka. Do you think Dante went to the dance?"

Rama squeezes my hand but plays it cool, smiling and waving to guests who throw curious glances our way. Yet, beneath his calm facade, he's trembling. I can't imagine what kind of trouble he's in—an Ascended Master losing his spirit walker's soul to a Demon Knight.

My guilt multiplies exponentially.

I'm so worked up that I can barely sit still. "Well, I'm not waiting around here any longer. I'm going to find Bailey." I stand slowly to gauge my equilibrium. As a spirit walker, I'm constantly absorbing the earth's energy, and losing my soul has not changed that. My head is clear, but my legs wobble, not so bad that they can't do their job, though. Michael returns pensive and uneasy.

"I've explained to my family, but my parents have arranged a private celebration at the house. For both of us. They're hoping you'll come, but if you're too—"

"Of course, she'll come!" Rama says overdramatically before I can bow out. His energy is as taut as a tightrope. He's desperate to appease Michael and project a sense of normalcy. So for his sake, I agree.

"Well, I guess I should change first." I'm still wearing my ceremonial clothes: blue shorts, brown leather vest, leather cuff bracelets, ankle boots, and weapons. Hardly after-party attire. We arrange to meet at the door in a few minutes.

I'm anxious for the private dressing chamber, so I quickly descend the steps and enter the labyrinth of people. I keep my head down to avoid being stopped by well-wishers. The fewer lies I have to tell, the better. This seems to work; however, my second heartbeat never leaves, indicating Michael ignored my wishes. He's hard on my heels and will bombard me with questions the moment we're alone. This is exactly what I want to avoid.

I see Milvi waiting for me outside the dressing chamber

at the edge of the meadow. She's one step ahead of me, and I succumb to the inevitable; privacy is not to be mine after all.

I stop and turn around. "Please, don't follow me. Don't make a scene."

"*I'm* not the one making a scene," Michael says, keeping his voice down. "Are you going to explain what happened up there? The truth, this time?"

The truth?

My whole body sags with defeat and shame. Oh, Michael, how do I explain that I've been involved with Dante? How do I defend his late-night visits or that he escorted me to a private demon nightclub to find a spellbook to create Ka? How do I make you understand why I put my trust in the demon whose only ambition is to Take my soul to Hell? And how do I admit that Dante has done precisely what he set out to do—and it's all my fault?

Even if the words came easily, I would never say them. At least not until we've performed the Apocatastasis and put my soul back where it belongs. The only thing to do now is reroute Michael's attention toward a different truth.

I pull him aside and clutch my hands in front of me. My Chelsea Light has powered down to about the size of a quarter. But it still glows and tingles, adding to my edginess. I calm myself, narrow my focus, and then offer Michael a soft smile. The only thing I want him to detect are my genuine feelings for him in this moment.

"To be honest, Michael, I was pretty shocked to feel three tugs on my heart. I mean, after all this time, I thought you didn't love me anymore. I was afraid I ruined everything."

He nods. "Yeah, I could tell. I thought you were going to jump me on the stage." He laughs lightly and then grows serious. "You didn't almost ruin us, babe, I did. I had several chances to let you know I still love you, but I was confused. I thought we were too incompatible. I thought my calling and your entire life were like night and day, and I couldn't see how it would work. But I've never stopped loving you. My love is unconditional. You know that, right?"

He has such an earnest expression that I feel my common sense fleeing. I want to wrap myself around him and kiss him in front of everyone—anyone. I don't care what they think because this hurts too much. The cravings are too strong. Not touching or kissing him is like having withdrawals.

"Babe," he breathes out, knowing what I want. He feels everything I feel, only stronger. Then he closes his eyes as though not seeing me will ease his own desires. As though it could put distance between our cravings. He grips the hilt of his sword while he struggles to overcome or control his forbidden emotions. These past weeks are the longest we've spent apart since we confessed our feelings, and it's been nothing but torture. I want him so much that I take a step closer.

"Babe, please," I whisper, unsure what I'm begging for. I'm feeling so much right now—reckless, scared, loved. So much love that it's intoxicating. When Michael opens his eyes again, they are liquid indigo, and I catch my breath. He blinks slowly, and I feel his love enter me through my eyes. It accelerates my second heartbeat, and I know we're headed for trouble. We're not thinking clearly. We're not thinking at all, only feeling.

Then he gives me that soft crooked smile, the one to build my life on, and says, "I've missed my sweet, candy kisses—my lightning in a bottle."

Tears spike my eyes as he whispers the lyrics of our song, "Electric Love," the one he says must have been written for us, about us. It's too much, and I feel myself break. I'm not strong enough to stop myself from touching him, and he's not strong enough to back away. So I lift my hand to cup his face, but Michael stiffens, and a heartbeat later, we hear Raph's voice call out.

"There you are! Hey, congratulations!"

Michael and I flinch apart. Raph pushes through the guests and wraps me in a hug. "Never had a doubt you could do it." He steps back and clasps my shoulders, grinning. I instinctively look away so he can't sense my desire for Michael. Or worse, notice my missing soul. There is a long pause, and I'm afraid it's too late; Raph has noticed that something is off. Or maybe he's caught his brother's unnatural emotions. Whatever made Raph hesitate, he doesn't act upon it now. He continues in his casual tone. "Hey, you're coming to our house, right? You know Mom and Dad planned a private party? Michael told you?"

Michael clears his throat. "Yeah, I was just telling her about it. In case she wants to stop by and—"

"Mom'll be bummed if you don't," Raph interrupts, ignoring Michael. He drapes an arm around my shoulder, leading me away. "So, you in?"

"Of course. I was just on my way to change."

Raph deposits me at the dressing chamber, where I turn and look back for Michael, but he is gone.

"Congratulations!" Milvi calls from inside and then throws her arms around me. She is strong and thin beneath a red silk dress. Her exuberance chases away lingering concerns about Michael and Raph for the time being. Since Raph didn't question my missing soul, I'm hoping I've also fooled Milvi. How long I can keep up the charade is another matter entirely.

Milvi and I sparred during my training, which gave me considerable respect for her fighting skills. She'll make a great guardian someday.

"I knew you could do it," she continues casually. "And remember, if you ever want your butt kicked again, just ask, and I'll make myself available." She laughs playfully. "You're going to Katarina's party, right?" She spins around without waiting for an answer. I follow her deeper into the cool, comfortable dressing chamber. It's basically every girl's dream closet—shelves of shoes, racks of dresses, skirts, pants, and tops. The walls are lined with shimmering gowns and accessory overload.

At a glance, the decor is 1940's chic—elegant blacks, grays, silvers, and creams. A stylish black rug takes up most of the gray marble floor, on which a glittering silver sofa rests next to a tailored dove-gray chair. Massive mirrors in heavy silver frames lean against the walls, and several delicate chandeliers sparkle overhead. A black armoire with mirrored doors stands in the corner next to an elaborate cream-colored sideboard with a silver tea set and a variety of little, colorful cakes. Milvi bites into a tiny frosted cake before sifting through the clothing for options in her size.

"It's a casual party so don't worry too much," she says, selecting black tights, a miniskirt, tall boots, and a silver top. She heads for one of the changing rooms while I stay rooted in place. The bloody clothes I shed before the ceremony are right where I left them, in an ugly heap outside my changing room door. I can smell Wolfgang's black demon blood from here. It splashed across my clothes when I decapitated him. The pungent odor was so foreign to me that I had to force down the bile in my throat; it's not something I'll ever forget. I never wanted to smell it again.

Just looking at my shredded pants—with *my* blood—makes my shins throb. Wolfgang got me once across my legs, but Chang`e's medicinal goop has eased the pain. Less than two hours ago, I almost died at the hands of a monster, and now my soul is probably on its way to Hell. How am I still standing?

I put the question out of my head. I have no regrets about anything I've done—creating Ka, which helped me become a spirit walker, or killing Wolfgang. Of course, I wish I'd kept a closer eye on Ka, but Wolfgang deserved what I did to him. And more. I won't waste another thought on him.

Lucky for me, I don't need to. My goal now is to do as Rama said. Ride this evening into the shallows and then get answers about Ka. The physical pain of losing my soul has dissolved. It's those dark visions accompanying it that worry me now. My instincts tell me I'm seeing what Ka is experiencing. As disturbing as the images are, I believe it's a good sign. It means Dante didn't actually kill her. So as bizarre as it sounds, I'm hoping he took her to Hell. Alive.

With my mind set, I move silently among the clothes, running my fingertips over silk and satin. Suede and wool. I don't care much about what I wear now, just that we get on with the evening. Eventually, I select something warm and modest: black skinny jeans, a thick gray sweater, and black ankle boots. I step into the dressing room next to Milvi's and strip down.

"Hey," she calls. "Rama told you about the transition, right?"

"Huh?" I sound muffled under the sweater sliding over my head. Milvi makes a few disparaging remarks about my Ascended Master and then explains the process.

Unlike guardians, who convert into spirit form in whatever clothes they might be wearing, spirit walkers will transition into the clothes they selected for their ceremonial attire. When I'm called to help a lost soul, I'll convert from human form into spirit form, and everything I wore during the holy sacrament—everything blessed—will appear. Clothing and weapons. I'm excited at the prospect of it all, especially saving my first soul. But now I worry that *my* missing soul might prevent me from helping someone cross over. So I add it to the list of questions I have for Rama, the moment we can be alone to discuss the newest mess I've gotten us into.

Once I've changed, Milvi says to leave my ceremonial clothes behind, so I arrange them with my weapons on the sideboard for safekeeping. Then we head out, working our way through the meadow. I'm focused on escaping but can't help noticing that people look differently at me. Not, *hey, she's missing a soul*, differently but with reverence or respect. A few even bow their heads. It feels weird like they're treating me above the others. When I ask Milvi, she just shrugs, but I think she's pretending ignorance. I drop it since I have enough on my plate to worry about.

Rama and Michael are standing near the door when we approach. Rama is fidgety and eager to leave. Michael has changed into jeans and a dark blue shirt. He is in the center of a crowd, swamped by congratulating pats on the back and vigorous handshakes. So many friends and warriors have come to offer their praise and young guardians to ask his advice. Their admiration and respect are apparent. Michael favors them with a patient smile because his mind is on other matters.

When he sees me, his face stills, then he pushes through the circle surrounding him, never breaking eye contact. We meet at the door, where Milvi entertains Rama with descriptions of the ceremony, holy dignitaries who've attended, or friends from Estonia. He listens politely. I haven't congratulated Michael, so I tell him now. He grins and tilts his head in a faint bow.

"And congratulations to you, too, spirit walker Sophia." His deep voice is soft and thick with emotion. "I'm happy for you. You've earned your place." His smile is warm and loving, and I know he means it. Michael is truly happy for me.

His gaze lingers longer than necessary. He wants to say more, but Rama is watching. Without a word, my Ascended Master steps between us and takes my elbow, deliberately guiding me out the door.

With no moon or stars, we are instantly swallowed by the night. Snowflakes dance around as we hike up the thick path leading to the Patronus farmhouse. It's a short trek that moves organically through trees, across an open field, and around Katarina's extensive garden. We're nearly there when I realize I'm not as cold as I should be. I stop and scoop snow into my hands. It's mildly chilly.

"Why don't I feel the cold?"

Everyone turns and looks back at me. Milvi laughs and smashes the snowball I've made. "Because you have spiritual energy rushing through your veins. Rama didn't tell you what to expect?"

Rama is distracted by more important issues. But he eventually comes around to the question. "Oh, for sure. I'll tell her what to expect. There just hasn't been time yet. Lots of changes coming, *wahine*. And for you, too, Michael. Now that you're a Halo."

Rama and Michael lock eyes for a moment, and then Michael gives him a sharp nod. He seems well aware of the duties and expectations required of an elite warrior. The details are lost on me. I don't want to think about Michael being called away or sent on a mission. We haven't had time to settle things between us. If he's called up now, we might not see each other for a very long time. The idea makes a knot of my stomach.

The Victorian farmhouse is situated at the top of a gentle hill. It's a glorious sight, with numerous peaks and dormers heavy with snow. Tall, beveled windows glow with soft light. Smoke drifts from the chimney, adding a pleasant, earthy aroma to the frigid smell of snow. We plod up the steps and onto the sprawling veranda, stomping snow from our shoes. Milvi bursts out laughing because Rama's huarache sandals have disappeared completely, and he looks like he's wearing two giant snowballs.

I manage a faint smile. Milvi reminds me that this should've been a night for celebration. Rama deserves some fun after all the stress I've put him through during my training. Unfortunately, I've ruined that, too. After we thank Michael's family for their good wishes, Rama and I will have to leave. I'm sure he's just as desperate to find Bailey as I am. We have to know what happened to Ka.

We pile through the back door and stop in the hallway, overcome by an angry, shouting voice coming from the living room.

"You promised to protect her! You gave me your word that nothing would happen to her! You're angels, for God's sake! How could you let this happen?"

Michael and I look quickly at each other. We can't comprehend what we're hearing. Or how it's even possible.

Milvi murmurs, "Uh-oh," and pushes past us. We follow her down the hallway and into the living room. I stop short.

"Dad?"

He whirls around, just as stunned to see me as I am to see him.

~

CPSIA information can be obtained
at www.ICGtesting.com
Printed in the USA
BVHW080308010323
659402BV00005B/54